Black Forest Burning

Lorelei Gray

Foxfoot Books Paperback

Foxfoot Books first edition January 2023

Foxfoot Books and colophon are registered trademarks of Countdown Media LLC.

www.foxfootbooks.com

ISBN: 979-8-9866361-2-2

Cover design by Sarah Whittaker

Manufactured in the United States of America

This book contains imagery and scenarios some readers may find upsetting. The world is a dark place, and so is this book. The Black Forest waits, enter if you dare.

Lorelei Gray

1

The end of the story.

Sadie rolled her eyes at May's spooky proclamation. She'd had enough of ominous warnings and riddles since they arrived at the castle. In front of them, the forest waited, dark and mysterious and probably full of death. Behind them, the castle—lurking, hungering for them to return, and *definitely* full of death. Sadie looked at the start of the path in front of them, a simple, flat dirt path, nothing special or magical about it. Sadie knew better, though.

What was left of their group crowded around the opening in the trees. Jenny, with her curly brown hair pulled up into a messy ponytail, was clutching her backpack straps and digging her nails into the nylon. Aiden and May stood irritatingly close to each other on the other side of Sadie. May was playing nervously with her hair while Aiden squinted into the trees as if looking for something. Travis, his white T-shirt already sweat stained, fidgeted behind them.

None of them had taken a step into the forest yet. Everyone was waiting for someone else to take the lead. This had all been Jenny's idea—to go into the forest to find her missing boyfriend, Ryan, his twin sister, Rain, and Eckert, the woman that took them. But now, Jenny seemed hesitant. Frightened. Sadie knew she would have to do what she always did: push her.

This time, literally.

Sadie took a step back and gently pushed Jenny over the invisible threshold, onto the path, and into the forest. Jenny made a soft, surprised yelp and turned around. She gave Sadie an annoyed look but didn't say anything. Jenny's statue-turned-wolf, Marble, growled at Sadie and glared at her with his intense black eyes. His gray, black, and white fur swirled mesmerizingly in the dappled shade of the trees. She'd been afraid of the wolf when Jenny first introduced him to the group, but now he was just another member of their rescue party.

"Oh shut it. We're *all* going," she grumbled in the wolf's direction. He looked away and lumbered heavily into the woods after Jenny.

Sadie followed the wolf into the forest, her skin prickling at the sudden chill of the shaded trail. Deep-green spruce trees, intermixed with peeling white birches, grew lush on either side of them. The trail was surprisingly smooth, hardened dirt, just wide enough to fit two people across. Sadie inhaled a strange smell, fresh and Christmassy, but almost too much so, like the strong fragrance was being used to cover up some *other* scent beneath it. Sadie felt uneasy as she scanned the trees for movement, or monsters, or anything else that might jump out and kill them. Next to her, Jenny stared stoically down the trail, lost in thought.

Jenny turned and met Sadie's gaze, giving her a weak smile. Sadie glanced behind them—the others were still standing on the other side of the tree line, wrapped in warm sunlight. Sadie felt very much that they should be heading *toward* that light, not away from it. She thought about Hannah and Cameron, who were walking safely down the road in that same sunlight, and felt an uncomfortable mix of jealousy and anger. *They should have come with us*, she thought bitterly. Dividing their group like this seemed like a mistake, a potentially deadly one. Cameron's idea to walk the road until they found help was reasonable, but Sadie knew it had more to do with Hannah's fear of the woods and her refusal to enter.

Travis, his pinkish skin shiny with sweat, his pale-blonde

buzz cut practically translucent, took a few steps down the path until he was standing with Sadie and Jenny in the shaded forest. May and Aiden were still in the sunshine, May's long dark-brown hair giving off a hint of red in the sun. Her arms were crossed over her chest, her signature bracelets weighing down her thin wrists. Sadie was about to yell at them to hurry up when Aiden turned to May and, in a squeaky voice, said, "Follow the yellow brick road!"

Sadie never understood Aiden's random movie references, but *this* one she knew: *The Wizard of Oz*. She saw May give him a courtesy smile and then step forward onto the path. Aiden ducked his head and followed quietly. He stood next to Travis; his olive skin and dark hair were a stark contrast to Travis's slightly sunburned, pale skin. Sadie pulled her attention from the boys and addressed the group.

"Well, we didn't all immediately die, so that's a good start," she said dryly. "Now what?"

"Now ... I guess we follow the path and ... hope it takes us where we need to go," Jenny replied, uncertainty dragging down her words.

"Hold on," Aiden said, his eyes brightening. He took a knife out from his backpack—it had a curved blade and a handle set with red stones.

Must be the knife he picked from Eckert's room, Sadie thought.

"Sadie actually gave me this idea," he said, throwing her a quick heart-stopping smile. He took the knife and dug a shallow *x* into a nearby birch tree, its white bark peeling away in thin sheets. "We can mark the trees so we can find our way back! I just hope it works better than those rose petals did."

Sadie's face burned at the memory of how ridiculous she had been—dropping rose petals to find their way back out of the ruins, then abandoning Aiden inside after throwing a temper tantrum. She'd liked him from afar for so long, but the delicate fantasy she had created had shattered when she actually got the chance to talk to him. She felt hot with shame, then realized it wasn't just the embarrassment that was making her feel warm. It was the tree.

It was on fire.

Aiden jumped away from the burning tree, his mouth agape. The x he'd carved into the pale skin of the birch was shooting out hungry flames. The others moved away from the fire with matching stunned expressions.

"What did you do!" Sadie yelled at Aiden.

"I don't know!"

"Someone put it out!" Jenny screamed, her face flushed.

In one quick movement, Travis dropped his backpack on the ground and tore his T-shirt off, revealing the bulk that put him in the heavyweight class of the school's wrestling team, and started hitting the fire with it. A few quick smacks of the shirt and the fire died out, leaving two wide scorch marks on the bark.

"Okay, there has to have been a better way to do that," May said, rolling her eyes.

Travis shrugged and pulled the now-singed T-shirt back over his head.

"Seriously?" Sadie said, noticing a scattering of small holes burned out of the fabric.

"What? It's fine," Travis said. "It's not like we're going to a fashion show."

Sadie shook her head and stared at the black x now burned into the tree. She felt disgusted—they'd been in the forest all of five seconds and had already started destroying it.

"Do you think all of the knives can do that?" Travis asked, pulling out the knife he had taken from Eckert's room, a small dagger with a handle made of a smooth dark green stone. He cut an x into the same tree, and Sadie winced. They waited in silence for the tree to burst into flames again—but it didn't.

Nothing happened.

"Lame," Travis said, slipping the knife back into its sheath and dropping it into his bag.

Jenny took out a knife in a black leather sheath with a swirly black-and-white marble handle that looked exactly like her wolf's fur. She awkwardly slid the knife out and walked over to the tree. She carved a tiny little *x*, then backed away quickly. Again, nothing happened.

May took out *her* knife—it had a broad, slightly serrated blade with a worn wood handle. It looked like the kind of knife you'd cut bread with, not wood, but May dragged it across the tree anyway. Again, nothing happened. Sadie thought about her own knife, shoved carefully into the outside pocket of her backpack. She didn't think anyone had seen her take the knife from Eckert's room, but all eyes turned to her, waiting for her to add her own *x* to the marred tree.

"What? I'm not doing that," she snapped. "None of the other knives did anything. I'm sure the one I have wouldn't either. Can we just move on? And maybe someone else can mark the trees as we go. I don't want to start a forest fire."

Sadie shifted uncomfortably and waited for them to stop staring at her. She didn't like damaging the trees like this—even if they were fairy-tale trees bent on their destruction. She also didn't like the idea of pulling out her pilfered knife and waving it around in front of everyone. She had hoped to keep it a secret altogether, but apparently it had never been one.

She brushed past Jenny and determinedly started down the path. She wanted to get this over with as quickly as possible— and she knew the sun wouldn't stay up forever. The last thing she wanted was to be stuck in this forest after dark. Sadie looked out at the trees surrounding them—green spruces, white birches, plump little bushes. It reminded her of the forests she'd seen underneath the castle when she and Jenny had saved Hannah from the Monsters' Ball. Except these trees weren't made of gold and silver—just regular wood and leaves. She glanced anxiously to her left and right, searching for anything that might jump out at them. If she came across one of those giant spider monsters in here ...

She shivered at the thought.

Sadie sensed Jenny coming up next to her. Marble was in step with Jenny, his long tail flicking back and forth.

"Are you okay?" Jenny asked softly.

No, I'm not okay, Sadie thought but did not say out loud. The path ahead could take them anywhere; they had no map, and the forest itself was full of unpredictable magic. She had no idea what they would face. After what they had experienced in the castle—dancing corpses, spider monsters, ghosts—it could be anything. She wasn't confident that they would even be able to find Rain and Ryan, and if they *did* find them ... she didn't know if they'd even be alive. She had been so quick to back up Jenny, to follow her on this crusade, but now that she was here, actually doing it, she started to question herself. *Why are we risking our lives for Ryan and Rain? Are two lives really worth more than our combined five lives? This doesn't make any sense.*

I never even liked Ryan, she thought bitterly. He was so one-dimensional, as deep as a kiddie pool. Everything was always so easy for him, with his blonde hair and perfect tan and that stupid guitar he brought everywhere. When Jenny had started dating him, Sadie had liked him even less. She never had any problem with his sister, Rain, but she barely knew her. Rain was almost boringly beautiful with her long golden-blonde hair and bright smile. The only thing marring her perfect appearance was a long vertical scar that ran down her chest from the multiple heart surgeries she'd undergone since childhood. Sadie didn't know much about Rain's heart condition, just that it kept her from doing a lot of things the rest of them took for granted. She couldn't help but wonder if Rain's heart was strong enough for whatever she was going through.

Regardless of how she felt about either of them, she'd apparently decided they were worth risking her life for. *No, not them*, she knew. *I'm not risking my life for* them.

Sadie could feel Jenny staring at her, but she looked straight ahead, refusing to meet Jenny's eyes. Anxiety trickled down her spine and arms, causing her to tremble slightly.

"Yeah, I'm fine," she said as evenly as she could. "I just want to get this over with."

Out of the corner of her eye, she saw Jenny nod slightly and turn away.

I'm not okay, she thought. *But no one needs to know that.*

2

Jenny walked quietly beside Sadie with her attention focused forward. She could feel a tension in the air, despite what Sadie had said. Their recently renewed friendship still felt fragile, and Jenny didn't want to undo the progress they'd made.

It was chilly inside the forest with the path completely covered in shadow. Jenny looked up at the canopy above them—just a few tiny cracks of golden light filtered through the thick leaves. It reminded her of something she'd learned in art class last year. She searched her mind for the word. *Kintsugi,* she remembered, the Japanese art of fixing broken things with gold to create something new. She had really liked the idea that something could be even more beautiful after it had broken.

As they walked, Jenny breathed in the fresh scent of the forest. Every Christmas season, Ryan would work at his uncle's tree farm, helping families with U-cuts, spraying the fresh green needles with fake snow, strapping trees tightly to the tops of cars. He always smelled so good after working at the farm, and her heart ached wondering where he was, what was happening to him.

She let her fingertips rest on Marble's back and drew some comfort from the soft warmth of the wolf's body next to hers. Marble had been in her life just over a day, but it felt like he'd always been there, and she had no idea why. What was he exactly? Why was he with her? He had followed them into the woods, so he wasn't tied to the castle the way Bannan and Sophie were, but he was clearly no ordinary wolf. He turned his large head to look up at her. It was almost as if he could hear her thoughts. She searched his dark eyes for answers but found none.

She glanced over at Sadie, who looked lost in her own thoughts. They continued down the trail in silence. Jenny looked furtively around, seeing nothing but identical trees as they made their way down the trail. She didn't know what it was she was looking for but hoped that she'd know it when she saw it. After what felt like almost an hour of uneventful walking, she finally saw something different ahead of them—a massive tree with a gnarled trunk and twisted branches.

The trail they were on split at the tree, heading in two different directions. They now had their first choice to make—which path would they take, left or right? Jenny glanced down both, trying to see as far down each as she could, but they looked exactly the same. No sign as to where either of them led.

"We shouldn't split up," Sadie said firmly, throwing Jenny a stern glance as if that was what Jenny might suggest.

"No, of course not," she responded, a little wounded. She wasn't stupid. Splitting up was the last thing they should do—the forest hadn't done anything strange yet, but she knew it was just a matter of time.

"Should we eeny, meeny, miny, moe it?" Travis said from behind her. She smiled faintly. It was a stupid idea, but it wasn't like she could think of anything better. She looked over at May hopefully.

"Do you have any idea which way to go?" she asked.

May frowned and shook her head. "No idea. We could try looking through the book for stories about split paths ... but it would take forever, and the answer in the story might not even be the right answer here."

Jenny looked down at Marble sitting next to her. "How about you? Which way should we go?"

Marble looked up at her with his dark, shiny eyes but made

no movement.

"Where's a caterpillar when you need one?" Aiden asked with a smile. Jenny stared at him blankly. She was starting to tire of his random nonsense comments. Even May, who had seemed to be enjoying them, was looking at him with confusion.

"No one?" he said, looking around at them. "'If she had kept going down *that* way, she would've gone straight to that castle!'" he continued in a high, slightly British-sounding voice. More blank stares. Aiden rolled his eyes and exhaled with irritation.

"*Labyrinth,*" he said bitterly, more to himself than them.

"Okay!" Sadie said, a little loudly for the quiet forest. "So let's just pick one and take it."

Jenny knew she was probably right but couldn't help but feel like they were missing something. She looked around the ground and scanned the fat, gnarled tree in front of them for anything telling, like an arrow carved into the trunk or something. But she didn't see anything except for hard, crusty bark and ... golden pears. She could have sworn they hadn't been there a moment before. She turned to the rest of the group to point it out, but before she could even open her mouth, Aiden was beside her, reaching into the tree and pulling at one of the shimmering gold pears.

"Aiden, no!" May, Sadie, and Jenny all yelled simultaneously.

A loud snap echoed through the forest as Aiden pulled the pear off the branch. He turned to look at them in surprise.

"What? It's just an—"

Jenny felt the earth beneath her begin to shudder and collapse, as if the ground were being sucked away from her and toward Aiden. She watched in horror as Aiden was pulled into the earth, pear still clutched in his hand. She tried to reach down to him, but the ground slid away underneath her, and she felt herself being pulled down after him. She lost her footing and fell to the ground, and the wind was knocked out of her lungs.

She scrambled backward, away from the expanding sinkhole. She felt Sadie grab on to her wrist and try to pull her back, but her hand slipped from Sadie's grasp as the ground continued to disappear from underneath her. One moment she was looking into Sadie's panicked face, the next all she saw was dirt and darkness.

3

Stunned, Sadie stood at the edge of the hole with her hand still outstretched. Everything had happened so quickly—Jenny and Aiden were there, then they weren't. All that was left was a gaping hole in the ground where they had been standing. It stopped expanding once Jenny had been sucked in, saving Sadie from the same fate.

"Where did they go?" Sadie yelled, her voice breaking. She fell to her knees and carefully leaned over to look down into the hole, but all she could see was darkness. A darkness she'd never experienced before. A darkness that felt like blindness. She looked quickly back at Travis and May, who were standing a few feet away looking panicked. Marble was whining and pacing back and forth around the opening in the ground. His tail slashed the air angrily.

"Jenny!" Sadie yelled into the hole. "Aiden!"

Sadie held her breath and strained to hear something—anything—coming from the bottom of the pit.

"Yeah?" she heard Aiden's voice echoing up from the darkness. A relief so strong it was almost painful washed over her at the sound of his voice.

"Are you okay?" she called down. "Is Jenny okay?"

"I ... I guess," Aiden replied, and Sadie couldn't tell if he was speaking softly or was just too far down to hear clearly. "Yeah, we're both okay. It's really dark down here. We can't see anything."

Sadie leaned farther over the hole, searching the darkness

for a sign of Aiden and Jenny.

"How far down do you think they are?" May asked, suddenly beside her on her knees, gazing down into the hole.

"I have no idea. It's so dark," Sadie replied, then called down, "How far down do you think you fell?"

A moment of silence passed, and then Aiden yelled back, "Hard to tell!"

"We need to get them out," Travis said.

"Obviously. But how?" Sadie snapped.

"Do we have a rope or something we can throw down to them?" Travis said, looking around the empty trail as if some such thing might magically appear.

"Yeah, I do," May said hesitantly. She moved aside a bright-orange rubber bracelet and another that looked like it was made with paper clips, then unlatched a bracelet made of black cord braided together. She pulled it off and began to unravel it.

"It's a paracord bracelet," she said, answering the unspoken question. "It unravels to eight feet of cord. We can throw it down and try to pull them up with it."

"What? That's insane!" Travis said appreciatively.

"Yeah, if they are less than eight feet down," Sadie grumbled.

"I have two of them," May replied, pulling a second, matching bracelet from her other wrist. "If we tie them together, it'll be almost sixteen feet. I don't know if that's enough, though."

Sadie leaned over and looked into the hole again. No matter how hard she strained her eyes, it was impossible to tell how far down they were; it was too dark.

May tossed the second bracelet to Travis. "Here. Unwind that one."

Sadie watched uselessly as May and Travis unwound the two bracelets. Thin black cord began to pool in front of them, and Sadie wondered if it would be strong enough to pull Aiden and Jenny up. After a few minutes of unraveling, May took the two ends and tied them into a knot, tugging hard on each end to see if it held.

"Okay, we have a rope," May said. "But we need something for them to hold on to so we can pull them back up."

"They can't just hold on to the rope?" Sadie asked, eyeing the black cord.

"They could, but it would be really hard for them to hold on. They'd hurt their hands pretty badly or their grip would slip and they'd fall back down."

"Okay," Sadie said, irritated. "So what then?"

"We need ..." May looked around them the same way Travis had, as if something might appear. Her eyes landed on something in the woods. "A branch."

May dropped the cord on the ground and walked over to the tree line. She bent down and picked up a few sticks and branches, examined them, then dropped them back down to the ground.

"What are you looking for exactly?" Travis asked, joining her.

"A branch thick enough to hold their weight," May replied, dropping another rejected branch to the ground. Travis looked up at the trees and pointed at something Sadie couldn't see.

"What about that one?" he said. May looked to where he pointed and nodded.

"Yeah, that one would probably work, but it's still attached to the tree, and I don't think—"

Travis, ignoring May, jumped up and grabbed on to the tree branch, breaking it off the trunk in one quick move. A loud *snap* echoed into the woods, and Sadie worried something out there might have heard it. Travis held out the branch to May who, looking a little startled, took it.

"Yeah, this should hold them," she said.

Sadie glanced down at the paracord lying on the ground in front of her. She didn't say anything. She didn't want to admit that she had no idea where May was going with this.

May sat back down next to Sadie with the branch in her lap and started snapping off the little sprigs of needles growing along the branch until it was smooth. She wound the paracord around the middle of the branch and tied it off in a complicated knot that Sadie figured probably had a name, but she didn't know it and certainly wasn't going to ask.

"There," May said, testing the tightness of the knot by pulling on the cord. "It should hold. I think."

"Heads up!" May yelled as she lowered the end of the cord with the stick attached into the hole. "I'm lowering down a stick, tell me when you can reach it!"

She fed more and more cord into the sinkhole, until Aiden finally shouted up that he had it.

"Okay, so this isn't great," May said, looking at the paltry two feet of cord they had left. She looked up at Travis standing over them and covering them in shadow. "Can you get me another branch like the last one?"

Travis nodded and rushed off to the side of the trail, looking around for another sturdy branch. Sadie sat in the dirt and watched it all numbly. She felt slightly overwhelmed by what was happening around her. May and Travis were moving so quickly, so efficiently, while Sadie just sat there not knowing how to help. There was another loud *snap*, and Travis returned with another branch.

"Perfect," May said, taking it from him. Travis grinned like a puppy who had pleased his master, and it made Sadie want to puke.

May repeated the process, removing the sprigs of needles and small offshoot branches and tying the paracord around the middle of the branch. Sadie examined May's creation with uncertainty. The branch was only long enough for one person to hold it.

"Okay, Travis, you're going to be doing most of the work,"

May said as she stood up. She held out the branch to Travis, who took it. "Grip it as close to the knot as you can, and slowly move backward. Sadie and I will wait at the hole to grab them as they come up. Make sense?"

"Sure, sure, make the guy do all the work," Travis said with a playful smile. He followed May's instructions and held the branch in the center, on either side of the cord. May kneeled down next to Sadie and yelled into the hole, "Okay, we're going to pull you up! Hold on to the branch!"

"We're ready!" Aiden yelled back. "Jenny's going to go up first!"

"Alright, Travis, you ready?" May said, turning to look at him.

"Ready," Travis said seriously from behind them.

"Okay," May said. "Travis, *pull*!"

Sadie heard Travis grunting behind them and his feet shifting on the ground as he pulled. The cord began to come toward her, inch by inch, with Jenny dangling at the bottom. Marble crouched at the edge of the opening, his long black nails digging into the ground. Sadie squinted into the darkness, trying to see her, and finally saw the branch come into view, with Jenny's hands clasped tightly to it.

"Almost there! I see her!" Sadie yelled. She couldn't believe this was working. *We're doing it!* Jenny's head came into view—her brown curls stuck to her sweaty, dirt-streaked face. Soon Jenny would be close enough to grab and pull up. Travis slowly continued to yank the cord, and Jenny was almost within Sadie's grasp.

Her eyes fell on the knot tied around the branch between Jenny's hands. The knot was loosening, and before she could shout out a warning, it came undone, releasing from the branch entirely. Sadie watched in horror as Jenny disappeared again into the darkness, leaving behind the echo of a scream.

4

Jenny fell backward, weightless for a brief moment, before she hit Aiden, who had been standing right below her. She felt him crumple underneath her, and they both hit the ground, with Aiden softening her fall. He cried out in pain as her elbow hit him in the stomach.

"Sorry!" she cried, scrambling to get off him, blind in the darkness. She felt along the ground until she hit a wall and stopped, using it to steady herself as she stood up. She looked around, eyes wide, trying to see anything—even just an outline—in the dark. She thought her eyes would adjust, but they didn't; everything around her was pure black. She only had a vague concept of the size of the space they were in, but it was enough for her and Aiden to move around freely without crashing into each other.

"Jenny, are you okay?" she heard Sadie call from above them.

"Yeah!" she called back. "What happened?"

"The knot came undone. Can you throw the branch back up here? We'll try again!"

The branch! Jenny must have let go of it when she fell. "Aiden, help me find the branch," she said, dropping back down to her knees and feeling around blindly. She bumped into Aiden a few times while they groped around for the branch. "Hey, what about your knife?" she asked, looking in the direction she hoped Aiden was.

"Oh, yeah! Hold on."

She heard some movement and then a disappointed groan.

"It's not working," he said. "I think it needs something flammable to stab."

Jenny thought for a moment about the copy of *Grimms' Fairy Tales* inside her backpack. It was certainly flammable, but it wouldn't burn for very long and then she wouldn't have the book anymore. No, better to wait it out in the darkness.

She crawled around some more, running her hands across the hard-packed earth. She tried not to think about what her hands might touch-if there were some horrible bugs or something worse on the ground. She started worrying the branch had been sucked into some void and lost forever when she felt something long and hard underneath her hands. She grabbed it and carefully stood back up.

"Got it!" she yelled. She readied herself to throw it up when she realized it felt a lot lighter than it should have. She hesitated, feeling the object in her hands with more focus, and realized it wasn't the branch. It was too smooth, with one bulbous end and ... She felt a smaller object attached to the other end and examined it with her fingers. It moved a little, and she could feel one, two, three, four, five smaller pieces on the very end in differing lengths. Jenny screamed and dropped the leg bone to the ground, rubbing her hands vigorously against her jean shorts and trying to get the feeling of the bone off her hands.

"What happened?" she heard Sadie call from above.

"There are bones down here!" Jenny screamed up at her. "I think they might be human!"

Jenny didn't *think* they might be human. Jenny *knew* they were human. Animals didn't have foot bones with toes like that. Her hands trembled, and she didn't want to feel around the ground again for the branch.

"Aiden?" she whispered into the darkness.

"Yeah, I'm still down here," she heard from somewhere on the ground. "I think I found it."

She heard him get up and felt him press the stick against her. "You should throw it," he said as she accepted the stick clumsily. "You're the pitcher of the softball team, and my arms are basically noodles."

She laughed awkwardly, not certain how to respond to his self-deprecating joke.

"Okay, heads up!" she called out to Sadie. "I'm throwing it!"

Jenny leaned back and chucked the branch like she'd seen during the javelin throw segment while watching the Olympics on TV. She'd never done it before, but she hoped she'd throw it hard enough to make it to Sadie. She watched it go up and up and disappear into the light.

"Got it!" Sadie yelled. "Hold on, we're going to try tying it back together."

Jenny nodded, though no one could see her do it. She turned and tried to find Aiden in the darkness but couldn't tell where he was. "Aiden?"

"Yeah?"

"Where are you?"

"Here," he said, patting her shoulder. She grabbed on to his arm. If she were able to see his expression, she might have been too embarrassed, but she felt adrift and lost in the dark and needed something to hold on to. Part of her was afraid if she didn't, he might disappear into the darkness and leave her there. Alone.

Aiden was Ryan's best friend, but she rarely hung out with him. She searched her mind for something to say to him while they waited. She thought about Sadie's long-suffering crush, but knew Sadie might actually murder her if she were to say anything to him about it.

"Are you okay?" he asked softly.

"Yeah," she replied. "I don't think I'll be taking up rock climbing when we get back," she joked weakly.

"If," he answered.

"If? If what?"

"*If* we get back."

Jenny felt like she'd been punched in the chest. She had been trying so hard not to think about it like that. She tried to focus on what was happening now, right in front of her, rather than what was waiting in the future. If she let herself think about it, about the possibility that they might never make it out of these woods ... Well, she just couldn't let herself think that way.

"Don't say that," she said as firmly as she could. "We're going to get out of here."

"Out of where?" he scoffed. "Out of this hole? Out of these woods? Out of the castle? Out of Germany?"

Jenny blinked in the darkness. Until this moment, she had thought Aiden was handling their situation better than anyone else; he was always ready with a joke or an idea. It had seemed like he was almost *enjoying* what was happening.

"Are *you* okay?" she asked. She heard him sigh next to her.

"I don't know. I thought I was holding it together pretty well, you know, trying to keep things light. But now ... I don't know. I really don't like being in this hole."

Jenny didn't blame him. It had been bad enough before she'd found the human leg bone. Now she was starting to feel claustrophobic, like the walls were closing in on them.

"I miss Ryan," he said so quietly Jenny almost didn't hear him. Jenny turned to look at where she knew he was standing but couldn't see his face. She had been so wrapped up in her own pain she hadn't for a moment thought about how all of this might be affecting Aiden. He had grown up with Ryan; they'd been neighbors and known each other their entire lives. Ryan had always been a constant for Aiden, she knew that much. Aiden's parents had divorced when he was ten, and at first it wasn't so bad. His dad had rented an apartment in town, and he'd still seen him almost as much as he had before the divorce. But then his dad had moved to another town a few miles away, then San Francisco, then he'd taken a commercial fishing job in Alaska, and now Aiden saw him only once a year over Christmas break. Aiden didn't have any siblings, and his mom worked a lot, so he was often over at Ryan's for dinner or sleepovers. They were together so often people would joke that Ryan, Rain, and Aiden were actually triplets.

Jenny knew she had changed things between them when she started dating Ryan. Maybe that was why she had always given Aiden some space. In the beginning, it was obvious that Aiden had resented her for coming between him and Ryan, for taking up Ryan's time. It seemed, though, that Aiden had finally accepted her. She knew she wasn't his favorite person, but they got along. Now here she was, clinging to his arm in the dark.

"He's the only one who *gets* me, you know? He gets all my references and was always down to watch old '80s movies with me when my mom was working late. He's just always been there, you know?"

Jenny stiffened slightly at Aiden's sudden outpouring. He'd never spoken to her like this before, and she had no idea how to respond. The moment felt incredibly fragile, like if she said the wrong thing, he'd shut down or even get angry.

"Yeah, I know. I miss Ryan too," she said weakly. She had no idea what else to say.

"We were supposed to go to college together and be roommates," Aiden continued. Jenny swallowed. Ryan hadn't mentioned any such plan to her. When they talked about the future, it was always left vague, but one thing had been constant: his focus was going to be his band. Aiden had tried, she knew, to learn guitar so he could be in it. She'd even heard him practicing at Ryan's once or twice. But he'd just never gotten the hang of it and had eventually given up. Music just wasn't his thing, no matter how much he wished it were. Jenny had always had a suspicion that he was even more jealous of Ryan's band than he was of her.

"Okay, ready?" Sadie called from above. Jenny felt a rush of relief.

"Yeah!" she called back quickly. They heard the branch fall and slap lightly against the dirt wall. Jenny felt around for it and grabbed it firmly on either side of the cord.

"Ready!" she called up.

She moved up as they pulled. Her arms ached as she held on, and her shoulder joints burned. With short jolts, she was pulled closer and closer to the light above them, and she held her breath, praying the cord would hold this time.

She looked up and saw the tip of Sadie's shoe at the edge of the hole. She was almost there. She looked around to see if there was anything she could hold on to if the cord broke again, but she saw nothing but weak little roots and dirt.

She reached the rim of the pit and felt Marble grab her by one of her backpack straps, and Sadie and May's hands wrapped around her arms to yank her up. Together the three of them pulled Jenny out of the hole, and she landed face-first in the dirt, out of breath and aching, but *out*.

5

Sadie fell backward as Jenny collapsed in front of her.

"Thank you!" Jenny coughed, pushing herself up into a sitting position. Jenny was covered in dirt; her clothes were filthy and her face was smudged. She saw that Jenny's hands were red and raw from holding on to the branch. Sadie glanced back at the hole where Aiden was still trapped.

"Alright, one more time," she said to the others.

"Hold on, I need a minute," Travis said, sitting down on the ground near Jenny. He rubbed at his large raw hands and winced. "Just a short break. Aiden's not going anywhere."

Sadie looked at Travis. His face was covered in sweat and his singed T-shirt was soaked through. Sadie felt a touch of guilt and nodded.

"Hold on, Aiden!" Sadie yelled down. "We need a minute!"

"Oh, sure, no problem!" Aiden yelled back. "I'll just hang out down here in this creepy black hole with a bunch of human skeletons! Take your time!"

Sadie smirked and sat back, away from the opening in the ground. She looked around the bedraggled little group. Everyone looked hot, sweaty, and tired, and the thought of having to do that all over again was not appealing.

May was behind her, fiddling with the knot and tying the two cords together, tightening and then trying to yank them apart. She seemed to be satisfied because she set the cord down and looked up, locking eyes with Sadie. Sadie turned quickly away to face Jenny.

"What's it like down there?" she asked.

"Dark. Dirty."

"That's it?"

"That's it."

Sadie glanced at the twisted tree with golden pears standing innocently across the hole from them. *Grab a pear and get sucked into the ground. Sure, great, why not?*

"So, do you think those pears do anything?" she asked the group.

Jenny took her copy of *Grimms' Fairy Tales* out of her backpack and opened it up to the table of contents. "Let's see, shall we?"

Jenny started reading, and Sadie sat awkwardly in the silence that followed. They all just sat there, waiting, staring at Jenny.

"Here's one about a juniper tree, but that's probably not it, right?"

"Definitely not," answered May, shaking her head. "I know that one. It's really high up there on the twisted scale."

"Ooh, what happens?" Travis said with a grin, leaning forward slightly, as if waiting for story time. May looked at him blankly.

"A woman kills her stepson, chops him into pieces, and feeds him to his father."

Travis's mouth fell open a little, and he looked like he might be sick. "Why ... why were these stories written? They're disgusting!"

May shrugged.

"Well there are stories about golden eggs, golden children, and, of course, golden keys, but I don't see anything about golden pears," Jenny said, still staring at the table of contents. "Wait." Jenny stopped reading and started flipping through the book, looking for a specific page.

"What? Did you find something about golden pears?" Travis asked. "If the story is gross like that last one, you can just keep it to yourself *thankyouverymuch*!"

"No ..." Jenny said, distracted as she read. "It's about Sophie. I found her story."

Sadie straightened and stared at Jenny. She thought of the young girl—a fairy tale character—who had worked in the kitchen at the castle, how she had *sort of* tried to help them. "What? What do you mean?"

"When I was in the kitchen, right before we left, she told me what her story was. She had these three beautiful dresses and a gross fur coat. She said they called her Allerleirauh."

"*All Kinds of Fur*," May said softly. "I know that story ... Poor Sophie."

"Do I even want to know?" Travis asked.

May shrugged again. "Probably not."

"Well, *I* want to know," Sadie said. "What's the story about?"

"Sophie ... Allerleirauh ... Ugh, it's gross," May answered. Jenny looked up from the book, apparently done reading.

"Her dad tries to force her to marry him," Jenny filled in as she slammed the book closed. "She runs away and works in a kitchen at a different castle. The king of that castle eventually marries her."

Sadie's stomach tightened. She thought about the young girl she'd talked with in the kitchen. If *that* was her story ...

"So why is she still in the kitchen then? Shouldn't she be a queen or something?" Sadie asked.

"I don't know," Jenny replied. "None of the stories so far have been exact matches to what's in the book."

"What is wrong with German people?" Travis yelled. "They're all a bunch of sickos!"

"They're just old stories," May said, shaking her head. "They're not real."

"Well they're real *here*!" Travis argued. He looked disturbed, his eyes shiny and his face flushed. May didn't respond.

Sadie shivered as a cool breeze blew past them—the only movement in the forest. She pushed away the disturbing story and tried to think about what they were going to do when they got back. *Hopefully Hannah and Cameron will be successful and there'll be help waiting for us when we get out of these stupid woods.* They'd be able to go home. She let herself fantasize for a moment: the comfort of her own bed and the safety her house and parents promised. She even looked forward to seeing her annoying siblings again. Sadie glanced back at the hole and felt the fantasy rip away from her. They were so far from home, so far from the end of all this.

"Hey, guys!" Aiden's voice echoed out of the hole. "Think you could get me out of here now?"

6

Jenny stood awkwardly at the rim of the hole, not knowing what to do. Travis was holding the branch, and May and Sadie were at the edge of the hole, prepared to grab Aiden like they had Jenny. It was a little strange seeing it from this angle, the not-inside-the-hole angle.

"Okay, throwing the branch down!" Sadie called before dropping the shorter branch into the pit.

"You got it?" she called. A moment passed. Then another. Jenny remembered how hard it had been to find the branch in the dark.

"Got it!" he finally called back.

"Okay, Travis, pull!" May yelled. Jenny watched as Travis huffed, pulled on the branch, and slowly walked backward, away from the hole. Jenny felt awkward standing there without a task and eyed May's thin arms and knobby elbows. She felt the defined muscles in her own arms from years of playing softball and was certain she had more upper body strength than May.

"Here, let me do it," she forced herself to say, gesturing for May to move aside. May looked up at her, puzzled, then seemed to understand and moved out of her way.

Jenny took May's place crouched next to Sadie and stared hard into the hole, desperately willing Aiden to appear. Travis was grunting and wincing, the branch cutting into his palms. Jenny stole glances at the cord, afraid it wasn't strong enough to lift Aiden. He was heavier than Jenny, but not by a lot. *He'll make it*, she told herself.

Travis pulled, bringing Aiden up inch by painfully slow inch until finally Jenny could see a slight glint in the darkness—the light reflecting off his eyes.

"He's almost up!" she yelled, reaching into the hole to grab Aiden's wrist. His hands were still clinging to the branch. She got a good grip and struggled to pull him up, her own arm burning. His legs scrambled at the side of the hole as dirt crumbled down into the darkness. Jenny could feel herself sliding forward. *No, not again!* She tried to get better footing, but kept slipping in the smooth dirt. Sadie reached in and grabbed him by his other arm, and she felt his weight lessen slightly. Jenny felt a warm, slightly wet something press against her lower back—Marble had bitten onto the back of her jeans and was pulling her away from the hole.

They yanked one more time, and Jenny let out a loud groan as she pulled Aiden over the edge. He fell onto Jenny's feet, which he hugged.

"Never have I been so happy to see feet," he said, out of breath but smiling.

Travis dropped the other branch and rubbed at his raw, blistering hands, and Jenny felt a twinge of guilt. *This is my fault*, she realized. *Anything that happens to any of them will be my fault.*

They moved away from the hole and sat down on the ground together, covered in sweat and rubbing their hurting hands, arms, and backs.

"So, I probably shouldn't eat this, right?" Aiden said, holding up the gold pear he'd pulled from the tree.

Jenny stared, bewildered, at it for a second, then snatched it from his hand and threw it as hard as she could into the forest.

"Okay ... guess not," Aiden mumbled.

"So, what have we learned?" Sadie said, looking at Aiden sourly.

"Don't take fruit from trees," he grumbled.

"Not just that! Don't touch anything you don't have to. We have to treat everything like it's a booby trap. We have to assume everything in this forest is here to kill us. Otherwise we're never going to make it out of here alive," Sadie said seriously, her expression dark.

"Heh, you said 'booby'" Travis said, throwing them a weak smile. Sadie rolled her eyes.

"Where did you get that?" Aiden asked, gesturing at the paracord lying lifeless on the ground, its purpose realized.

"Oh man, get this—they're *bracelets*!" Travis said, grabbing May by the wrist and holding her arm up. "May's bracelets!"

May pulled her wrist out of Travis's grasp and scowled at him. She leaned over, picked up the two cords tied together, and started wrapping them loosely around her hand.

"Paracord bracelets?" Aiden responded, admiring both the cord and May herself. "How do you keep getting cooler?"

Jenny glanced over at Sadie, who was glaring at Aiden and May. May didn't seem to notice the glare as she finished wrapping the cord into a tidy ring around her hand. She looked as if she were considering putting it back onto her wrist, then stuffed it into her backpack and zipped it shut. Aiden watched her with interest, then looked back to Jenny when the cord was out of view. May, too, was looking at her, waiting for direction. Jenny rubbed at her aching shoulder and looked around the group. She was a terrible guide, she knew, but this had been her idea. Her expedition. Jenny stood and slapped the dirt off her clothes as best she could.

"Come on, let's keep going," she said. "We'll go ..." Jenny looked in both directions and shrugged, then gestured to the right. "That way."

"Why that way?" Travis asked, peering down the path.

Jenny frowned. "I don't ... really ... know. You have a better idea?"

"The right path it is!" Travis said with a grin.

The group stood to follow Jenny down the path to the right. May and Aiden fell behind the rest of them as Aiden spoke quietly to her. Jenny felt Sadie at her side and glanced over at her. Sadie hadn't said anything when Jenny chose the path for them all, and a sour expression pinched Sadie's face.

"What's up?" Jenny asked.

Sadie looked over at her, startled. "What?"

"Are you okay?" Jenny asked for the second time since they'd entered the forest.

"I'm fine," Sadie spat, her eyes pinned to the ground.

Once again, Jenny dropped it.

They continued down the path in silence, each deep in their own thoughts. As she walked deeper into the forest, she felt her skin pucker with goosebumps and the tip of her nose grow cold. She glanced at Sadie and saw her rubbing at her bare arms. It was getting colder, quickly. Jenny looked up at the blocked-out sky, but it didn't seem much darker than it had the last time she'd looked up. It seemed to her that the deeper they went into the forest, the colder it got.

She stared down the long dark path winding ahead of them and felt a little sick.

She had no idea where they were going.

7

Sadie sped up slightly, walking a few steps ahead of Jenny, to avoid any more annoying questions she may feel like asking. She wasn't in the mood to talk. She hated feeling this way—so *less than*. It wasn't even about Aiden anymore, she realized. She was just used to being the strong one, the logical one. May and all her German folklore and survivalist-genius stuff took that from her. She didn't know who she was anymore. She felt like a shadow—following dutifully and adding nothing—a secondary character in someone else's story.

She wasn't even supposed to be on this trip, she remembered. Hannah had talked her into it. If she had just said no, she'd be safe at home right now and everyone here ... would be in exactly the same situation. Her being here didn't make any difference.

"Did I ever tell you guys about the time I fought a shark and won?" Travis called from the back of the line. "I was surfing over at—"

The group groaned loudly in unison. Sadie couldn't help smiling a little. She'd never liked Travis, before. She had found him loud, obnoxious, and self-involved. Teachers seemed to find him endearing—despite constantly interrupting classes, he never seemed to get into trouble. They would just smile and shake their heads and move on.

Sadie had seen another side of Travis, though. Two years ago, at the beginning of their sophomore year. After school one day, she'd gone to Seashore Donuts and had seen Travis there with some other guys from the wrestling team. It was a popular place to go right after school, and there was always a long line of kids waiting for donuts. Travis and his friends were towering over a freshman boy, and the energy inside the shop was all wrong. Tense. She'd felt it the moment she walked in. Travis and his friends were trying to cut the line in front of the freshman. Sadie watched from the back of the line as they poked at him, mocked his hair cut, and eventually shoved him out of the line and took his place. The kids behind them watched with sour expressions but didn't say anything. She remembered how infuriated she had been that day, how she'd stormed to the front of the line and placed herself between the freshman and Travis. She'd yelled something about how pathetic it was for them to embrace the bully stereotype so fully and pulled the freshman back into the line.

She might have said some other things, she couldn't really remember. She just knew that Travis and his friends had left the shop without any donuts that day, shamed by a girl half their size. Sadie glanced back at Travis, his T-shirt pockmarked with burn holes, his hands raw from saving Jenny and Aiden, his skin sunburned red. She wondered if he remembered that day. She wondered if he realized that had been her.

She tried to block out Travis's yammering and focus on what was happening around her. She tried to look for clues, anything that might help them find Ryan and Rain, but everything looked the same. Trees and bushes blurred together into one mass of green, brown, and white. It felt like she'd been walking on a treadmill, moving but not actually getting anywhere.

She felt this way right up until she stepped forward and found herself no longer on the path, but in a small clearing. It had happened so quickly that she felt a little whiplashed. She hadn't seen the clearing ahead; she was just suddenly *in* it. Soft grass dotted with tiny white flowers stretched out in front of her, and little white butterflies floated through the air. Sunlight poured in through the large gap in the canopy. It was warm, beautiful, and peaceful, and she felt herself relax a little. To the left, at the far end of the clearing, Sadie noticed a small cottage with a thatch roof and ivy growing up the walls.

The calm Sadie had been feeling melted away. She wasn't a fairy-tale expert like May, but she knew a few stories that featured little cottages in the woods, and none of them were good. Light glinted off a large object resting in front of the cottage, and Sadie squinted to see what it was: a long rectangular box with what looked like a glass lid. It sort of looked like ...

"A coffin," Jenny finished the thought for her.

"So, this is where we just, like, walk right through to the other side, right?" Aiden asked, gesturing toward the path that stretched across the clearing and disappeared into the woods on the other side. "Or did you want to go look inside the random creepy coffin?"

Sadie looked from the cottage and coffin to the path ahead of them. Walking quickly through the clearing and back into the woods, back onto the path they'd been following, did seem like the safest plan. They didn't know, though, what was inside the cottage. Maybe Ryan, Rain, and Eckert were all inside and this would be the end of their adventure. Something inside her told her it wouldn't be that easy.

"We have to check it out," Jenny said hesitantly. "I don't want to go over there either, but we have to see if Ryan and Rain are inside. Or if there are any clues ... or something. We don't really have an option."

"Yeah, I thought you might say that," Aiden said. "I just want to state that, for the record, this is way worse than picking a pear."

Sadie couldn't help but smirk. Aiden wasn't wrong.

"Alright, I'll go first," announced Travis. "Ladies—and Aiden—stay behind me."

Sadie thought she might actually strain her eyes from

how frequently she was rolling them at Travis. Usually she'd push him out of the way, reject his blatant savior sexism, but right now, after everything … she figured she'd let Travis take the brunt of whatever might be waiting in that cottage if he insisted.

Sadie followed slowly behind Travis as they made their way to the glass coffin. Jenny and Aiden were close behind her, but May kept back a few paces. Sadie wondered if she should be back there with May, the one person in their group that had any idea what to expect from these fairy tales. She forced herself forward, behind Travis, and when he stopped, she peered around him to get a look at the coffin.

"Okay, now *this* one I know—*Snow White*, right?" Travis said with a sheepish smile. The coffin lid was made completely of glass so they could easily see into it. Sadie saw a girl about their age with long pitch-black hair, pale skin, and lips the bright shade of fresh blood. The simple pale-blue nightgown she wore spread out at her sides, which reminded Sadie a little of making snow angels. She was the most beautiful person Sadie had ever seen. She was breathtaking, but something wasn't right here. A warning bell started going off inside her head.

"This isn't right, is it?" Sadie said, glancing up at the others gathered around the coffin. "If this is Snow White, why is she in the coffin? Everyone knows this story—she's put under a spell, but a prince comes along and blah blah kisses her and she wakes up, happily ever after. So why is Snow here *still* in the coffin?"

"I don't know," Jenny answered slowly, her face scrunched up in thought. "Maybe … maybe the story isn't over yet. Maybe we're, like, in the middle of it?"

Sadie glanced around the clearing and noticed the others doing the same. If they were in the story, seven little men might suddenly show up. Or the prince. Or the *witch*.

"The story might not be playing out the way we remember from the Disney movie," May said. "The story in the book has differences from the movie. This might be different from both."

"I think we should just keep going," insisted Aiden. "Just go back to the path and keep going. I don't want to be here when her seven friends come back, do you?"

"I don't think we need to worry about that," said May, gesturing to six small moss-covered headstones, all in a row. They'd all been so focused on the glass coffin that they'd walked right past them without noticing. Sadie followed the others as they walked closer to the headstones. She noticed Travis linger at the coffin, still staring down at the girl inside.

Sadie looked at the little headstones and shook her head slightly. *Something* definitely *isn't right here.*

"Oh no," Jenny said, putting her hand to her mouth and turning away. Jenny was a few feet from Sadie and had been looking at the end of the row of headstones. Sadie took a few steps forward and saw what Jenny had seen: a small deformed skeleton resting in the grass to the left of the last grave.

"He was the last one," May said softly beside her. "He buried the rest of them, but there was no one left to bury him."

Sadie stared at the bones and didn't feel afraid or disgusted, just sad. She thought about how miserable it must have been— to watch all of your friends die one by one. Sadie's eyes flicked up to the rest of the group. They were purposefully staring at the headstones, not the body. The headstones had something written on them, but it was in a language none of them understood. *That doesn't really matter, though*, Sadie thought. *We know what their names were.*

"This is too creepy," Aiden said, backing away from the graves. "I think we can all agree it's time to go."

"No, we can't go yet! We have to look inside the cottage first," Jenny insisted. Sadie glanced over at the small, dark cottage. On the outside, it was cute with its thatch roof and round little windows, but she could almost feel a sort of misery emanating from it.

"But what if going into the cottage sets it off or something?" Aiden pushed back.

"Maybe we can just look in the windows," Jenny offered. "Just take a little peak and then run away."

Sadie eyed the small cottage just a few yards away from them. If there was something in there, wouldn't it have come out by now? The house looked quiet and abandoned.

Sadie moved toward the house, her body making the decision before her mind had.

"Sadie!" she heard Jenny whisper-yell from behind her, but she didn't turn. Didn't stop. All she had to do was look in a window. Not difficult. As she got closer to the house, she saw that it was in worse shape than she had realized. Thick cobwebs clung to the eaves, and ivy grew wild over the walls. Where there wasn't ivy, Sadie could see cracks and small holes peppering the walls. The front door was off its hinge a little, propped against the jamb, rather than securely shut. It was not unlike Eckert's bedroom door after they had broken it down. Sadie made her way to the front window, wiped the thick dust from the glass, and peered inside.

It was dark inside the cottage, with tiny pinpricks of light coming in through the cracks and holes in the walls. She could make out a long wooden dining table with eight chairs wrapped around it and a sink filled to the brim with dirty dishes. Everything was coated in dust. No one had been inside this cabin in years.

Sadie sighed and turned back toward the group. They were all gathered by the glass coffin, watching her. She could see Jenny's hopeful expression even from this distance. *Great.* Sadie wished she didn't have to be the one to disappoint Jenny. She walked away from the dilapidated cottage and shook her head slightly as she approached the group.

"There's no one in there, it's all dusty," Sadie said. "I don't think anyone has been in that house in a very long time."

Jenny nodded and looked away.

"This might sound crazy, but hear me out," Travis said, still staring down at the girl in the coffin. "What if we wake her up?"

May, who had been trying to read the writing on one of the little headstones, whipped her head around. "Yeah that's a *great* idea, no way *that* could go horribly wrong!"

"Yeah, dude, that's a terrible idea. Like award-winning bad," Aiden agreed. "Ryan and Rain aren't here. Let's keep going." Aiden turned and made his way back to the path and paused once he reached it. "Well? Coming?"

Sadie looked from Aiden on the path to Travis by the coffin, then at Jenny who wasn't looking at any of them but instead had that faraway look she so often got.

"Yeah, Aiden's right, we should leave," Sadie said firmly, willing the others to follow.

"We can't just leave her here like this," Travis said, his eyes locked on the girl inside the glass coffin. "What if her prince never comes? What if she's not really Snow White but like ... What if she's like us?"

It had never occurred to her that the girl in the coffin might not actually be Snow White. Was it possible, she wondered, that Travis was right? What if this was a real girl, just like them, who had wandered into the woods and had become trapped in this fairy tale? The thought made her pause.

"I'm going to try and wake her up. The rest of you go stand by chicken Aiden."

Before anyone could say anything, Travis lifted the lid of the coffin in one swift motion. Sadie watched in horror as the lid swung upward and fell to the ground beside the coffin. Sadie turned away and covered her face, expecting shattered glass to fly out at her, but it didn't break. She didn't know if the grass was soft enough to break the lid's fall or if the lid was indestructible. She lowered her arm and looked back at the open coffin. The girl inside was now fully exposed.

Sadie's body was tense as she scanned and rescanned the clearing for any movement. Her imagination went wild with visions of zombie-dwarf protectors climbing out of those little graves, a witch with claws and spells swooping in to stop them from waking Snow White. A painful few seconds passed in silence as they waited for something horrible to happen. Nothing did.

"See? Everything is fine," Travis said, smiling and staring down at the girl in the coffin. "True love's kiss, right, May?"

"Well, yeah, but I'd hardly call this true love!" May yelled as she backed away from Travis and the coffin. "You're just going to be some weirdo kissing a corpse."

"She's not a corpse!" Travis yelled back. "In the story she's just asleep."

May shook her head and moved farther and farther back until she was next to Aiden on the trail.

"Travis, please don't do this," Jenny pleaded, her hand on his bulky arm. "Please. Remember what *just* happened to Aiden and me? We were lucky we were able to get out. You have no idea what is going to happen."

But Travis wasn't listening. He shook off Jenny's hand and leaned down over the girl's pale face, paused, then kissed her once on her bloodred lips.

Travis brought his head up from the coffin and looked inside, expectant. Sadie saw his eyes widen and mouth drop open in a desperate *no*.

Sadie looked into the coffin and watched as the girl's body quickly disintegrated. In just a few seconds, all that was left of the beauty in the coffin was a pile of snow-white ashes. Sadie stared, horrified, at the pile of body-shaped ashes that had taken the place of the beautiful girl. Sadie hoped fiercely that the girl had just been a fairy-tale character and not ... real.

"Okay, definitely time to go now," Sadie said, grabbing

Jenny by the arm and dragging her down the path to where May and Aiden waited. "Go, go, go!" she yelled at them as she pulled Jenny behind her.

"What about Travis?" Aiden said, gesturing at the small mountain of a man standing forlornly over the coffin.

"Move it, Travis!" Sadie screamed at him. Travis moved slowly away from the coffin and followed them dejectedly as they made their way across the clearing and to the other side, where the forest began again. Sadie didn't hesitate walking back into the shadowy world of trees. Anything was better than staying near that coffin.

"What happened?" May asked once they left the clearing.

"Turned into ashes," Sadie replied simply.

"Huh. Interesting."

"Well if she wasn't dead when we got there, she certainly is now," Aiden quipped.

"*Aiden*," Jenny snapped, eyeing Travis, who was moving slowly behind them with his head drooped and eyes fixed to the ground. Sadie couldn't feel sorry for Travis even if she wanted to. She was full of bubbling anger at the pure, stupid recklessness of what Travis had done. She bit back the harsh words that waited eagerly in her mouth. She knew this wasn't the time to lose it. It didn't matter now, anyway. What was done was done.

"I'm sorry," Travis muttered. "I'm not sure what came over me. It felt ... I felt like it would work. Like I had to do it. To save her. But she's gone now. I ruined it. I killed her."

"It's just another one of these fairy tales," Jenny consoled him. "It wasn't real. She wasn't real."

Travis nodded glumly but did not look up or respond. Sadie turned away and focused on the path in front of her. In a moment, Jenny was beside her, with Marble trailing behind. Sadie watched the wolf loping easily behind them and realized she hadn't seen him in a while. She couldn't remember him being at the clearing at all. *Where had he wandered off to?*

Sadie pushed the thought away. The comings and goings of Jenny's fairy-tale wolf didn't matter. She eyed Jenny next to her, who seemed withdrawn and a little shaky.

"That girl just ... disintegrated into nothing," Jenny said, shaking her head in dismay. "Why? That's not part of the story. Do *any* of these fairy tales have happy endings?"

Sadie noticed Jenny's eyes glistening with unfallen tears. She knew this wasn't really about Snow White or Travis. There was only one story Jenny was really worried about—and that story was still playing out somewhere in these woods.

They just had no idea how it would end.

8

Jenny still felt nervous, despite the distance they had put between themselves and Snow White. The dwarves were long dead, but there were still a witch and prince that could potentially pop up. She stole glances at the others and saw nothing but dark thoughts written across their faces. They had been walking in silence, a palpable tension in the air, since leaving the clearing. Jenny tried to make herself relax. Nothing had come chasing after them. It was possible that was it. Still, Jenny's eyes flitted back and forth, terrified something would jump out at them at any moment.

She was starting to feel a little claustrophobic too, as the trail seemed to be slowly shrinking around her. The path, once wide enough to easily fit two people side by side, was now so tight they were forced to walk single file. Jenny was in front, and Marble drifted behind her like a shadow. She insisted on going first, though she would have much preferred being somewhere in the middle. This expedition into the woods had been her idea. She should take on the most risk.

As she walked, Jenny struggled to keep herself balanced. Her heart pounded painfully in her chest with the fear of what might be waiting for them around every corner, but at the same time, she was incredibly bored. Walking down an unchanging path with no conversation or distraction was starting to take its toll on her sanity. Jenny winced as a branch reached out and scratched her bare arm. The path had become so tight that she had to bend and weave to avoid the branches reaching out at her. She wondered if the trail was going to continue to shrink until it didn't exist at all. Then what? They'd have to retrace their steps all the way back to the pear tree, where the path had split. The thought of having to backtrack, of losing all the time and energy, made her groan internally. *Please*, she begged the forest silently, *please don't be a dead end.*

As if the forest were listening, Jenny saw the path start to widen, then she saw the path disappear. With an abrupt lurch forward, she felt herself falling off the trail and sliding down a steep bank. She landed hard on the ground, her whole body aching. Marble was close behind her, though he made his way down the bank in a much more graceful fashion. She winced as she looked down at her legs, which were now sporting a scattering of scratches from the fall.

"Jenny!" she heard Sadie call from above her.

"Yeah, yeah. I'm okay! I'm o—" she broke off when she saw what she'd landed next to. She was just a few feet away from the edge of a murky deep-green pond. Shadows from the trees above it played on the surface, and large lily pads with even larger bright-white blooms floated silently as cinnamon-colored cat tails jutted out here and there, looking like magic wands. It was beautiful, something you might see in a Monet painting, but something about it made Jenny feel sick inside. A memory pricked at her brain, sending shivers of an unwanted familiarity through her.

It was just like the pond they had seen that first day at the castle, on their way back from the well. Jenny didn't notice as her friends carefully made their way down the steep bank toward her. She didn't hear them call out to her, didn't feel Sadie's hand on her shoulder. All she heard was the soft movement of the water against the shore. All she felt was a deep desire to drown herself in it.

"Jenny!" Sadie yelled into Jenny's face. She forced her gaze away from the water and tried to focus on Sadie. *Focus*, she commanded herself. *Ignore the pond. Ignore it.*

"What's your deal?" Sadie asked, a tinge of worry under the irritation in her voice.

"Don't, ah, don't look at the water, or touch the water. Avoid the water!" Jenny's voice was strained and broken; she hardly recognized it. The others stared down at her quizzically. Jenny herself wasn't even sure what she was warning them against.

"Oh, dude, look!" Aiden said, breaking the tension Jenny had created with her sudden nonsensical outburst. She glanced over to where Aiden was pointing and saw a deer—the first animal they had seen since entering the forest. It was beautiful, ephemeral—a shimmering gold with long velvety ears. It was standing on the other side of the pond, staring at them with large hazel-green eyes Jenny felt oddly drawn to. The deer felt *familiar* to her somehow. But that didn't make sense.

A sharp gasp cut through the air from behind her. Jenny turned to see May, whose eyes were set on the pond—or rather on something *in* the pond.

Jenny followed her gaze, and her breath caught. Next to her, Marble's eyes were locked onto the figure in the pond as well, and a low growl emanated from his throat. Jenny watched, horrified, as a head covered in long, tangled seaweed-green hair floated along the surface toward the deer. Then, as if feeling their eyes on it, it turned slowly to stare back at them, and Jenny froze. Its dead eyes, cloudy orbs protruding from its sickening bluish-white face, met hers. Its mouth was hidden just under the surface of the water. Jenny felt her heart hitting against her rib cage, begging her to *run*. She tried to breathe slowly and calmly, tried to keep control of herself. Not knowing what lurked under the water was eating at her. Her mind quickly filled in the gaps in the worst ways it could, and she tried to shut it off, tried to make the visuals stop. *Please, please, please don't...*

The head was staring right at her. It wasn't looking at

anyone else but her. A wild thought rushed through her—*what if it can hear me? What if it can hear my thoughts?*

The head slowly rose out of the water, just a few inches. Just enough for Jenny to see its mouth—a round, gaping hole in its face with hundreds of tiny, sharp teeth. She was reminded of when she had gone swimming in a lake with her cousins during a family trip to Minnesota and had come out of the water completely covered in leeches. She'd had nightmares about those leeches for years afterward—their sucker mouths all over her body, chewing into her flesh. Her cousins had thought it was hilarious—her running away from the lake, screaming, and tearing at her own skin.

This creature had the mouth of a leech. It looked like some nightmarish combination of mermaid, leech, and corpse.

"A nixie," May said behind her. Jenny turned to see May backing away from the pond. "Get away from the water. Don't look at it!"

The others backed away, but Jenny couldn't move. The nixie's eyes locked her in place; her entire body felt frozen. She *couldn't move.*

And then the creature simply looked away, and her body relaxed. She could feel her limbs again, could move again. The nixie turned its attention back to the deer, who was still standing at the edge of the water, staring at them with its wide hazel-green eyes. It didn't move as the nixie floated closer and closer to it. Hot panic filled Jenny. The deer wasn't moving.

"Come on, we need to get away from here *now*," Sadie said, pulling her arm.

"But what about the deer? It's going to get the deer!"

The thought of that disgusting pond creature touching the beautiful deer made her sick.

"It's just a deer," said Aiden softly from behind Sadie. "Sucks, I know, but I'd rather not watch what happens when that *thing* catches it."

The others had started to make their way down a path that led away from the pond, the deer, and the bloodthirsty nixie. Jenny looked back at the golden deer, shining there in the shadows. The nixie was only a few yards away from it now. She stared at the beautiful animal, trying to think of what she could do. She had no idea what a nixie could do or what it was capable of–and she really, really didn't want to find out. But the deer was so innocent, so helpless. Jenny's throat closed in on itself. There was something on the deer's chest she hadn't noticed before, but now it was so clear. A long vertical scar ran down its chest. The same scar Rain had from her heart surgeries.

"Rain?" she whispered. "Could ... could that be ..."

She felt someone brush past her and was nearly knocked over. Travis was running toward the deer, something flashing in his right hand as he ran around the perimeter of the pond.

"Hey! Hey, ugly! Look at me!" he yelled, his eyes locked onto the deer as he called out to the nixie. Jenny watched the nixie stop and look at him, a low hissing sound emanating from its sucker mouth.

"What is he *doing*?" Sadie said from beside her.

"I don't know, but come on!" Jenny said, running after Travis, with Marble by her side. She didn't bother to look to see if the others followed her, she just knew she couldn't stand there and watch, doing nothing. Maybe it was just a deer—but they hadn't seen any other animals the entire time they'd been in the forest, not even a squirrel or bird. No, there was something special about this deer, even if it wasn't Rain.

She glanced at the pond to see where the nixie was—it had hesitated only for a moment when Travis had yelled at it, but it was now quickly making its way through the water toward the deer, leaving trembling waves in its wake.

"Move away from the water!" she yelled at the deer. "You need to get away from the water!"

The deer still didn't move. The nixie was coming out of

the water now, and Jenny nearly vomited. The stench of the creature was overpowering—a combination of rotting meat and expired eggs. She quickly pulled her T-shirt up to cover her mouth and nose and tried to focus on getting to the deer before the nixie.

Ahead of her, Travis had put himself between the deer and the nixie, the knife with the handle made of dark green stone he had chosen from Eckert's room flashing in his hand. The nixie's body was almost entirely out of the water now, and Jenny struggled to understand what she was seeing. The top half looked mostly like a human woman—except for its horrifying mouth and bluish skin. The bottom half was worse, though—it was just a black, slimy mass, like a slug or a ... leech. The mouth, the bottom half ... All Jenny could think was *leech*.

"Don't let it touch you with its mouth!" she screamed to Travis.

"Yeah, no shit!" he yelled back. He slashed the air in front of him with the knife, pushing the deer back from the water with his body. The deer faltered under Travis's weight and began to stumble backward, away from the pond. The nixie let out a high-pitched hissing sound and lunged at Travis, who was trapped between the deer and the nixie, unable to move out of the way. Travis screamed in pain as the nixie dragged its long fingernails across his chest. He lurched away from the nixie's reaching arm and slashed it with the knife. The nixie screamed and drew its arm back, its white eyes turning red. A sickly green liquid oozed out of the nixie's arm, and it started to retreat back into the water.

Jenny finally reached the deer and guided it back toward the other side of the pond. "Come on, shh, it's okay. Come on now," she whispered to the deer. The deer seemed like it understood her and had finally shaken off the nixie's spell as it followed her down the trail. Behind her, Travis was still at the water's edge, yelling profanities at the now-cowering nixie, daring it to attack him again. The nixie sunk into the water, disappearing completely under the surface, and did not come back up. Travis wiped the nixie's green-ooze blood off the knife on a nearby patch of moss, and Jenny could see his arm was shaking.

"Travis, come on, let's get out of here!" she called out to him. He turned, and she gasped as she saw the five long gashes running from his left shoulder down to the bottom of his rib cage. The T-shirt he'd been wearing was ripped open, and blood soaked through.

"Oh no, Travis!"

"It's fine, I'm fine," Travis said as he nudged her forward, back down the trail. He looked down at Marble, who was walking quietly at her side. "A lot of help you are, eh?"

Jenny looked down at the wolf, embarrassed. If she had asked him to help, would he have? Would Travis have been able to avoid getting injured? Would Marble have even done anything at all? What was the point of having a magical wolf if it didn't help her friends?

They reached May, Aiden, and Sadie with the deer and gestured for them to follow. They turned quickly down a path leading away from the pond, hoping it was the right one. She had no desire to stop in that clearing or stay there another moment.

"You okay, man?" Aiden said, putting a hand on Travis's shoulder. "I can't believe you did that!"

"I couldn't let another beautiful thing die," Travis mumbled in response. Jenny was surprised to see him so serious—he'd been quiet since watching Snow White disintegrate, but she had figured he was just embarrassed about what had happened. Now Jenny saw it was something deeper than that.

"May, what was that thing? You said 'nixie'?" Aiden asked. May nodded, her eyes glued to the trail ahead of her. "Nixies are like ... fairies, I guess. They show up a lot in *Grimms'*

Fairy Tales. That would be a water nixie. I ... It wasn't what I imagined they'd be like."

"Yeah, aren't fairies supposed to be beautiful? With, like, butterfly wings and sparkles?" Aiden joked dryly. May shrugged, but Jenny figured that was pretty close to what May had been imagining.

Once they were out of sight of the pond, they stopped and tried to collect themselves.

"Here, let me help you," May said, pulling Travis's ripped and burnt shirt over his head as he winced. "Oof, this is bad," she said softly as she examined the gashes across his chest. She pulled a water bottle out of her backpack and a towel she must have taken from the castle.

May poured some of the water onto the towel and began gently patting Travis's wounded chest. Jenny could see him trying not to wince but noticed tears gathering in his eyes. The deer walked over to Travis and gently pressed her forehead against his cheek. He smiled faintly and stroked the deer's neck as May continued cleaning the wounds on his chest. Jenny watched his large hand run across the vertical scar on the deer's chest.

"So, this is going to sound a little crazy, but ... I think that deer might be Rain," Jenny said awkwardly. May stopped cleaning Travis's chest and looked at the deer. Aiden and Sadie also stopped rummaging through their backpacks and looked at the it. Travis quickly withdrew his hand from the deer's chest and Jenny saw a flush of pink rush from his neck upward. The deer looked at Jenny with her large hazel-green eyes. "Uh, are you ... are you Rain?" she directed to the deer, trying to push past how stupid she felt asking that.

The deer nodded, and a collective gasp echoed around the group. Jenny didn't even feel surprised. After everything she had seen and experienced here, a person turning into an animal felt almost ... normal.

"*Rain*?" Travis said, eyes wide. "Uh, sorry for, uh, petting you ... Oh man, you're, like, totally naked right now, aren't you?"

"Travis, if you weren't so injured, I'd smack you," Sadie said with a glare.

Jenny couldn't help but smile, *that* was the Travis she knew.

"How did you know this deer was Rain?" May asked, her head tilted to the side slightly.

Jenny gestured at the deer's chest. "The scar. It's, uh ... Well, Rain has a scar like that. Her eyes, too, are the same color as Rain's ... but honestly, it was a feeling more than anything else."

May shook her head. "Crazy."

Jenny stiffened slightly at the word, then relaxed. Of course she knew what May meant. It *was* crazy. *All* of this was crazy.

"Okay, so yes or no questions again," Sadie said. "Rain, do you know where Ryan and Eckert are?"

The deer nodded. Jenny's heart fluttered with excitement. *Finally! Something good is finally happening!*

"Are they also deer?" continued Sadie.

Rain shook her head. No.

It's Rumpelstiltskin all over again, Jenny thought, a little annoyed. "Can you take us to Ryan?"

Rain nodded.

"Well that'll have to wait until morning," Aiden said. "It's getting dark quickly. We won't be able to continue until it's light out again."

Jenny looked around and noticed for the first time how dark it had become. She couldn't see more than ten feet away, and it was getting darker by the second.

"Do you think we're far enough away from the pond to camp here?" she asked no one in particular.

"Yes. Water nixies are tied to their bodies of water. They can't leave the water entirely," May replied. "I think."

"Yeah, but what about other nixies?" Travis asked, his eyes darting around the clearing.

May shrugged.

"We need to gather some wood while we can still see," Aiden said, pulling out the knife with a curved blade and a handle set with red stones. Jenny remembered the tree on fire—Travis's now-shredded shirt was still pocked with burn marks from putting it out. "I can start a campfire with this!"

"I'll go with you," Sadie offered. "Jenny, keep asking Rain questions. Try to learn as much as possible. May, keep helping Travis."

Jenny saw May roll her eyes, but Jenny didn't argue. She just nodded. Jenny felt exhausted from the long day of walking and the recent adrenaline surge. Having Sadie take charge was more of a relief than an irritation.

Jenny watched Sadie stand up and start moving toward the tree line. Aiden looked at Sadie, surprised, then back at May. "Here, why don't you keep this until I get back?" Aiden said as he set the knife down next to May. May didn't acknowledge him and continued working on Travis's ripped-up chest. Aiden looked a little hurt as he joined Sadie.

Jenny didn't like watching Sadie and Aiden disappear into the trees, away from the safety of the path and the group. No one else seemed concerned, though, and she tried to shake off the anxiety coursing through her.

They were just gathering some fire wood, she told herself, what's the worst that could happen?

9

As Sadie and Aiden walked silently through the trees together, she started to get a strong feeling of déjà vu. Every few steps, they'd stop and pick up a stick to add to their campfire collection, but conversation was nonexistent. She couldn't help but think about the last time she'd been alone with Aiden, when she'd blown up and abandoned him in the ruins. Nothing bad had actually happened to him, he was fine, and yet she couldn't stop feeling guilty about it.

"Um, listen, I just wanted to say, ah, sorry, I guess," she muttered, more to the ground than to Aiden.

"Sorry? For what?" Aiden leaned down to pick up another stick. Sadie swallowed, trying to force herself to say what she knew she had to.

"Just, you know, for the other day in the ruins, when I sort of stormed off and left you there."

"What? Oh, right. Yeah, it's fine."

It's fine?

"That's it?" she blurted out. It had taken everything she'd had to utter the apology, and he was acting like it didn't mean anything. Like *she* didn't mean anything.

Aiden stopped gathering sticks and looked at her with a seriousness she'd never seen in him before.

"Charlotte is dead. Rain is a deer. My best friend is missing, and Travis was just attacked by a pond creature—so yeah, you ditching me during a walk isn't ranking real high on the list of things I care about."

Sadie felt like she'd been slapped. For once in her life she was actually speechless. Aiden turned away from her and continued picking up wood. Her skin tingled with embarrassment, and her hands started to tremble. She wished she could disappear into the woods—anything to be away from Aiden and this moment.

She was struck with an intense need to run. It was the same feeling that had flooded her that day in the ruins behind the castle. She turned away and felt her muscles tense, her body preparing to take off, to run out of the woods, away from Aiden, away from all of this painful awkwardness.

This time she stopped and forced herself to turn back around to face Aiden instead. His arms were nearly full of sticks, and she had only a small handful. He had his back to her still, and she was relieved—she didn't think she could stand him looking at her right now. She started gathering wood as quickly as she could and didn't say anything else. He was right, of course. She felt incredibly stupid and self-involved. It was so obvious Aiden didn't like her. Why had she been holding on to some weak chance he might change his mind? And why did she even care? They were dealing with life and death here, for real, and she was preoccupied by a stupid crush? She had never hated herself before—not until that moment.

"I think this is enough for now," Aiden said without looking at her. "Let's go back to the others."

She nodded pathetically at his back, then noticed something flash bright red in the distance. She squinted her eyes to try and see what was so red in all this green and brown.

"Aiden, do you see that?"

"See what?" Aiden replied, exasperated. Sadie pointed toward the small splash of red in the distance, and he turned to look.

"Uh, yes. I very much see that."

The red figure was too far away to distinguish. Sadie

couldn't tell if it was a person, an animal, or just a piece of clothing hanging from a tree branch. They stood motionless, watching. The red was there among the trees, then it was gone.

"Should we be worried about that?" Aiden asked. Sadie didn't know how to respond. It was just a flash of color, far away from them. But it was the first flash of color like that they'd seen since entering the woods.

"I'm ... really not sure."

"Let's get back to the others," Aiden said nervously, looking over his shoulder, back toward the path they had strayed from. She nodded and followed him through the thick brush when Aiden stopped abruptly in front of her.

"What's going on?"

"Uh, this bridge was definitely not here a minute ago," he said, pointing ahead of him. Sadie leaned to look around Aiden and saw a small cobblestone bridge arched over a wide, rushing creek that had *also* not been there a minute ago.

"This can't be good," Aiden said, setting the wood he was carrying on the ground. Sadie added the few sticks she had to his pile. "This is the way back to the trail. Across that bridge ... that we never went over."

Sadie stared at the creek and the innocent-looking bridge. Maybe they had just missed it? No, how could they have missed walking over a creek? Sadie wasn't as well versed in fairy-tale lore as May, but even she knew this was trouble.

"What should we do?" she asked, looking around for another route back to the trail. She couldn't see one and, in fact, couldn't tell where the trail was at all. "Are you sure this is the way back to the trail?"

"Well, I *was* sure," Aiden said, scratching his head and squinting at the bridge.

Sadie turned around in a circle, looking for anything that might direct them back to the path and their friends, but all she saw were trees, more trees, and even more trees.

"I feel like crossing that bridge would be really, super stupid," she said finally.

"Agreed."

"We're going to have to do it anyway, aren't we?"

"Yup."

Sadie took a deep breath and looked around one last time.

"You first."

10

Jenny's back made a *c* as she leaned over her copy of *Grimms' Fairy Tales*, trying to read as much as she could in the quickly fading light. She absentmindedly stroked Marble's back with her free hand. The wolf, Jenny was relieved to find, showed no interest in Rain despite her deer form. He seemed to know the deer wasn't really a deer.

"What are you doing?" Travis asked Jenny as he tried to ignore the pain May was causing as she cleaned his chest wounds.

"I'm looking for stories with people turning into deer in them," she replied without looking up from the book. "I found one that might fit—it's called *Little Brother, Little Sister.*"

May looked up from Travis's chest, the damp towel hovering over the next moldy claw mark. "That sounds promising, seeing as how it was a brother and sister who were kidnapped."

Jenny nodded and went back to reading. "So, in this story, two children run away from their evil stepmother, but she finds them and puts spells on all the springs in the forest. The little brother drinks from a spring and is turned into a deer." Jenny looked over at Rain, who was hovering next to Travis, her pelt shimmering even in the growing dark. "Did a spring turn you into a deer?"

Rain nodded.

"Well, that's progress!" Travis said, stretching his neck to see Jenny over May's head. "Does it say in the story how to turn her back?"

Jenny turned to the book and scanned through the story, looking for the solution to their deer problem. Her heart sunk when she found it.

"Kill the witch that cursed the spring," she said, looking over at Rain. "Do you know where the witch is that cursed the spring?"

Rain shook her head no.

Sadie felt a coldness run through her. How were they going to find the witch that had cursed the spring if Rain didn't know where she was? And even if they did happen to find her, how would they kill her? She looked sadly over at Rain.

"Keep looking," said May. "Look for stories with any kind of animal transformations, not just deer. See if there is something in a different story."

"Mm, good idea," said Jenny. She studied the stories in the book until it became too dark to read. Jenny looked up from the book and was surprised that she could barely see the others just a few feet away.

May stood up and stepped back from Travis, then tossed the bloody towel off to the side of the trail. "The wounds need to air out," May said. "Hopefully by tomorrow they'll be healed enough to not stick to his shirt, but I don't know. Travis may have to be shirtless for a while."

"You know, I think the nixie might have cut my leg too—might just have to go pantless as well," Travis said with a strained smile. Jenny wondered if he was just leaning against that tree or if the tree was actually holding him up.

"Ha ha," May replied sarcastically. She picked up her own copy of *Grimms' Fairy Tales* and leaned down, squinting at the words briefly before giving up and setting the book to the side.

It was comforting to hear one of Travis's gross jokes, even if the delivery wasn't as enthusiastic as usual. Travis was a lot of bluster and bad jokes, but Jenny knew he had another side to him, a side he rarely showed to other people. Jenny herself had only ever seen it in fragments—little moments here and there. One time she saw him gently pick up a snail from the middle of the sidewalk and move it to the other side so it wouldn't get stepped on. She'd seen him break up more than one fight at school, and everyone knew he worked after school and weekends at the grocery store in town, when he wasn't at wrestling practice or a match. She knew other things too. Things most people *didn't* know.

Last year, she was leaving the apartment of a little girl she sometimes babysat when she ran into Travis's mom and dad. They'd been drinking and were struggling to get to their own apartment a few doors down. Jenny tried to avoid the clumsy couple, but Travis's mother grabbed her by the arm as Jenny tried to squeeze past them. Jenny remembered the woman's eyes were slightly yellow, and her dark eyeliner was smudged. His mom stared at her, hard, for a long, horrible moment before speaking. "Who are you?" she yelled in Jenny's face. "What are you doing here?"

Travis came out of their apartment and steered his parents inside. Stunned, Jenny stood motionless as she watched, not sure what to do. She listened to the delicate tap of flies as they hit the overhead fluorescent light. Travis paused, half inside his apartment, then turned to face her.

"Don't tell anyone about this," he said softly. "Please."

She nodded, and he went inside and shut the door. They'd never spoken of that night, and she had never told anyone about it. A few months later, his dad ran his car off the road and straight into a field of radishes. He was arrested and got a DUI. It'd been written about in the crime section of their local newspaper.

Jenny thought about her own dad, how inconsistent and unpredictable their relationship was. There were days when they got along just fine and would even joke around with each other, but other times he was controlling and infuriatingly unfair. He'd treat her like she was some naive little girl instead of the person who made most of the meals, did the laundry, and had even started doing the grocery shopping when she got her driver's license. When her mother finally went to the psychiatric hospital, it had been a relief—but even though she was unstable and sometimes violent, her mom had still managed to take care of them. With her gone, Jenny felt like it was up to her to keep everything together.

Jenny snapped herself out of the spiral she was falling into. She couldn't let herself get lost in all that, not now. Not here. She turned to look at the place Sadie and Aiden had cut into the woods. "They should be back by now, don't you think?"

"It hasn't been that long," May replied. "But do you think we should go looking for them?"

Jenny stood, walked to the edge of the path, and tried to see if she could see them through the trees. It was too dark, and she knew going after them would be a mistake. She'd probably get lost herself. She looked down at Marble, whose dark eyes glinted in a slim slice of moonlight. "Marble? Can you find them?"

Jenny didn't know if Marble could understand her, but it was worth a shot. The wolf flicked his long tail behind him and turned away from her. He slipped into the woods, and in a moment, he was gone—one with the darkness of the forest.

11

Aiden took a hesitant step onto the cobblestone bridge and paused. "Okay, nothing horrible has happened yet." He took another step and another until he was halfway across. Sadie watched nervously, still not trusting the bridge that had appeared out of nowhere. Aiden looked back at her and shouted, "Come on!"

Sadie grumbled softly to herself as she made her way onto the bridge and met Aiden at the center. "See? It's fine," he said, flashing a smile. Sadie tried to smile back.

This bridge isn't so bad, she thought. It was a little slippery with moss but there wasn't anything scary about it. Not really. The sound of the creek moving underneath them, the sound of water on rock, was almost relaxing. She let out a relieved breath and started to follow Aiden down the other side of the bridge.

"Who's that stomping on my bridge?" a deep voice roared from somewhere underneath them, drowning out the sound of the creek. Sadie jumped and grabbed Aiden's arm reflexively, looking wildly around her for the source of the voice.

"Of course," Aiden said, his smile gone, worry clouding his eyes.

"Who's that stomping on my bridge?" the voice roared even louder, causing the bridge to tremble slightly underneath them.

"Go, just go!" hissed Sadie, pushing Aiden forward. He made his way quickly down the other side of the bridge. Sadie was right behind him when she felt something strong and damp clamp on to her ankle. She screamed and tried to pull away from the massive, putrid green hand holding on to her. Aiden turned at Sadie's scream and came running back up the bridge to her.

"It's going to be okay," he said quickly, leaning over the bridge slightly to peer down at whatever had hold of her.

"What are you doing! Get it off me!"

Then the hand pulled. Sadie slipped on the moss and fell forward, hitting the stone bridge hard as her leg was pulled out from underneath her. The hand started dragging her back the way she had come, and then she felt her legs go over the edge. She stretched her arms forward and tried to grab hold of the cobblestones, but her hands slipped on the smooth, slimy rocks. "Aiden! Your knife!" she yelled, kicking at the hand with her free foot.

"I left it at camp!" Aiden grabbed Sadie's hands and tried pulling her away from the edge. The hand pulled too. Sadie screamed again, this time in pain, not fear. She felt as if she were being pulled apart.

"I'm going to gobble you up!" the voice from under the bridge roared. Something odd stirred in Sadie. She should be—and was—terrified, but something about what the voice had just said sounded familiar and almost comforting, even. It felt like something she'd heard a long time ago—in school? She was reminded of glue sticks and nap mats.

"Ah! It's the billy goats one!" she called out triumphantly.

"What?" Aiden yelled back as he continued to try and pull Sadie from the troll's grasp.

"The stupid fairy—*uhg*—tale! The troll under the—*ow!*—bridge! Eats the goats!" Sadie was out of breath and not sure she was making any sense. Her arms burned from Aiden's fruitless pulling, and her ankle felt like it was being squeezed in a vice where the troll's hand wrapped around it. Slimy moss had rubbed off the cobblestones and was covering her entire front, and her clothes were damp with rank muck.

"Right!" Aiden said, understanding. He thought for a moment, then yelled to the troll, "You don't want her! She's too skinny!"

"Hey!"

"There's a fatter girl coming soon! You should eat her instead!"

Sadie winced at Aiden's words, but they were familiar. That's how the goats had escaped: the promise of a larger meal on the way. The hand stopped pulling, then released her.

"Go on, then," the voice grumbled.

Sadie looked up at Aiden in shock. It had worked! He helped her up, and they ran the rest of the way off the bridge and a little farther for good measure. They stopped, and Sadie looked behind them—no scary trolls were chasing them down. She was breathing hard and noticed Aiden was too. His face was covered in sweat, and he looked shaken.

"Thanks," she said, looking away. "For, uh, you know, not leaving me to be eaten by a troll."

Aiden grabbed her by the shoulders and made her look at him. She was just inches away from him, and her heart was beating wildly in her chest. *What is happening?*

"Sadie," he said seriously, "I would never, ever let you get eaten by a troll."

Sadie burst out laughing, a nervous, strained laugh, and Aiden smiled back at her. His hands slipped off her shoulders, and the moment was over.

"Let's go now, before some other fairy-tale thing pops up," he said, starting to turn, then stopped. "Damn it! We left all the wood behind!"

Sadie groaned. He bent to gather more wood, and this time she joined him in earnest, loading herself up with as much wood as she could carry. They heard voices on the other side of the tree line and found they were merely steps away from the trail and their friends.

"We have returned triumphant!" Aiden called as they stepped out of the trees. He and Sadie dropped the firewood they'd gathered in the center of the trail. "I am Aiden, Destroyer of Trolls!"

Sadie smirked. "It's more like, Aiden, Convincer of Trolls."

"Hey, let me have this," Aiden said, smiling, his eyes twinkling at her.

"I'm sorry, *what*?" asked Jenny.

"Ah, you know, the ol' *troll under the bridge trying to eat you* thing, no big deal," Sadie said as casually as she could. Jenny stared at her with her worried face on. Sadie waved a dismissive hand at her. "Really, we're fine. It was nothing compared to that nixie." She stole a look at Travis, who didn't look any better than he had when they'd left.

Aiden dropped to his knees and began arranging the firewood into a sort of teepee shape in the center of the group. Sadie sat down a short distance away and watched him curiously. Her mind was racing with what had just happened in the woods—and it wasn't the troll she was thinking about.

"Log cabin method is better," moaned Travis from his place on the ground.

"Oh, shut up," Aiden replied playfully, continuing to lean the wood pieces up against each other.

"Did you guys see Marble out there?" Jenny asked, pacing back and forth at the edge of the trees.

"No, why?" Sadie said, following Jenny's gaze into the woods.

"I sent him in to find you ... but I guess he didn't. You didn't see him out there?"

"No, we didn't see him," Sadie replied, looking into the forest herself. She wondered if the wolf would be crossing that bridge too. She wondered if trolls ate wolves. She swallowed the dark thought back. "I'm sure he'll be back. Nothing is going to mess with that guy!"

Jenny cracked a small smile. "Sure, right."

Jenny moved away from the tree line and sat down next to Sadie on the ground.

"May, toss me my knife," Aiden said, turning toward May and extending a hand.

Sadie tried to focus on watching the fire being built instead of thinking about what had happened in the woods. Had she imagined the moment they'd had? Was it nothing, and Sadie was just creating something that simply wasn't there? She felt a little whiplashed by the whole experience.

May leaned toward Aiden, and her long braid slipped from her shoulder and swayed slightly between them. Aiden smiled at May and accepted the knife. Sadie bristled at the brief exchange.

A little flower of jealousy started to bloom inside her. She took a few deep breaths to try and break up the tension she felt inside her chest. *Stop it*, she told herself. *Grow up.*

A sudden *whoosh* of flame startled Sadie out of her thoughts. Aiden had lit the pile of sticks with his knife, and a raging fire was now burning in the center of the trail. The heat felt nice against her skin, and for the first time all day, she noticed that she was hungry. *Really* hungry. Her stomach hurt, and she was starting to feel a little weak.

Jenny opened her bag and pulled out a single loaf of bread.

"Where did that come from?" Sadie asked.

"Sophie," Jenny replied. "She gave it to me right before we left the castle. Probably should have brought more food than this, though, huh?"

Sadie shrugged. She eyed the others, but none of them were pulling out any food. She had hoped they wouldn't be in the woods long enough to need much food, but that was stupid and way too optimistic.

"So ... is Jenny the only one who brought any food?" Sadie

asked, hoping one of them would come through.

"I brought some food," May said, leaning over to grab her black backpack. Sadie cringed. *Of course she did*. She watched as May pulled out a large wedge of red-rind cheese and a long string of sausages wrapped in paper.

"Nice!" Aiden said as he reached for a sausage. May slapped his hand away.

"We need to ration what we have," she said, exasperated. "We don't know how long we'll be in this forest, and we know we can't eat anything we find here. We *do* know that, right?" May eyed Aiden seriously.

"Yeah, yeah, don't pick random fruit, I know," he mumbled, withdrawing his hand from the string of sausages.

"I'll cut up small portions for everyone and save the rest for tomorrow." May pulled out her large knife with the worn wooden handle and started sawing at the chunk of cheese. Next to her, Jenny had started tearing the bread into small chunks. Sadie looked awkwardly around the circle. Everyone seemed to be doing something, *helping* in some way. Everyone except Travis, but he was injured. She started to feel small and useless again.

"How do you know all this survivalist stuff?" Aiden asked May.

"You mean like bringing food and water with you when you go into the woods?" May said sarcastically, rolling her eyes.

Aiden's face reddened. "Uh, not just that. The paracord"— Aiden looked around and gestured at Travis—"the first aid."

May smiled softly, as if remembering something bittersweet, then the smile faded.

"My dad taught us," she replied. "He wanted us to be able to be self-sufficient. He'd take us on these survivalist backpacking trips. He taught us how to purify water, make a shelter ... hunt our own food."

May's eyes looked shiny in the flickering firelight. She stood up and handed Aiden part of a sausage and a piece of cheese, then started distributing the rest of the food to others without another word. Sadie watched as May moved around the group, and felt unsettled. There was something about May's explanation that nagged at her. Like something was missing, had been intentionally left out.

The fire shifted with the breeze, causing shadows to dance across their faces. Sadie shivered and inched a little closer to the campfire. She stared into the flickering flames and watched gray smoke rise from the burning wood and disappear into the sky above them. She thought of when her own dad used to take her camping—*just* her. None of her older siblings ever wanted to go camping, but she always did. Every summer, he'd take her on one trip, usually to Yosemite National Park. It was just car camping, nothing too rugged, but it was the only time in her life when it was just the two of them. No annoying older siblings, no mom even. She didn't really remember them talking about anything special. No movie-esque bonding montages. She just remembered being happy. Then her mother got pregnant again with her little sister, and the trips stopped. They were always going to stop, she knew, but that didn't make it hurt any less.

May's hand dipped into her line of sight, holding a chunk of cheese and part of a sausage. "Here you go," she said, gesturing for her to take the food from her outstretched hand. Sadie hesitated, then took the food.

"Thank you," she said begrudgingly. May took a portion for herself, then placed the remaining food into her backpack. A chunk of bread dangled in front of her face, and she looked up to see Jenny waggling it at her. She took the bread, and Jenny sat back down next to Sadie—she'd already given everyone else a piece, and Sadie hadn't even noticed she'd gotten up.

Sadie flinched as she felt something furry rub against her arm. She turned to see the wolf staring at her. No, not at her. At her food.

"Marble!" Jenny squealed. The wolf took his gaze off Sadie and made its way around her to Jenny. With a soft *thump*, the wolf lay down next to Jenny, his large head facing the fire. "I feel bad," Jenny said softly to Sadie. "I feel like I should give Marble some of my food, but it's not much. Do magical stone wolves need to eat, you think?"

Sadie eyed the large beast resting on the other side of Jenny, curled up like a house cat.

"I really don't know," she said. She didn't mention that Marble had been staring at her food just moments before. Jenny needed to eat.

Jenny nodded and started nibbling on her piece of bread. Sadie looked back at the fire and forced herself to eat her own food. She was hungry and needed to eat, but her stomach felt tight. Out of the corner of her eye, she saw Jenny slip Marble her entire piece of sausage. Sadie shook her head and held out what was left of her own sausage to Jenny.

"Here," she said as she waved the sausage at Jenny. "Take it. You need to eat."

Jenny's face flushed. "You saw that? I can't take your food, Sadie. I'm fine. Really."

"Just take it. I'm not even that hungry," Sadie lied. "Just don't give it to that wolf."

Jenny hesitated, then took the sausage from her and ate it in one bite.

"So, does anyone know any good ghost stories?" asked Travis with a forced grin, the wounds on his chest clearly still hurting him.

"I think we're *in* a ghost story," Aiden said sardonically.

"You guys remember the ghosts in the castle library?" May said softly, her eyes staring down at the fire. Everyone started nodding, the light from the fire flickering across their faces. Sadie thought of the old woman in the peasant dress, forever napping, the fashionable couple from the 1920s, the teenage girls with ponytails and neon workout clothes.

"Sure, how could we forget?" Aiden said next to her.

"Well ... do you guys think that there are ghosts back home too? Haunting the places they died?"

Sadie swallowed and thought about this. If ghosts existed, they'd be *everywhere*. In every house, on the roads, in hospitals and jails, everywhere. The idea creeped her out.

"Oh man, I don't know," Travis said. "I mean, if there are ghosts here, then it makes sense that there could be ghosts other places too, right?"

"Maybe," Jenny joined in. "But maybe it's special to the castle—like the fairy tales are. Those *could* be the only ghosts that exist."

Sadie watched May, who hadn't taken her eyes from the fire but was nodding slightly.

"I don't know if I want there to be ghosts or not," May said. "Is being a ghost better than just ... not existing anymore at all?"

Next to Sadie, Jenny was looking straight up and blinking rapidly, which is what she would do when she was trying not to cry. Sadie wondered if she was thinking about Charlotte. Sadie had believed Jenny when she'd told them she'd seen Charlotte's body inside the wall, and she herself saw the painting of Charlotte as a bride. But something in her still refused to believe it, even now. It was just too strange. It felt like Charlotte had just left, or had stayed behind. *Gone forever* wasn't a feeling she was familiar with.

Rain was curled up on the other side of the fire, near Travis. Sadie wondered if it was because of Marble—Sadie had been afraid of the wolf when she'd first seen it. She imagined being a deer would make the wolf seem even scarier.

"I don't know. I guess I'd rather be a ghost," offered Aiden. "I don't want to just disappear."

Sadie studied May's face, which was softly lit by the

campfire. Her eyes were wide and unblinking, staring into the fire but also staring *past* the fire, at something no one else could see. She was gently pulling at the bracelets on her right wrist. Sadie remembered when she had first noticed the bracelets, that first day when they'd hiked to the well. *So much has changed since then*, she thought. She remembered the question she'd asked May at the well, that May hadn't answered.

"May, where did you move from again?" she heard herself ask. Sadie didn't like mysteries, and May was one she really wanted to solve.

May's eyes flicked from the fire to Sadie, and the lost look disappeared. Her eyes were sharp, focused, and full of suspicion.

"A small town in Washington," May answered curtly. It was the same thing she'd said when Sadie had asked her that first day.

"Oh, really?" Travis said, shifting his head to look at May. "My older sister goes to college in Seattle. What town are you from?"

"You wouldn't have heard of it," she replied coldly.

"Try me!" Travis persisted. "Is it near Seattle?"

"Hey, didn't something happen in Washington last year?" Aiden said, glancing toward May. Sadie watched as the color drained from May's face.

"Lots of things happened in Washington last year," she said tersely. Sadie noticed, though, how her eyes dropped back to the fire.

"Ugh, these cuts are starting to itch," Travis said, groaning. "Must ... not ... scratch ... must ... not ... scratch ..."

"Definitely do not scratch those!" May yelled, the spell broken. "Don't touch them at all, and try not to get dirt or anything in them. You don't want them to get infected."

Sadie looked around at the dirty ground they were all sitting on.

"Yeah, good luck with that," Sadie muttered under her

breath.

"I don't know about you guys, but I'm super tired," Jenny broke in, then yawned for effect. "Should we take turns sleeping or something?"

"Probably a good idea," May said. "I'm not that tired. I can take the first shift if you want."

"I'll stay up with you!" Aiden said, smiling.

"Ah, that's really not necessary," May started, but Travis interjected.

"Good idea, bro. We should do it in pairs. Keep each other honest."

Travis attempted to make himself more comfortable by leaning against the tree, and Jenny lay down and nestled against her wolf. Sadie tried to make herself as comfortable as possible on the hard ground, using her backpack as a makeshift pillow. She closed her eyes and tried to clear her head, tried to sleep. She heard the soft crackle of the fire and low whispering between May and Aiden. *Great. Exactly what I want to listen to as I try to sleep.*

She tried to focus on the sound of the crackling fire and not whatever Aiden and May were talking about. Before long, it was all white noise, and Sadie drifted to sleep.

12

Jenny woke up in pain. Her feet and legs hurt from all the walking they had done the day before, and her back ached from sleeping on the hard ground all night. She slowly sat up and rubbed her neck, which hurt from sleeping at a weird angle. Marble's deep black eyes opened and stared at her, but he didn't move to get up. The fire Aiden had started the night before was now just a few glowing embers, and she was happy to have had Marble's body for warmth during the cold night. Sadie was still asleep on the other side of Marble, playing big spoon, her body wrapped around his. Jenny couldn't help but smile.

On the other side of the firepit, Aiden and May were nestled together underneath both their jackets, and Jenny felt a soft pang. Seeing them like that made her miss Ryan. She had been trying so hard not to think about him too much, not to miss him like this. She didn't want it to fog her judgment or distract her. But now, in the blue dawn of morning, she allowed herself to think about him. To worry. Where was he? Why had he been separated from Rain? Why was Rain a deer? Questions flooded her mind, and she felt so frustrated that Rain was *right there* but couldn't answer them.

Wait, where's Rain?

Jenny looked around the clearing but didn't see the golden deer anywhere. Panic rushed through her, and she looked again, her eyes not believing what she didn't see. Travis stirred and slowly sat up. He was the only one without a buddy to keep him warm. Jenny followed his motion, then gasped. He had slept shirtless to keep the fabric of his shirt from sticking to the fresh wounds, and she could see the five claw marks across his chest. Except they didn't look like they had yesterday. They looked much, much worse.

A dingy brownish-green mold was spreading outward from the claw marks. It had grown quickly overnight and was already making its way over his shoulders and down his stomach.

"Oh, Travis ..." she started, but he looked down before she could warn him and let out a surprisingly high-pitched scream when he saw the mold growing on his body. May and Aiden jolted up and away from each other, and Sadie was on her feet in a flash.

"Oh. My. God," Sadie said, gaping at Travis's molding chest.

Travis leapt up and started slapping at his chest, clawing at his own body and trying to scrape off the mold. Jenny was reminded again of the leeches that had covered her that day at the lake years ago. How she, too, had clawed at her own skin to rip them off.

"Travis!" Jenny yelled, running over to him. "Travis, you need to stop! It's going to make it worse!"

Travis's eyes bulged, and he continued to claw at himself as if he couldn't hear her. She tried to grab his wrists, but he yanked them away. She felt movement behind her and then suddenly heard a loud *slap!*

Sadie was standing next to her, the hand that had just slapped Travis across the face now up and ready to slap him again.

"I've been wanting to slap you for a long time, so go ahead, keep freaking out! I'd love to keep slapping you!"

Travis stopped tearing at his skin and stared blankly at Sadie. Tears ran down his cheeks, and a terror Jenny had never seen before haunted his watery blue eyes. In addition to the claw marks, Travis's chest was now covered in long red scratches where he had scraped the mold away. He had green sludge all over his hands and underneath his fingernails.

"I don't understand," May whispered a few feet away. "I cleaned it ..."

"Well not good enough, apparently!" Sadie snapped.

"Sadie, come on, this isn't May's fault and you know it," Jenny said.

"Wait, where's Rain?" Aiden asked.

"Gone. I don't know," Jenny said, slumping down to the ground in front of Travis. She felt a heaviness come over her, and all she wanted to do was lay down on the ground and close her eyes until this all went away. She had felt bolstered by finding Rain, but now Rain was gone and Travis was infected with some sort of magic mold. Her entire body hurt. She was tired and hungry and cold, and it was too much. It had all become too much.

She rubbed her forehead, a headache quickly developing.

"Ew! What is that?" Aiden yelled, pointing at the ground. Jenny whipped her head up and looked at where he pointed. On the ground, rifling through Sadie's backpack, was ... a tiny man. He was about the size of a rabbit and dressed in what looked like a long nightgown in various shades of green. Instead of hair, he had a scattering of tiny mushrooms growing from his head. He looked both delicate and grotesque at the same time. He didn't seem to care that he'd been caught, he just kept digging through Sadie's bag.

"A gnome!" May gasped.

"Hey! Stop that!" Sadie yelled, picking up a stick from the ground and throwing it at the little man. A shimmering gold figure slipped gracefully from the forest and walked slowly toward the gnome. Jenny watched, confused by Rain's sudden appearance. *What is she doing?*

With one quick movement, Rain dropped her head and snatched the gnome by the shirt with her mouth and lifted him off the ground. Jenny stared dumbfoundingly at the tiny man hanging from Rain's mouth. He was wiggling and fighting like a fish on a hook.

"What ..." Jenny was at a complete loss for words. She looked up at Rain and gestured at the small man in her mouth. "Uhm, why ... What ..." Jenny stammered, unable to pull her gaze from the little man.

"It's a gnome, right?" May asked, moving toward Rain. Rain moved her head to look at May, jostling the little man and causing his mottled brown skin to turn almost as green as his nightshirt.

"Why was he going through my stuff?" Sadie interjected, leaning forward to get a closer look at the creature.

May shrugged and picked up Sadie's bag from the ground. "What do you have in here?

Sadie snatched the backpack out of May's hands and scowled. "Nothing! Nothing interesting, anyway."

"Okay, so what are we supposed to do with this thing?" Travis grumbled from his place on the ground. He looked sick and had dark rings under his eyes. The mold had already grown over the places he had scraped off just minutes earlier.

"Maybe he can help us?" Jenny asked.

Sadie drew closer to the gnome dangling from Rain's mouth.

"Do you speak English?" she asked. The gnome covered his ears with his hands.

"I think you're too loud," May said. Sadie glared at May but lowered her voice to a whisper.

"Do you speak English?" she asked again, quietly.

Jenny heard a tiny voice respond but couldn't make out what it was saying. Sadie waved them over, and they all gathered around the dangling gnome.

"Say it again," she whispered.

"I speak all languages," the tiny squeak of a voice said.

Jenny's heart thundered in her chest. Finally! Something useful! Someone who answered questions without using rhyming riddles.

"Do you know how to change Rain back to a human?" Jenny asked as quietly as she could.

"What? Who?" the tiny voice asked, annoyed. "No. What?"

Jenny's brief spark of hope was extinguished.

The gnome looked over at Travis, the mold now covering his entire torso, and grinned. His tiny teeth looked like little gray pebbles in his mouth, flat edged and grimy.

"I offer a trade—I'll tell you how to fix the large man if you give me what I want."

Jenny perked up. "What do you want?"

"What, like our firstborn child?" Aiden scoffed.

May punched Aiden in the arm. "Seriously, Aiden? *Seriously*? Have you not read *any* of these stories?"

Aiden rubbed at his arm sheepishly and shrugged.

"There are a lot of stories where gnomes ask for firstborn children. Like, *a lot*," May explained. "You trying to give him ideas?"

"Sorry," Aiden mumbled.

The gnome had covered his ears again when May started yelling at Aiden. He slowly lowered them when they stopped speaking.

"No, no firstborn children. Takes too long. I want something *now*."

Jenny heard Aiden whisper to May, "What do they do with the firstborn children?"

"Not now," she hissed back.

"So what, then?" Jenny asked.

The gnome turned to look at Sadie and grinned a horrifying smile, so wide it seemed to cut his head in half. "*You* have something I want."

13

All eyes were on Sadie. She looked at the little man swinging from Rain's mouth. How could someone so vulnerable demand anything from her, and what could she possibly have that he would want? Terrifying thoughts streamed through her head. *What if he wants a body part? Or my eyes? Or my voice like in* The Little Mermaid? *Wait,* The Little Mermaid *isn't a Grimms' fairy tale, is it?* She watched him dangle harmlessly and tried to appear confident.

"Or," Sadie said, "you fix Travis and our friend here will let you go."

The gnome glanced up at Rain and shook his head. "She'll have to let go eventually. I am very patient and heavier than I look. Bad deal. I want what is inside that bag."

Sadie held on to the bag a little tighter. She thought through everything that was inside her backpack, and there was only one thing she could think of that he might want.

"The knife," the gnome said, confirming her suspicion. The gnome refused to break eye contact with Sadie despite the gentle swinging from Rain's mouth. She glared back.

"Knife? How do you even know I have a knife?"

"I can smell it," he said, sniffing the air with a gross snuffling sound. "I smelled it the moment you entered the forest."

Sadie could feel the small lump in the bag that was her knife, a small dagger carved from one piece of black stone. She didn't want to give it to him. She looked down at the bag and then back at Travis, considering.

"Seriously?" Travis yelled. "It's just a knife! I'm being eaten alive by ... by ... *mold*!"

"Yeah, well, *your* knife sure came in handy, didn't it?" Sadie snapped, remembering how Travis's knife had saved them from the nixie.

The gnome grinned at her again. "You don't even know what it does, do you?"

This was true. Sadie *didn't* know what it did—if it did anything. But from the moment she had picked it up from the desk in Eckert's room, she'd known it did *something*. The fact that the gnome wanted it only proved this. He didn't want any of the others' knives, so hers must be special. How special? What would she be giving up?

"Honestly, why is this even a question?" May said, looking at Sadie with disgust. "It's just a knife, and Travis needs help. Just give him the stupid knife."

May telling her to hand over the knife only made her want to keep it more. She glanced quickly at Aiden, who was looking at her with no expression at all. She looked over at Jenny, who was looking at her as if she felt sorry for Sadie.

"Give him the knife," Jenny urged gently. "You know you have to."

"Fine!" Sadie unzipped her bag and pulled out the knife. It was smooth and shiny in her hand, and she didn't want to let it go. It was beautiful, but more than that, it was *special*. She had something *special*, and she was being forced to give it up for stupid Travis? What if they needed it later? She glanced up, hoping someone might interject on her behalf, but all she saw were expectant faces.

The gnome's pupilless eyes widened and latched onto the knife in her hand. He reached out to take it from her, but she moved it out of his grasp.

"Yeah, right. Fix Travis first, then you get the knife."

The gnome glared at her and crossed his arms.

"Fine," he hissed. "You have to wash the wounds with water from the nixie's pond. Has to be the nixie that did the damage, though. Can't just pick any pond you want. Has to be from *her* pond."

Sadie closed her eyes and groaned. She really, really didn't want to go back to that pond. She opened her eyes to see everyone's faces mirroring her own. *No one does*. The pond wasn't far behind them; they'd had to stop walking pretty soon after leaving the pond because it had been getting dark. Still, going backward bothered her. It didn't feel right.

"Cool. Cool cool cool cool," Travis said as he leaned his head against the tree that was propping him up.

"How are we supposed to clean his wounds with the pond water when the nixie is still there? Won't she just attack us again?" Jenny asked, frowning.

The gnome shrugged. "Not my problem. Now give me the knife and let me go!"

Sadie rubbed her thumb up and down the smooth handle of the knife in her hand. They'd gotten what they needed from the gnome—did she really have to give him the knife? What was he going to do about it?

"Nah, I think I'll keep it," she said. "That wasn't really that helpful. Not really worth giving you the knife."

The gnome glared at her and mumbled something she couldn't hear under his breath.

Jenny turned and gave her a worried look. "Sadie, what are you doing?"

"I don't think it's a good idea to go back on a deal with a magical creature," May said seriously. "We don't really know what he can do."

"I feel like if he could do anything, he would have done it by now," Sadie said, peering at the small man still dangling comically from Rain's mouth.

"Doesn't matter if you give me the knife now," he sneered

at her. "You made a deal—the forest will make you keep it."

Sadie was about to ask what that meant, but in one swift movement, the gnome slid out of his green nightshirt and fell to the ground. Sadie stared, stunned, at the naked little man in front of her. "Ugh!" She turned away, averting her eyes from the creature's repulsive body.

"Don't let him get away!" Aiden yelled, but it was too late. Sadie forced herself to look back at the naked gnome, but he was gone.

"We'll never find him," May said stoically. "He blends right in."

Sadie felt the eyes of the group land on her and stay there. She met them with a scowl. "What? What was I supposed to do? He was too fast!"

"It doesn't matter," said Jenny. "He's gone, but at least we know how to cure Travis now."

"And you got to keep your stupid knife," added May darkly. "For now, anyway."

Sadie suddenly felt embarrassed to be holding the knife. Why had she made such a big deal about it? She didn't even know what it could do. She returned it to the side pocket of her backpack and slid the bag over her shoulders. She held tightly to the straps and tried to act like nothing had happened. "Well, are we going back to the pond? We're wasting daylight here."

Jenny looked wistfully at Rain. "Sorry, Rain. We have to fix Travis first. Then you can take us to Ryan, right?"

"And you know where he is?" Sadie added. Rain nodded. Sadie felt a sudden surge of optimism. They knew how to help Travis, and they would be taken directly to Ryan instead of continuing to wander around the forest aimlessly. Rain was still a deer, but they could figure that out later. It suddenly didn't feel so impossible.

Aiden helped the much larger Travis up from the ground, who winced when he moved. He held his head up, making a point not to look down at the mold quickly growing over his body.

They walked in silence back down the trail to the pond they had raced away from just last night. Sadie sorted through her thoughts, trying to think of a plan for how they were going to wash Travis without him—or anyone else—getting taken by the nixie. When she reached the edge of the clearing where the pond was, she stopped and turned around.

"Okay, so what's the plan here?"

Blank faces stared back at her.

"Anyone?" she asked.

"Well, we could create a diversion," Aiden offered. "Distract the nixie while Travis washes that stuff off him. We have his knife still ..."

Sadie avoided eye contact with Aiden but nodded. It was probably their best and only option. "So who is volunteering to be the distraction?"

More blank stares.

"Wow. Thanks, guys. Don't all volunteer at once," Travis said dryly.

"I'll do it," said Jenny. "It's my fault you're here in the first place, my fault this happened to you. I'll be the distraction."

Sadie's stomach tightened. Jenny was probably the last person she would have picked to do this. "I'll help," Sadie offered, surprising herself a little. "You two"—she gestured at Aiden and May—"help Travis wash as quickly as possible, then get away from the pond."

Sadie turned back to look at the pond and saw two grayish, empty eyes staring at them from the center of the pond. It already knew they were there.

Sadie grabbed Jenny's hand and led her to the far side of the pond, where Rain had been standing when they found her. Travis slipped her the knife, and she put it up the sleeve of her sweatshirt to hide it. It poked into the palm of her hand as they walked, and she tried not to wince.

"Okay, we're going to stand very close to the pond, but not touching it, and see if she starts to come near us," she whispered to Jenny. "Just follow my lead, and if I tell you to run, you run, got it?"

Jenny nodded slowly, worry shadowing her eyes.

They made it to the other side of the pond and creeped slowly to the edge of the water. Sadie felt her feet start to sink into the thick muck surrounding the pond's edge. She took a step backward, yanking her feet out with a disturbing sucking sound. "Watch out for this mud," she muttered to Jenny behind her.

Sadie looked up at the surface of the pond, trying hard not to blink. The surface was completely smooth. The top of the head and the eyes she had seen had disappeared underneath the water. Sadie anxiously scanned and rescanned the entire surface of the pond.

"Alright, time to make some noise," she said. "Hey! Nixie! I want to talk to you for a sec, come here!"

"Yeah! Come here! Where are you?" Jenny added in a broken voice.

Sadie eyed May, Aiden, and Travis at the other side of the pond. They were a few feet from the water, waiting to see where the nixie was before getting too close. A ripple in the center of the pond caught her attention. The seaweed-green head bobbed to the surface, its white eyes fixed on Sadie. The head slowly floated toward them, but as it did, it seemed to change. Sadie became transfixed—the hideous corpse-like creature was transforming! The lank, scummy hair softened and curled, and the face rippled until it was no longer pale and bloated but beautiful and blushing. Deep-green irises bloomed in the center of the cold white eyes. As she got closer, Sadie could see more of her; her bare shoulders and breasts were now out of the water, and the pond was lapping at her skin. *This can't possibly be the same nixie*, she thought. This nixie was beautiful, nothing like the horrible creature they had seen before.

"Hello?" she ventured. "Who are you?"

The nixie smiled, and Sadie's heart fluttered. She wanted nothing more than to swim out to her.

"My name is Egel," the nixie replied in the most soothing voice Sadie had ever heard. "I grant wishes. What do you wish for?"

What do I wish for? Sadie had a lot of wishes ... but she couldn't seem to remember them right now.

A scream broke her concentration on Egel, and she looked around angrily at whoever was making such a horrible sound. She looked down and realized she was ankle deep in the pond. Jenny was screaming and pulling at her arm, but she didn't move an inch. Everything felt far away and unreal, as if she were watching a movie with the sound turned down so low it was just a light buzzing. She didn't like it. She wanted to go back to Egel. She pulled her arm loose from Jenny's grip and turned back to the beautiful pond fairy, who was so close now she could almost touch her. She reached out to her, and Egel reached out too.

Sadie saw a quick movement to the left of her, then heard a bloodcurdling scream that sounded like a thousand nails being dragged across a chalkboard. The beautiful creature was gone, and all that was left was a slimy monster with the face of a leech screeching and holding its shoulder.

"Come on!" Jenny yelled from beside her, and this time she was able to move. Jenny pulled her out of the water and didn't stop dragging her until they were away from the pond and at the mouth of a trail. Sadie leaned against a tree and tried to shake the fog from her head.

"What ... what happened?" she asked groggily. She felt like she had been pulled from a deep sleep, and she had a horrible headache.

"The nixie entranced you," May said behind her. "We were too far away to do anything, and by the time we got here, Jenny had already saved you."

Jenny ... saved me?

Jenny was bent over, her hands on her knees, shaking and hyperventilating. Tears ran down her flushed cheeks. *That Jenny?*

"That was amazing!" Aiden said, patting Jenny on the back.

"What happened?" Sadie repeated.

"You were just staring at the nixie and slowly walking toward it," Jenny replied, her breath slowing. "I screamed and tried to pull you back, but you couldn't hear me. Finally I was able to pull the knife from your sleeve when I grabbed your arm. Then I ... I stabbed it."

"Stabbed it good!" Travis said. Sadie looked over and saw Travis standing tall, his chest its normal pinkish color. Not a speck of mold to be seen. The claw marks were gone too. "Can I have my knife back now?"

Jenny paled. "Uh ... I ... I dropped it. In the pond."

They all turned to look at the pond.

"Well, that's gone forever," Aiden said.

"What happens when a nixie gets ahold of a nixie-killing knife?" Sadie asked, fear trickling through her.

"Let's not find out," Aiden replied. "Rain? You ready to take us to Ryan?"

Rain nodded and nudged past Sadie to follow the trail they were at the mouth of. *This is where Rain was when we came along before*, she realized.

They started down the trail after Rain, but Sadie couldn't help stealing one last glance at the pond. It was calm; there was hardly a ripple. No sign of the nixie.

She couldn't believe she had fallen for the nixie's trick. She had completely lost control of herself—she didn't want to feel that way again. She swung her backpack off one shoulder and unzipped the pocket she had placed her knife in. She reached in to take it out, but when she dipped her hand into the pocket, she felt nothing. She dug through the main compartment, but the knife wasn't there either. She looked frantically around for some explanation, but saw nothing.

Her knife was gone.

14

Jenny followed Rain into the forest and tried to shake off the trembling in her arms and legs. She needed to sit down, to get control of herself, but they were *so close* to finding Ryan. She didn't want to slow them down.

As Jenny trekked through the woods behind Rain, she thought about the hideous pond creature and how it had almost killed Sadie. She thought about how panicked she'd been when she thought Sadie was going to be taken away. She'd lost Charlotte; she wasn't sure she could handle it if she lost Sadie too. Jenny cringed as she thought about how it had felt stabbing a knife into the creature's flesh. Its skin was delicate and waterlogged, so the knife had pierced through easily. It was the extra push she had to give to get it to go deep into the nixie's shoulder that made her feel queasy.

She tried to focus on what was ahead of her, but that had its own issues. Rain's deer butt swayed back and forth in front of her, her small white tail flicking left and right. She knew this wasn't Rain's body, but it still made her uncomfortable to be seeing it from this end. Jenny prayed Rain wouldn't forget she was there and start pooping, then Jenny immediately felt guilty for worrying about that.

The trees were thick Lon either Ger side of them, as they had been on other parts of the trail, but the canopy above seemed a little thinner. Dappled light fell across the path ahead of them, and there was an odd sweetness in the air. Jenny breathed in deeply, trying to place the smell. Cookies. It smelled like freshly baked cookies.

Distracted by the cookie scent, Jenny didn't notice Rain stop until she collided into her back end.

"What's wrong? Are we there?" Jenny asked.

Rain nodded, and her long, velvety ears twitched nervously.

Jenny peered over Rain's body at the clearing ahead of them. A strange little cottage made of what looked like candy sat quietly in the center of the clearing. It was a simple structure—one story and made of gingerbread walls with a peppermint chimney and sugar-glass windows. Different colored gumdrops decorated the exterior, and a chunk of dark chocolate served as the front door. Scattered all around the outside of the house were large, shiny chunks of hard candy. It was the cutest thing Jenny had ever seen, but she couldn't enjoy it. She knew which fairy tale this was.

The others collected behind her, their eyes wide and mouths drawn tight.

"He's in there, isn't he?" Jenny asked Rain.

The deer nodded slowly.

Jenny felt sick. Ryan had been trapped inside the house of a child-eating witch for three days. *Three days*. Jenny couldn't bear to think about what might have been happening to him all this time.

"Is he ... is he okay?"

Rain's head didn't move. She didn't know.

Next to Jenny, Marble was growling, his eyes fixed on the house made of candy. Even *he* seemed to know the story of *Hansel and Gretel*. Jenny rested her hand on Marble's back, and let the soft swirling fur slide between her fingers. She stroked him to calm herself.

"Come on," Jenny said as she mustered every bit of courage she could. "We have to save Ryan."

She took one step forward, then stopped abruptly. Marble was standing in front of her, his hackles raised and ears back.

"Marble? Come on, we have to do this. Get out of the way."

She tried to walk forward again, but Marble pushed his considerable weight against her, forcing her back toward the trail.

"Anyone else think we should listen to the magical wolf?" Aiden said awkwardly.

Jenny whipped around to glare at Aiden. "And do what? I'm not leaving this forest without Ryan. I don't care what I have to do to get him back, *I'm getting him back*. You're all welcome to stay here, I don't blame you. You've taken me this far. I can do this on my own if I have to."

"Yeah, right," Sadie said. "You're not going in there alone."

"I fought a pond monster. I think I can handle a candy house," Travis added.

"Yeah, sure. Fine. Let's all go die," Aiden said with a dramatic wave of his arm.

Jenny could feel the fear practically coming off May next to her. May's eyes were glued to the cottage, and she was slowly shaking her head.

"May, will you please stay here with Rain? I don't want to leave her alone out here, and she obviously can't come with us."

May looked at her, surprised. Jenny could see the gears working inside her head. Gratitude flushed May's face, for the briefest of moments, then was gone. She nodded.

"Remember, in the story they kill the witch by pushing her into the oven. I don't know if it will be exactly the same, but that's all we have to go on."

"Knives out, everyone!" Aiden said as he pulled the fire-setting knife from his bag. Travis glared at him, and Jenny felt guilty for losing Travis's knife in the pond. "Ah, sorry, man. I forgot."

Sadie, too, looked glum and did not open her backpack to get out her knife.

"Sadie? Where's your knife?" Jenny asked.

Sadie lowered her head and mumbled something Jenny couldn't make out.

"What?"

"It's gone, okay?" She said louder, annoyed.

Gone? The last thing the gnome had said before it disappeared echoed in her head. *You made a deal—the forest will make you keep it.*

"Seriously?" Travis turned to Sadie. "The knife was more important than saving me from flesh-eating nixie mold, and you already *lost it*?"

Sadie looked away and shrugged moodily.

"The gnome," May said for her. "The deal had to be kept."

"So, two knives down," Aiden interjected. "Jenny, what about you? You still have your knife?"

She did. She pulled it out of her backpack and was struck again at how beautiful it was. It had swirling blacks, grays, and whites in the stone handle, just like Marble's fur. The weight of it felt nice in her hand, and she felt a little less vulnerable.

"May?" Aiden urged.

"Ah, my knife is sort of ... like a bread knife?" May replied, pulling out the wide, flat serrated knife with its worn wood handle.

"Oh, right. Well, better than nothing!" Aiden said with a forced smile.

Jenny looked down at the wolf, who was still blocking her path to the cottage.

"You have to let me go," she said softly to the wolf, hoping he could understand her. "This is why we're here."

The wolf looked behind him at the candy cottage and back at her. He slowly shook his large head. *No.*

The tiny bit of confidence she had managed to dig up inside her crumbled. The only other time Marble had tried to stop her from doing something was when she opened the hidden door in the castle. She would have died like Charlotte if it weren't for him pulling her away from the opening. She glanced past him at the cottage waiting in the distance. She should have listened to him then, and she should probably listen to him now. But she'd come all this way, and she wasn't leaving without Ryan. She kneeled down in front of Marble and wrapped her arms around his neck. Softly, so only he could hear her, she whispered into his fur.

"I have to do this," she whispered. "Please help me."

She pulled away and looked deeply into Marble's magnetic eyes, willing him to understand. The wolf stared at her for a few tense moments, then ducked his head and moved out of her way. Jenny stood and let out a deep breath. She gestured to the others and started walking toward the cottage, knife in hand and Marble by her side. Travis, Aiden, and Sadie followed close behind.

"So we're going in with no plan?" Travis asked.

"The plan is to go in, get Ryan, and get out," Jenny snapped. That was as much of a plan as she was going to come up with.

"Ah, good plan," Aiden said. "We're *definitely* not all going to die horrible deaths."

Jenny ignored Aiden's sarcasm and continued toward the cottage. As she neared the house, the chunks of hard candy scattered around the yard started to take shape. They were different sizes, some only a few feet high and others the same height as she was. Each step she took brought the small candy sculptures into focus.

Children. They were all statues of children carved out of some sort of translucent hard candy. There were around thirty just in front of the house, and she saw more wrapping around the sides. Each glistened a different color—deep red, punchy orange, lime green. She stared down at the little statues, startled by the detail carved into each of their faces. The statue directly in front of her was of a little girl, her hair in a perfectly carved pair of braids. Jenny bent to look closer at the statue and was amazed at how intricately the little girl's face had been carved. Faint eyelashes, the turn of the pouting mouth, wisps of hair coming loose from her braids—all perfectly rendered in hard lemon-yellow candy.

Nails suddenly dug into her arm and pulled her backward. She whipped around to see Sadie's stricken face.

"What are you doing?" Jenny hissed at her.

"L-look." Sadie gasped out, pointing toward the cottage. Jenny turned, and her eyes followed where Sadie was pointing. Her breath caught in her throat. There was a statue she hadn't noticed yet. It stood closest to the house, behind the other statues. Its body was made of a deep-red hard candy, but its head ...

"Ms. Eckert," Travis said before turning away and vomiting into the grass. Aiden's face went white, and he slowly started walking backward, away from the house. Then he started running.

"Seriously?" Sadie snapped as she watched him go.

Jenny was frozen in place; she couldn't stop staring at the grotesque sculpture in front of her.

Ms. Eckert's real head was sitting on top of a candy neck, her eyes open and staring at them. The last time Jenny had seen Ms. Eckert, the woman had been terrifying, formidable. Now her long white-blonde hair had been cut off, and her cheeks had salty traces of tears running down them. The skin of her neck melted seamlessly into the red candy, and Jenny struggled to understand what she was looking at.

The icy-blue eyes that had once sent shivers through Jenny blinked. Sadie jumped backward, but Jenny was still locked in place. She couldn't move. She felt like she had that first day, when she had to walk across that rickety bridge, only much worse. She was stiff with fear, and her brain was no longer communicating to the rest of her body.

"Go away," Ms. Eckert's head hissed at her. "Leave!"

Jenny's mouth fell open in shock. Ms. Eckert was ... alive?

"What happened to you?" Jenny whispered back. "Where's Ryan?"

"Jenny, we really need to rethink this," Sadie said, pulling at her arm. "We need to go back and talk about this."

Jenny pulled her arm out of Sadie's grasp and took a step closer to the cottage.

"Stupid girl, run away," Ms. Eckert hissed again.

"What happened to you?" Jenny repeated. "What is this?"

"Piece by piece," Ms. Eckert said, unmeasurable pain in her voice. "Every time she eats a piece of me, she replaces it with candy. My head is the only thing left. She's keeping me this way on purpose—to torture me."

Jenny gaped at Ms. Eckert. Her entire body had been eaten already. She hated Ms. Eckert for taking Ryan and Rain into this cursed forest, but she never would have wished *this* for her. The thought of Ryan made her feel like she might faint. *Three days*. They'd been gone *three days*.

"Is ... is Ryan ..." Jenny couldn't finish the sentence. Tears were flowing and she couldn't stop them. She was living in a nightmare that just kept getting worse.

"Is Ryan still alive?" Sadie asked for her.

Jenny stared hard at the ground, dreading the answer.

"Yes, still alive. I still hear him in there. She started with me, lucky boy," she said with a scoff.

Jenny felt her nails digging painfully into the palms of her hands and forced herself to loosen her fists. "Why? Why did you do this?" she spat, anger overcoming her fear. "Why did you bring him here?"

Eckert looked past Jenny at something Jenny couldn't see. Eckert sighed. "When I was a little girl, my brother and I wandered into these woods. We found this house and went inside. The witch captured us, but we escaped. I thought we had escaped. I made it out of the forest, but my brother ..."

fresh tears fell from her eyes and splashed onto her candy chest. She looked down to her right at the statue of a little boy. "I thought he was right behind me."

Jenny stared at the small statue next to Eckert. He had plump baby cheeks and big eyes. He was wearing overalls and a T-shirt; she could see the little latches of the buckles. He couldn't have been more than six years old.

"Is that ..."

"Yes. She ate him a long time ago. Now I'll be gone soon too. This is where I belong anyway, with Jonas."

Jenny felt like she was going to throw up, like Travis had. She looked at the cottage's dark chocolate door and the little sugar-glass windows. Was the witch inside, watching them?

"Please," Jenny pleaded. "How do we kill the witch? How do we save Ryan?"

"The boy is inside the house in a locked cage. I don't know how you get him out. My knife"—Eckert flicked her eyes to the left—"over there. It's the only thing that can kill the witch." Jenny followed her gaze, and she saw it about ten feet away, slightly hidden by grass. It had a short, sharp point, and the red handle looked like it was made of the same shiny hard candy the statues were made of. "I tried pushing her into the oven when we were children, but it barely slowed her down. The knife is the only way. I spent over twenty years looking for it. For what? She had me before I even got to the door. I dropped it."

"You *dropped* it," Sadie said, her eyes narrowed at Eckert.

"Run away while you still can," Eckert said flatly.

Jenny wanted nothing more than to run far away from this horror show, but there was no way she was leaving Ryan behind. She quickly walked over to where the candy knife was lying in the dirt and picked it up. Eckert had failed, but there was no reason *she* would fail too. If the witch was inside, then she already knew they were there and there would be no way to surprise her. Might as well just walk right in.

"I'm going inside. I'm getting Ryan," she said shakily, trying to control her voice as best as she could. Travis was standing a short distance away, his arms wrapped around himself and his eyes watery. Sadie looked at her and slowly shook her head.

"Jenny, this is crazy," she said. "I know you love Ryan, but we could *all* die in there! I personally have no desire to be slowly eaten!"

"I know. You two are going to go back to May and Rain. I can't risk your lives. I can do this by myself."

"Yeah, right!" Sadie exploded. "You're going to take on a child-eating *witch* all by yourself? Eckert tried, and look at what happened to her! How on earth do you think *you're* going to succeed?"

"Jenny, she's right. You can't go in there," Travis said quietly. "None of us can. It's too dangerous."

Jenny felt her insides turn to stone, and she tried to shut off the part of her brain that told her they were right. She tried to drown out all the voices in her head screaming at her to run far away from here and never look back. But she knew she couldn't do that. She looked down at Marble, who was staring up at her with his big black eyes. It felt like he, too, was begging her not to go inside.

"Go back to May and Rain," she told her friends again, pushing past Sadie. "I have Marble." She blocked out Sadie's pleas for her to stop and focused on the chocolate door ahead of her. She forced herself to walk the short length to the door, took a deep breath, clutched the knife as tightly as she could, and kicked the door open.

She held the knife up, ready to stab anything that attacked her. But nothing did. Marble slinked into the room ahead of her, sniffing the objects intently. She looked quickly around the small one-room cottage, but it was empty—the witch wasn't there. She saw a small oven, an open fireplace with a large black hanging cauldron, and a dining table big enough to fit one. Her eyes fell on a little bed on the right side of the room, with a patchwork quilt folded neatly on top. Jenny struggled to imagine a witch this evil sleeping in a bed like a normal person.

"Jenny?" a weak, hoarse voice she barely recognized said from across the room. There, next to the giant stove, was a metal cage built into the wall of the house. Marble's head lifted at the sound of Ryan's voice, but he did not move toward the cage. Marble slinked to the front door as she rushed over to the cage and grabbed at the bars.

"Ryan! Ryan, are you okay?" Jenny said, tears streaming down her face again. He looked sick, and his eyes were red rimmed.

"Get me out of here," he gasped. "Do you have the key?"

Jenny stared at the giant lock hanging off the door of the cage, and panic rippled through her. Key?

"I just have this knife," she said, showing Ryan the candy knife. "Where does she keep the key?"

Ryan hit his head against the bars of the cage in anguish.

"She has it on her at all times," he groaned.

Jenny searched the small cottage for anything she could use to break the lock open. There were no tools or anything else that would do any damage to the lock. Then a strange idea struck her—the knife. She rushed back to the cage and aimed the point of the small candy knife into the lock's hole, then pushed.

The lock disintegrated in her hand, crumbling like a piece of old cake. She yanked open the cage door, and Ryan crawled out of the cage, favoring his right hand.

She threw her arms around him and hugged him as tightly as she could. He pulled away, glaring at her. "We don't have time for this, she could be back any moment."

Then it struck her—if the witch wasn't inside the cottage, that meant ...

"Sadie, Aiden, and Travis are outside!" She grabbed Ryan

by the hand to help him up but quickly pulled her hand back when she felt something hard and smooth where his hand should have been. Horrified, she stared at the shiny purple rock-candy hand connected to Ryan's wrist. He moved the hand behind him, out of her sight, but she couldn't unsee it.

"Ryan, your hand—"

"We can talk about it later. Right now we need to get out of here!" He pushed past her and Marble, then rushed out the doorway. She followed close behind, her mind racing with what she had seen. *The witch already started eating him.*

Outside, she saw what looked like a little old woman in an apron and ankle-length dress. Her gray hair was wrapped into a bun on top of her head. She was talking to Sadie and Travis, who looked transfixed by the old woman. Marble growled and lowered his body in an attack position in front of her.

"It's her," Ryan whispered.

15

Sadie stared at the little old woman in front of her. She had a sweet, caring face etched with wrinkles and exuded warmth. A scent of freshly baked cakes wafted off her. Sadie wanted nothing more than to be swallowed up in the old woman's warm embrace. Next to her, Travis seemed to be feeling the same way. He didn't look sick anymore. Instead, he was smiling in a way she had never seen before. His whole face looked relaxed, like he was calmed by the old woman's presence.

Sadie couldn't remember exactly what she had just been doing. Were they taking a walk together? Why would she be taking a walk with Travis? Where were they? Her mind felt foggy, like she could see the vague outline of the truth, but that was it.

"Oh, dear, you two look tired. Are you hungry? I just finished baking a lovely chocolate cake. Would you like to come in and have some?" the old woman offered in a sweet, gentle voice. Sadie wanted nothing more than to go inside the cute little cottage and eat some cake. That sounded wonderful.

She smiled at the old woman and nodded. She did feel very tired and very hungry. What good luck it was that she ran into this wonderful lady.

The old woman's smile faded, and she turned to look at something by her cottage. Sadie felt a slight chill as the woman's warm gaze left her. She wanted to be in the gaze again; she didn't want to be cold and alone anymore. The old woman did not turn back to her. Instead, she was staring at the two people that had just come out of her house. They looked like they might be her age—a boy and a girl. Sadie squinted at them. They looked vaguely familiar but she couldn't quite place where she would know them from. School, maybe?

"You're being a very naughty boy," the old woman said. "You know you should be in bed, you're still so weak."

Sadie looked closer at the boy and saw that he in fact did look weak. He looked sick, and Sadie wondered why he wasn't obeying the nice old lady and staying in bed where he belonged. He did look *awfully* familiar, though, and it nagged at her. The fog in her head started to evaporate, and she realized that she knew who he was—Ryan. *Jenny's Ryan*, she reminded herself. And the girl next to him, of course, was Jenny. Sadie felt relieved that she had finally put it together. The longer the old woman focused on Ryan and Jenny, the clearer her head felt.

"Sadie, run!" Jenny screamed, surprising her. *Run?* Like a tidal wave, everything came crashing back to her—where they were, what they were doing there, and who this old lady must be.

"The witch," she whispered. The witch had done the same thing to her the nixie had. *I can't believe I fell for that trick again.*

The witch quickly turned around and grabbed Sadie's long ponytail, gripping it hard and pulling Sadie to the ground with a shocking strength before she could get away. She screamed out in pain, her scalp on fire.

"No one is going anywhere," the witch snapped. She turned to Travis, who was still standing there looking dumbstruck.

"Sweet boy," the witch said with a kindness Sadie now knew to be fake, "would you mind holding her for me? Don't let her go. She'll hurt herself. Soon we will all go inside and eat some cake. Won't that be nice?"

"Travis, no! Get out of here!" Sadie yelled from the ground. Travis ignored her and walked over to where they were huddled.

Sadie was on the ground, and the witch was bent over her, her clawed hand tangled in Sadie's hair. Travis grabbed Sadie by the arm and pulled her up. His large hand wrapped firmly around her arm. She tried to pull away, but he didn't loosen his grip. He didn't even look at her.

"Such a good boy," the witch cooed, patting him on his flushed, fleshy cheek.

"Let me go!" Sadie yelled, punching at Travis with her free arm. The witch grabbed her chin in her bony hand and came inches from her face. The witch's breath smelled like burnt sugar with an undertone of rotting meat. Sadie felt her stomach pull, and she worried she was going to throw up. She averted her eyes, avoiding eye contact with the witch as best she could. The witch opened her mouth, and a long tongue—too long for a human tongue—slipped out and ran the full length of Sadie's face, leaving a trail of saliva down her cheek. Sadie cringed, disgusted, and tried to move her head away.

"Mmm, you're going to be tasty. I can tell," she whispered, then broke out laughing—a true witch cackle. Sadie winced at the sound, but in her peripheral vision, she saw a quick movement, something dark and low to the ground. The witch screamed directly into Sadie's face. The sound tore at her eardrums, and the putrid smell of her breath was overwhelming. Sadie faltered but Travis held tight to her arm, and she didn't fall.

The witch looked down, and so did Sadie. Marble had the witch's leg in his mouth. He shook his head violently, whipping back and forth, like he was trying to tear the witch's leg off. The witch grabbed the wolf by the scruff of his neck, and Marble let out a high-pitched yelp, releasing the witch's leg. With a flick of her wrist, she tossed the massive wolf away, as if he were nothing but a child's toy. He landed with a thud on the ground. Sadie stared at the fallen wolf and cold dread flowed through her body from her eyes to her toes. The witch was strong—*really* strong. The witch shook her leg, the one Marble had bitten, and started walking toward Jenny and Ryan. Sadie twisted her neck to look back at Travis. His eyes were still glazed over, still under the witch's spell.

"Travis, you need to let go of me," Sadie begged. "Just look at her! She's the *witch*."

But Travis maintained his grip and continued to stare forward, into nothing, like he couldn't hear or see what was happening right in front of him. She struggled against him but quickly tired herself out. She was weak. Too weak. Sadie looked desperately around her for help, for anything she could use. Marble was slowly getting up from the ground but was clearly in pain.

The witch walked past her collection of candy statues, pausing briefly when she reached Eckert, then continued toward Ryan and Jenny. *Why aren't they running?*

In one quick movement, the witch grabbed at Jenny, going for her hair the same way she had Sadie's. Jenny dodged the lunging witch and tried to stab her with the candy-handled knife, but missed.

"Don't look her in the eyes!" Sadie yelled. She now saw too clearly what had happened to Eckert. Eckert had never had a chance against the witch's hypnotism. But maybe Jenny did.

Behind her, she felt an odd warmth that quickly transformed to burning. She whipped around to see what remained of Travis's shirt was on fire. Travis let go of her arm and hit himself until the flame went out. Sadie locked eyes with the person standing behind him. Aiden was there, red-stoned knife in hand.

"Sorry, man, but you were out of it," he said. "I didn't know what else to do."

"So you lit me on *fire*?" Travis yelled.

"Finally," Sadie said, rubbing her sore arm. "We have to help them, just don't look the witch in the eyes, and try not to listen if she talks to you. We have to stay in control."

Travis and Aiden nodded solemnly.

They split up and surrounded the witch. Sadie looked around for anything she could use as a weapon, but all she saw were the rows of hard-candy children. She looked down at what was once a little girl with pigtails but was now just a lifelike statue crafted from grapefruit-pink candy. The statue reminded her of her little sister back home, and a hot fury raced through her. *It's not fair,* she thought heatedly. It wasn't fair this witch had taken so many lives that were not hers to take. All these children—robbed. Robbed of a life.

She looked up at the witch; she had hold of Jenny now and threw her to the ground even harder than she had the wolf. Sadie wasn't going to let her take any more lives. The witch was leaning over Jenny, her back to Sadie. Sadie locked eyes with Aiden a few feet away and made a stabbing motion at him. His face crinkled in confusion, then smoothed as he put her pantomime together. Fire knife in hand, he ran at the witch, but she was too fast for him. The witch made a sound that was something between screaming and laughing and smacked Aiden across the face with the back of her hand as he approached her. He went flying and landed twenty feet away. Sadie stared at his motionless body, willing him to move, to stand. To be alive. Aiden stirred but did not get up. Travis ran to where Aiden landed and bent to his knees at his side. Sadie turned away from the boys, back to the witch.

She felt movement next to her and looked down to see a battered Marble standing at her side. She heard him release a pained sigh, then he moved toward the witch, winding his way carefully through the candy statues. He stayed low to the ground and moved slowly, until he was just a few feet away from the witch and Jenny. He crouched, his muscles tense, and leapt on top of the witch, his mouth searching out the witch's neck. The witch stood up and shook the wolf off easily, like rain from an umbrella. He went flying again and slammed into two of the candy statues before crumpling to the ground. Sadie winced and tried not to look at the wolf's motionless body. Sadie hovered behind the candy statues, not sure what to do. The witch was stronger than the wolf, and she had no weapon.

Oh, Jenny, I'm so sorry, she thought, her heart breaking.

Suddenly a high-pitched scream blasted her back a few feet and shattered the sugar-glass windows of the gingerbread house. It was like a bomb had gone off. She found her balance again and looked back to where the witch had been—and saw Jenny.

Jenny's curly brown hair was a tangled mess, and she had mud smeared on one side of her face. Scratch marks covered her arms, and she was breathing hard. In her hand was the candy knife, dripping with a brownish-red syrupy substance. At her feet was a bundle of clothes, nothing else.

"You did it!" she choked out. Jenny looked up at her like she had just woken from a dream but wasn't sure if she was really awake or still sleeping. Sadie made a step toward her but stopped when she saw Ryan wrap her in his arms. Jenny buried her face into his shoulder.

Sadie looked away from the couple and saw the hard-candy sculptures melting all around her. "J-Jenny?" she called out. "Something is happening!"

Jenny pulled away from Ryan to look around her at the liquefying statues. Wisps of white smoke rose from the brightly colored puddles and took the foggy shape of children. Everywhere Sadie looked, a statue fell and a spirit rose up. She looked over at where Eckert had been and gasped. She turned away, horrified at the sight of Eckert's decapitated head lying lifeless on the ground.

A ghost taller than the rest appeared, with an ankle-length dress and a long braid of hair down her back. She was transparent and smoky, but Sadie recognized Eckert easily. She watched, breathless, as the ghost took the hand of a little boy next to her. She and the boy followed the rest of the ghosts, dispersing from the cottage and into the woods before they disappeared from view entirely.

The cottage started to fall apart once the children had gone. The gingerbread walls and chocolate door cracked, the peppermint chimney broke into shards and slid down the sinking roof.

Sadie watched, fascinated, as the whole structure crumbled to the ground.

16

Jenny dropped the candy-handled knife to the ground and looked up at Ryan. She'd missed being held by him and wanted to enjoy this moment. She closed her eyes and soaked in his warmth and let herself stay in the bubble they had created. She knew when she opened her eyes she would still be in the Black Forest, still trapped among fairy tales, still not knowing how they would ever escape these woods.

She knew she couldn't stand like this forever. She slowly opened her eyes and looked up at Ryan. He looked exhausted; his eyes were bloodshot, and his heavy lids were struggling to stay open. Jenny pulled away slightly and looked around her. The children were gone, and the cottage was nothing but a pile of broken candy. Something on the ground caught her eye, and she turned away in disgust.

Eckert's head was still here. Jenny had seen her ghost go off with the others and her candy body melt away, but her head had never been eaten. It was faced away from her, thankfully, and all she saw was her ragged blonde bob of hair. Jenny clenched her teeth and tried not to vomit as tears filled her eyes. Ryan led her away from the decapitated head, away from the candy cottage debris, and back toward the tree line. She reached to take his hand and gasped. It was *gone*. Where there had been a shiny rock-candy hand, there was now just empty air. Ryan noticed her looking and pulled down his sleeve to hide his stump. Jenny had hoped that once the witch was vanquished, Ryan would get his hand back. She cursed herself for being so stupid. Charlotte was dead. Ryan's hand was gone.

She met Ryan's eyes and saw something there she had never seen before—a darkness. Defeat. Like the light that had always filled him had been suddenly snuffed out.

"Ryan—"

"Have you seen my sister?" he said, cutting her off. "We were separated." His eyes scanned the area around them.

Jenny hadn't prepared herself to tell Ryan about Rain, and the worry in his tired, reddened eyes pulled at her heart.

"Yes, but—"

"What?" he looked at her with panic in his eyes. "What happened? Where is she?"

Jenny winced, afraid of how he was going to react. He'd already been through so much, and to now learn his sister was a deer ... Jenny swallowed.

"She drank from a cursed spring and was turned into a deer. But don't worry, we'll figure out a way to turn her back. I promise."

"A ... a *deer*?"

"Come on, I'll take you to her."

Jenny led Ryan to the path, where Sadie, Aiden, and Travis were waiting for them. Aiden and Travis looked rattled and a little scraped up but otherwise okay. Travis's shirt, which had now been burned twice and torn open by the nixie, hung off his frame in tatters. Both boys rushed to meet them and threw their arms around their found friend, cheering with a vibrant, shaky energy that came from narrowly escaping death. Ryan hid his missing hand from them, and Jenny didn't mention it. If Ryan wasn't ready to talk about it, she wouldn't make him. It horrified her that he had been mutilated, but after seeing Eckert, she was just relieved he was still alive. Sadie lingered behind like a wavering shadow. Jenny left Ryan to his friends and made her way over to Sadie, then stopped. She saw Marble limping slowly over to them, and she let out a relieved breath.

He didn't have any visible injuries that Jenny could see, but he looked like he was in pain. She crouched down and ran her hand across his back, and he nudged her shoulder softly with his head.

"What is *that*?" Ryan shouted, moving away from Jenny and the wolf.

"Oh, sorry, this is Marble. He's, ah, my wolf, I guess?" Jenny said, not really sure how to explain Marble. *She* wasn't even really sure what Marble was.

Ryan looked at her as if she were crazy, and Jenny started to squirm a little under his demanding stare. She stood up and struggled to think of what to say.

"He's fine, really," Jenny said softly, touching Ryan's arm. "He won't hurt you. He's been helping us."

Ryan didn't respond, but he tore his gaze from the wolf and looked down the path that led to his sister. He turned back to Jenny. "That way?"

Jenny nodded and they all made their way down the path and up the small hill where they had left May and Rain. She could see them waiting in the distance, the sunlight shimmering off of Rain's golden coat.

"That"—she pointed at the deer—"is Rain."

She wrapped her arm around his waist and gave him a gentle squeeze she hoped was comforting.

"It will be alright," she said softly.

"You don't know that," he snapped, pulling away from her. She stared at him, stricken. He'd never snapped at her before. "I'm sorry," he said, letting out a deep breath. "I'm exhausted, and my head is all ... scrambled."

Sadie, Travis, and Aiden slipped past them and continued toward May and Rain. Jenny's face burned knowing they must have overheard Ryan snap at her.

Ryan continued up the hill to where the others were waiting for them. Jenny drifted behind him dejectedly. When they got to the top, Travis was sitting on the ground, still shaken, and Sadie was pacing around like an agitated cat. May stood next to Rain, her dark eyes twitching between her and Ryan suspiciously.

"So, what happened?" May asked. "Where's Eckert?"

Jenny looked over at Ryan, who was staring at Rain, his eyes glossy.

"Ah, let's take a little walk," Aiden suggested, taking May gently by the arm and steering her away from the group. "I'll fill you in."

Jenny tried to thank Aiden with her eyes, but she didn't think he noticed. None of them wanted to relive what had just happened, and she thought maybe it was better for Rain not to know. Not yet, anyway.

"Let's stop here for a bit," Jenny told Sadie, Travis, and Rain. "Ryan needs to rest, and we need to figure out what to do now and how to get back." Jenny said, ignoring the look of impatience Sadie shot at her. "Ryan, are you hungry?"

"No," Ryan tore his eyes from Rain and met hers. "The witch has been force-feeding me for the last three days. I am exhausted, though. I can't remember the last time I slept."

"We really need to keep going," Sadie said, shooting daggers at her. "I know he's tired, but we have to get out of these woods as quickly as we can, before something *else* happens."

Jenny knew she was right, but looking at the state of Ryan, she doubted he would be able to make it very far before collapsing.

"I know, but he needs to rest. Just for a little while."

"I'm right here," he snapped. "Don't talk about me like I'm a little kid!"

"Sorry, I know. Sorry. Why don't you try to sleep? And we'll work on finding a cure for Rain in the book."

Ryan nodded begrudgingly and looked around before selecting a spot a little off the trail to rest. He lowered himself to the ground carefully and lay down in the grass. Rain trotted over to him, folding her legs to lay next to him. He put his shaky hand on her back and stared deeply into her eyes, looking for the sister he knew was inside the deer's body.

"I'm so sorry," he whispered to her. Rain rested her head on his shoulder briefly, then curled up next to him.

Jenny bit her lip and watched Ryan with Rain. He looked exhausted, pale, like a quickly dimming shadow of who he used to be. He had managed to hide his missing hand from the rest of the group, but she knew it wouldn't be long before someone noticed.

The adrenaline that had been pumping through her fizzled out, and she was left feeling drained. She pushed past that and dug out her book of fairy tales from her backpack. Sadie shook her head but dug out her own copy of the book. Jenny gestured for them to move away from the sleeping siblings. They were still within eyesight, but hopefully they'd be able to talk without waking them.

Jenny and Sadie sat down on the ground and started thumbing through pages, looking for any stories that might explain what happened to Rain and how they might be able to fix her. Aiden and May returned, her face looking a little more pale than usual.

"We're taking a little break," Jenny told them as they approached. "Ryan and Rain need to rest for a little while. We're trying to find a cure for Rain in the meantime."

May nodded and without argument took out her own book and started reading. Aiden and Travis, who hadn't thought to bring their books, stood awkwardly and looked around as if they might find something to do.

"Why don't you guys use this time to rest too?" Jenny offered, knowing they must feel as tired as she did. "Take a little nap. We'll wake you when it's time to go. Oh, and, Travis?"

"Yeah?"

"I think it's time you say goodbye to that shirt."

Travis looked down at the scraps of material that were once a T-shirt and smiled sheepishly. He pulled off the shirt and dropped it on the ground. Jenny half expected him to make some comment about her just wanting to see him with his shirt off, but he didn't say anything.

Travis and Aiden found their own spots in the grass to lay down and rest. In just a few moments, they could hear Travis snoring and Aiden mumbling softly in his sleep. Jenny couldn't help but feel jealous. She had barely slept the night before, and her entire body hurt from fighting the witch. Still, there was work to do. She forced her eyes open and began reading.

They'd been sitting like that, bent over their books reading, for about half an hour when May broke the silence.

"I think I found something."

Jenny looked up from her own book. "What'd you find?"

"In this story, *Jorinde and Joringle*, Joringle is turned into a bird, and the thing that turns her back is a flower. It says, 'He had found a flower as red as blood with a shimmering pearl in the center. He picked the flower and went with it to the castle; everything the flower touched was released from the magic spell,'" May finished with a smile.

"Wait, read the description of the flower again," Sadie said, leaning toward May slightly.

"Erm ..." May searched for the line she had read and found it again. "'Red as blood with a shimmering pearl in the center.'"

"I've seen a flower like that before!" Sadie said excitedly. "On the hike to the well that first day. On the way back, I saw Eckert reach down and pick a flower that was red with a pearl in the center. At the time, I convinced myself I had just seen it wrong, but now ..."

"Were there others there?" May asked. "Besides the one she picked?"

Sadie frowned. "No, just that one."

"Well, if there was one, there are more. Now we know what to look for at least!" Jenny said, smiling warmly at Sadie.

"I wonder what Eckert did with the flower," Aiden said from behind her, making Jenny flinch in surprise. "Think it's still in her room somewhere?"

"It is!" Jenny said, a bit too loudly. "I can't believe I didn't remember! When I was digging through her desk, I saw a red flower. I hadn't paid that much attention to it, but I remember seeing it there."

Jenny felt a warmth spreading through her. Things were coming together. They'd saved Ryan, and now they knew how to save Rain too. They weren't going to get out of this unscathed, especially not Ryan, but they were going to get out of it.

"I think it's time we wake up Ryan and Rain," she said, excited to tell them the news.

They got up and walked over to where Ryan and Rain were still sleeping. Jenny felt guilty waking them up. She knew they needed much more sleep than this, but Sadie had been right when she said they needed to get out of the forest as quickly as possible.

She gently touched Ryan on the shoulder, and his body jerked away from her. He stared up at Jenny, wide-eyed and frightened.

"It's okay! It's just me. You're okay. You're safe."

He awkwardly stood up, denying Jenny's offer to help with a shake of the head.

"We, uh ... we think we found out how to turn Rain back," she said quietly, the excitement she had felt from the good news draining away.

"What is it?" he asked without looking at her.

"A flower," May answered. "We think there's one in Eckert's room back at the castle."

"Great, let's go," he mumbled, and started walking down

the path in the opposite direction of where the gingerbread cottage had once stood. Travis pushed himself up off the ground with a huff and moved in front of Ryan, blocking his path.

"Hold on," Travis said. "Can you tell us why we're here? Why did Eckert drag you guys into the woods?"

Jenny shot Travis a look he ignored.

Ryan looked at them all looking at him and took a deep breath.

"You don't have to do this right now," Jenny said softly, resting her hand on his arm. He flinched away from her slightly.

"No, it's fine. Eckert used us as bait, basically. The gingerbread house would only show itself to kids—specifically twins. When she was a kid, she and her twin brother were in these woods and were captured by the witch. She managed to escape, but he didn't. She tried to find the gingerbread house over the years but was never able to. She told us she wanted to kill the witch. I think some part of her had hoped her brother would somehow still be alive after all these years, but he was long dead."

Jenny felt sick as she remembered the cute little boy she had seen next to Eckert, his pudgy cheeks and wide eyes.

"Nothing went how she planned it. The second we got there, the witch was on us, hypnotizing us. Eckert and I froze but Rain managed to get free and run into the woods. The witch put Eckert and me in separate cages. She—" he broke off and looked at Rain. "God, I am so glad you got away." Tears filled his tired, bloodshot eyes.

Jenny didn't want to think about what would have happened if she hadn't.

"The witch, ah, ate Eckert," Ryan continued. "Piece by piece."

Jenny saw May's face drain of all color, and Travis looked like he might throw up again. She trembled thinking of it:

Ryan in that cage watching as Eckert was dismembered and eaten, knowing he was next. Jenny thought of all the time they had wasted back at the castle. If only they'd gotten there faster, maybe Ryan would still have his hand. She felt sick to her stomach.

"Dude, you are so lucky," Travis said, shaking his head. Jenny's eyes flitted nervously to Ryan, he pulled at his sleeve and looked off into the distance.

"Well, not entirely," Ryan said slowly. He hesitated, then lifted up his arm for the group to see. He pulled his sleeve up to reveal his missing hand. His wrist ended in a stump that was covered in pale-pink scars, and she could hear collective gasping all around her. Jenny didn't look at how the others reacted. She kept her eyes glued on Ryan. His dirty blonde hair fell over his eyes, hiding them and their expression.

"I don't want to talk about it, but I know I can't hide it either. So let's just all move on, okay?" Ryan pulled his sleeve back down. "Please?"

They all nodded silently, biting back any questions they had. Jenny was relieved no one was pushing him to talk about it.

"Hey, man," Travis said, breaking the awkward silence that had been growing longer and longer. "I had mold growing out of my chest, so, you know. Don't worry. We fixed that, and we can fix this."

Maybe we'll be able to fix Rain, Jenny thought. Not his hand, though. That was gone forever. Like Charlotte. Jenny glanced up and saw the same thought painted on Ryan's withdrawn face. He forced a smile and turned away. Jenny had never seen a forced smile on Ryan's face before. It was heartbreaking.

"Well, what are we waiting for?" Ryan said, turning back to look at them all standing there awkwardly in the middle of the path. "Let's get the hell out of here."

17

Sadie's stomach made an embarrassing groan she hoped no one else heard. She had been trying to ignore it, but she couldn't any longer—she was starving. Dehydrated. Weak. She pushed the discomfort away and focused on the trail ahead. They were going back to the castle; she could eat when they got back.

As they walked, Aiden and Travis filled Ryan in on what he had missed when he was imprisoned in the gingerbread witch's cottage. Travis reenacted his fight with the nixie, and Aiden told him about the troll under the bridge and the pit beneath the pear tree. Ryan listened politely, letting Aiden and Travis exhaust themselves storytelling, then stopped in the middle of the trail. Everyone stopped with him.

"I've been afraid to ask," Ryan said. "But I can't take not knowing anymore. Where are Cameron, Charlotte, and Hannah?"

Travis and Aiden's excitement died, and Jenny's face grew dark. Sadie looked around, wondering who would speak first. When no one did, she stepped up. She started with the easy ones.

"Hannah and Cameron are walking back along the road we came in on," Sadie explained. "They are going to get help and bring it back to the castle. Hopefully they'll be back by the time we get to the castle."

Ryan's tense expression softened, and he nodded. "What about Charlotte?"

Sadie's stomach twisted, and she looked at Jenny to see her

reaction. She felt, somehow, that the telling of Charlotte's fate wasn't her right.

"Ah, Charlotte ..." Aiden started, but couldn't finish.

"Charlotte is dead," Jenny said firmly from beside Ryan. Sadie watched Jenny, waiting to see what was going to happen next. She prepared herself for a breakdown, but Jenny just continued walking and didn't say anything more. Ryan opened his mouth as if to ask more questions, but Sadie caught his eye and shook her head no. He closed his mouth, and no one said another word as they continued down the path to who-knows-where.

Sadie scanned the woods as they walked, alert for the next nightmare, but so far, she'd seen nothing interesting at all. Tree after tree, bushes, branches, leaves. She didn't see a single bird or squirrel, no butterflies or even mosquitos. It was as if nothing could live in these woods, nothing except the fairy tales. Once or twice she thought she saw a small flash of red in the distance, like she had last night with Aiden when they were gathering wood. Every time she tried to focus on it, though, it disappeared, leaving Sadie to question whether she had actually seen anything at all.

Sadie looked up and tried to gauge what time it was by where the sun was in the sky, but under the thick canopy of trees, it was nearly impossible. It seemed like it had dipped past high noon, at least, so she knew it was the afternoon, but she didn't have a clearer idea than that. Still, she was sure they had a few hours left before it started to get dark. Sadie, now leading the group, picked up her pace. She didn't want to spend another night on the ground in this stupid forest.

Sadie moved quickly down the trail but grew more and more concerned as the path continued to stretch on ahead of her. She couldn't see anything but trees and the trail in front of her, and she had no idea where it was leading them. The idea that the trail would lead them safely out of the forest seemed almost laughable, yet here they were, trusting it. *We don't have any other options*, Sadie thought miserably. If the trail diverged again, she would have no idea which direction to go.

Her tennis shoes had been beaten up before they entered the woods, but now the soles were so thin she could feel every little pebble she stepped on. Her feet and ankles were sore, and her stomach pinched with hunger. She slowed to ask if they wanted to take a break—when she saw it.

"The well," whispered May, suddenly next to her. Sadie stared in disbelief at the little stone well they had gathered around for lunch that first day at the castle. The clearing was exactly as she remembered it: green grass dotted with little white flowers. Sunlight poured through the gap in the trees, making the scene look warm and welcoming. She was struck with an odd sense of déjà vu, and she could almost see her past self sitting in the grass with Hannah, blissfully ignorant of what was about to happen to them.

Sadie stepped off the path and into the clearing after May, who was already making her way toward the well. Sadie looked around, feeling disoriented. The trail had taken them through switchbacks and turns, and it had been impossible for her to know which direction the castle was, but she'd thought they'd been heading toward it, not around it. The well was on the opposite side of the castle from where they had entered the woods. She shook the thought away and shrugged to herself. Nothing made sense anymore.

"Are you sure it's the same one?" Ryan asked as he entered the clearing with Jenny.

"Pretty sure," May said, running her hand along the mouth of the well.

"Great! We know how to get back to the castle from here," Travis said.

"Well, sort of," Jenny said slowly. Sadie glanced behind her to see Jenny's worried face. "Remember, last time we went back the same way, but it was ... different."

Sadie nodded. She did remember. It had been really disconcerting.

"Yes, but we *did* make it back," Aiden countered.

"It's the best chance we have," Sadie agreed.

Sadie walked around the well, toward where the trail had been that first day. When she reached the tree line, she saw the opening—though she wasn't sure if it was the trail they had come in on or the one they'd used to leave. It didn't really matter as long as it led them back to the castle.

Sadie remembered then—the pond. They had passed a pond on the way back.

Travis seemed to have remembered it the same time she did because he groaned. "A pond is that way," he complained.

"That's fine," Jenny said. "We know what to do—and *not do*—this time. We'll avoid another nixie."

"Another what?" Ryan asked.

"The evil pond fairy that attacked us earlier," Aiden answered.

Ryan looked blankly at Aiden, then nodded. "Right. Of course. The nixie."

Aiden and Travis moved toward Sadie and the trail, and she stepped aside to give them room to look at it. Sadie looked back at the stragglers—May lingered at the well, examining the stonework, and Ryan and Jenny were still on the other side of the clearing. Rain drifted gracefully through the clearing, bending to nibble on the grass. *What are they doing?* she thought, annoyed. *Now is not the time to just wait around for something else to happen.* Sadie was about to yell for them to hurry up when Jenny gasped.

"Guys?" Jenny's voice called from the other side of the clearing, low and tense. Sadie looked beyond her, into the forest, and saw a pair of yellow eyes gleaming at them from the trees. Marble was at Jenny's side, growling at the invisible creature. Sadie's breath caught when she saw two large black paws step out of the darkness.

"Time to go, Jenny!" Sadie called, gesturing to the path behind her.

Ryan listened and slowly moved backward, toward Sadie and the trail, but Jenny seemed locked in place. "Jenny!" Ryan hissed, pausing when he reached his sister, her ears erect and twitching, her golden coat shimmering in the sunlight. Marble moved in front of Jenny, growling, but Sadie saw that he was still limping from his fight with the witch. He was weak. Sadie's mind raced, trying to figure out what to do, when the creature stepped entirely out of the woods.

The lion was enormous, twice the size of Marble, his head framed with a long, shaggy mane. Sadie's eyes flicked from Marble to the lion—the lion wasn't brown like normal lions; it had the same swirly black, white, and gray fur that Marble had. They looked like they were part of the same collection—a menagerie of marble animals carved by some unknown entity. Sadie didn't know what to make of it.

The lion skirted the outside of the clearing, walking around Jenny and Marble, its yellow eyes gleaming with hunger. Sadie realized too late what it was doing—it was putting itself between Jenny and the rest of the group. By the time she noticed what was happening, there it was, between Jenny and the rest of them—with its swirling black-and-gray fur and thrashing tail. It raised its massive head toward the sky and roared, a guttural, angry sound that shook the branches of the trees and made the ground tremble underneath her. Sadie took a step back, toward the trail to the castle. She eyed Marble, once so mighty in her eyes, now puny and weak next to the lion. After releasing its roar, the lion lowered its head and crouched closer to the ground, its body tense. Then it lunged.

Marble met it, and they fell together in a heap of swirling fur and gnashing teeth in front of Jenny. At the same time,

Rain balked, pushing past Sadie and galloping down the path behind them, toward—she hoped—the castle. *Shit.*

"The lion scared her," Ryan said, looking at the path Rain was running down, then back at Jenny, who was still trapped behind the fighting animals.

"Go," Ryan said to them. "Catch up with her; don't lose her. I can't lose her again."

"But what about—"

"Go!"

Sadie didn't move, stunned at the sudden chaos. Ryan shook his head angrily at her and turned to Travis. "Go after my sister!"

Travis didn't hesitate. He turned and took off running after Rain.

Sadie looked at her friend as the lion and the wolf fought; her eyes were wide with fear. *There's nothing I can do*, Sadie realized, defeated. She had no weapons, no magical abilities. All she could do was stand there and *watch*. She thought of the castle, how there must be weapons there, something they could use. *Too late*, a whisper inside of her head teased. *You'd be much too late.*

Sadie knew the voice in her head was right, but she couldn't just stand there doing nothing. She searched the clearing, frantically looking for anything that could be used as a weapon. All she saw was the well, which May was hiding behind, and a few rocks that were far too small to do any damage if thrown. The lion wouldn't even feel it.

"Just go!" Ryan yelled at her, placing his body in front of hers. "There's nothing you can do, just go!"

"But—" Sadie felt her arm being pulled and turned to see Aiden. She stumbled after him as he pulled her up, onto the path, and out of the clearing. She yanked her arm away.

"What are you doing?"

"Saving your life, *again*," he said, his hand back on her arm.

"Leaving Jenny and Ryan to die? And what about May?"
Aiden let go, looking guilty.

"I'm not leaving them," she insisted, turning back toward the clearing.

But there wasn't a clearing. There wasn't a trail. Just dark forest so dense she couldn't force herself through it, no matter how hard she tried.

Jenny, May, Ryan ... were *gone*.

18

Jenny watched, frozen in place, as Marble fought the lion. What looked like black oil sprayed from where Marble had ripped into its flesh. The lion roared and wrenched itself free from the wolf and lunged at him again, its large jaws closing around Marble's throat. Her wolf made a heartbreaking high-pitched yelp as he fell to the ground with the lion on top of him.

"No!" Jenny screamed. Tears ran down her cheeks as she paced around the two entangled animals. It was hard for her to tell where Marble started and the lion ended; their matching fur swirled together as they fought. Black puddles of blood started to form all around them. She looked all over the clearing, frantically trying to think of some way to help. She saw Ryan near the tree line, waving at her to come toward him. May was huddled behind the well, peering out, wide-eyed and pale.

Ryan slowly approached the tangled creatures, his hand outstretched toward her. They didn't notice him approaching, just continued growling and tearing at one another. Jenny shook her head at Ryan. There was no way she was going to get past the fighting animals. Ryan gestured to the well on her right and yelled over the loud snarls and roars, "Go around the well!"

Jenny looked at the well, where May was crouched. She could go around; the well would give her some safety from the lion. She hesitated, and in that brief moment, the tangled animals slammed into Ryan. She watched, helpless, as he fell hard to the ground.

Ryan managed to roll clear of the fighting animals, then

looked furiously up at her. He gestured toward the well again. "Jenny, come on, just run over here!" Ryan yelled.

She saw her path out—around the well, away from the fighting wolf and lion, and into Ryan's arms. They'd escape down the path and make it safely to the castle. For the briefest moment, Jenny allowed herself to envision this happy ending. But in it she wasn't happy.

"I can't leave him," she said, shaking her head sorrowfully. She knew how stupid she was being. She didn't care.

Ryan looked at Jenny in a way he had never looked at her before—with disgust. She knew he couldn't understand. She didn't expect him to. She wasn't going to just leave Marble to fight the lion alone, and she wasn't going to just stand there and watch him get torn apart. *I have to do something*, she thought fiercely.

Then she remembered—she still had her knife.

Jenny shakily pulled out the knife with the swirly black-and-gray handle. She'd stabbed a nixie and a gingerbread witch; she could do this. No problem. The creatures made horrible snapping and growling sounds as they continued to fight in front of her.

Jenny edged closer to the lion and the wolf, watching anxiously as they tumbled around on the ground; she didn't know if she would be able to stab the lion without accidentally stabbing Marble. She inched closer, trying to find an opening, when the tumbling suddenly stopped. Marble was pinned to the ground underneath the giant paws of the lion, its black claws digging into Marble's flesh. Marble's head turned weakly toward her. She stared into his dimming eyes, and something broke inside of her. He wasn't fighting anymore. The lion, triumphant, leaned down and wrapped its jaws around Marble's neck.

It was like she left her body and something else took charge. Suddenly, she was on top of the lion, one hand gripping its mane and the other driving the knife into its bulky neck as hard as she could. A chilling roar escaped the lion as it released Marble and fell to the ground beside him. Jenny fell on top of the dying lion and felt its soft body turn rigid. Underneath her, there was no longer the bleeding body of the lion that had attacked them, but now a smooth marble *statue* of a lion. Her knife jutted out of its neck, locked into the stone. She tried to pull it out, but it didn't budge. She let go of the knife and quickly scrambled off the lion statue. She looked at the handle of her knife sticking out of the lion—it was made of the same swirly marble her wolf had been made of before she had brought him to life. It was the same marble the lion was now made of. She turned her attention to her wolf, who was lying in the grass, unmoving, his breathing just a shallow rattle, his head in a puddle of black blood that was pouring from the wounds in his neck. She dropped to her knees at Marble's side, tears streaming down her cheeks as she stroked his blood-soaked face.

"You're going to be okay. Please, please be okay," she begged.

Marble had repeatedly fought to keep her safe, and she hadn't been able to do the same for him. If she had remembered the knife sooner, maybe he would still be okay. She buried her wet face into his fur and held him against her. His body was limp in her arms. A large gash ran across his neck, and part of one of his ears was gone. She stared into his deep, sweet eyes that had always looked at her with love and trust and watched as the life drained out of them. She bent her head over him and cried until her throat closed up and her chest burned. Tears dripped down her face and were lost in the swirling grays and blacks of Marble's fur.

His eyes closed.

The tears wouldn't stop flowing as she continued to hold his body against hers. Her heart hurt so badly; there was a physical pain in the center of her chest. She clung to Marble's body and closed her eyes, forcing the world around her to cease to exist. There was no sound except for her own sobbing. She knew Ryan and May were there watching her completely fall apart. She didn't care. They would never understand how this felt. She sensed someone moving behind her, and a hand fell on her shoulder. She forced her eyes, burning and puffy from crying, open to look at Ryan crouched next to her.

"I'm sorry, Jenny," he said. "I really am. But he's gone, and we really need to go. We don't know what else might be coming for us."

Jenny nodded weakly and looked down at her wolf. His eyes were closed, and his fur was wet with blood, but he was still beautiful. She leaned over and kissed the wolf gently on top of his head between his ears and whispered goodbye.

She let Ryan help her off the ground. Her whole body felt weak, and her legs were shaky underneath her. They made their way to the trail that would hopefully take them out of the forest and stopped at the tree line. They turned to see that May was still standing by the well, her hands resting on the stone lip of the opening.

"May? What are you—" Jenny stopped as she saw something move in her peripheral vision. She turned to focus on where she saw the movement and closed her eyes tightly when they fell on Marble's body. She hated that she would have the vision of him like that, lying dead in the grass, burned into her mind forever. She looked over at May, who was still standing by the well, but May's attention was directed toward something on the ground.

"Jenny, look," Ryan said softly, pointing at Marble. "He's ..."

"Alive!" Jenny screamed, letting go of Ryan's hand and rushing back to where Marble was slowly starting to stand up. He stood on all four legs and shook his body like a dog shaking water off after a bath. The wounds on his neck and body slowly disappeared into the swirls of his fur. "I can't believe it! He was ... he was *dead*!" She threw her arms around Marble's neck and hugged him harder than she probably should've, but she didn't care. He was *alive*.

Over by the well, May snorted and shook her head.

"What?" she said, offended by May's levity.

"True love's kiss," May said with a small smile. A second passed before Jenny understood, then she laughed too. It was a laugh filled with more pain than joy, but it burst out of her, and the tightness in her chest released a little.

Ryan wasn't laughing. He turned and started walking silently toward the path. She let Marble go and tried to collect herself. Her nerves were completely frayed, and she wasn't sure how much more she could take.

Marble stretched his body and yawned, showing rows of his sharp moonlight-white teeth. She smiled down at him and ran her hand along his back. More tears slipped down her cheeks, but now she was crying out of relief. For the few minutes he was dead, Jenny had felt impossibly lost and empty. She needed him more than she'd realized.

"Time to go back," she said to the wolf, who looked up at her as if he had no idea he'd just been dead.

Jenny looked over at May, who was still standing by the well, peering down into it. It reminded Jenny of the last time they had visited the well, that first day at the castle. She had been afraid that May would to throw herself into it. She was starting to have the same fear now.

"May?"

Jenny took a few steps toward her, and May looked up at her with an odd determination in her eyes.

"Do you remember the story of Mother Holle?" May asked. Jenny blinked. "I told it the last time we were here."

"Yeah, I guess, but why—"

"Mother Holle grants wishes. Gives treasures. If you're worthy."

Jenny didn't know where May was going with this or what

she was supposed to do with that information.

"Wishes?" Ryan said from the mouth of the trail, turning back toward them.

May nodded and looked back into the well.

Jenny looked down at the stump where Ryan's hand used to be. She knew what he'd wish for.

"But how does it work?" she asked, hesitantly. "We haven't exactly had the best luck with the fairy tales we've interacted with so far."

"Yeah, I know," May agreed. "I'm not entirely sure. In the story, the girl is thrown down the well—but that's not a very appealing option."

All three of them were now standing around the well, gazing into its darkness. May took off her backpack and pulled out the long knife with the flat blade and wooden handle she had taken from Eckert's room. "This knife has a few of the same symbols carved into it as the well does," she said, gesturing at the marks scratched into the stone. "That's why I grabbed it."

"I wonder what they mean," Jenny said, biting her bottom lip, deep in thought. She knew they should leave—follow the others out of the forest and back to the castle. But something about the well pulled her to it.

"It doesn't matter," Ryan said ruefully, "if we don't know how to use it."

Why would this fairy tale help them when every other story had tried to kill them? Jenny stared into the darkness of the well and felt stunned that they were even considering this. The reality was, though, that once they got back to the castle, they were basically back to square one. They'd saved Ryan and Rain, but Ryan was missing a hand and Rain was a deer. If what May said was true, and this Mother Holle person actually could grant wishes ... It didn't matter, though. They had no idea how to use the well to get to Mother Holle.

May groaned, and her hands clenched at the stone of the

well, her knuckles turning white. Jenny wanted a wish, too, but May seemed overly obsessed with the idea. She wondered what it was that May wanted so badly.

Marble got up from his place on the grass and walked over to Jenny. She winced at seeing his left ear—the top half was missing but no longer bleeding. He looked up at her as if he was trying to tell her something. He lifted one large black paw and tapped it against the side of the well.

"What's he doing?" Ryan asked, a slight annoyance tinging his tone.

"I'm not sure," Jenny said. "It seems like he's trying to tell me something about the well, but I don't ..."

Marble pawed at the side of the well again and stared at her. She bent down to look at the place he had been pawing at. The well was made of uneven stones of all different shapes and sizes, mortared together and worn smooth with time. One of the rocks, she noticed now, was oddly round in comparison to the others. It jutted out, too, slightly, from the rest of the well.

"It looks like a doorknob!" May said excitedly, now crouched next to her.

"A doorknob? Let me see," Ryan said, joining them on the ground. "I guess it does, kind of."

May reached out, wrapped her hand around the round rock, and tried to turn it, but it didn't move. May's face fell.

Marble stared meaningfully at Jenny and pawed at the well again. She shook her head.

"I don't understand what you're trying to tell me," she said to the wolf. Marble let out a breath that sounded almost irritated and pawed at the well again.

"If that's a doorknob," Ryan said slowly, "then does that make the area around it a door?"

May and Jenny looked at Ryan and then back at the well. A door.

May grinned. "And what do you do when you come to a

locked door?"

"You ... knock?" Jenny said uncertainly.

May rapped her knuckle lightly on the side of the well three times and then sat back. The ground began to tremble slightly underneath them, and the well, only about four feet high, suddenly rose out of the ground until it loomed above them. The section of the well May had knocked on shuddered and creaked open, revealing darkness.

"What the ..." Ryan stared in disbelief at the now seven-foot-high well and the opening.

May's dark eyes sparkled with excitement. After everything they'd been through, she had never seen May like this before. It unnerved her a little. Something felt ... off.

"Come on," May said, walking carefully through the opening. A second later, she was swallowed up by darkness, and they couldn't see her at all.

"May!" Jenny yelled into the well.

"What? Come on, there are stairs," May replied from inside the well, a touch of annoyance in her voice.

Jenny looked at Ryan, who was looking at the opening.

"I don't know about this," Jenny said. "*Willingly* entering another fairy tale? After what happened to you and Rain ... and Charlotte ..."

Ryan nodded, then looked down at Marble.

"The wolf helped us open it, right?" he asked.

"Yeah, I guess ..."

"And the wolf is on your side, so he wouldn't help put you in danger, right?"

Jenny stared down into Marble's warm eyes and felt a calmness come over her as it usually did when she looked at him. Marble had tried to stop her from opening the door in the wall at the castle, had tried to stop her from going into the gingerbread house, had protected her from the lion. Marble was always trying to keep her safe. He wouldn't push her into something dangerous, would he?

"Yeah ..."

"So this should be safe then, I think," Ryan finished. "I'm going in."

One, two, three steps, and Ryan, too, disappeared into the darkness.

Jenny chewed nervously on her bottom lip and looked around the clearing. She really, really didn't want to go in there. She eyed the path that she thought led back to the castle—back to the rest of their friends. She briefly considered taking the path instead, leaving May and Ryan to their dangerous adventure.

But no, she couldn't leave him again. Not after what had happened to him. She had survived everything else this forest had thrown at her—she'd survive this too. She took a deep breath and stepped into the well.

She turned to call for Marble to join her, but when she did, she didn't see the clearing—all she saw was worn gray stone. The door had disappeared. Panic raced through her—they were trapped.

"The door's gone!" she yelped into the darkness. She felt around for Ryan, and he took her hand.

"Here, hold on to my hand," Ryan said. "Only one way to go now. May is already making her way down."

Jenny waited a moment for her eyes to adjust to the darkness—the only light was coming from the opening at the top of the well, and that light was already obscured by the thick forest canopy above. It reminded her of the hole she and Aiden had fallen into under the pear tree. She couldn't see Ryan clearly and wished she could see his face. She never would have thought Ryan would be so eager to get trapped inside another fairy tale. *Is getting his hand back so important that he'd risk all three of our lives?*

Ryan went ahead of her, and she followed close behind. A panic she was embarrassed by started to fill her chest. She felt slightly betrayed by Ryan, she'd been forced to do something she hadn't wanted to do, something she didn't know if she'd even come back from. Being separated from Marble didn't help either—it felt wrong being apart from him. He had become her shadow, *part* of her. She didn't know if that lion was the only monster nearby. *What if something else attacks Marble while we're down here?* She tried to ignore the fear and guilt swirling around inside and focus on Ryan in front of her. The stairs spiraled down the well to a dark bottom they couldn't see.

"What if it never ends?" she whispered.

"No, it will end. It will," he replied firmly. He didn't look back at her as he said it but instead continued walking down the stairs. Ahead of them, May was rushing down far too quickly, and Ryan picked up his pace to catch up with her. Jenny followed dutifully, wondering what on earth had gotten into them both.

Wishes. What was worth putting all three of them in this kind of danger? A chance to fix things. To get Ryan's hand back, turn Rain back into a human, bring Charlotte back to life. To get out of here. When she thought of everything that could be gained by doing this, she started to understand their determination. *Yes,* she admitted. It was worth the risk.

In the darkness, Jenny had no sense of time—she had no idea how long they'd been descending the staircase. Finally, she saw a light ahead of her and nearly collided into Ryan as they landed at the bottom of the well. A door just like the one they had used to come in stood in front of them. Warm light outlined the closed door from the other side.

"Well, here we go," May said with a breath. Jenny watched as May pushed the door open, and was nearly blinded by the sunlight that came flooding into the well.

Outside the well was nothing like the forest they'd been trapped in the last couple days. It was bright, open farmland, with rows of mounded vegetables stretched out on one side of them and long golden grain swaying softly on their other side. A path led toward a small dot of a house Jenny could just barely make out in the distance.

"Now what?" Ryan asked May.

"We go that way," May replied, pointing toward the house. "If we help everyone we come across, she'll grant us our wishes. At least, that's how the story goes anyway."

Jenny didn't have to say what they were all thinking—that the story could easily go a different way, a less desirable way. It didn't matter now. They were committed.

May led them down the path, with Ryan close behind and Jenny lagging slightly after him. May seemed so different all of a sudden—she had been really helpful before, of course, but this was the first time Jenny saw her really take charge. As they walked toward Mother Holle's house, Jenny enjoyed the warmth of the sun on her skin. She'd been covered in shade for so long. It felt good to feel the sun again. The cloudless sky above them was a pale blue, and as she looked up, she realized there was no sun. She felt it, but there was no fireball in the sky. The oddness of this made Jenny feel uneasy, and suddenly she didn't enjoy the warmth anymore.

As they walked, Jenny stared at the crops of vegetables growing on her left, and her stomach grumbled, reminding her how little she'd eaten in the last few days. Plump heads of green cabbages bumped up against vines with thick cucumbers, and the cucumbers made way for bright red tomatoes. Jenny remembered all too well what had happened when Aiden had taken the golden pear from the tree. She pushed aside the hunger and temptation and tried to focus on the trail ahead instead of the food surrounding her.

"So, is there something we should be looking for?" Ryan asked May. Jenny saw May shrug her shoulders ahead of her.

"In the story there's some bread, apples, then—"

Jenny jumped as May was cut off by a sound she had never

heard before. Her hands reflexively leapt to her ears to try and block out the noise. It was like some horrible combination of all the worst sounds in the world: nails on a chalkboard, the high-pitched whine her dog Hamilton made any time someone came to the door, silverware in a garbage disposal, her dad cracking his knuckles. Every sound that ever made her cringe was combined to create this ear-murdering noise.

"What is that?" Ryan yelled.

"It must be the bread! We have to take them out!" May yelled, and pointed at a stone oven just a few yards away. It looked like an old-fashioned pizza oven, just sitting on the side of the path.

Despite her natural instinct to run *away* from the horrible sound, they ran *toward* it. When they came to it, they peered inside and saw three loaves of perfectly browned bread. The awful noise was definitely coming out of the oven, almost as if the bread itself were screaming.

"Please, make it stop!" Jenny yelled. Her eardrums were on fire, and she was worried they might actually burst if she had to listen to the noise any longer.

"Look for something to take them out with!" May yelled to them, and they all looked hurriedly around the oven for something they could use to remove the bread. There was nothing there, though, except a tree stump and a few dandelions.

"We're running out of time!" May said, looking anxiously into the oven. May's eyes widened, and she tore her backpack off and pulled out the flat knife she'd taken from Eckert's room. She used it to push the bread toward the opening, but there was nothing to scoot the loaves onto, so she grabbed it with her bare hand. She set the loaf down on a nearby tree stump and repeated the task for the remaining loaves. Tears were in her eyes, and Jenny just stood there, frozen in shock at what May was doing. Ryan looked embarrassed and wouldn't meet her eyes when she looked over at him.

In a few seconds, May had all three loaves out of the oven, and the screaming stopped. Jenny felt a painful ringing in her ears replace the screaming. May stood next to the bread, tears in her eyes, staring down at the hand she'd used to pull the loaves out. Jenny winced as she saw bubbly yellow-tinged blisters growing like mushrooms on the inside of her palm and up her fingers.

"Oh, May," Jenny said, tears filling her own eyes.

"Why did you do that?" Ryan snapped. "You're crazy!"

Jenny flinched at the word, and before she could stop herself, she turned and snapped back at Ryan, "No, she's not! She did what she had to do!"

The words left her mouth with conviction, but she didn't really believe them. She knew the bread had to be removed, but there must have been another way. They just hadn't been smart enough to figure it out in time.

Then the screaming started again, only louder. Jenny's hands whipped up to cover her ears, and May looked down at the bread in shock. May seemed to realize something and picked up the bread knife she'd set down next to the loaves on the tree stump.

She hesitated, then cut into one of the loaves of bread. The screaming faded slightly. She cut again and again, until the bread was in uneven slices, then she did the other two. When she finished cutting up the last one, the screaming completely stopped. The warm smell of freshly baked bread filled the air, but the screaming had killed her appetite.

"How did you know to cut the bread?" Ryan asked.

"I didn't really," May said. "It was just a guess."

"Lucky guess," Ryan muttered, shaking his head. "I hate this place. Nothing makes sense."

"May, your hand—" Jenny started, but May cut her off.

"It's fine," May snapped, dropping her hands to her sides. "I'm fine. Let's keep going."

"May ..."

"Let's keep going!" she insisted, whirling away from her and moving down the path in long, fast strides.

She and Ryan caught up to May easily, but neither of them could find the right thing to say. Jenny couldn't help but stare at May's burnt hand and at Ryan's missing hand. She felt strangely alienated by what had just happened. She thought about how much suffering they'd all been through—Ryan had lost his hand, Hannah had had the life nearly sucked out of her, Travis had been injured by the nixie, Rain had been transformed into a deer, and Charlotte had *died*. Now May's hand was burned and blistering. Jenny felt her stomach churn, and she couldn't help feeling like it was all her fault. She hadn't had to suffer like they had, not really. She was still okay, and that felt wrong to her.

"What are the other things we have to do?" Ryan asked May carefully.

"In the story there's an apple tree that we need to shake, then we have to just, like, clean Mother Holle's house," May replied without turning around.

"That doesn't sound so bad," Ryan said, attempting a weak smile May couldn't see anyway.

"Yeah, well, taking bread out of an oven didn't sound so bad either," she said flatly.

They continued down the path, toward the cottage in the distance, and the farmland slowly turned into barren ground with nothing but small tufts of brown and dried grass scattered here and there. Jenny was disturbed by the sudden shift and knew there must be a reason for it. After a few minutes, they approached the only thing thriving in the wasteland—the most massive apple tree Jenny had ever seen. The trunk must have been ten feet wide, and the branches reached up so high she couldn't see the tops of them. The apples were a sickly green and oddly shaped. As Jenny came closer, she started to make out familiar features—a nose, a mouth, and empty sockets where eyes should've been. The apples were tiny shrunken heads.

"Ugh!"

May cringed and looked quickly away. Ryan took a step closer, fascinated by the tiny apple heads.

"I ... I don't understand," Jenny managed to squeak out. "Are we supposed to knock those ... *heads* down?"

May shook her head, eyes frozen on the ground. "The trunk is too big, too sturdy. We can't shake the tree."

"Shake me, shake me, my apples are all ripe," the tree whispered, the voice creepily gleeful, as if it enjoyed the thought of them being grossed out by it.

May groaned.

Ryan went over and kicked at the tree, but nothing happened. He tried running into it, but all he did was hurt his shoulder. The tree wouldn't budge. The shriveled apple heads remained where they were, giggling grotesquely down at them. Jenny watched Ryan's futile attempts to shake the tree and noticed how gnarled the trunk was—it almost looked like there were footholds molded into the tree. Her heart pounded as she realized what they had to do.

Correction, what *she* had to do.

She walked over to the tree and mapped out her route up to the nearest branch—knots were in all the right places for her to be able to climb up. She dropped her backpack on the ground and tested the first foot- and handhold. The tree didn't move or break or suck her in like the pear tree had tried to do.

"Jenny, what are you doing?" Ryan said, a look of shock painted across his face.

"We have to shake the branches, not the trunk, and we have to climb up there to do it."

May glanced down at her burnt hand, and Ryan's face flushed as he looked down at the stump where his right hand used to be. Jenny was the obvious choice.

Jenny tried to forget about them, about everything, as she carefully made her way up the knobby tree trunk. She forced herself to look up, never down. No reason to look down. As she thought this, her eyes flicked away from the next handhold and down at the last one. Her foot slipped as she saw how high she had already climbed. She started to feel dizzy, and the world shifted just enough to make her feel motion sick. *I'm going to fall.*

No, you're not, she told herself. She often had these little arguments with herself when she was being pessimistic. She continued to pull herself up and finally reached the first branch. She sat on top of it and tried to avoid looking at the revolting heads dangling below her.

"Watch out!" she called to Ryan and May as she leaned over and slowly started pushing and pulling at the branch. It barely moved—but it was enough. She watched as the little green heads dropped from the branch and fell to the ground below. She thought she could hear tiny little screams, but it could have just been in her mind. The first branch was clear of heads, and she looked up to the next one. She made her way up the tree this way, shaking each branch she came to until all the heads had fallen off. She became laser focused on the task, and the heads ceased to bother her. Up and up and up she went, until finally she reached the top of the gigantic tree. She looked up and saw there were just a few left. There were no more branches to climb onto, so she held tight to the trunk and moved her entire body back and forth. The heads started to fall—but this time they were falling *on* her. She tried not to scream as she felt them smack against the top of her head. She forced herself not to let go of the tree even as she felt tiny mouths biting into her arms, her legs, her scalp. She pressed her forehead to the tree trunk and tried to shield her face as she continued to shake the tree. Everything inside of her was screaming, and she fought the all-encompassing urge to let go of the trunk and slap the heads off her.

She gave one last exhausted shake, and no more heads came down. She was done. She looked at her arms wrapped around the trunk—she had three heads attached by sharp little teeth on her left arm and another two on her right. Her vision blurred as her eyes filled with tears.

"Get off, get off, get off, get off!" she screamed at them. She shook her arm as much as she could without letting go of the tree, but they remained attached to her skin. She'd have to ignore them until she got down to one of the branches. She started to inch down the trunk of the tree, making a point to stare forward at the dull brown bark instead of the five sets of empty sockets pointed at her. She made it to a branch and carefully situated herself so she was sitting with her legs firmly wrapped around it. She forced herself to remain calm and not move too quickly or do anything else that would result in her falling to a very nasty death at the bottom of the tree. An image of the heads rolling toward her on the ground to eat her flashed in her head, and she cringed.

She swallowed hard as she reached her shaking hand to the first head attached to her arm. If she pulled, it'd likely take a chunk of her flesh with it. She thought of the time she'd found a tick plump with blood stuck in her armpit when she went to take a shower at her grandparents' house after a long hike in the backcountry. She'd never seen one before and screamed for help, forgetting she was naked except for a towel wrapped around her. The bathroom had filled with every member of the family—her grandparents, mother and father, uncle and aunt, and two cousins. She'd stood there, mortified, as the adults argued about the best way to remove a tick. If you plucked it out wrong, the head would stay inside your skin and cause an infection. Her uncle had flipped open his Zippo lighter with a click and announced it was best to burn it off. She'd gaped at him in horror as he moved the flame toward her underarm.

The apple heads hadn't burrowed into her skin like the tick had, but their tiny sharp teeth were gripping it hard. *It's biting me, so that must mean it's at least sort of alive*, she thought. She stared at the little bumps of noses on their faces—yes, nostrils. They had nostrils.

I can't believe I'm doing this. It took every ounce of willpower to reach over and pinch the first head's nose shut. After a few moments, it began to shiver and then released her arm. She threw it down as quickly as she could before it tried to latch onto her again.

She did the same thing to the rest of the heads on her arms until all that was left were their tiny bite marks. Pinpricks of blood seeped slowly from each of them, but it wasn't as bad as she had thought it was going to be. She looked down at her bare legs and saw that a few more of the heads had managed to attach themselves to her calves and her shoe. She suffocated them all until they released their hold on her and dropped to the ground below.

Blood trickled down her arms and legs from the bites as she continued working her way down the tree. She looked below her to find the next foothold, and it didn't bother her anymore, being this high. If she could climb down a tree with those horrible things attached to her, she could do anything. A small glow of pride flickered inside of her.

Finally, she was back on the ground. She carefully made her way through the minefield of apple heads to where May and Ryan were sitting. They stood up as she approached, and she saw their eyes widen as they took in her arms and legs—now almost entirely covered in blood.

"It's not as bad as it looks," she told them with a smile. "We just leave them there, right? We don't have to take them with us?"

May shook her head. "I don't think so."

They continued quietly down the path toward the little

house, each lost in their own thoughts. Jenny noticed new vegetables had sprouted up on either side of them as they moved farther away from the apple tree. She saw rows of turnips, their little heads poking slightly out of the ground with sprigs of delicate green leaves sprouting up, and thick vines growing along the ground with bright orange pumpkins popping up here and there. Jenny's stomach pinched. She was so hungry, and she again tried to ignore the food growing just a few feet away.

She walked behind Ryan, watching his arms determinedly swing back and forth as he moved. His blonde hair was dirty and stuck to his scalp with sweat. If she had come up behind him out in the real world, she never would have recognized him. Even how he moved was different. Jenny remembered the outgoing, lighthearted guy Ryan had been and wondered if she would ever see him again.

As they approached the house, Ryan slowed. The cottage had white walls and a triangular thatch roof. Flowers of every color grew from window boxes, and a little white cat yawned and stretched on the porch. It was very different from the gingerbread house he had been imprisoned in, but still. She saw the fear in his eyes.

"We're sure about this?" Jenny asked.

"We came this far," Ryan replied stiffly.

May responded by walking up to the cottage door and gently knocking.

The door opened, and there stood a hunched-over woman with gray hair in one long braid down her back. She wore a simple brown dress with a white apron. She looked exactly like Jenny expected her to look—like every witch in every book she'd ever read as a child.

"Such good children," the old woman said with a large smile, revealing grotesquely large, stained teeth. "Such good little helpers. Come, come inside now." The woman waved them into the cottage, and they followed. Ryan lingered a moment on the threshold. Jenny knew he was still thinking about the gingerbread house and what he'd lost there. She tried to give him an encouraging smile. He sucked in a deep breath and entered the cottage.

The old woman sat down in a rocking chair and sucked on what looked like a corncob pipe. She blew purple smoke rings toward them and smiled her toothy grin again.

"You made it all the way here. You saved the bread and shook the tree, and now you get your wish. So go on, tell me what your wish is."

Jenny couldn't believe this was happening. She'd expected more tests, more tasks. May had said they'd have to clean her house. After everything they'd gone through, something was finally going right. She let herself smile.

"Wait, *one* wish?" Ryan said, concern pinching his face.

"Oh, ho! Do we have a greedy little child here?"

May grabbed Ryan by the arm and pushed him slightly behind her. "No, no, Mother Holle. Don't mind him. He was just … confused. One wish is very generous."

Jenny's eyes flicked from Ryan to May to Mother Holle, and the tiny flame of optimism she had been feeling moments before was doused out. *One* wish. Why hadn't it occurred to her that they might just get *one* wish?

"Excuse me, Mother Holle," Jenny interjected, "but may we have a minute to decide what our wish will be?"

"Of course, my dear, one minute you may have."

The tall wooden cuckoo clock behind her started clicking as the minute hand wound itself quickly up to the twelve, then started ticking forward. *Oh no.* She had said a minute, and now that's all they get, Jenny realized. *One* minute.

"Okay, let's figure this out quickly," Jenny said, her eyes flicking back to the clock. "What's the best wish we could make?"

Ryan eyed the stump where his hand used to be, and Jenny felt a twinge in her stomach. She didn't want to have this conversation, but they were literally on a timer.

"I know you want your hand back," she said as gently as she could, "but Charlotte is *dead*. I think we have to wish for Charlotte to be brought back."

"What about my sister? She can't stay a deer forever!"

"There is another way to help Rain," Jenny argued. "The flower. We know where at least one is. I'm sure it'll work. There's no other option for Charlotte."

"I know Charlotte is important to you, and it's terrible that she died," Ryan countered, "but what about getting out of here? There's no point in bringing Charlotte back if none of us are able to leave."

Jenny exhaled and stared down at the ground. He had a point. *Maybe we'll be able to find another way*, she thought hopefully. But there was no guarantee they would, and wasn't sure they'd be able to leave at all without using the wish. She felt the fight slip out of her. He was right, she knew. It was the right wish, but it didn't make her feel better.

"I know. You're right, Ryan," she acquiesced. "I guess we should—"

Jenny never got to finish her sentence.

"I wish my brother never killed anyone!" May yelled, her back to Jenny.

Jenny stared, dumbfounded, at the back of May's head.

The old woman smiled. Ryan and Jenny stood there, helpless and stunned into silence.

"Granted."

19

Gone. Sadie stood gawking at the dense forest, where just moments ago the path had been. Now thorny brambles and thick-trunked trees blocked their way. Jenny, May, and Ryan had been right there … and now they weren't. Travis had chased after Rain, and both were long gone, back to the castle, Sadie hoped. Now it was just her and Aiden.

"What do we do?" Aiden asked behind her. Annoyance bubbled up inside of Sadie. If he hadn't grabbed her … She sighed. It didn't matter now. She waited a moment before turning to face him, taking a few breaths first.

"I don't know," she said finally. "We can stay here and wait, see if the path reappears, or …"

"Or we can keep going. Back to the castle," he finished for her. Aiden looked as enthusiastic about these options as she felt.

Sadie crossed her arms and looked up at the thin cracks of light coming through the canopy high above them. Before they knew it, it'd be night again. Her stomach ached with hunger, and she was starting to feel weak. She looked back guiltily at the place the path had been.

Sadie never thought she'd be abandoning Jenny in the woods. When she had volunteered to come with Jenny on this insane rescue mission, it was to keep Jenny safe. And she had failed. She had no idea what was happening to Jenny right now, what that monster was doing. Sadie strained to hear something, anything, but the woods were as silent as ever.

"Let's wait a few minutes," Aiden offered. "If they don't come out, we'll keep going—back to the castle."

Sadie nodded. She looked around for something to sit on but didn't see anything that looked even remotely comfortable. She gave up and sat down in the dirt, then looked up at Aiden towering above her. "You gonna sit or what?"

Flustered, Aiden sat down across from Sadie, and they waited together in the middle of the trail. It felt strange to Sadie, to just sit there, waiting. For days now, *something* was always happening. The annoyance she felt toward Aiden for pulling her out of the clearing ebbed, and she felt completely drained. She wasn't sure how much more she could take.

Across from her, Aiden drew random scribbles into the dirt with a small stick he found. "Do you think Travis and Rain made it out of the forest?" he asked, without looking up at her.

"I don't know," she said honestly.

"It's crazy," he continued, still staring down at the dirt, "that just a few days ago, we all came here together. One big group. And now we've all been separated, and Charlotte is dead, and Rain is a deer ..."

Sadie watched Aiden, curious where he was going with this. None of this was new information. She wondered why he was bringing it up now.

"Yeah?" she prompted when he trailed off.

"I don't know. It's just ... everything feels different now. And all of this fairy-tale stuff ... it's not like the movies I've seen. It's not beautiful or fun. It's just dark and sad and wrong. We're not going to get a happily ever after. We'll be lucky if we get out of here at all. And Ryan—"

Aiden's voice cracked, and he stopped talking a moment, gazing fiercely out at the woods. Sadie waited for him to continue what he was saying, but he didn't. She squirmed in the awkwardness of the sudden silence. She never knew what to say or do when people got emotional around her.

"Knock it off," she said, opting to use what she felt most comfortable with: tough love. "We will either get out of here and on with our lives or we won't. There's no point in grieving what hasn't happened yet. It's like getting onto a boat and announcing it's going to sink. Yeah, it might sink, but you're on the boat, and it's pulling away from the dock, and lamenting your *potentially* impending doom doesn't help anyone."

Aiden looked up from the crude symbols he'd been tracing into the dirt and gaped at her.

Ah, I guess that probably wasn't the right thing to say, she thought.

"Sorry, I didn't mean that." She sighed. "I'm just exhausted, starving, and worried my best friend is being torn to shreds by a lion. I'm tapped out."

Aiden nodded. "I'm sorry too," he offered. "I know I'm being annoying. I'm just not sure how much more of this ... this *evil* ... I can take."

"Yeah, I feel you."

They didn't speak again for a while; Sadie was lost in her own thoughts and certain Aiden was struggling with his own. As the time continued to tick by, Sadie grew tired of waiting. It wasn't in her nature to sit and do nothing. She ran through the facts in her head for the hundredth time. Jenny and the others hadn't come back, and there was no indication that they ever would. There was only one way to go on the trail they were on. It was getting late, and soon it would be dark. Everything pointed to them needing to continue and leave their friends behind, but it turned her stomach. She felt like she was betraying Jenny.

Sadie peered down the path, and something she hadn't noticed before caught her eye. A tiny flash of red on the ground. She stood up, shaking the tingling sleep from her legs, and walked over to the red object. As she got closer, she almost didn't believe what she was seeing—a single red flower with a shimmering pearl in the center.

"Is that it? The flower that can change Rain back?" Aiden asked, suddenly next to her. She jumped slightly in surprise.

"I hope so. I think so." Sadie bent down and carefully plucked it from the ground. She peered into its center and fought the urge to touch the single pearl. She didn't know how this magic worked, and she didn't want to ruin it by doing something stupid.

"We need to go back to the castle," Aiden said softly. Sadie knew he was right. Now that they had the flower, they had to get it to Rain as soon as they could. They had been hoping the flower Jenny had seen in Eckert's room was the one that could change Rain back, but they didn't know if it was still there, or dead, or even the right flower. What Sadie held in her hands was definitely the right flower. She could just *feel* it somehow. She *knew*. She had to get to Rain before she lost it, or it got damaged, or—like her knife—something in the forest took it from her.

"I know," Sadie replied, throwing one last hopeful glance over at where they had come from, but it was still just dense forest. No path, no Jenny, nothing but the still, eerie silence of the woods.

20

Jenny stared at the back of May's head and tried not to vomit.

"What did you do?" Ryan yelled, grabbing May by the arm and forcing her to face him. Tears streamed down her pale cheeks, and she stared down at the ground, refusing to look up at them.

Jenny blinked, and they were no longer in the sunny valley, no longer in Mother Holle's little cottage. They were back in the clearing. The well was back to its normal size, sitting there as if it were nothing other than an old, dried-up well.

All three of them looked around, surprised at the sudden change of scenery. Marble nudged her leg with his snout, but she was too focused on May and Ryan to pay attention. Her blood was pounding in her ears, and her vision was blurring.

Ryan was gripping May's shoulders and shaking her. "What did you do?" he repeated. "Why? We're all going to die here because of you!"

"I don't care!" she screamed back at him, wrenching herself free of his grasp. She was sobbing now, and trembling. She sat down on the ground and stared at her bracelets, her long pale fingers gently touching the ones on her left wrist.

"My orange bracelet is gone," she whispered. "It worked."

Jenny tried to pull herself out of shock to try and understand what was happening. She walked over to May and stood over her, not willing to sit down next to her.

"Tell us what is going on," she said, anger heating the words she had tried to say as coolly as possible.

May continued to stare at where a bracelet used to be, her tears dried up now.

"You all wanted to know where I'm from," she started, her voice hoarse from crying and screaming. "I'm from Sunset Springs."

Sunset Springs. The name of the town instantly made her feel ill. She knew now why May had avoided telling them—everyone knew about what had happened in Sunset Springs.

"The shooting," Ryan said softly. "Your brother was the school shooter."

May nodded.

"He killed forty-two people and himself," she whispered to the ground. "Teachers, my friends, my—" She looked up at them now, her eyes shining. "But not anymore. It didn't happen. I fixed it."

Jenny rubbed her forehead. There was no way for her to have known that May was the sister of the Sunset Springs shooter. She hadn't remembered the kid's last name, had made a point to forget it, even. *Murderers don't deserve to be remembered.*

But of course May had remembered. Jenny had never really thought about the families of school shooters before—the parents, the siblings, what happened to them *after*.

"We moved to Crescent Bay for a fresh start," she continued, sniffling. "People kept throwing rocks through our windows. Spray-painting horrible things onto our house and cars. We had to leave. You understand why I did it, right?" she said, looking at them with wet eyes. "I had an impossible opportunity to reverse what happened. To bring all those people back. I had to—"

"Maybe they weren't supposed to come back," Ryan spat at her. "Did you even consider what they might come back as? Zombies, or just insane from having been dead for almost a year!"

May shook her head. "No, they didn't come *back* because

they never left. It never happened. *It never happened.*"

Ryan shook his head and walked away from them. Jenny didn't know what to say. She was shocked by Ryan's callous response, but she understood his anger. If May told them this before, argued her case for using the wish this way when they had been talking about it, would they have agreed? Forty-three lives were more important than ten, until one of those ten lives was your own. She grew sick wondering if she would have done the right thing. *It doesn't matter now,* she told herself firmly. *It's done.*

"I'm going back in," Ryan said, a fire in his hazel eyes. He knocked on the well with his fist, at first softly and then harder and harder until his knuckles split open and blood ran down his fingers.

"Ryan, stop!" Jenny cried, pulling him away from the well. It wasn't opening. Mother Holle was finished with them.

"Ryan, let's go. It's not going to open. It's over. We need to get back to the others. To your sister."

Ryan blinked, and Jenny started to see the Ryan she knew come back to her. The wild fury that had fueled his pounding had dissipated.

"Rain. Right," he said numbly. He let her lead him to the path as May followed a few steps behind them.

Jenny didn't really remember any details about the path from before except for the pond, so she wasn't entirely sure it was the right one. It was, however, the *only* one available to them, so they took it. They walked in silence, each lost in their own dark thoughts. The tension between Ryan and May was so tight she was afraid anything she said would cause them both to snap.

Jenny was still floored by May's revelation, a hundred thoughts swirling around inside her head, but she knew she needed to focus. She pushed the thoughts away and tried to take in her surroundings, tried to remember anything from the last time they'd walked this path. It all looked the same to her, though. Thick trees, green darkness. It felt like they should be out by now, but she wasn't sure. *We should have at least passed that pond by now*, she thought.

She considered how they had taken one path in and a different one out last time. Was this the first path, then? The one without the pond? Or a new path entirely? Would it lead them back to the castle or to certain death? She was exhausted and wasn't sure how much longer she could walk. The blood on her arms and legs from the shrunken heads biting her had dried and was starting to itch. She scratched at her arm and watched as the brown flecks floated to the ground. She started to feel a strange satisfaction as she scratched the dried blood off her. The tiny flakes disappeared into the dirt as she walked and scratched. Soon she had one whole arm cleaned of blood, although there were still the bite marks themselves. She held both arms out in front of her and compared the now-clean arm with the still-crusted one. She began working on her second arm.

The forest began to feel more comfortable, the path a little wider and a little smoother. She looked behind her to see Marble was still following, his eyes darting back and forth as if on the lookout for something.

"My, what big eyes you have …"

Jenny stopped abruptly, looking wildly around for where the voice had come from. Ahead of her, Ryan continued walking, but behind her, May had stopped when she had.

"Did you hear that?" Jenny asked, her heart pounding.

"No. Hear what?" May looked around the forest furtively, concern knitting her eyebrows.

"No-nothing, I guess."

Marble moved ahead of her, and Jenny continued walking, watching the wolf's bushy tail slap back and forth. Marble stopped, his ears pricked.

"My, what big ears you have ..."

Jenny whipped around to face May. "You didn't hear that?"

May shook her head slowly.

Jenny couldn't tell where the voice had come from—it didn't sound like it had come from behind, or in front, or off in the trees ... It sounded like it was inside her own head.

"What's going on?" Ryan called back to them, annoyed. "Let's go!"

Jenny swallowed and took a few steps forward while Marble walked gracefully ahead of her. As she watched him move, she saw him for the first time not as her companion or protector, but as what he was: a *wolf*. Fear trickled through her, and she wondered what had changed. As if he could hear her thoughts, Marble turned and looked back at her, his black lips pulled back in a canine smile, revealing rows and rows of sharp white teeth.

"My, what big teeth you have ..."

21

Sadie's stomach was empty and aching from hunger, and her legs felt rubbery. She forced herself forward, trudging down the path with the red flower resting delicately in her hands. She was afraid to look away from it; she had this irrational fear that the flower might just disappear if she stopped looking at it.

She was also afraid she might trip and fall and lose the flower that way, so she was walking at a painfully slow pace. It annoyed even her how slow she was going. She couldn't imagine how annoyed Aiden must have been.

"Tell me a story," Aiden said from beside her. "I'm bored."

Sadie wanted to tell him he should just enjoy this quiet moment of boredom after everything they had been through and what still lay ahead. Instead, she made a slight *hmmm* sound and tried to think of something to say.

"Do you have any siblings?" Aiden prompted.

"Yes." She almost laughed at the question. "Three sisters and a brother."

"What are you? Oldest, youngest?"

Sadie remained focused on the flower as she talked to Aiden. "No, I'm nothing. Second youngest."

"Must be nice having so many siblings," he said wistfully. "I'm an only child. It can get kind of lonely sometimes."

Lonely was not something Sadie ever felt at home. There was always someone yelling or taking too long in the bathroom or eating all the food.

"It's not that great, having siblings," she grumbled. "You're not missing out."

Sadie glanced up from the flower to check out the trail ahead. It looked just like the trail behind them, and Sadie hoped they weren't caught in some horrible fairy-tale loop. She was sick of these woods, sick of this trail, sick of holding this stupid flower.

"Do you have any idea how much farther it is?" she asked, already knowing the answer.

"No. But we must be getting close," he replied. "Right?"

Sadie didn't respond as she continued her slow march forward. She felt disgusting. She was covered in sweat and dirt, and she was sure her hair was a mess. She could smell her own odor and Aiden's too, and all she wanted was a meal and a hot shower.

In the shadowy forest, the light hadn't changed much, but she felt it getting colder. She could tell the sun was edging away from them, and she started to walk faster.

"Which one of your siblings is your favorite?" Aiden asked. She was confused as to why Aiden suddenly cared so much about her siblings, but it was a relief to get her mind off their current situation.

"Well I don't know my brother very well. He's thirty and married and lives in Virginia. I don't see him much."

"Wow! That's a huge age gap."

"Yeah, my parents started young and then must have forgotten to stop," she said bitterly.

"What about your sisters? Are you close with your sisters?"

Sadie thought about her sisters. Sylvia was a senior in college and Sybil, a sophomore. They both still lived at home and commuted to school, so they were around a lot. They mostly ignored Sadie but fawned over her baby sister, Sarina. No, she wasn't close with any of her sisters.

"No, not really," she answered.

"That's kinda sad, don't you think? All those siblings and

you aren't close with any of them? I would love to have even just one sibling. Another person going through all the same things as you are, who completely understands you and will be there for you for your entire life. That sounds amazing."

Sadie snuck a peak at Aiden and saw him staring ahead, his expression distant and sad.

"No one will ever completely understand anyone else, sibling or no," she said seriously. "It's just not possible. People are complex and irrational and unpredictable."

"I guess." Aiden shrugged. "I just think it would have been nice to have had someone around."

"What about your parents?" she asked.

"My mom works a lot," he said, not looking at her. She waited a beat for him to talk about his father. The silence stretched on, and she decided not to push the topic.

"When this is all over, maybe I could come over sometime," he said, a little sheepishly. "I want to know what a house full of people is like."

Sadie looked at him in surprise and felt her eyes water a little. *Am I crying?* she thought, horrified. She blinked the tears back before they fell. *Why am I getting so emotional?* She felt like this conversation was getting way too sensitive. She panicked, trying to think of a way to change the subject.

"Yeah, sure. What else are you looking forward to when we go home?" Sadie wasn't confident they *would* get home, but this felt like an easy way to distract Aiden from whatever dark thoughts had entered his brain.

"My bed," he said with a weak smile. "I am so sick of sleeping on the ground, and the castle's beds weren't much better. How about you?"

"Food," she said, almost in unison with an angry gurgle from her empty stomach. "I want a cheeseburger and a milkshake and a burrito and—" her stomach gurgled again, louder this time. Aiden laughed.

"Yeah, I'm hungry too," he said. "We really didn't do a good job of packing for this little adventure."

"Yeah, I just didn't think—or didn't *want* to think—we'd be in the woods this long." She stopped walking and looked behind her, hoping uselessly she'd see Jenny and the others coming toward them. Shadows from the branches above shifted eerily on the ground. The trail behind them was empty and quiet.

"This feels wrong," she said softly, guilt making her empty stomach twist painfully. "They should be with us." Sadie thought about the terrifying lion Jenny, May, and Ryan were trapped with in that clearing. The chances of them surviving ... Sadie didn't want to think about it, but she couldn't help it. She'd left her best friend to die. Aiden had left *his* best friend to die. What a great pair they were.

"I know," Aiden said as he looked behind them too. They stood that way, together, staring down the path that led back to their lost friends. Their potentially dying friends. "There's nothing we could do."

She knew he was right, but that didn't make her feel any better. She looked down at the delicate red flower in her hands. The small pearl in the center shimmered, and she reminded herself why they had to keep going. She couldn't save Jenny, but maybe she could save Rain.

Sadie looked up at Aiden and nodded.

"Onward?" Aiden asked.

"Onward."

22

"Enough!" Jenny screamed, closing her eyes and covering her ears. "Just stop it!"

Jenny breathed in and out too quickly, and she started to hyperventilate. She tried to slow her breathing and removed her hands from her ears. She slowly opened her eyes.

Darkness had taken over the forest, and May and Ryan were gone. The path itself seemed different, the trees had slightly changed. A low mist hovered over the trail, and moonlight spilled through the branches overhead. The white in Marble's coat shone brightly against the darkness, as if it were reflecting the moonlight. His ears pricked up, and his tail began swishing violently back and forth. He turned and looked into the woods, as if he were waiting for something to appear among the trees. She shivered as she realized how cold it had suddenly become. Jenny could see her breath, wisps of white in the cold night air. It had been a little chilly the nights they'd spent in the forest, but this was *freezing*.

"Marble?" Jenny whispered, "What happened? Where are we?"

Marble responded by pacing back and forth, looking deep into the woods one moment, then pausing to sniff the air or turn his ears a different direction.

"What ... what are you looking for?"

Jenny watched helplessly as the wolf continued his agitated pacing. Jenny looked in the direction they had come from, then back in the direction they had been going. They were on a different path, she knew, but it still didn't make sense to go *back*. Did it?

She rubbed at her arms to try and warm herself, but it didn't help. Her ears started to hurt from the frigid air, and her body trembled with uncontrollable shivers.

"Come on," she said as she continued the way they had been going. She walked a few steps and turned to see Marble wasn't following. "Marble?"

Marble stared at her with his sparkling black eyes, then turned and started walking the opposite direction—back to where they had come from. Jenny watched him retreat and started to panic. She didn't want to go backward. That couldn't be right. But she also didn't want to lose Marble and be left alone there in the cold and the dark. Marble slunk ahead of her, slowly making his way down the path, and Jenny had no choice but to follow. She wrapped her arms around herself as she forced her stiff legs to move forward.

They'd been walking only a few minutes when Jenny saw a small puddle of deep red in the middle of the trail. Jenny stopped, but Marble continued toward the puddle, and when he reached it, he leaned down and sniffed it. Jenny's stomach churned, and she thought she might be sick. Then Marble took the red puddle into his mouth and pulled it from the ground. Jenny couldn't believe what she was seeing. He padded back to her, dropping the puddle of red at her feet. She leaned down and picked up the deep-red cloak. The material was surprisingly heavy and a little scratchy. She guessed it was made of some sort of dyed wool. It was small, clearly intended for a child. Jenny's eyes darted from the cloak in her hands to Marble. A new terror rippled through her as she realized where they must be. They were in the *Little Red Riding Hood* story. And in that story, Jenny knew, the wolf dies at the end.

Jenny's hands shook, and her teeth clattered painfully against each other. She looked down at the warm cloak in her hands and grimaced. She didn't want to put it on, but she was starting to worry about hypothermia. She pulled the cloak around her shoulders and tied it closed across her chest. The cloak was small on her. It barely fell to her hips, but she suspected it was meant to be at least knee-length. As she pulled the hood over her head, her teeth stopped clattering, and the shivers that had racked her body ebbed. She was still cold; her skin was covered in goose bumps, and her hands were numb, but the cloak helped more than she had expected it to.

Marble gave her an intense look she couldn't read before turning and continuing down the path. She pulled the heavy wool cloak tightly around her as she followed, her mind racing with questions. *Why was the cloak lying on the ground? Where is the girl who should be wearing the cloak? By putting it on, am I taking over the role of Little Red Riding Hood?*

Mostly, though, she wondered where they were going. She squinted into the darkness. Their path was lit only by moonlight, and she cursed the woods. She had been *so close*. She had found Ryan, was almost out of the forest and back to the castle ... and now she was lost. She had no idea what happened to Ryan and May or if they were okay. *Why was I taken into this fairy tale and they weren't?*

A flicker of light in her peripheral vision made her stop. She peered through the trees, careful to keep both feet planted firmly on the trail. In the distance, she saw flames dance and jump from a small campfire. She couldn't feel the heat this far from the fire, but she could imagine it. She pulled the cloak more tightly around her and desperately wished she were near that fire. As she thought this, she noticed a small path weaving through the trees toward the campfire. It wasn't like the trail she'd been on, which was smooth dirt and seemed like it was supposed to be there. This one looked like it had been created by wild animals, or people stomping through the woods, flattening branches and grass down to create a small walkway.

Jenny knew leaving the trail and going down this goat path

would be a mistake. Someone, she knew, had to have started that fire. From where she stood, she couldn't see much, just the glow of the campfire and the cold darkness surrounding it. She couldn't tell if someone was there, warming themselves, but she doubted someone would light a fire and then just leave. She was about to turn away, to forget the campfire and continue down the trail, when she felt Marble's large body rub up against her legs as he passed her. She watched as the wolf, hunched down and ears flat against his head, made his way down the rough path and toward the mysterious campfire.

"No! Come back!" she hissed at him, hoping he would listen, hoping he would stop and come back to her. But he didn't even pause as he continued to stalk down the overgrown path.

Jenny looked down at the toes of her hiking boots, which were just barely over the line between the trail she was on and the path her wolf had gone down. Marble was almost out of sight now, and Jenny had to decide—stay on the trail or follow the wolf into the woods? Everything inside her told her to stay on the trail, but she trusted Marble.

Reluctantly, she took a step onto the overgrown path, then another. She forced herself forward, looking furtively around her for any sign of danger. Branches reached out and snagged on the wool cloak as she walked by, and she tripped more than once on an exposed tree root or rock. She pulled the cloak tighter around her and hurried to catch up to Marble. She was nearing the campsite. She could hear the intermittent snaps and cracks of the wood being burned and smell the smoke. She stopped as she reached the edge of the clearing and started to panic. Marble was gone. She crouched down and peered through a twiggy bush at the campsite. She felt a subtle shift in temperature, a slight warmth emanating from the fire toward her.

The campfire was roaring but somehow contained by a

perfect circle of smooth stones. A man sat on a tree stump on the other side of the fire. He was hard to make out past the flames, but even from where she was, she could tell he was a large man. He was wearing a red plaid jacket and dark pants, and she could hear him humming as he ran a cloth over a rifle. Jenny's heart beat a little faster. In the *Little Red Riding Hood* story, a huntsman kills the wolf, and *that* was definitely a huntsman. *Marble, where are you?*

Jenny turned away from the campsite and searched the trees as best she could in the dark. She looked for any movement, a swish of his tail, the gleam of his eyes in the moonlight, but saw nothing. Panic rushed through her as she realized he had abandoned her. She didn't understand why he had led her out here only to leave her. *Maybe*, she realized, *he hadn't been leading me here.* She had followed him, but maybe she wasn't supposed to. The wolf wasn't the best at communication. *I should have stayed on the trail*, she thought bitterly. She slowly stood up from her crouched position, but stayed low, and searched for the path she'd taken to get there. She would just retrace her steps and go back to the trail. The trail was safe—at least safer than where she currently was. Her whole body froze as she realized the path was gone. It had been a bit overgrown, but now there was nothing at all. Just trees and thick bushes and thorny brambles. She couldn't see the main trail and wasn't even certain which direction it was in.

Jenny felt a chill as something moved behind her, blocking the emanating warmth from the campfire. She tensed and slowly turned around to see the huntsman looming over her, the rifle he'd just been cleaning hanging from one hand. He ran his tongue across his chapped lips as he peered down at her. There was a hunger in his eyes, a need that made Jenny's stomach churn and made every alarm bell inside of her go off.

"It's not safe out here," the man said, his voice deep and full of gravel. "Not for *you*."

23

"Never thought I'd be so happy to see that ugly thing," Aiden said from a few steps ahead of Sadie. She glanced up from the flower to see that they'd left the forest. The castle was looming dark and intimidating across the river. She squinted, the sunlight bright and harsh after being in the dim forest for so long. She raised a hand to shield her eyes from the sun and saw the rickety bridge connecting where they were to where they needed to go. Aiden went across easily, but Sadie hesitated, looking back at the forest behind them. She had hoped Jenny and Ryan and even May would have caught up with them, that they would all cross this bridge together. But no one came out of the forest, and Sadie knew there was nothing she could do but move forward and focus on the task at hand. Helping Rain was the only thing she could do right now.

She made her way across the bridge and felt it sway unnervingly from side to side. She hadn't been afraid of the bridge before, but things were different now. She could easily see beneath the bridge; there was no troll there, but she still felt the ghost of a hand clutching her ankle, and she blanched.

She shook off the memory of the troll and walked carefully across the bridge, her eyes glued to the precious red flower in her hand. A strong wind rushed her when she reached the middle of the bridge, and she reflexively curved her body around the flower in her hands. The bridge shook wildly, and she struggled to maintain her balance. *I am not going to fall off this bridge*, she thought fiercely, *and I'm not losing this flower.*

The wind died down as quickly as it had come, and she continued across the bridge, stepping carefully over the gap where one of the boards had broken off. A few more steps and she made it to solid ground, letting out a breath of relief. She looked up from the flower to see Aiden watching her. His dark hair shifted slightly in the breeze, and when she looked at him, she no longer saw a schoolgirl crush, she saw something more: a friend.

She smiled and followed him around the side of the castle to the front, where she saw the fountain of the creepy handless girl, front steps, and head of poppy-colored hair.

"Hannah!" She walked faster toward her and Cameron, who was sitting beside Hannah on the ground. Travis, who had been pacing around and flailing his arms as if mid-story, stopped when he saw them and grinned. Rain was resting, curled into a perfect golden croissant shape on the ground. Seeing the group safe, alive, and in one piece—even if one of the pieces was deer shaped—warmed her. Careful not to harm the flower, she made her way quickly over to them and was relieved to see Hannah unharmed. Some distant part of her felt like she should still be angry with Hannah, but she couldn't be. All she felt was relief that Hannah was okay.

"What happened?" Travis asked eagerly, his eyes flicking to look behind them. "Where's everyone else?"

"We don't know, we were ..." Sadie wasn't sure how to explain it. "Sort of forced out."

"The forest closed us off from Ryan, Jenny, and May," Aiden explained. "We waited for a while, but nothing happened. The only thing we could do was to continue down the path back here."

"So you don't know if they're okay?" Travis asked, his large, sweaty face creased with worry. He was still shirtless, the skin on his torso red from a sunburn or from when Aiden had lit his shirt on fire, Sadie wasn't sure.

"No," Sadie said softly, guilt spilling into her heart.

"But Sadie found that flower, see!" Aiden said, gesturing at the precious cargo she still had in her hands. The group gathered around to stare at it.

"The book said we just need to touch her with it," Sadie said, looking at Rain, who had raised her head up to watch them. "Rain, come here."

Rain slowly stood up from the ground and walked toward her, the others moving out of the way to make room. Sadie's heart pounded as she realized this might not work. They were acting on a barely similar story they hoped was related to Rain's situation. If this didn't work ... there was no plan B. She held the flower toward Rain and gently ran it across the deer's long golden back. Where the flower touched Rain, a shimmering red powder was dusted along her back. As Sadie pulled her hand back, the red powder lifted into the air, spreading like a bloody fog all around Rain and wrapping her up until they couldn't see her anymore. The flower in Sadie's hand broke into tiny pieces, like red-and-white confetti. She let the fragments slip from her hand and fall to the ground.

"Rain!" Hannah yelled, her green eyes wide and afraid.

Just as quickly as the shimmering red fog had come, it dissipated, and standing in front of them was no longer a deer, but a human girl.

A very naked human girl. Rain's delicate figure was creamy and pale, and her tangled waves of long honey-gold hair cascaded down her shoulders. The thick scar from her heart surgeries ran vertically down the center of her chest.

Sadie smacked Travis's gawking face and yelled at him to look away. Aiden and Cameron, she noticed, already had. *Good boys*.

"Oh, wow, okay," Hannah said, her face flushing. She took her own sweatshirt off and tried unsuccessfully to cover Rain with it. "Guess we should have thought of this, huh?"

Sadie turned to Cameron, who had his back to the girls.

"Cameron, go inside and grab some of her clothes from her room. Break down the door if you have to–I don't think anyone will stop you."

"But it's not safe!" Hannah objected.

"It'll be fine," Sadie said. "Remember what May said? Eckert took that room's cursed try-to-kill-you object out. It's just a harmless room now."

She saw Cameron nod and turn away. He didn't hesitate as he went up the stairs and into the castle they'd all been relieved to escape. Even though she was the one who had told him to go in there, it felt wrong to go back inside. Dangerous.

"He'll be fine," she said to Hannah as confidently as she could manage. "And don't sneak any peeks, you two!" she yelled at Travis and Aiden.

"I would *never*!" Aiden exclaimed in a ridiculous Southern belle accent.

Sadie, too, tried to avoid looking at Rain's naked body, but it made it awkward to talk to her.

"Rain, are you okay?" she asked the ground.

"Ye—" Rain's voice broke as she tried to speak. She cleared her throat and tried again. "Yes, I think so. Talking feels weird."

"How long were you a deer for?" Hannah asked. Travis must have told them about Rain, Sadie realized. She wondered what else he had told them.

"I'm not really sure," Rain replied hoarsely. "Three days, maybe four?"

Sadie shook her head. It was amazing that Rain and Ryan had made it out at all.

"Where's my brother?"

Sadie didn't know how to answer that question.

"He, ah, well, I don't know," she said simply. No point in trying to soften it. "Last time I saw him, the lion was attacking Jenny. He made us leave to make sure you were okay. He really loves you, Rain."

Sadie wasn't used to talking this way. It felt like she was reading lines from a play she had been mistakenly cast in. But it felt like the right thing to say, even if it felt wrong coming out of her mouth.

"I'm not looking!" she heard Cameron yell from the castle steps. He came toward them, his head down and arm outstretched, holding the pulled-out handle of Rain's roller suitcase.

"I didn't know what you'd want, so I just grabbed everything and shoved it in this," Cameron said, his eyes still averted. Hannah took the suitcase from him with a smile and what Sadie could have sworn was a fluttering of eyelashes and set it down on the ground. Hannah unzipped the suitcase and sifted through clothes until she pulled out a yellow sundress and some underwear. Rain took them and dressed quickly.

"You guys can look now," Rain said, amused.

"I didn't see much," Travis said as he looked up and approached them, "but what I did I see ..."

"Yeah, I'm gonna stop you right there," Sadie said with a glare. "We're moving on now, and you're forgetting whatever it is you think you saw."

Rain let out a light laugh and shook her head of long golden hair. "I really don't care," she said. "I've been naked this entire time!"

Sadie thought of everyone petting her, sleeping next to her. It was sort of funny in a disturbing way.

"Well, we're glad you're back," Aiden said with a smile.

"Now what?" Travis asked.

"We ... wait." Sadie said, not knowing what to say. "We wait for Jenny and Ryan to come out."

"And May," Aiden added, pointedly.

"Yes, and May," she said with an eye roll.

"Shouldn't we go back in after them?" Travis asked.

"There's no way to know that we'd find them, or that we wouldn't end up lost ourselves. We were lucky to make it out of there," Sadie replied, knowing the logic behind what she said but still feeling guilty.

"I ran away when I saw the gingerbread witch, leaving Ryan there by himself," Rain said quietly. "I ran away when I saw the lion attack, leaving Ryan behind again. I'm tired of running away. I'm not leaving my brother in there to die."

A guilty hush fell across the group. Sadie had told herself leaving the woods, leaving Jenny behind, was the only option they had. Now it was starting to feel like a weak excuse she'd used to save herself. Jenny had made them go into the woods to find Ryan and Rain. Jenny hadn't let fear keep her from saving the people she loved. Sadie looked up at the setting sun. The sky was turning pink at the edges. Night was coming. Sadie shook her head.

"No, I'm sorry Rain, but you can't go back in there. Not now. The reality is—" Sadie broke off, hating what she was about to say next. "The reality is that by now either they killed the lion or the lion killed them. Either way, there's nothing we can do."

"Is that what you told Jenny when she wanted to go into the forest to save Ryan and me?" Rain snapped back. "If you guys hadn't come for us, Ryan would have been eaten, and I'd still be a deer. Don't tell me there's nothing we can do!"

Sadie glared at the golden girl, thinking she had liked Rain better as a deer.

"Whoa, okay. Let's all calm down," Travis said, sliding between her and Rain. "Rain, I hear you. We all want to get them back, but it's getting dark, and if we go back in now, we'll have to stop before we even get close to them. I think the better plan is to rest here and first thing tomorrow go back for them. Right, Sadie?"

Travis urged her with his eyes, and Sadie looked around to

see everyone else's eyes on her, too, waiting. "Yes," she forced out, low and angry. She hated being pushed into a corner, hated being accused of not caring about Jenny and the others. She thought about the lion, how weak Marble was, how they didn't have any weapons. What Sadie had tried to ignore, tried to deny, rose to the surface. There was a good chance Jenny and the others were already dead.

She looked at Rain's shiny hazel eyes and flushed cheeks, her tangled golden hair. Sadie knew how bad their chances were—but Rain wasn't ready to face it.

"Great, so in the meantime, maybe we can just all take a break, sit down, and bring the pieces together," Travis continued.

"Pieces?" Hannah asked.

"The pieces of the story," Travis explained. "None of us know the *full story*, right?"

"What do you mean?" Rain asked as she wiped the tears from her eyes with the back of her hand.

"From the beginning," he said, gesturing at Rain. "What happened to you the day you went missing?"

"Oh," Rain said softly, and sunk down to the ground. Equally tired, the rest followed, until they were all sitting on the ground in a slightly lopsided circle. Sadie hesitated but eventually joined them, not wanting to create another scene.

Rain's birdlike frame inhaled and exhaled. She looked around the circle and seemed to be considering what to say.

"Ms. Eckert tricked us into going into the woods with her," she started slowly. "She said we had to help her gather some wood for a big bonfire we were going to have later. We were so stupid. She made us go farther and farther, collecting wood, until we came across a strange little cottage made of candy. The second I saw it, I knew. Somehow I knew." Rain shook her head. "I remembered how weird Eckert had gotten when talking about the *Hansel and Gretel* story, then when she led us to this candy cottage in the middle of the woods, I thought she was some psycho serial killer or something. I just turned and ran."

Rain stopped and looked down at the ground. She pulled at the little blades of grass in front of her. "I thought Ryan would get away too, but ..."

"Don't do that," Travis said sternly. "It's not your fault. It was good that you ran when you did. After what happened to Eckert ..."

Sadie grew sick as the memory of Eckert's head on top of a candy body came back to her. And Ryan's missing hand. Travis patted Rain on the leg.

"We all know what would have happened."

Rain nodded miserably. "I got lost right away," she continued. "I wandered around and around and eventually got really thirsty, and I drank from the stream–that's when I turned into a deer. It was really weird, like the hulk, kind of. My clothes ripped apart as my body changed, and I had to walk on four legs instead of two. It took me a bit to get it. I kept falling over. It was probably for the best, actually. After I became a deer, my senses became much stronger. I could hear things insanely well. That's how I found the candy house again. How I found you too, actually."

"So it wasn't a coincidence that you were at the pond when we were?" Travis asked.

"No. I had heard you tromping around and had been making my way toward you when I ran into the nixie, and, well, you know the rest."

Yes, they knew the rest. Sadie looked over at Hannah and Cameron, who were sitting so close together their knees were touching. They looked tired, a bit rumpled, but unscathed.

"So, Hannah, what happened to you guys? Did you ..." Sadie was about to ask if they had found a way out of here, but she already knew the answer to that question.

Hannah shook her head. "It was so annoying! We walked down the road for hours, *hours*, Sadie, and when we stopped to rest ..."

"We saw the castle behind us," Cameron finished for her. "Right there. Like we'd been walking on a treadmill."

"So we gave up and just came back here. We thought about trying to find you in the woods, but that seemed like a really bad idea."

Sadie thought of everything they had encountered in the woods—the nixie, the gnome, the cannibalistic witch, the massive lion. Sadie had been angry that Hannah had refused to go with them, but now she was glad she hadn't. She couldn't imagine what seeing those things would have done to Hannah. She didn't know if Hannah would have even survived. Sadie nodded. "You did the right thing."

"We've been sleeping out here because Hannah refuses to go back into the castle," Cameron said as he took his glasses off and wiped them on his shirt. Sadie couldn't tell from his tone if he was annoyed with Hannah over this or simply stating a fact. He put his glasses back on and looked around the circle.

Sadie glanced up at the castle and wondered what they were going to do for the night. She was hungry, dirty, and exhausted—but she didn't have a strong desire to go back into the castle either.

"Well, if story time is over ..." Sadie shifted to get up.

"Wait! What happened to you guys?" Hannah asked. "Travis had just started telling us about the pear tree and the hole."

Flashes of the nightmares she'd experienced in the last few days flooded her mind, and she closed her eyes tightly, trying to force the thoughts away. She didn't want to talk about what happened. Didn't want to relive it.

"Right!" Travis shouted. "The pear tree! So, there we were, minding our own business when resident genius Aiden here ..."

Sadie tilted her head up to the dimming sky and cringed. It was going to be a long night.

24

The huntsman loomed impossibly large above Jenny. He smiled menacingly, showing uneven, stained teeth. The rifle he'd been cleaning was in his hand.

"Don't you know there are wolves in these woods?" the man continued. "They like to eat sweet young things like you."

Jenny thought she'd happily face a whole pack of wolves if it got her away from this man. He was massive, at least eight feet tall with muscles bulging underneath his red plaid jacket. He rested his rifle against one shoulder and watched her intently. She had to answer him, she knew, but didn't know what to say. Didn't know what to do. Marble was gone, it was freezing cold even with the red cloak, and she was lost. In the story, the huntsman saved Little Red Riding Hood from the wolf. But in *her* story, the wolf was good—so what did that make the huntsman?

He reached out and grabbed Jenny by the arm, his sausage-size fingers wrapping around her bicep painfully. "Come," he demanded. "Warm yourself by the fire. In the morning you may take your leave."

Jenny had no other option but to allow him to drag her through the bushes and into his campsite. The roaring fire did warm her, ceasing her shivers and smoothing her goose bumps. She began to wonder if she had been wrong about the man, if she'd misjudged him due to his size. *Maybe Marble led me to him on purpose, maybe he can help me*, she thought, desperate for that to be true. He guided her roughly around the fire, and instead of returning to the tree stump he'd been sitting on before, he stopped at a fallen log. He set his rifle on the ground, leaned up against the log, the barrel pointed to the sky, and sat heavily down next to it. He pulled Jenny by the arm to sit beside him. He was uncomfortably close; the tree trunk was barely long enough to fit the two of them. She hated the feeling of his body pressed against hers, the smell of onions and dirt coming off him.

He let go of her arm and reached into a small woven basket she hadn't noticed before, removing a piece of cake and a bottle of wine. Her stomach grumbled at the sight of the cake.

"I like you," the huntsman growled as he broke the piece of cake into two pieces. "You're not like other girls. You're quiet."

He handed her one of the pieces of cake, and she took it. She stared at it in her hands, starving but afraid to eat it. She felt his eyes on her and, not knowing what he'd do if she refused, brought the cake to her mouth. He grunted in approval as she took a bite and slowly chewed. The cake was dry and brittle, with a faint taste of ginger. As she chewed, it felt like the cake was soaking up every ounce of moisture she had in her mouth. She struggled to swallow the first bite and, once she managed it, didn't want to take another.

Jenny's eyes darted around the campsite, taking in her surroundings and searching for an exit route, a weapon, anything that she might use if she needed to get away from the huntsman. There wasn't much—just the roaring fire, the man's gun and basket, and what looked like a large burlap sack on the ground next to the stump he'd been sitting on when she got there. It was the same type of sack she'd seen in Sophie's kitchen back at the castle, full of potatoes. The opening was tightly tied shut with rope. As she stared at the bag, she was sure she saw it move, but dismissed the thought. It was probably just a trick of the light—just an illusion created by the flickering flames and the shadows they cast.

"You don't need this anymore," the huntsman said through a mouth full of cake. He pulled the hood of the cloak off her head and started fiddling with the tie across her chest. She shrunk away from him, and he glowered at her. She quickly reached up, untied the cloak, and let it fall away from her body. He grabbed the cloak from the ground and stuffed it into the now-empty basket at his feet. The fire was producing more than enough heat to keep her warm, but without the cloak, she still felt cold and exposed. She shifted uncomfortably under his gaze and started to wonder if he would be able to catch her if she tried running. He was larger and stronger than she was, but with all that mass, she wondered if it would slow him down—at least enough for her to get away and hide. She eyed the gun sitting at his side. *He wouldn't have to chase me*, she thought miserably, *he could just shoot me.*

She scanned the woods for Marble again, desperate to see any trace of him among the trees. *Why would he leave me like this?*

Jenny's eyes were drawn back to the burlap bag on the ground. She was certain this time it had moved. She watched with increasing uneasiness as the bag twitched and wiggled on the ground. Whatever was inside definitely didn't want to be.

"What ... what's in the bag?" she murmured, speaking to the man for the first time.

Instead of answering, the man pushed the now-open wine bottle at her.

"Drink," he barked at her. Hands shaking, she took the bottle from him. The cake was one thing, but wine? She had no idea what sort of effect fairy-tale wine might have on her. The weight of the bottle in her hands gave her an idea, though. If she was quick enough, she could hit him over the head with the bottle and get away. He wouldn't be able to shoot her if he was concussed. He was too tall, though. Sitting next to him, she was far too low to get the right angle. She'd end up hitting him in the shoulder.

"I'm cold," she tried, slowly standing up. She started walking toward the fire, waiting for him to grab her again, to stop her. But he stayed sitting, an amused look on his broad face. He rubbed at his dark beard and watched her. *If I knock him out*, she thought, *I'll at least have time to grab the cloak.*

"Drink!" he demanded again. She didn't want him standing up, so she quickly brought the bottle to her lips and pretended to drink. She felt thin streams of wine drip down her chin and splash onto her T-shirt. Out of the corner of her eye, she saw him nodding, seemingly satisfied by her charade. She kept the bottle up to her lips as she walked back toward the log, and before he could stop her, she swung the bottle down toward his head. Wine flew out in red arcs as she wielded the bottle, most of it spilling down her front. As the bottle hit his head, a sickening *thwack* echoed throughout the quiet woods, like a baseball bat hitting a tightly packaged pound of ground beef.

She tightly held the bottle upside down, by the neck, the rest of the wine draining onto her shoes and into the dirt. The huntsman, dazed, looked at her for a brief moment before his hand flew to his rifle. She swung the bottle again, but he was ready for her this time and wrapped his hand around her wrist and squeezed. She cried out in pain, and her hand released the wine bottle.

The huntsman threw her to the ground and was on top of her before she realized what was happening. He pushed her face into the dirt, and she lost feeling in her legs as he leaned his massive weight on them. *This is it*, she thought as she felt his hands wrap around her throat.

"I was wrong," he growled into her ear, his hot breath moist on her face. The smell of onions and alcohol mixed together, and she gagged. "You're just like all the rest."

Her vision went black as he pressed on her windpipe,

cutting off her oxygen. She couldn't move, could barely think, but she could *feel*. She felt a surge of rage—she had made it so far, been through so much, had saved Ryan from a powerful *witch*, and here she was, being strangled to death in wine-soaked dirt by a man. A big man, but still just a man.

He let out a deep yell, and she felt his hands leave her neck, and her vision slowly returned. She saw flames, she saw darkness, she saw Marble. Jenny scrambled up and away from the huntsman, who was now on his back and struggling underneath the wolf. Jenny turned away, horrified, as Marble's sharp teeth bit into the man's neck and blood began to spurt out in every direction.

She forced herself to look back, and she watched, dismayed, as Marble whipped his head back and forth, the man's neck still in his jaws. "Marble, stop!" she cried, looking away from the quickly growing pool of blood and the man lying in it. Marble let go of the huntsman's now-shredded and broken neck and trotted past Jenny, straight to the burlap sack. He made a soft whimpering sound and nosed at the bag, then looked up at Jenny.

Jenny tried to avoid looking at Marble. Her sweet, loving wolf had turned into a monster right before her eyes. His mouth was stained red with blood, and his eyes were shining with an unsettling excitement. He whined again, this time pawing at the burlap sack. Jenny walked toward the bag, but she felt detached from her body. Everything had happened so fast. Her neck hurt where the man had choked her, and the coppery smell of fresh blood permeated the air.

The burlap bag was still moving, squirming, and she could now hear a soft, muffled sound coming from inside. Jenny hesitated, then slowly bent down to the bag. Her hands trembled as she struggled with the rope knotted around the bag's opening. After a few seconds, she managed to untie it, letting the rope slip from her hands and onto the ground. Her pulse beat loudly in her ears, and her vision was starting to get dark around the edges. She blinked hard a few times and tried to focus. Jenny pulled the bag away from the creature inside and gasped when she saw what it was.

A girl. A little girl. She couldn't be older than eight or nine and had long blonde hair that looked like it had once been neatly put into braids but was now messy and snarled. She was wearing a red wool dress that looked like it had been made with the same material as the cloak Jenny had been wearing. Her bright blue eyes were wide and frightened, and a white gag filled her mouth and cut into her rosy cheeks. Jenny quickly untied the gag and threw it to the side.

"Untie me," she whispered, her voice hoarse.

Jenny then noticed that the girl's hands and feet were tied together with rope behind her back, like she was a roast pig. She quickly undid the knots, and the girl sat up, rubbing at the red welts encircling her wrists.

"You set him free," the little girl said, gazing at the wolf beside her.

"What? What do you mean?"

The girl turned her attention to Jenny. "My wolf. He'd been turned to stone. You broke the curse."

"I broke the ... curse?" Jenny thought about how she'd touched the stone wolf and given him a name. How that simple act had somehow transformed him into a flesh-and-blood wolf. She'd thought it was a statue magically made alive, not a live wolf that'd been magically turned to stone. Her head started to hurt thinking about it.

"Are you ..." Jenny swallowed, feeling awkward asking such a strange question, "Little Red Riding Hood?"

"Little Red Cap," the little girl corrected. "They call me Little Red Cap."

Jenny rubbed at her forehead, confused. Little Red Riding Hood ... Little Red Cap ... she guessed they meant the same thing.

Jenny suddenly remembered the bleeding corpse lying right behind her.

"Ah! Don't look!" Jenny cried, raising a hand to cover the girl's eyes. The girl shook her head and pushed Jenny's hand away.

"It's fine, nothing I haven't seen before. Where's my cloak?"

Jenny stared at her, horrified. *Nothing she hasn't seen before? What has this little girl gone through?*

Jenny stood up, skirting past the mutilated body of the huntsman, and picked up the basket from the ground, the cloak still stuffed inside. She brought it to the girl and handed it to her.

"Is the basket yours too?" Jenny asked. Little Red Cap nodded, and she took out the cloak and wrapped it around herself. She pulled the hood over her mussed hair and tied the cloak shut at her throat. "But the cake and wine are gone. Now I have nothing to bring to my grandmother."

Jenny couldn't understand how the little girl could be thinking of gifts for her grandmother at a time like this.

"I don't understand what's happening," Jenny said as gently as she could. "I thought the huntsman was supposed to be the good guy in your story?"

"*The* huntsman?" the little girl asked, raising an eyebrow. "There are many huntsmen in these woods. He's just one of them."

"Okay, so this is a bad huntsman? In your story there is a huntsman—a different one, I guess? He saves you from—" Jenny broke off and looked at the wolf.

"From who? Him?" the little girl gestured at Marble and shook her head as a small, sad smile slipped across her face. "No, it's the opposite. The wolf saves me from *him*." She nodded toward the corpse behind her. "And the others."

The others. Jenny felt sick.

"I don't understand," Jenny replied, shaking her head.

"I don't know what story you've heard, but it's not right," the girl explained. "The huntsmen, they are ... not good guys. They are hunters. They hunt *me*."

Something Eckert had said on their first day suddenly echoed in her mind. She'd been talking about the *Little Red Riding Hood* story. What had she said? *The moral of the story ... was that young women should not talk to or trust strangers.*

"Oh." Jenny looked at the little girl and was worried she might vomit.

"Ever since I lost my wolf ... my story has been *wrong*. I found him in that garden behind the castle, but he was a statue."

Jenny thought about this as the fire behind her crackled and spat. She knew where this was going. Marble wasn't *Jenny's* wolf, never had been. She'd just been ... *borrowing* him. Jenny watched as Marble sat beside the little girl, her small hand resting on his back. They looked right together, somehow. Little Red Cap and her wolf.

Jenny's legs started to feel shaky, and she slowly lowered herself to the ground. She was losing Marble, she knew, and there was nothing she could do about it. Nothing she *should* do about it. Marble left the girl's side and sat down in front of Jenny, his magnetic eyes staring into hers. Ignoring his bloodstained mouth, she wrapped her arms around him and buried her face into his fur. She had just watched him tear the throat of a man apart in a matter of seconds, but he still made her feel safe. Marble had been her sole source of comfort, of strength, the last few days. He had saved her from being just another corpse in the castle wall, had fought against the gingerbread witch with her, and had actually *died* protecting her from the lion. But he was so much more than that—he was her friend.

She looked at the little girl standing just a few feet away. The red welts on her ankles and wrists were still there, and her cheeks had dried salt streaks on them from crying. She looked so fragile, so young. So vulnerable. He was her wolf. He belonged with her, not Jenny.

Marble pressed his forehead against hers. His fur was soft and comforting against her skin, and though she tried to fight it, tears began to drip down her cheeks. He slowly stepped away, and she let him, her arms slipping off him and dropping to her lap. She knew this was the right thing, but everything inside her felt wrong. The wolf rejoined the little girl, and Jenny's heart broke a little.

"Thank you for bringing him back to me," the girl said. "We're going back to our story now—it's time for you to go back to yours too."

My story?

Jenny watched, her throat swollen and eyes burning with tears, as the forest around her grew blurry, the colors running together. She felt the ground shift slightly underneath her. She closed her eyes tightly, and when she opened them, she was no longer at the campsite, was no longer staring at Marble and the little girl in the red cloak. She was back on the trail. It was a hot summer day again, and she was alone.

25

The sun was nearly gone, and the world grew dim around them. Travis had told Hannah and Cameron everything they had experienced in the forest, despite Sadie's attempts to quiet him. She hadn't wanted Hannah to have those images in her head. She watched her friend closely as Travis talked. Hannah's already pale face grew paler with every story he told.

Sadie's stomach ached, and the hunger she'd been trying to ignore was scratching at her insides. She looked around at the rundown group around her. Travis was still shirtless, his bare skin red and filthy with dirt and dried pond water; Rain was trying to force a hairbrush through her tangled mess of hair, wincing each time it caught on a snarl; and Aiden ... Aiden was dirty, like all of them, but still somehow managed to look good. Sadie could smell her own rank body odor seeping through her dirty shirt. She glanced up at the castle looming just a few yards away from them and wondered what they were going to do. No one wanted to go back inside, but it didn't make a lot of sense to Sadie for them to suffer out here when everything they need was *right there*. Clean water, fresh clothes, warm beds, toilets, *food*. Sadie's stomach gurgled angrily at the thought. They would have to go inside eventually.

Sadie glanced over at the edge of the castle, hoping she'd see Jenny. She knew Jenny was probably dead, but she still held on to a sliver of hope that she'd see her come around that corner.

"So what's the plan for tonight?" Sadie asked the group. They looked back at her with blank faces. "Do we go back inside, back to our rooms? Or sleep out here?"

"We've been sleeping out here," Hannah answered. "It's been fine."

Sadie remembered sleeping on the ground the last two nights, and the idea of another night sleeping on hard earth didn't appeal to her.

"Is the castle even really that dangerous?" Travis asked. "I mean, we know how it works now. Our room's objects were those little statues—we can just chuck them out of the room and be totally safe. Right?"

Travis had a good point, for once. They knew the dangers all too well now, and she was pretty confident she could avoid any fairy-tale monsters. After everything she had experienced in the woods, the castle didn't even seem that bad.

"I don't think we should split up," Aiden said cautiously. "We just found each other again. And there's safety in numbers, right?"

"I'm staying with Hannah out here," Cameron spoke up. "It really hasn't been that bad."

"Then I'm staying out here too," Aiden said, leaning back on his arms in a demonstration of nonchalance Sadie didn't quite believe.

"I'm used to sleeping outside now," Rain added. "So I'm fine staying out here."

Sadie thought about the bed in her room. It hadn't been the most comfortable thing in the world, but it was definitely better than the ground. She looked at Travis, the only other holdout.

"Fine! Outside it is," he grumbled. "I need to get cleaned up at least, though. And I need a new shirt."

"You definitely do," Aiden agreed. "I could use a shower too."

"Yeah, man, I didn't want to say anything, but you really stink," Travis said, waving his hand in front of his face theatrically.

"You're one to talk!" Aiden replied, looking embarrassed.

"We *all* need to shower," Sadie interrupted. She could manage sleeping outside another night, but she couldn't last another minute without a shower and fresh clothes. "But let's do the buddy system. No one goes anywhere alone."

Sadie thought about going to her old room, then remembered that their last night in the castle, she and Hannah had moved into Jenny's. All of her stuff was in Jenny's room, but Sadie didn't have the key. She looked over at Hannah. "You don't happen to have the key to Jenny's room, do you?"

"No," Hannah shook her head.

"Perfect," Sadie groaned. "All our stuff is in there!"

"You can use my shower and borrow some of my clothes, if you want," offered Rain, gesturing at the poorly packed suitcase on the ground. Sadie looked at Rain's tiny frame and nearly laughed at the idea she would fit into any of Rain's doll clothes. Then she thought about May, Rain's roommate. May was skinnier than Sadie but about the same height. Wearing May's clothes was the second to last thing Sadie wanted to do—the last thing was to stay in her current filthy clothes.

"Great," she finally said. "Lead the way."

Cameron and Hannah remained outside while Travis and Aiden returned to their room to shower and change. Sadie watched them go up the stairs ahead of her and felt a strange jab of absence as Aiden disappeared from view. Rain turned down her hallway, and Sadie followed her to her room, which Sadie recognized immediately by the kicked-in door. Cameron had taken her orders to heart and kicked the thing in. She couldn't help but smirk.

Inside, Sadie pressed a chair against the door to keep it shut and asked Rain where May's clothes were.

"That dresser," she replied as she put her suitcase on the bed.

Sadie hesitated a minute, feeling very strange about rifling through May's things. She was almost afraid of what she might find in her drawers. Sadie dug through May's clothes until she found a black T-shirt and some gray cotton shorts she was pretty sure would fit her. The shirt had some stupid band name written on it—the Cranks—but it was the best option she had. Sadie heard the bathroom door click shut and the water turn on. She sat on what must have been May's bed and awkwardly waited for Rain to finish bathing. She'd been careful not to go through May's things any more than necessary, but now faced with an empty room, her curiosity began to get the better of her. There was something off about May, that much she was sure of, but she had no idea what it was. She shook off the desire to poke around May's stuff. She was about to lay down when she noticed May's pillow. *Gross*, she thought. Not wanting to put her face on a pillow May's face had been on, she shoved the pillow off the bed and onto the floor. As she did, something else went with it, and Sadie heard a light clatter of something hard hitting the floor. Sadie bent over the edge of the bed and saw something lying next to the pillow.

It was a diary.

Sadie sat, frozen, staring down at May's diary. Everything she wanted to know about May was right there in front of her. She would never even know Sadie had read it.

She stared down at the diary—a small black moleskin notebook. Everything inside her wanted to pick it up and read it as fast as she could, but something held her back. It was wrong, she knew, to read someone else's diary. It was possible she didn't even want to know what was written in there. Sadie chewed on her bottom lip, and she struggled with the decision. Rain would come out soon, and she'd miss her chance.

She gave in and snatched the notebook off the floor and opened it. What she saw, though, didn't make any sense. The diary was filled with dates and writing but there were huge gaps throughout the whole thing. It was as if someone had come along and erased certain sections and not others. She heard the water turn off and quickly put the diary back, with the pillow on top. A moment later, Rain entered the room, her long golden hair wrapped in a towel on top of her head.

"All yours!" she chirped. Sadie attempted an innocent smile but wasn't confident she'd been successful. She grabbed May's clothes and felt guilt prick at her, then walked into the steamy bathroom. As she bathed, Sadie thought about the diary. Was it possible May had gone through and erased parts of it, worried this very scenario might occur? It hadn't *looked* erased. There were no faded ghosts of words; it was just empty, like there had never been any writing there at all. Plus, the writing that *was* in there was in black ink. Ink doesn't erase.

Sadie washed the dirt and grime out of her hair and felt a little sick. She hadn't actually read any of the words in the diary, but she had looked. That was enough for her to hate herself a little. She wanted to be better than that. Why did she care so much about May's secrets anyway? May, who she might never see again.

I don't, she told herself fiercely. *I don't.*

26

Jenny was alone. She looked around, expecting to see Ryan and May, but no one was there. She stood up and looked for any sign of where she might be. She had assumed she'd be brought back to where she'd been when she was dragged into the *Little Red Riding Hood* story, but now she wasn't sure. Was she in a different fairy tale? Or had she been put back on the wrong trail? As she looked around, she noticed an arrow carved into one of the nearest birch trees. Above the arrow the initials *R. A.* were roughly carved. *Ryan Andrews.*

He … he left? How long have I been gone?

Jenny wrapped her arms around herself and rubbed at her bitten, scratched-up skin Her neck felt bruised from when the huntsman had tried to strangle her, and her clothes were stained with wine and blood. She felt shaky, like she was just seconds away from completely falling apart. She wanted to curl up in a ball and sleep and escape this nightmare. She missed Marble already. With him gone, everything felt colder and darker. Ryan had abandoned her in these woods—the woods she had entered to save *him*. For the first time, Jenny felt a hot rage bubbling up inside of her toward Ryan. *He just left me here.* Anger shoved aside sadness, and she felt it filling her up, pushing away any other thought or feeling. She hated Ryan. She hated the castle, these woods, and every single fairy tale she'd had to endure. She was *so sick* of being attacked and afraid. She didn't want to be afraid anymore. She wanted to feel powerful. She wanted to be the thing *others* were afraid of. For once.

She let out a scream of anger and frustration that hurt her throat but somehow made her feel a little better.

Jenny glared at the arrow Ryan had carved into the tree for her and stormed past it. She walked as quickly as she could down the trail toward what she hoped was the castle and out of these stupid woods. She focused on the trail ahead, refusing to look into the forest surrounding her. If she didn't see anything, she couldn't be pulled into anything, she hoped. She was knifeless, wolfless, and friendless, and she was painfully aware of how vulnerable she was.

She tried to ignore the itching from the apple-head bites. What if they became infected with some incurable fairy-tale disease? She thought about what she went through to get to Mother Holle, to get a wish, and what May had done. Anger sizzled underneath her itching skin. The entire time, May had known. From that first day at the castle, May had been oddly focused on that well. She'd known the Mother Holle story. Back then, May couldn't have known it was real, but still. It all felt so premeditated.

Jenny had been understanding, at first, about what May had done—stealing the wish to save the people her brother had murdered. But had they had a chance to think about it, to talk things through, maybe they could have come up with a wish that helped *everyone*. Now they were all still stuck here with no clue as to how they would escape. She hoped Hannah and Cameron had been able to find help. *Maybe*, she thought, *I'll get back to the castle to find that help has arrived. There will be cars to take us out of the forest and far away from any more fairy tales.* She held on to the warm thought as long as she could before it grew cold. Something inside her knew it wasn't going to be that easy. When had *anything* been that easy?

As she walked, she realized there wasn't a single part of her body that didn't hurt. Her calves were tight, her feet tired and blistered, her neck was bruised, and, of course, there were the bites. Her hand drifted automatically to her side to where Marble usually was, her muscle memory obscuring her actual memory for a moment.

She continued down the path and tried not to think about anything. She was almost successful, when she saw something small skitter out of the forest and stop in the middle of the trail ahead of her. It was too small and too far away for her to be able to tell what it was, but she was in the Black Forest—so it was definitely not something good. Then another small creature came out of the woods, and another, and another, until the entire trail was blocked off.

They're trying to stop me from leaving, she realized. She stopped and watched the creatures, waiting for them to make a move. They didn't make a sound, didn't move toward her. They just stood there. Jenny took a few steps forward, then a few more, until she was close enough to see what they were.

They were gnomes, tiny little people in various shades of green and brown, similar to the one they had captured at their campsite. Some had leaves and small branches growing from their bodies, and one had a large grayish mushroom sprouting from the side of its head. Others were covered in moss, and one looked like it was made of rock. They stood shoulder to shoulder, blocking her path. They were so short she could easily just step over them, but she was afraid of what they might do if she came too close.

"Move, please," she said as calmly as she could. A tittering of sounds ran across the line of gnomes, a sound like rocks being hit together and branches snapping in half. *Are they ... laughing?*

The sound was incredibly grating, and Jenny clenched her teeth in irritation. She tried to keep herself calm, but she was in pain and hungry, exhausted, and sick of things getting in her way. She didn't care anymore about what the gnomes might do to her. She was sick of playing these games, sick of being forced into these situations. *If Marble were here ... but he's not. And he never will be again.*

Something inside her brain snapped. She stormed over to the line of gnomes and without hesitation started kicking them out of her way. She watched with satisfaction as they flew away from her and bounced across the trail. She grabbed every gnome that lunged at her and threw them as hard as she could back into the forest. In a matter of seconds, she had cleared the trail entirely of gnomes and was looking for more to kick.

"Now listen to me!" Jenny yelled into the woods. "I am leaving this forest, and nothing is going to stop me! The next gnome I see, I'll stomp to death, you hear me?"

Silence answered her. She was breathing hard, and her heart beat painfully against her rib cage, but she also felt exhilarated. She almost wished they would come at her again.

But they didn't.

Fueled with fresh energy from her fight with the gnomes, Jenny marched confidently down the path, and within minutes, she found herself out of the woods and at the edge of a cliff. A river churned and spat below, and a familiar bridge swung slightly, almost menacingly, in the breeze.

She looked up at the castle she had hoped to never see again and let out a breath of relief. She had made it. A slightly hysterical little laugh escaped her mouth, and her whole body trembled a little. *I can't believe I made it out.*

She crossed the rickety bridge and didn't look back.

27

Sadie froze as a scream echoed out at them from somewhere deep in the woods. The chatter stopped as everyone listened. A long silence dragged out as Sadie waited for another sound, another scream, something. She didn't know who the scream belonged to, but she knew it had to be either Jenny or May. She didn't think Ryan would sound so high pitched. *This is bad. This is very bad.*

She looked at her friends sitting around her on the ground. They had all finished showering and changing and had brought what they could from the rooms they had access to outside. Pillows and blankets were scattered across the ground in preparation for the campout. Sadie felt awkward in May's clothes; they were a little tight on her, and she didn't know how May would react when she saw her in them, if May ever saw her wearing them at all. They'd been in the middle of discussing food when they'd heard the scream.

"Ooookay, so are we all just going to pretend we didn't hear that?" Travis asked, gesturing toward the woods.

"What do you suggest we do about it?" Cameron asked, giving him a wry look. "You want to go back into the woods and see where it came from?"

Travis's face reddened, and he looked down. "No."

Sadie wasn't sure how she felt about the scream. On the one hand, it meant at least one of them hadn't been killed by the lion, but on the other, she didn't know what else they may have run into on the way back to the castle. She and Aiden had made it out without any other attacks, but who was to say Jenny and the others would be so lucky?

She stared at the path that led around the castle and to the footbridge they had all come across to get back here. Her heart skipped as she saw two figures come around the corner.

Ryan walked toward them quickly, with May trailing behind. Sadie waited for Jenny to come around the corner after them, but when she didn't, she knew. The scream had come from Jenny.

Sadie stood up and stomped over to Ryan, who was making a beeline for his now-human sister. Sadie blocked his way and ignored his irritation. "Where's Jenny?" Sadie demanded, her heart beating so hard it hurt as worst-case scenarios flooded her mind.

Ryan pushed past her and wrapped his arms around Rain in a tight hug. Sadie glared at his back and made a move toward him but felt someone grab her arm. She turned to see Aiden standing beside her.

"Just give them a minute," he whispered in her ear, sending chills running through her body. "They've been through a lot."

Sadie felt a little guilty. Ryan had lost his hand and his sister, and here she was, human again. Aiden was right, she knew. She had to give them a minute. But she didn't have to give *May* a minute. She whipped around, pulling her arm out of Aiden's grasp, and made her way to May. May looked at her, startled. She eyed Sadie up and down.

"Are those my clothes?"

"Yup, get over it," Sadie spat. "Where's Jenny?"

May pulled at her long hair nervously and looked over at Ryan.

"Um, well, I don't know—"

"What do you mean you don't know!" Sadie yelled. "She was with you. Now she isn't. What happened to her?"

"Sadie—" Aiden tried calming her again, but this time she

ignored him.

"Where is she!" Sadie demanded.

May's eyes grew glassy with tears, and Sadie fought the urge to slap her. She felt the others gathering behind her.

"I don't know!" May yelled back. "We were walking, and she was there and then she wasn't. She just disappeared!"

"What do you mean *disappeared*?" Sadie asked, irritation burning through her.

"Sadie, give her some room. Let her explain," Hannah said softly from behind her. Sadie took a step back and crossed her arms.

"I'm waiting."

"That's it! That's all I know, I swear!" May started crying and rubbed fiercely at her eyes. Sadie hadn't liked May before, but now she *hated* her.

"What happened with the lion?" Travis asked. "Can we start there?"

"We killed the lion ..." Ryan answered, now separated from his sister and standing among them.

"*Jenny* killed the lion," May corrected, and Ryan glared at her.

"Yes, *Jenny* killed the lion," he spat back at May. Sadie had never seen Ryan this angry before. He'd been mad when Travis had pretended to throw Rain into the well their first day at the castle, but that was nothing compared to this. Sadie looked between Ryan and May and knew something wasn't right. Something had happened.

"And then?" Sadie urged, as gently as she could, to avoid Ryan's rancor being redirected at her.

"Jenny killed the lion," Ryan repeated, continuing his story. "And then—"

"And then you abandoned me in the woods."

28

"Jenny!" Sadie yelled, throwing her arms around her. Jenny flinched; the bites on her arms hurt as Sadie squeezed her. Sadie let go of her and stepped back, looking a little embarrassed. Jenny smiled, surprised and warmed by her friend's enthusiasm. Just a few days ago, Sadie had hated her. That felt like a lifetime ago now.

She looked at all the familiar faces directed at her and stopped when she saw a slight girl with long golden hair standing next to Ryan.

"Rain! You're human again!" Jenny said, amazed. "I can't believe it. The flower in Eckert's room worked?"

"No. Actually, Sadie found one growing on the way back," Aiden said proudly.

Jenny was happy, for the briefest of moments, until she saw Hannah and Cameron were there too. Her smile faded.

"What are you guys doing here?" Jenny blurted.

"Well nice to see you too, Jenny," Cameron joked.

"Sorry, I mean, I just thought you were getting help ... I hoped—"

"Yeah, that didn't work," he interrupted. "Short story shorter: we never really left."

Jenny frowned, confused. They'd just been sitting here this whole time? She looked at Hannah questioningly, but she just shrugged.

"Wait," Sadie said, gesturing at Jenny's arms and legs. "What *happened* to you?"

Jenny looked down at herself and winced. Her arms and legs were covered in small red welts from where the shrunken apple heads had bitten her. Her clothes and shoes were covered in wine and blood. Gnome blood, or the hunter's blood, or both—she didn't even know.

"Really big mosquitos," she lied, and looked away. She hoped Sadie wouldn't press her on it. Jenny glanced at May and saw she had put her black sweatshirt back on; its sleeves long were enough to cover her burnt hand. She wouldn't be able to hide it forever, Jenny knew. Eventually they'd have to tell them what had happened. But not now.

Sadie looked at her suspiciously, her head slightly tilted, and her hands on her hips. Sadie could always tell when she was lying.

"Okay, well what happened after you killed the lion?" Sadie persisted.

"And where's your wolf?" Aiden added.

Jenny reflexively looked down to where Marble would normally be standing. She jerked her head back up, annoyed with herself.

"We found the trail and followed it back to the castle," she said simply, avoiding eye contact with Sadie.

"That's not—" Ryan started, but Jenny glared at him as fiercely as she could, and he shut his mouth. The last thing they needed right now was a huge blowup about the stolen wish.

"As we were coming back, I was dragged into another fairy tale," Jenny continued, then narrowed her eyes at Ryan. "Tell me, Ryan," she said as she took a few steps closer to him. "How long did you wait for me after I disappeared? A whole five minutes?"

Jenny felt the tension in the air—tension *she* was creating. This wasn't what she had wanted to say, but it had just come out. There was too much anger inside her of to bite back.

A cool breeze slipped across the back of her neck, sending

shivers through her body. The scent of the ocean and roses made her heart stop.

"*I* wouldn't have left you in the woods," a familiar voice whispered into her ear.

29

"Uh, you see the tall creepy guy too, right?" Aiden said, his head cocked sideways. Sadie glared at Bannan, a man she'd only seen once before but recognized immediately. His dark hair was perfectly windswept, his gray eyes stormy and intense. He wore oddly old-fashioned clothes, but somehow it didn't look odd on *him*.

"Yeah, we see him," Sadie snapped.

Jenny was stuck between Bannan and Ryan. Jenny moved away from Bannan to stand next to Ryan, even though she had just been yelling at him. She could see Jenny's hands trembling slightly at her sides, though Sadie wasn't sure if it was out of fear or anger.

Bannan's eyes drifted off Jenny and slid across the rest of them with a look of boredom. His gaze stopped on Ryan, and his demeanor darkened.

"Who are *you*?" Ryan asked, breaking the silence that had overcome the group.

Bannan looked back at Jenny, who had crossed her arms and was now glaring back at him. She said nothing.

"It's complicated," he said, his voice tired. "I'm trapped here, like you are."

Jenny snorted, and everyone turned their attention to her.

"Oh, please," she burst out. "He's a *fairy-tale character*," she spat. "He's not like us at all. He killed Charlotte!"

"How many times do I need to explain this to you?" Bannan yelled back, his cool, bored tone transforming into sizzling anger. The air around them felt staticky and alive.

Jenny rolled her eyes and tossed back a limp lock of hair from her face. "Sure, your *story* killed her. Same thing."

"Okay," Sadie interjected before she knew what she was going to say. "Uh, let's all just take a beat, okay?" Bannan was staring at Jenny, and Jenny was glaring right back at him.

"Why are you here?" Sadie tried, hoping the answer wouldn't make things worse.

"I'm always here," he said vaguely, then looked at her for the first time. "I've been waiting for *her*."

"Who? Jenny?" Ryan asked as he took her by the hand. Sadie tried not to roll her eyes at the obvious demonstration of ownership.

"Ah, so this would be Ryan, then?" Bannan replied, not to Ryan or to Sadie, but to Jenny. She nodded. Bannan's dark gray eyes dipped down to Ryan's other arm, hanging limply at his side. Bannan smirked. "Was he always missing a hand?"

"Enough," Jenny snapped. "I'm here, you see me. Now go. Leave us alone."

Bannan let out a deep breath and looked away from the couple.

"Wait," Sadie said, worried he would disappear into thin air the same way he had arrived. "We need to get out of here. How do we leave?"

They had run out of options, and now that they were back at the castle, it felt like they were truly and literally back to square one. They needed to try everything and everyone at their disposal.

"Ha," he scoffed. "Leave? There's no way to leave, except …"

"Except what?"

Bannan glanced conspiratorially around the group. "There's one way, but it's impossible."

"What!" Jenny said, her voice so high it hurt Sadie's ears.

"This whole time you knew a way to leave and you didn't tell me?"

Bannan shrugged and looked up at the castle looming above them. "Like I said, it's impossible."

"Well, we're out of possible options," Sadie snapped. "So why don't we give it a shot?"

Bannan's eyes slid over the group and landed on Sadie. She locked eyes with him and refused to look away, refused to back down.

"Do you know how this castle came to be?" he asked, dropping his gaze, his tone flat and uninspired. When no one responded, he continued.

"A long time ago, there were two brothers—Jacob and Wilhelm Grimm. They were obsessed with folklore, and they were certain that the stories were true. They searched for years, collecting the oldest stories they could. They were mostly concerned with the ones about magic and fortune. They were very poor, you see, and obsessed with money. They thought if they looked hard enough, for long enough, they would come across something—or someone—with the power to change their lives."

"We know all this already," Cameron interrupted. "Ms. Eckert told us all about it on our second day here, during the tour."

"Right, but there's more to it than that," he said, crossing his arms. "You see, the brothers ended up *finding* what they were looking for: *magic*. Pretty soon, money wasn't what they were after any longer. They wanted *power*—and they found it. One day, they came across Rumpelstiltskin. They had heard all kinds of stories about him—that he could give you anything you wanted if you could just get through his riddles."

"He didn't seem very powerful to me," Travis mumbled. Sadie thought of the decrepit, blind old man behind the front desk and couldn't help but agree with Travis.

"The brothers made it through Rumpelstiltskin's riddles and were granted one wish," Bannan continued, ignoring Travis's interjection. "They knew from stories they had heard that magic could be tricky, that when granted a wish, it'd often turn out to be a curse. So, they thought they could beat it—they thought they were smarter than Rumpelstiltskin. They asked for power, power over all the Black Forest's magic."

Sadie tried to follow what Bannan was saying. She remembered staring up at the portrait of the Grimm brothers during the tour. How ridiculous they had looked in their old-timey clothes. Imagining them as powerful was difficult.

"Rumpelstiltskin had to grant it, even though it was giving them power over him as well. A deal is a deal, after all. He gave them a book full of blank pages and told them that they would have power over every fairy tale they wrote inside of it. They combed the forest, collecting witches, princesses, magical objects. They trapped them all inside the book."

"Hold on, what?" Cameron interrupted incredulously. "How is that supposed to work? They write stories in a book and then ..."

"It meant they could control the outcome of any magical interaction. They could collect gold from witches without any repercussions. They enjoyed *the company* of beautiful princesses."

"Ew," Sadie blurted, unable to control herself. "Disgusting."

"Yes, not very gentlemanly," Bannan continued. "They were easily bored, though, so they never stopped traveling and collecting stories for their book. Then Wilhem died, and Jacob was left alone with the book and free to do what he wanted. He holed himself up here, at Schloss Finster, obsessed with the book and what he could do with the fairy tales within."

"Schloss Finster?" Ryan asked.

"Dark Castle," May mumbled. Sadie was surprised it had taken May this long to say something. Something was up with her, Sadie knew, but now was not the time to try and figure it out. Her mind was already spinning, trying to keep up with Bannan's story.

"That's one thing we don't understand," Jenny said. "How did we end up here? Mrs. Braun didn't ... didn't bring us here on *purpose*, did she?"

The thought that their English teacher had done this to them intentionally gave Sadie a jolt. That wasn't something that had ever occurred to her—but she *was* gone. *What if she brought us here for a reason?*

"No," Bannan said bitterly. "No one comes here on purpose. The castle is like a living thing—it moves, it hunts. It intercepted you, placed itself between you and where you were supposed to go."

Sadie's skin crawled at the thought of being inside a living thing, a living castle.

"Anyway, where was I? Right, Jacob. He holed himself up here with the book and eventually grew bored. He decided to use the book on other people—and not just enemies. Anyone. Anyone who made the mistake of coming here. He managed to figure out a way to pull the stories out of the book and embed them into the castle. He enjoyed ... *playing* ... with people. He even placed Rumpelstiltskin at the front desk as a harbinger— his sole purpose being to warn people of what awaited them. Jacob felt it was only fair to give them a hint, a chance to escape. Of course, no one ever did.

As Jacob aged, the idea of immortality took hold of him. Why should someone so powerful die? he thought. He realized he'd had the key to immortality in his hands all along. As he neared death, Jacob wrote *himself* into the book. He disappeared from the real world—but he did not die. He's here, somewhere, living in a fairy tale of his choosing. I've looked for the book over the years. I thought if I could find it, I could somehow undo all this. Set us all free, stop all the death and misery. But I haven't been able to find it."

Sadie stared at him and tried to process everything he had said. The thought that all of this had happened to them because hundreds of years ago one old nutjob decided to live forever made her clench her fists. She didn't know Jacob, but she hated him. *How dare he?*

"Okay, that's something," Cameron said, more to himself than the rest of them. "There's a book, and we need to find it. Simple enough."

"Yeah, right," Aiden said. "If Mr. Creepy Magic Man over here has been looking for it for—what, centuries?—and couldn't find it, how are *we* supposed to?"

The group grew quiet, staring into space or at the ground or at the person they hoped would come up with the right answer. The plan. She felt Jenny and Hannah's eyes on her.

"Well, we have to try," Travis said with a forced smile. "What else have we got to do?"

"So what if we find the book? Then what?" Cameron asked.

Bannan hesitated.

"We destroy it," May said, staring at Bannan.

"Yes, you destroy it," he nodded.

"What happens to you if we destroy it? To Sophie? To *Charlotte*?" Jenny asked, her voice tight and strained.

Sadie watched Bannan suspiciously. How could they trust him? He was a fairy-tale character, and not just any character but a *villain*. His whole purpose for existing was to *kill women*. And here they were, enthralled with every word he said. Sadie found herself shaking her head.

"How can we trust you?" Sadie said coldly. "You may not have killed Charlotte yourself, but you're still the reason she's dead."

Bannan looked up at the castle looming over them. He had the look of someone who wasn't just physically tired but emotionally tired too. For a brief moment, Sadie felt a little sorry for him, but she quickly pushed that away.

"You really don't have a choice," he finally replied with a small shrug.

That she did believe.

30

Jenny's hand was starting to hurt clamped in Ryan's. He had taken it when Bannan appeared, and had been increasing the pressure with every word he said. She was still angry with Ryan and wanted to yank her hand from his grip, shake out her sand-filled fingers, but the way he was glaring at Bannan kept her still.

"Okay, I believe you," Rain said, taking a step closer to Bannan. Sadie scoffed and rolled her eyes but didn't interrupt. "What does the book look like? Where should we look? How do we destroy it?"

All good questions.

"Yes, well that's the problem, isn't it?" he replied with a mocking smile. "I don't actually know what the book looks like, or how to destroy it. As to where you should look ... I could tell you where I have already looked, but it's possible I've missed something."

"So you're useless?" Ryan snapped beside her. Jenny winced at his hard voice. The bones in her hand ached from his tightening grip.

Bannan shrugged.

As they were arguing, the sun had dipped below the horizon, and the light was quickly fading into darkness. Jenny didn't know what time it was, but she knew it would be pitch-black soon. She looked around at her friends and saw a bunch of exhausted, starving people, some of them wounded. They had *just* escaped the Black Forest, and Jenny didn't have it in her to start a new adventure right that minute.

"I think we should start looking tomorrow," she said, watching for the others' reactions. "It's almost dark, and we need to rest. I'm exhausted."

"Yeah," Ryan agreed. "I haven't really slept in days now, aside from that brief nap in the woods. We've all been through a lot today."

Jenny looked around at the bedding and pillows scattered across the ground. They must have decided to sleep outside, she realized. Jenny couldn't blame them for not wanting to sleep inside the castle, but sleeping outside, exposed, didn't seem like the best idea either.

There was a light cough, and their attention was brought back to Bannan, who they had forgotten for a moment was still standing there.

"What?" Jenny said crossly. "Unless you know anything else that could help us, why don't you do your little disappearing act and leave us alone?"

Bannan looked hurt and eyed Jenny's hand still locked inside Ryan's.

"As you wish," he said with a slight bow. Then he was gone.

"*The Princess Bride*," said Aiden automatically.

"I seriously doubt he's seen that movie," Jenny replied, shaking her head. She pulled her hand out of Ryan's and flexed her aching fingers. "Or any movie, for that matter."

Jenny felt Sadie's eyes on her.

"You still haven't answered any of our questions," Sadie said. Jenny had hoped Bannan's appearance would have diverted their attention, but Sadie was stubborn. Jenny took a deep breath, trying to loosen the tightness in her chest.

"We were walking back to the castle, and I was pulled into a fairy tale—*Little Red Riding Hood*. I don't want to go into the details, please don't make me, but I had to leave Marble there."

Jenny looked around at her friends, who were all looking

at her pitifully. She felt Ryan put an arm around her, but she shrugged it off and moved away from him.

"I need a shower," she said, breaking the awkward silence. "And food. I'm going inside now." She turned toward the castle.

"Wait!" Sadie said, stopping her. "We have a strict no-one-goes-alone rule. I'll go with you. You still have your room key? My stuff is in your room."

Jenny nodded distractedly. She'd kept her room key. She considered arguing with Sadie. All she wanted was to be alone. She couldn't argue with the logic of the buddy system, though.

"Fine, come on," she said, gesturing for Sadie to follow her.

Jenny walked up the few steps, pushed the door open, and let the cool darkness of the castle swallow her. Sadie followed behind, uncharacteristically quiet, and Jenny felt bad about lying to her. She just didn't see a point to going into the details of the *Little Red Riding Hood* story or revealing what May had done with their wish. No good would come from it, and they needed to stick together. She had no idea how they would react if they knew what May had done—and why.

"I was really worried about you," Sadie said softly behind her. "I thought you were dead."

Jenny paused at the bottom of the stairs and turned around. It was the first time since she'd returned that she really looked at Sadie. She was wearing a tight black T-shirt with "the Cranks" written on it. She tilted her head, confused.

"What are you wearing? Don't get me wrong, it kind of suites you, but—"

"Don't start with me," Sadie said, rolling her eyes. "I had to borrow some of May's clothes. The first thing I'm doing when we get up to the room is changing."

Jenny smiled and relaxed a little.

They made their way up to the fourth floor, and before Jenny had a chance to prepare herself, she was staring at the smooth, blank wall at the top of the stairs. The wall that hid horrors Jenny knew she would never be able to get out of her mind. Horrors she knew would haunt her for the rest of her life. The strength she had felt withered away, and her hands trembled at her sides.

"I know," Sadie said softly as she placed a hand on Jenny's back and guided her to the left, down the familiar hall that led to her room. Once she was a few feet away from the wall, Jenny was able to calm herself and force back the hot sobs she felt building in her chest. She willed herself to shake off the despondency that had taken her over. She couldn't let herself fall apart every time she saw that wall.

At her room's door, Jenny shifted her backpack to one shoulder and dug around in an outside pocket until she pulled out her key bracelet. She'd hated having it but had known she couldn't just get rid of it. She opened the door, and they went into the room Jenny had never wanted to enter again. It was just as they had left it—the beds were unmade, and Charlotte's shoes were lined up against the wall. She glanced at the blank space where the portrait of Charlotte had been.

Jenny dug some clean clothes out of her bag: black leggings, underwear, and a shirt so long it could be a dress. She left Sadie in the room and escaped into the bathroom, relaxing as the door clicked shut behind her.

She caught her reflection in the mirror and barely recognized herself. Brown curls jutted out here and there from her ponytail, and her arms and legs were pockmarked with bites. Her face had smudges of dirt and blood on it. She looked like she'd been killed and buried, then had to dig herself out of her own grave.

Jenny turned the water on in the bathtub and didn't wait for it to fill before getting in. She tossed her dirty clothes on the floor and climbed into the uncomfortable clawfoot tub, the water hot and steamy. Jenny grabbed a chunk of lavender soap from the small table by the tub and began vigorously scrubbing her legs and arms. The blood and dirt turned the water a disgusting brown. She drained the tub and refilled it, then let herself sink into the hot water. She scrubbed at her dirty, greasy hair with the scented soap, then lay there a moment, just staring up at the ceiling.

Help me.

Jenny sat up in the tub and looked around the room for where the voice had come from. The sound of crying echoed around the bathroom.

Please, help me.

"Shut up!" she screamed at the voices, realizing these were the same voices she had heard every night in this room. The voices that had lured Charlotte to her death.

"Are you okay?" Sadie called through the door.

"Do you hear them?" Jenny called back.

"Hear what?"

Jenny shook her head. She needed to get out here.

She rinsed off as quickly as she could, dried off, and dressed. She couldn't hear the voices anymore, which was a relief, but she didn't want to be there a second longer.

She opened the door to see Sadie standing there, no longer wearing May's black T-shirt. She'd changed into her own clothes and looked much more herself in a loose-fitting blue T-shirt and jean shorts. Sadie looked at her with concern.

"Are you okay?" Sadie asked.

"It's fine, I'm fine. Let's just grab our stuff and go."

They packed up all their things and pulled the blankets and pillows from the bed. Just as they were leaving, Jenny paused, looking at the shut closet door. She set down her duffel bag and blankets, walked over to the closet, opened the door, and pulled out the painting that had been removed from the wall. Charlotte's wide, bright blue eyes looked back at her. Jenny hesitated, not sure what she was doing or why, then flipped the frame over. She set it on the bed and pulled a small pair of nail scissors from her toiletry bag and slowly cut the painting out of the frame.

"That seems like a bad idea," Sadie said quietly from the door.

"I don't care," she said as she released the painting from the frame. She took one last look at Charlotte's face, then carefully rolled up the painting and secured it with one of her hair ties.

"Now I'm ready."

Jenny didn't know why she had suddenly decided to take the painting. It was just that the thought of leaving Charlotte there, even if it wasn't really her, made Jenny feel sick.

They lugged their things downstairs and outside and dropped them on the ground among the other piles of bedding and clothes. It was completely dark now, but someone had found a few small glass lanterns, and candles were flickering away inside of them, creating a warm glow over the area. Jenny's stomach ached, and she looked around to see if anyone had gotten any food, but didn't see anything.

"Have you all already eaten?" she asked, a little annoyed.

"Ah, no, we were ... not sure ..." Aiden stumbled on his words.

"Okay, I'll go and talk to Sophie," she said, not waiting for Aiden to finish his sentence. She turned to go back into the castle. Sadie followed, and Jenny prickled. It was a little annoying not being allowed to go anywhere by herself. Inside the castle, Jenny pushed the doors to the kitchen open and looked around the empty room for Sophie.

"Sophie!" Jenny called into the empty, echoey space.

"You came back," a soft voice with a thick German accent said at her side. She jumped at the sudden presence and relaxed when she realized it was just Sophie. She stood, her head tilted, studying Jenny like she was some sort of specimen in a lab. She was wearing the same pink-and-white pin-striped dress and faded green apron she always wore. *She looks so young*, Jenny thought, and she cringed when she remembered what Sophie's fairy tale was about. Her own father demanding she marry him. *Disgusting.*

"Yes, we came back," Jenny finally replied, trying to slow her breathing and push away the memory of Sophie's story. "We're all starving. I was wondering if you had some food you could give us."

Sophie nodded and began moving around the kitchen, grabbing bowls and ingredients and other objects Jenny didn't recognize. Sophie stoked a fire in the small hearth and moved a large cauldron into the flames. The smells that started steaming out of it made her stomach tight with hunger.

Jenny thought about Bannan and the book they would begin searching for tomorrow. She didn't trust Bannan, and the idea that there was some magical book that would solve all their problems seemed a little unbelievable.

"Sophie," she called to the girl still busying herself around the kitchen. "There's something else—a book. We're looking for the original copy of *Grimms' Fairy Tales*. Do you know where it might be?"

Sophie stopped cutting carrots and frowned, tilting her head as if thinking.

"A book? Did you look in the library?"

Jenny closed her eyes and tried to remain calm. "Not just any book, a very important book."

"I don't know what you're talking about," Sophie said with a shrug, and turned back to her chopping.

What if the book isn't even real? The thought made Jenny feel sick to her stomach. *Did Bannan lie to us about that? But why would he lie?*

She wasn't sure of anything he said. *If I find out he's just been wasting our time...* Jenny let the thought drop. She realized there wasn't anything she could do to him. He had been right— they didn't have any other choice than to believe him.

Jenny smelled baking bread, and her stomach made an embarrassing groaning sound.

Sophie gestured at the large pot, then at a stack of bowls and loaves of bread that appeared on the table in front of them. "Stew, bread."

Jenny opened her mouth to ask Sophie more questions, but felt them die on her tongue. Sophie didn't know about the book, or if she did, she wasn't going to tell them.

"Thank you. I'll tell the others to come get some."

Jenny filled a bowl with steaming, meaty stew and set a chunk of bread on top. Sadie did the same, and they made their way carefully back out of the castle and to the others. Outside, the steam poured off the stew in ghostly white wisps.

"Go into the kitchen. Sophie made us some food," Jenny told the group as she sat down on the edge of the fountain to eat. Sadie hesitated, then sat down next to her. Jenny watched as everyone else moved toward the castle to get food. Everyone except Hannah.

"Hey," Hannah said, standing in front of them. Jenny looked up at her, confused.

"You're not hungry?" Jenny asked, taking a big bite of stew. It was salty and thick with beef and potatoes and carrots. It might've been the best thing she had ever tasted. As she swallowed the food, she felt warmer inside.

"No. Uh, I mean, Cam is getting me a bowl." She shifted uncomfortably. Jenny rolled her eyes and put another spoonful of stew in her mouth to keep herself from saying anything.

"Oh it's *Cam* now?" Sadie teased next to her.

"What? Oh, no, I mean—" Hannah's face bloomed bright red. "Well, I'm gonna let you two eat!" Hannah scurried away to her pile of bedding and started fussing with the blankets.

Jenny dipped some of the bread into the stew and took a large bite. She turned to see Sadie not eating, but staring at her intently.

"So, are you going to tell me what *really* happened in the woods?"

31

"Something *else* clearly happened. It's written all over the three of you," Sadie pushed. If she was going to get Jenny to tell her anything, now was the time, when no one else was around to hear or interrupt.

Jenny's expression darkened, and she looked away.

"What exactly happened to Marble?" she tried. Maybe she could get the story out piece by piece.

"Little Red Cap took him back," Jenny said between bites.

"What do you mean?"

"I said I didn't want to talk about it," Jenny snapped. Sadie winced. She stared at Jenny, who seemed to her a wholly different person than the last time she'd seen her just hours ago. *Something more had to have happened*, Sadie thought. Sadie racked her brain for something else she could ask Jenny, anything that might give her a clue to what had happened.

"What's up with May?" she ventured. She wasn't entirely sure something had happened to May, but she was acting off too, and it was worth a shot.

Jenny finished her stew and set the empty bowl down on the ground. She stood up, and Sadie bent her neck to look up at her. In the shaky candlelight, Jenny was hardly more than a dark silhouette, her face was unreadable.

"You'll have to ask *her* that," Jenny said before walking away.

Sadie sat alone on the edge of the fountain, the half-finished bowl of stew in her hands. She quickly finished eating and set the bowl on top of Jenny's. The others started filtering outside and were just starting to eat their dinners. Sadie felt tired watching them. The stew was warm and filling, and she felt unbelievably tired. She looked at the little islands of blankets and pillows scattered across the ground and couldn't remember where she'd put hers. She watched May pass in front of her but didn't say anything. It wasn't the right time.

"Hey," Aiden said as he sat next to her. "You finished yours already?"

"Yeah, it was really good." She offered a weak smile.

Aiden followed Sadie's gaze and looked out at the rest of the group in their various places on the grass. Cameron and Hannah were huddled together, Travis was eating alone on the castle steps, and May was off by herself, and so was Jenny. She watched as Jenny put together her bed for the night a little away from the others. She didn't see Ryan or Rain, and guessed they must still be inside.

"It's good to have everyone back together again," Aiden said, stirring the hot stew with a spoon.

"Yeah," she said, eyeing the distance between each of them. They were together again, sure, but it didn't really feel like it. Her eyelids grew heavy, and she had to shake her head a little to try to wake herself up.

"You look really tired," Aiden said, looking at her.

"I *feel* really tired."

"Do you know where you're going to sleep?"

Sadie looked out at the islands of bedding and still couldn't remember where she'd dropped her bundle. She guessed it didn't really matter.

"I don't know, somewhere over there," she gestured widely at the yard.

"You can sleep over by me if you want," Aiden said calmly, spooning food into his mouth. Sadie waited a painful few seconds before he swallowed and spoke again. "Over there."

Aiden pointed to an area with bedding piled up higher than the other bundles. It looked like he'd taken as many blankets and pillows as he could and made a small mountain. If she weren't so tired, the prospect of sleeping next to Aiden would have her heart beating so loud he'd hear it. At the moment, though, the only thing she really cared about was lying down and closing her eyes.

"Sure," she finally managed. "Looks like you squirreled away a lot of bedding."

Aiden smiled and shrugged. He set his empty bowl on the ground next to hers and Jenny's and stood up. He offered her his hand. "You ready for bed?"

"*So* ready."

They tiptoed around the others, careful not to step on anyone, and stopped at Aiden's pile of blankets and cushions. Aiden bent over and separated out a blanket and pillow, then tossed them aside. Sadie watched, half-asleep and a little delirious, as he took the remaining blankets and folded them into a makeshift sleeping mat, then put the last blanket on top with a pillow at the end.

"There you go," he said, studying his work. "The best bed in the yard."

Sadie smiled and thanked him, then crawled onto the "bed" and pulled the blanket over her. She lay down on her back and enjoyed the comfort of an actual pillow. "Mmm, so comfy," she said, drunk with exhaustion.

She sensed Aiden making his own bed next to hers, not too close but not too far away either. She turned her heavy head toward Aiden and saw him watching her.

"What?" she said, yawning.

"Oh, nothing."

Aiden's face was the last thing she saw before sleep overtook her.

32

As Jenny put together her bed, she wished she didn't have to spend another night on the hard ground. She looked around at the others preparing their little areas and listened to the soothing crash of the river nearby. She raised an eyebrow as she saw Sadie and Aiden lay down together. Sadie had peppered Jenny with questions about what had happened to her in the woods, but clearly things had changed here too.

Jenny settled onto her makeshift bed and pulled a blanket on top of herself. She lay back and stared up at the stars in the clear night sky. It was beautiful. She never saw so many stars back home. It was usually overcast, or there was too much light pollution. She wished she could enjoy it. Instead, all she could think about was tomorrow. The thought of searching the entire castle made her feel even more tired, and she let her eyes close.

"Can we talk?" a familiar voice said above her.

Jenny opened her eyes to see Ryan standing over her. He looked sheepish and awkward, and the hardness she had felt toward him softened a little.

"Sure."

Ryan lowered himself down to sit next to her, and she sat up. Everyone had spread out, so no one was close enough to hear them.

"About the woods," he started, staring down at the ground and pulling at strands of grass. "We waited for you, but it was getting dark, and we had no idea where you had gone or when you would be back. You have to understand—it was the only thing we could do."

Jenny stared off at a point over his shoulder, not wanting to make eye contact. She knew what he said was true, and had it been reversed ... she wondered if she would have done the same thing. *No*, she thought. *I went into the woods to save him. I never would have just left him behind.*

He looked at her almost like he used to—*almost*. The love was there, she could see it in his eyes, but there was something else behind it. A resentment. Her gaze trailed down his arm to his missing hand. Had she gone after him sooner, he would still have two hands. If none of this had happened and they were all out here just having a fun night under the stars, he'd probably be playing his guitar and cracking jokes.

"Jenny, I'm sorry," he whispered. "I shouldn't have left you."

Part of her wanted to hold him, tell him it was okay. But the other part wouldn't let her. She took his remaining hand instead and gave a soft squeeze. It was the best she could do right now.

"Can I sleep here with you?" he asked, giving her his best pouty face.

"Sure." Jenny let go of his hand and lay back down. She pulled her blanket over herself and stared up at the stars as Ryan struggled to put his bed together next to her. After a few minutes, he went still.

She snuck a glance at him and saw he had his back to her. She stared at the back of his head, his sandy-blonde hair curling slightly at the edges. She thought of all the times she'd run her fingers through it. *We should be cuddling*, she thought. She should have her head resting on his chest and be falling asleep to the soothing sound of his breathing, like she'd done so many times before. Now his back was turned to her, and there was an unfamiliar tension between them. Even though he was right there, right beside her, she missed him.

She'd gone into the forest to save Ryan, but she had failed. Ryan wasn't the same person anymore, and neither was she.

33

Sadie opened her eyes and flinched in surprise—she wasn't expecting to see Aiden's face just a couple feet from hers. His eyes were closed, his dark eyelashes fluttering gently on his cheeks as he dreamed. His mouth was slightly open, and she was pretty sure there was a drool stain on his pillow. He was beautiful.

She considered staying there, staring at him like a lunatic, but wasn't sure how she'd respond if he suddenly opened his eyes and caught her. She slowly sat up, careful to not make any noise and wake up Aiden. It was early. The sky was a warm pink, and the sun was just starting to peek over the treetops. A light dew had settled over them all; the blankets and pillows were damp with it.

She looked around and saw that everyone else was still asleep. She'd never been a morning person; she was surprised she was the first one awake. She hesitated, not sure what to do. Waking everyone up seemed cruel, but they had a book to find and a curse to break. She was already starting to feel antsy sitting there doing nothing. She pushed the blanket off and rose to an awkward squatting position as she tried to stand up without making noise. She watched Aiden's face as she stood, looking for a sign he was waking up, but his eyes remained closed and his breathing, even.

Sadie had slept in her clothes, so she didn't bother looking for her things and slipped on the shoes she'd left at the foot of her makeshift bed. She tiptoed around Travis and Rain as she made her way out of the minefield of friends and let out a breath of relief when she was past the sleeping area. As she made her way up the castle steps, her stomach grumbled—she was hungry again. She paused at the front door, remembering her own strict buddy-system rule. Sadie glanced back at the others. None of them stirred, so she decided to break her own rule and go in alone.

She carefully opened the heavy castle door and shut it behind her and softly as possible. Inside, she glanced at Rumpelstiltskin's still-empty desk and shook her head. She had a feeling that he could fix it all if he wanted to but that he just chose not to, and his hiding from them only irritated her more. She turned toward the large painting on the wall of the Grimm brothers and looked up at it. She wanted to look into the faces of the two psychopaths that had caused this all to happen.

The same two miserable men she'd seen that first day in the castle stared back at her. One man was sitting, and the other was standing next to him, a hand resting on the sitting man's shoulder. The man sitting down had a book in his hand, opened to some unknown page. They both had terrible wavy, ear-length hairstyles: the standing man's hair was a dirty white, like unwashed sheep wool, and the other's was a dishwater brown. She couldn't tell which brother was which, but it didn't matter. She hated both of them.

She hated them with every cell in her body, and just looking at their two ugly old-man faces made her want to punch them. She examined the ornate frame around the painting. It looked heavy and expensive. Sadie got onto the little chaise that sat underneath the painting and pushed the frame up so it unhooked from the wall, then let it fall onto the castle floor with a loud *bang*.

She glanced over at the desk to see if her vandalism would cause Rumpelstiltskin to appear, but it was still empty. She jumped off the chaise and looked down at the men, now lying on the floor, staring up at the gaudy chandelier hanging above.

"Not so important now, are you?" she snapped. Sadie stared down at the large painting on the floor and realized she hadn't really thought this through. She didn't have a plan for the painting; she'd just wanted it off the wall.

"You want some help with that?"

Sadie turned to see Jenny standing behind her, her hands on her hips and an amused expression on her face. Sadie was glad it was Jenny and not one of the others. Sadie grinned.

"You want to destroy it with me?"

"More than anything."

They took turns stomping all over the painting, focusing primarily on the two men's faces. Then Sadie held it up slightly so Jenny could smash the frame with her foot. It broke in two easily, and they tore the rest of it apart, chucking pieces of gold-painted wood in every direction. When they finally ran out of steam, the painting was frameless, torn, and covered in footprints. Sadie felt a little twinge of guilt. They'd just destroyed a historical piece of art. The thing probably belonged in a museum somewhere.

"Now what should we do with it?" Sadie asked Jenny, who had sat down on the chaise and was breathing hard. Jenny looked up, her face flushed and eyes shining.

"Let's have a little bonfire later," she said with a smile.

Sadie laughed and shook her head. She kind of liked this new Jenny. The old Jenny never would have done this with her; she would have been too scared she'd get into trouble or something. Sadie bent over and unceremoniously rolled the painting up and shoved it underneath Rumpelstiltskin's desk and out of sight. "To keep it safe, for later," she said. Jenny nodded and kicked the broken pieces of frame underneath the chaise, as if that would keep their friends from seeing what they'd done. It didn't matter. Sadie was pretty sure the others would just be mad they hadn't been there to join in.

"I was going to see if Sophie had the breakfast buffet out," Jenny said. Sadie nodded and followed her into the dining room.

The dining room was just as it had always been, except Sadie looked at the other "guests" sitting at the small tables differently. She knew now that the people surrounding them weren't really there. Just the ghosts of who they used to be remained. Sadie tried not to look at them and instead focused on the buffet running along the wall. It was like it had been every morning—full of steaming eggs and flaky pastries and a number of other breakfast dishes. Sadie wondered who it was all for. If they weren't here, would the buffet still be here, sitting uneaten?

Sadie approached the buffet and picked up a plate, then noticed Jenny was still at the door.

"I'm going to wake the others," Jenny said. "We should all be on the same timeline."

Sadie nodded at Jenny and turned back to the food. The stew last night had been delicious, but she was excited for some variety. She dished out a little bit of everything, just like Hannah had that first day, then made her way through the ghosts and into the Red Room.

34

Jenny watched as the rest of the group began rising up from their beds on the ground. They stretched out stiff backs, rubbed their eyes, yawned, put their shoes on. They'd all slept in their clothes, too tired to change into something else, and everyone looked a little rumpled.

"The buffet is up. Come inside and eat. We'll talk about the game plan inside," she announced to the group. Groans and nods told her they'd all heard her. She turned to go back inside the castle and get her own breakfast when Ryan called for her to wait up. She stopped and turned, then watched him hurry his way past the others and finally stop in front of her.

"Hey, we're okay, right?" he asked softly. His blonde hair was a mess, and he still looked tired, with bluish circles under his bloodshot eyes. He looked the worst of all of them, and for good reason, she knew. She took a deep breath and remembered how frightened she'd been when she realized she was alone in the woods, that he had abandoned her there. Then she thought about all the good times before that, before this nightmare of a trip, and tried to stay in the warm bubble of those memories. Kissing him in front of his locker, hearing him cheer for her at her softball games, the time they'd gone skinny-dipping in the ocean and had to immediately get out and put their clothes back on because of how freezing it was. She smiled at the memory and tried to push her anger aside.

She wanted to go back to how things used to be—fun, sweet, easy. But Jenny knew something had changed inside of her. It was like a little piece of her love for him had broken off and was lost forever.

She did still love him, though. He was looking at her with those sad eyes, and she felt the pull to hold him, to take care of him. She wrapped her arms around him and rested her head on his shoulder. She felt his arms encircle her, and they stood that way for a moment, until Jenny saw the others making their way over to them. She pulled away and left a quick kiss on his cheek.

"Yeah, we're okay," she replied, then turned so he couldn't see her expression. She didn't want her face to give her away. She didn't want him to see that she was lying.

She sensed him behind her as she entered the castle and made her way to the dining room. Inside, she eyed the buffet table covered with silver platters of food. A bowl of hard-boiled eggs sat next to a tray of steaming croissants fresh from the oven. There were platters of fruit and cheese, shiny red beets, and fat, soft pretzels with large grains of salt. Jenny hurried to the buffet, starving and not caring if she looked overeager.

At the buffet table, Jenny filled her plate and felt an uncomfortable sense of déjà vu. She had done this all before, but it was very different this time. She envied the Jenny of last week, the Jenny who'd still thought this was going to be a fun trip.

A soft cough from next to her drew her out of her thoughts. It was Ryan, holding his plate in one hand, his other arm hanging at his side. She glanced at his empty plate, then at him, and was horrified at how long it had taken her to realize he wasn't able to serve himself.

"Sorry! What, ah, what would you like?" she said, her face warm with embarrassment.

Ryan told her what he wanted, and Jenny put a little of each on his plate. They made their way down the buffet line this way, and Jenny was relieved when they reached the end. They took their plates into the Red Room and sat down at the long banquet table they had spent so much time around. Jenny slid into a chair next to Sadie, who was already halfway through her meal, and the others took the remaining chairs scattered around the table. Everyone except Cameron and Hannah.

"Where are Hannah and Cameron?" she asked, worried.

"Cameron took some food out to Hannah. They're eating outside," Travis said.

"Seriously?" Jenny blurted out before she could stop herself. "It's daylight." She shook her head and stabbed at the food on her plate. She'd been patient with Hannah after what had happened to her at the Monsters' Ball, but the rest of them had been through far worse now and weren't being such babies. *Hannah must not realize we may never leave here*, Jenny thought. If they failed to find the book, if they had to stay here, sooner or later she'd have to come inside.

Still tired, no one felt much like talking and instead focused on eating. As she bit into a warm croissant, small flakes of buttery pastry sprinkled onto the table. Jenny tried to come up with a plan for the day. She wasn't very optimistic that they'd manage to find the book right away. If Bannan had been looking for who knew how many years and hadn't found it, how were they supposed to? Jenny tried to push aside the pessimistic thinking and focus on the plan. They would have to split up to search as much as possible as quickly as possible, but she didn't love the idea. They had *just* reunited.

She finished the last of her croissant and wiped her hands on her shorts. She stood up to get the group's attention and cleared her throat.

"I know this isn't going to be a popular plan," Jenny started, "but we need to split up in order to better our chances of finding the book."

Aiden groaned at the other side of the table. Jenny ignored him and pressed on.

"We'll break into three groups of three. Ryan, Rain, and I

will be in one group." Jenny hadn't discussed this with Ryan or Rain, had just come up with the plan that moment, but she didn't anticipate any argument. She knew Ryan would want to stay near his sister, and she knew she needed to stay near Ryan. She looked around at the waiting faces. "Sadie, Aiden, and May, you'll be together," Jenny continued.

"So that leaves me with Hannah and Cameron?" Travis asked, sounding disappointed.

"Yes." Jenny waited for him to argue, but he just nodded and went back to finishing his breakfast.

"We should start with—"

"Let's wait until we're done eating," Aiden interjected. Jenny looked at him, surprised at the interruption. "Cam and Hannah should be part of this conversation."

Jenny felt the blood rush to her cheeks, making her face feel uncomfortably warm. Aiden was right, she shouldn't have started this without them. She'd been so annoyed they weren't there. She had finished eating and didn't want to sit back down and wait for the rest of them to finish.

"Sure, of course," she said, moving away from the table. "I'll see you all outside."

35

Sadie watched Jenny leave the Red Room, then Sadie worked through the start of Jenny's plan in her mind. She didn't know if Jenny had set her up with Aiden and May on purpose or if it had been random, but either way, she was pleased. She wanted to be with Aiden, and she wanted a chance to talk to May without Jenny or Ryan around too. This was perfect.

Sadie quickly finished the food on her plate and followed Jenny. Outside, it was bright and already getting hot. She shielded her eyes with her hand and squinted across the yard they'd slept in the previous night. Blankets and pillows were scattered everywhere, and Cameron and Hannah were sitting on one of the blankets eating their breakfast picnic-style. Hannah waved to Jenny, but Jenny ignored her, walking past her and Cameron to the fountain. Jenny picked up one of the copies of *Grimms' Fairy Tales* that was lying on the ground and started reading it, or at least she *pretended* to read it. From the castle steps, Sadie looked from Hannah's hurt expression to Jenny's blank one and hesitated. She didn't want to answer any questions Hannah might have—*Is Jenny mad at me? Why is she mad at me?*—and didn't want to bug Jenny and have that irritation redirected at her instead. She debated with herself for so long that the others began spilling out of the castle doors behind her, forcing her down the steps.

Jenny seemed to be pulling them all into her orbit, Sadie noticed. Everyone, even Hannah and Cameron, were gathered in front of the fountain, waiting for Jenny to speak. Jenny stood up, leaving her fountain perch with the book she was reading—or pretending to read—in one hand.

"We're going to split up into three groups to search for the book," she repeated. "Hannah, Cameron, and Travis, you'll all be in a group together."

Sadie saw Hannah nod and smile at Cameron. Travis threw one heavy arm around Cameron's shoulder and gave him an uncomfortable-looking side hug.

"We'll all start inside the castle. Ryan, Rain, and I will search the rooms, starting on the fourth floor," Jenny continued. "Travis, Hannah, and Cameron, why don't you start with the library?"

Travis groaned, and Cameron nodded agreement. Sadie appreciated Jenny taking control, but she knew where she wanted to search first, and it *wasn't* inside the castle.

"We'll start with the ruins behind the castle," Sadie announced. "Weird things seem to happen there—well, *slightly* weirder things than everywhere else."

"Great," Jenny said, a little too dismissively for Sadie's taste. "We'll meet back here, in front of the fountain, before dark. Good luck." Jenny turned toward the castle and began walking through the group without any other instruction. Sadie watched her, a little bewildered at Jenny's sudden coldness.

"W-wait!" Hannah yelled, her face flushed and eyes shining. "I don't want to go back in there. Can't we look out here?"

Sadie tried not to audibly groan. She loved Hannah, but she was quickly becoming a nuisance.

"Hannah," Jenny said with a slight edge to her tone, "we've *all* been through a lot. We're *all* risking our lives right now, and honestly you're being really selfish—"

"Okay!" Hannah screeched, cutting off Jenny. Sadie winced at the sound of Hannah's strained voice. "I get it. I'm sorry. I'll go inside."

Sadie watched, stunned, as Jenny turned away from

Hannah without another word and made her way up the castle steps. It wasn't like Jenny to talk to Hannah, or really *anyone*, like that. She watched as Jenny, Ryan, and Rain disappeared into the castle. Sadie turned to Hannah and saw how red her face was, how shiny her eyes were.

"Hannah ..."

"It's okay, Sadie. She's right," Hannah said, wiping at her wet eyes. "We don't have the luxury of fear anymore."

Hannah turned and walked toward the castle without another word, eliciting a shrug from Travis and a dark look from Cameron.

"Good luck," Cameron said distractedly before following Hannah.

"Maybe I could go with you guys instead?" Travis asked Sadie quietly.

"Ah ..."

"Kidding, it's fine. We'll be fine!" Travis said, then turned and slapped Aiden on the back. "Take care of the ladies!"

Sadie and May rolled their eyes almost in unison, and Aiden shook his head. They watched as Travis caught up with Hannah and Cameron, and all three of them disappeared into the castle after a brief hesitation at the doors. Sadie felt strange, watching them go. She felt the absence of Jenny and Hannah, a growing coldness surrounding her. She had just gotten them both back, and here she was, separated from them again. She eyed May and Aiden, who in turn were eyeing her.

"To the ruins?" May asked. Sadie was a little surprised May was directing the question at her, and noted a subtle shift in May's whole demeanor. So far May had been a know-it-all, a little sarcastic, a touch irritating, but now she seemed ... humbled? She studied May as May waited for Sadie to respond. Something was definitely off, and she was determined to find out what. But not right this second. Sadie sighed.

"Yes, to the ruins," she answered.

"You're not going to leave me in there again, are you?" Aiden said playfully.

Sadie groaned and walked away without responding. She felt like a completely different person from the one who had run away from Aiden. So much had changed in just a couple days. She couldn't imagine herself acting that way now. She heard them follow behind, and in a few minutes, they were standing in front of the broken iron gate. Roses in every shade of red grew wild over the crumbling walls, and thorny vines wrapped around the bars of the battered gate. It reminded her, briefly, of a book she had been forced to read a few years ago in school: *The Secret Garden*. She'd never understood why that book was so popular. She had found it painfully boring.

"I haven't been here," May said softly, examining the thorny rose vines growing voraciously across the broken stone and iron.

"It's not so bad," Aiden replied.

Sadie rolled her eyes. Not so bad. Yeah, in comparison to everything else they'd been through, this would be a piece of cake.

Yeah, right.

They walked through the broken gate and made their way through the ruins. Everything was more or less as Sadie remembered—crumbling stone walls of varying heights, overgrown rose bushes, statues of sleeping animals and people scattered throughout. The only thing missing from the last time she was in there was the wolf statue.

"So we're looking for a book," Aiden said as if they had already forgotten why they were there. Sadie bit back the snarky comment rising in her throat.

"Yeah," she said instead.

"A book of unknown size and color," he continued.

"Uh-huh."

"A book that *could*, for all we know, be invisible."

"You got it."

"Cool, just making sure."

Sadie smirked at her and Aiden's banter. She felt like she understood his sense of humor much better now than she had the last time she'd been in the ruins with him. They continued through the broken structure, stepping over partial walls and avoiding thorny vines that had grown into the path. May quietly followed behind her and Aiden.

"Where are we going?" Aiden said, turning to Sadie suspiciously. "You seem to be going somewhere specific."

"Yeah, I want to check out that tower," Sadie replied, pointing at the tower poking into the sky in the distance. "Something really weird happened to me there, I think the book could be there."

"Really?"

Sadie shrugged. She didn't have a clue if the book had anything to do with the tower, but she knew there was something special about it, something that was being protected by magic. There must be a reason she'd ended up back where she came from when she tried to go through the tower door before. As they continued toward the tower, she looked around for the book, but it was a futile exercise. Everything was covered in such thick rose vines—the book could be anywhere. It could be two feet from them, and they wouldn't even know. Sadie eyed May behind her. *Now,* she thought. *Now's my chance.* Sadie slowed her pace until she fell in step with May.

"So, May," Sadie said as casually as she could, "what really happened after we were separated in the woods?"

May's shoulders stiffened, but she did not stop walking.

"Nothing," May finally said after a few moments. Sadie wasn't surprised by May's response. She knew having May tell her what had actually happened was a long shot. It didn't matter, though. Now Sadie knew for sure that something had *definitely* happened. She was about to press May harder when

Aiden stopped ahead of them and turned around.

"Uh, Sadie, I don't really know where I am going."

"Right, sorry," Sadie said, forcing a smile. She moved ahead of May and Aiden and continued to lead them to the tower. She passed the sleeping pig statue, then the collection of stone chickens, then the maid with the broken broom. She'd made a point to remember these landmarks the last time she was there, and they led straight to the tunnel they'd need to go through to get to the tower. They came to the only wall not broken and falling apart. It stretched up and was far too high to climb over. The only way to the tower, she knew, was through the tunnel. As they approached the dark opening in the wall, Sadie recognized the two sleeping guard dog statues on either side of the opening. They were the largest animal statues she'd seen, apart from Jenny's wolf, and their legs stretched out as if they'd been running in their sleep.

"That's it," Sadie said. "The tunnel I went through before."

She glanced at May to see her reaction. She looked almost ... bored.

"What is it, May?" she asked, annoyed.

"Well, obviously this is *Briar Rose*," she said flatly, looking down at the two statues of sleeping dogs. "Sleeping Beauty," May explained when she saw Sadie and Aiden's blank expressions. "When the princess is cursed, the entire kingdom is put under a sleeping spell. We passed *a lot* of sleeping people and animal statues on our way here. I'm guessing the princess is at the top of the tower."

"Well, let's go get us a princess," Aiden said as he took a step into the tunnel, then paused. "Sadie, anything I should know about before I go in here? Monsters? Quicksand? Skeletons?"

"No, nothing like that," Sadie replied. "Just watch out for the spiderwebs."

36

"You were a bit harsh with Hannah," Rain whispered as she pulled her long blonde hair back into a ponytail.

"I guess," Jenny said, eyeing Ryan. He was looking straight ahead, lost in his own thoughts. "I'm just really tired. Of everything. You two have suffered the most and I just … I just snapped."

"It wasn't so bad, really, being a deer," Rain said. Her wide eyes still looked doe-like to Jenny.

Jenny shook her head and opened her mouth to respond but stopped when she saw Hannah, Travis, and Cameron enter the castle.

"So, you're gonna need keys, right?" Travis said, pushing past them. They stared up at the key cabinet behind Rumpelstiltskin's desk. The small man was nowhere to be found. Still hiding from them, she guessed. Or had something else happened to him?

"Or do you want to kick in every door, Cam?" Travis continued with a half smile.

"Nah, I'm good," Cameron replied, looking at the floor shyly.

Travis moved behind the desk and looked up at the delicate key bracelets hanging from the tiny hooks. Many of the hooks were empty—the keys to Eckert and Mrs. Braun's rooms were gone, as were the keys to their own rooms. Travis removed the keys that were left and tossed them on the desk.

"Those are to the rooms on the second, third, and fourth

floors," he said, gesturing at them. Jenny felt overwhelmed looking at the key-covered desk. There were so many of them. It would take them forever to get through every single room.

"We'll start at the top and work our way down," Ryan said, shoving the keys into his pockets.

"Let's meet back here in the lobby when we're done, or once it gets dark, whichever comes first," Cameron said.

Done. When we're done. Jenny didn't know what that would mean—would *done* mean they had failed? Would *done* mean they had found the book? Would *done* ever come at all? If they didn't succeed, they'd be spending another night at the castle. How many more nights would they have to spend there?

"Come on, Jenny," Rain said, snapping Jenny out of the spiral she had started to lose herself in. Travis, Cameron, and Hannah were already making their way down the hallway toward the library, and Ryan was halfway to the stairs. She hurried after Rain to catch up with Ryan and forced herself to follow them up.

Jenny paused when they reached the fourth floor landing and the smooth wall Charlotte's body was behind.

"Are you alright?" Ryan said, touching her shoulder gently. "Is this where—"

"Yes," Jenny interrupted. "Let's just ... let's just keep going." She wasn't going to let herself have another breakdown.

As they walked down the hall, Jenny remembered the first night they had been there, a night that felt like years ago now. She remembered how Ryan had walked her up to her room, how Charlotte had caught them about to kiss. Jenny's throat felt sore and her eyes stung as she remembered that night. How innocent everything had been. She wanted to shake the memory of herself and tell her to run, to run far away from this place.

"Let's start at the end of the hall and make our way back toward the stairs," Ryan said without looking at her. She wondered if Ryan had been remembering that night too, or if it even lived in his head anymore.

"Sure."

They reached the last door on the left, and Ryan pulled out the tangle of key bracelets from his pocket. He moved as if to pick out one of the keys but paused and quickly drew his arm back. Ryan, his face red, held the keys out to Jenny. She jerked forward awkwardly and sifted through the keys until she found the one with 408 on it. He handed the rest of the keys to his sister without looking at her, and she took them without saying anything.

"Well," Ryan said with a breath, "go on."

Jenny's hand shook as she placed the key in the lock. Neither Ryan nor Rain had experienced a room fairy tale yet. But she had. She had no idea what they'd find behind that door.

"Wait, should we knock first?" Rain said softly. "What if someone is in there?"

"If someone was in there, they'd have this key," Jenny explained.

"Right, but still, it feels weird not knocking first."

"Okay, sure," Jenny acquiesced and knocked three times on the door, then waited.

Nothing happened. Jenny strained to hear anything moving behind the door, but it was quiet.

Jenny took a deep breath and pushed the key into the lock. The door opened with a soft click, and they slowly made their way into the room. Rain took the key from the lock and let the door close behind her.

It was a simple room, with two small beds covered in thin brown blankets that looked like they'd be itchy. There were simple wood floors, stone walls, and no decorations of any sort. Jenny tossed her copy of *Grimms' Fairy Tales* on the bed. She wondered if they were even going to find any use for the book, but it was the only thing they had that might help them.

"Okay, so, look for a book, I guess," Jenny said, uncertainty creeping into her voice. She hoped they'd know it when they saw it, but they really didn't know what they were looking for. "It might not be an actual book," she continued, "it might be a picture of a book, or a statue of a book, or ... I don't know. Just look for anything book-like, I guess. But don't touch anything! Remember that any item could be linked to a fairy tale we don't want to be thrown into."

"We *know*, Jenny," Ryan said, a tinge of exasperation in his voice. He brushed past her and went into the bathroom. Jenny shrugged it off and started searching the room. She dropped onto her stomach to look underneath the first bed, then moved over to look under the second. Nothing but dust and cobwebs. She pushed herself off the floor and made her way over to the closet and opened it. Again, nothing, except a soft coat of dust. She closed the closet door and saw that Ryan was still searching the washroom and Rain was examining a small item sitting on top of the sole dresser. An object. Jenny thought of the small statues she saw in Travis and Cameron's room, and the rug in Sadie and Hannah's room.

"Rain, don't—"

"Little pot, cook," Rain said, reading aloud the small inscription on the little black pot. Jenny hurried to her side to stop her, but she was too late. Rain turned, surprised. "Oh, hey, this is weird, isn't it?"

The little black pot on the dresser began to shiver. Jenny grabbed Rain and pulled her away from the dresser.

"What's happening?" Rain asked, her eyes glued to the shaking object. In a moment, Ryan was with them and was staring at the small pot too.

"I *just* told you not to touch anything," Jenny tried to keep her voice even and calm, but the pot was shivering faster now.

"But I *didn't* touch it ..."

Jenny clenched her teeth to keep herself from yelling at

Rain. *It's not her fault.*

"We have to get out of here," Jenny said, her heart racing. "We have no idea what that thing is going to do, but it's not going to be good."

Jenny pushed Rain toward the door, but Ryan was already pulling at the door handle. The door wouldn't budge. Then the porridge came. Hot, steaming porridge began flowing from the little pot, faster and faster until they were all ankle deep in the thick sludge. Jenny breathed in the overwhelming scent of cinnamon and spices wafting off the porridge.

"This is ridiculous," Ryan spat, still fighting with the door. "We're not going to be taken down by a breakfast food!"

Jenny tried to keep calm, but she was filling with panic as quickly as the porridge was filling the room.

"What are we going to do!" Rain yelled, the porridge continuing to flow unchecked from the pot.

Jenny pulled her legs through the thick cement-like sludge to where the pot sat. She reached out to grab it, but the moment her hands closed around it, she pulled them back with a scream. Her palms were bright red and burning from the searing iron pot.

"Stupid, stupid," she mumbled to herself before grabbing one of the brown blankets from the nearest bed. The rough fibers scratched her burnt hands, but she ignored it as she tried again for the pot.

She wrapped the blanket around the shaking pot and managed to get ahold of it. She picked it up with both hands, but it fought against her, shaking and thrashing in her grasp. She almost dropped it a couple times but managed to hold on. She made it to the far side of the room and threw the small pot through the glass window.

Glass shattered as the window broke and the pot disappeared from sight, falling the four floors down to the ground.

"It still won't open!" Rain shouted as she pulled uselessly at the doorknob.

"Come on, get up on the bed," Ryan said as he extracted one leg, then the other, from the thick pull of the porridge. He grabbed Jenny by one arm and pulled her onto the bed with him, her legs sticking for a moment in the warm porridge before releasing. Sitting on the bed with Ryan, she tried to think through alternative options. She'd managed to get rid of the pot, but that hadn't worked, so ...

Then she saw it. The little pot was back on the dresser where she had taken it from, porridge continuing to flow out of it at a rapid pace. She turned and saw the window she'd thrown it out of was now unbroken. *Shit.*

"Rain, forget the door, come up here!" Ryan yelled at his sister who was now knee deep in porridge. "We need to think!"

Rain started laughing, but tears ran down her cheeks. "You know, this is almost funny. Porridge! Death by porridge!"

"Rain, you need to get it together!" Jenny yelled back at her. "Come on, move it!"

Rain's laughter died as she focused on Jenny. She slowly pulled herself through the porridge until she was within reach. Jenny grabbed her and pulled her up, with Ryan helping with his one hand.

Jenny eyed the book of fairy tales she had set down on the bed when they first walked in, and grabbed it. She flipped open the cover and started scanning the titles in the table of contents, praying something would pop out at her.

"What are you doing?" Ryan asked, leaning over her shoulder.

"Trying to find this story. Maybe there's something ..." Jenny stopped. "There! *The Sweet Porridge*!"

Jenny flipped through the book until she got to the story and let out a sigh of relief when she saw how short it was, barely one page long. She read it quickly and grinned.

"Little pot, stop!" she yelled, desperately hoping she was right.

She blinked, and it was over. The pot stopped moving, and the porridge stopped flowing. The chaos of the room settled, and the porridge grew cool. Jenny eyed the door—the door that opened inward.

"The porridge is blocking the door from opening," she said despondently. "We're going to have to ..."

"What? Eat our way out?" Ryan scoffed.

"No, just move the porridge out of the way. Here, let's move it into the closet."

The three worked on pushing porridge away from the door and into the closet. They threw handfuls of it onto the beds. They filled the bathtub and sink with it, then the bathroom itself. Finally they'd cleared enough away to open the door. They spilled into the hallway and slammed the door behind them.

Jenny looked down at her clothes, which were surprisingly dry and porridge-free. The burns on her hands were still there, but they weren't too bad.

"I guess the porridge stays in the room?" Rain said, examining her own clean clothes.

Jenny nodded and sunk down against the wall to sit on the floor. She was exhausted from pushing porridge around, and her arms and back ached. She just felt *so* tired.

"Okay, so what have we learned?" Ryan said, in a soft, playful way that reminded Jenny of what he used to be like. A small glimmer of his old self. Jenny watched him with hope.

Rain rolled her eyes. "Don't read things written on the little pots."

"Better not to read *anything*," Ryan said, his tone turning serious. "Or touch anything."

Rain nodded and avoided making eye contact with either of them.

"So," Ryan said, offering his hand to Jenny, still sitting on the floor. "Shall we see what's behind door number 409?"

37

Sadie made her way through the tunnel with one arm across her face. She *was not* going to get another face full of spiderwebs. They made it through quickly, and Sadie found herself in the same courtyard she'd been in before. There were walls on all sides that were still overgrown with weeds and rose vines. The tower waited for them across the courtyard, the small door she'd tried to go through before was set into the stonework of the tower.

"There," Sadie said as she pointed to the little door across the courtyard. "We need to get through that door somehow. Last time I just ended up back where I came from."

"What do you mean?" Aiden asked.

"Just, like, you know ... back *there*." Sadie pointed toward the tunnel they had just come through. Aiden looked at her quizzically, and Sadie was too tired to try and explain it. "Come on, I'll show you."

Sadie led Aiden and May across the courtyard toward the tower door. The overgrown weeds shooting up through the cracks in the stone floor slapped at her bare legs and made her skin itch. She made sure to avoid stepping on the thorny vines growing like hidden snakes among the long weeds. She stopped in front of the door. The two stone soldiers were still slouched on the ground on either side, asleep.

"Go ahead, try to go through it," Sadie directed Aiden, gesturing at the door. Aiden gave her a nervous look, then pushed it open.

"It's not even locked. I don't see what the—" Aiden broke off as he stepped across the threshold and looked back at them through the open door.

"See?" Sadie pointed at the sleeping dog statues on the ground. "Same statues. Same everything. It just brings you back to the beginning."

"Interesting," May mused quietly. "Someone really doesn't want anyone going inside this tower. In *Briar Rose*, the prince just has to cut through the vines to get through. Aiden, come back in here."

Aiden obeyed, stepping back through the door and into the courtyard. They let the door close behind him.

"This door is here for a reason," May said after a moment. "We just ... need to figure out how to open it the right way."

"The right way?" Aiden echoed, looking back at the door.

"Yeah. We're clearly not opening it right the way. Otherwise it would lead us inside." May pointed at the tower looming above them. "See the window? There's something up there."

Sadie squinted as she looked up at the small window May was pointing at. The tower was the only thing still intact within the ruins. It had a little window. The door didn't work the way doors normally do. *Something* was up there. Something important.

"But how?" Aiden asked. "How do we get the door to open the right way?"

The three of them stood there for a minute in silence, thinking. Sadie tried to remember what she knew about *Sleeping Beauty*. It was one of the more boring fairy tales. The princess was cursed because they didn't invite the mean fairy to her birthday party ... or something. She grows up in the woods with the good fairies, only to prick her finger on the spindle anyway and fall into a forever sleep until Prince Charming comes along and kisses her. Sadie couldn't remember there being a door he had to get through, though. She stole a glance at May, who seemed to be just as stumped as she was.

"A key," Aiden said slowly, looking furtively between the two girls. "The door has a keyhole." Aiden pointed at the door, which indeed had a keyhole. Sadie wondered how she hadn't noticed it before.

"Makes sense," May said, nodding slightly.

Sadie groaned. Now they were looking for a book *and* a key and had no idea where to look for either.

"We can go check the key cabinet behind Rumpelstiltskin's desk," May offered. "I don't know where else to look for a key. The cabinet seems too obvious, but ..."

"But what other options do we have?" Sadie finished for her. May shrugged in response.

"So, back to the castle?" Aiden asked.

Back to the castle.

38

Jenny, Ryan, and Rain moved in and out of the next few rooms without incident. The objects of each room became easy to spot and therefore easy to avoid. The problem was that they didn't feel especially confident as they crossed each room off the list. They looked in closets and under beds and felt around for any hidden compartments—but the reality of it was that they could easily be missing something. Jenny wondered if they were just distracting themselves with busywork. It might take them *years* to find the book, if they ever found it at all.

Jenny paused as they reached her old room. She'd just been inside it last night; she knew the book wasn't there. She thought of the voices she had heard when she was soaking in the tub and shivered despite the stuffy heat of the hallway.

"That's my old room," Jenny told them. "It's not in there."

Ryan nodded and slipped his hand into hers. Jenny was relieved he didn't insist on looking. She never wanted to go inside that room again. They passed by and stopped at the room next to Jenny's.

"Okay, here we go again." Rain sighed as she pushed the key into the lock.

They entered the room and looked around nervously. Though this was the sixth room they'd explored, they knew better than to let their guard down.

It was a simple room. There were bare floorboards under their feet and unpainted stone walls. They separated to search, but something felt off to Jenny. In the other rooms, the cursed objects were pretty obvious. One room actually had a live goose sitting on golden eggs. It was odd, of course, but it was almost a relief to immediately know where the object to avoid was. In this room, though ...

Jenny examined the dresser, the walls, the small closet. There was nothing out of the ordinary, no obvious magical object. Which meant the object could be anything. Jenny bit her lower lip nervously as she looked around the room.

"Nothing," Rain said as she stood up from looking underneath the beds.

"Nothing," Ryan echoed as he returned from searching the bathroom.

Something still didn't feel right. *Is it possible not all of the rooms have a fairy tale attached to them?*

Rain moved to leave when a loud ticking stopped her midstep. Jenny looked above the door to see a small clock she had somehow missed before. The minute and second hands were ticking forward abnormally quickly, making their way around the clock until they both stopped abruptly at the twelve.

"Yeah, that can't be good," Ryan said.

Rain moved quickly to the door and tried to open it. Jenny was not surprised when it didn't budge.

"And that's even worse," Ryan said as he grabbed his sister and pulled her away from the door and the clock above it. Jenny, too, moved away from the clock and to the other side of the room. They looked around feverishly, not knowing what was going to happen but knowing *something* would.

The room suddenly grew icy, and Jenny could see her breath create small clouds in the air. She rubbed at her bare arms as she looked frantically around the room. *Something is happening,* she thought, panic rising through her. Her eyes locked onto the stone wall on the right side of the bathroom door. Steam rose off it, and a little boy stepped out of it and into the room. Rain screamed and raised her hand to her chest. Jenny felt the blood drain from her face, but she didn't move.

The little boy's skin, hair, and clothes were white, as if the color had been completely drained from him. What looked like steam was wafting off his body in little wisps. He didn't look at them or move toward them, but instead walked over to a spot by the door and bent down. The boy began scratching at the floorboards with his hands, slowly at first, then faster. He appeared to grow more and more distressed as he clawed at the floor. She expected the disturbing sound of nails scraping against wood, but there was no sound at all. It was like the whole room had been muted.

Jenny looked over at Rain and Ryan and saw that they, too, were transfixed, watching the boy. Ryan must have felt her looking at him because he turned and met her eyes.

What do we do? Jenny mouthed, afraid to speak in case the sound drew the specter's attention, afraid to speak and find her voice was muted too.

Ryan shook his head helplessly.

The quiet of the room was broken as the frozen clock came back to life. The hands ticked forward past the twelve. The ghost disappeared.

Jenny rushed over to the door and tried to open it—but once again it wouldn't move.

"Why is this happening!" she yelled, giving the stubborn door a kick. She had just started to feel like she was getting the hang of the castle, that she knew what the rules were. Now it felt like she'd been tricked. She knew nothing.

"Calm down," Ryan soothed, running his hand slowly up and down Jenny's back. "We'll figure this out. I promise."

Jenny tried to force a smile, but it felt strained.

A *tick, tick, tick* above her interrupted her thoughts. The clock's hands were moving again, just as they had a minute ago.

They ticked quickly around the face until they stopped again at the twelve. Jenny looked over at the wall the ghost boy had come through and held her breath.

Again, the boy drifted into the room, ignored them, and scratched at the floorboards in the same spot he had before. Jenny realized they were now stuck in some bizarre loop. Something would have to be changed if they were ever going to be allowed to leave. But what?

"Hey," Jenny forced out, relieved to find that she hadn't been muted. "What are you doing?"

The boy did not respond or look up at her. He just pounded his small hands against the floor in frustration and vanished again when the clock ticked forward.

Jenny stared down at the part of the floor the boy had been clawing at. She glanced at Ryan, who appeared to be thinking the same thing. He walked over to the spot and crouched down to examine it. He knocked, first on the place the boy had been scratching at and then all around it. Jenny noticed the change in tone when Ryan knocked over the area of the floor the boy had been obsessed with. *Hollow.*

"Rain, toss me that key, would you?" Ryan asked, gesturing at his sister.

Rain tossed it to him, badly, and it landed with a harsh clatter onto the floor next to him.

Ryan picked up the key, jammed it into the space between two floorboards, and leaned his weight on it slightly. One of the boards popped up, revealing a small compartment. Jenny moved closer to peer inside. "What's in there?"

Ryan reached inside the hole and pulled out three little tarnished copper coins.

"Pennies, I think," he said.

Tick, tick, tick. The clock's hands were moving again.

"Watch out," Rain gasped. "Get away from there before he comes!"

Ryan and Jenny moved away from the hole in the floor and stood between the beds, their eyes glued to the solid wall they knew the ghost would soon step out of. The clock's hands stopped on twelve, and once again a chill hit the room. Jenny shivered and wrapped her arms around herself. The boy stepped out of the wall again and floated over to the hole they had made in the floor. Jenny watched anxiously, uncertain how the ghost would react to what they had done. The boy didn't bend down this time, didn't scratch at the floorboards or disappear. He slowly turned to face them.

Jenny's blood turned to ice in her veins. The boy's face wasn't grotesque. It was just very pale. His wide, sad eyes moved away from her and landed on Ryan's closed hand.

"Ryan," she hissed, "the pennies! Give him the pennies!"

Ryan looked down at his closed fist as if he had forgotten he was holding the coins. He opened his hand and offered them to the ghost. The ghost boy drifted closer to Ryan, the frigid fog blowing off his body and chilling the air around them even more. He looked at the pennies in Ryan's hand and smiled softly. Not a smile of joy, but of relief, maybe.

Jenny watched, captivated, as the boy's form became more and more translucent until all that was left was a few wisps of mist.

39

After trudging as quickly as she could back to the castle, Sadie was becoming increasingly impatient and frustrated with every dead end they came up against. The most recent of which was a completely empty key case.

"The others must have taken the keys to search the rooms," Aiden groaned. He peeked around the tall podium desk and started pulling out drawers. "Maybe there's something in here."

There wasn't, of course. Nothing except the painting of the Grimm brothers she and Jenny had shoved underneath it. If Aiden noticed it, he didn't say anything. Sadie thought of the frightening little man that had spouted riddles at her from behind the desk and wondered if they would ever see Rumpelstiltskin again.

"Well, now what?" Aiden asked as he leaned forward, his elbows propped on the desk and his head resting on his hands.

"I think they were going to search the library. Let's check there first," Sadie replied with a sigh. "Maybe they have the keys."

The library was eerily the same as the last time Sadie had been inside. There were the floor-to-ceiling bookshelves on either side of the room, the same ghosts in the same places, the large stained-glass window in the far back. The only difference, she noted, were their friends pulling books off the shelves and throwing them onto the ground.

"Uh, whatcha doing?" Aiden asked as a thick book fell with a loud *thwack* at his feet.

Hannah whirled around with an odd look on her face. She was flushed, and her eyes were red rimmed and shining.

"Sadie!" Hannah pulled her into an uncomfortable hug. Sadie grimaced; they'd parted just an hour ago. Hannah pulled away just as quickly and looked at Sadie seriously.

"Sadie, we found ... we found ..." Hannah's green eyes grew dark and wet, and Sadie was worried she would start crying.

"We found Charlotte," Cameron finished for her, his voice soft and somber. His eyes diverted to the ground.

Icy tingles ran through Sadie, and her skin broke out into goose bumps.

"What ... what do you *mean* you found Charlotte?" Sadie gasped. "You mean her ... her corpse?"

"No, not her corpse," Cameron replied as he pointed across the room. Sadie followed to where he was pointing and saw her, facing a bookshelf on the other side of the library. Her eye-catching white-blonde bob was perfectly styled, her curvy figure enhanced with one of her trademark red dresses.

Sadie realized that Jenny was the only one who had seen Charlotte's dead body inside the wall. She felt an unexpected jolt of excitement—*maybe Jenny had been wrong*. Her thoughts tumbled around inside her head as she stared at Charlotte on the other side of the room. She couldn't wait to tell Jenny that Charlotte was okay after all. She imagined Jenny's face, so dark and downturned lately, brightening at the news.

"Sadie, wait—"

Sadie moved past Cameron and waved away his words. She walked quickly past tables and chairs until she reached Charlotte, who was reaching for one of the books on the shelf. She chose one and looked down at it, then put it back and reached for another.

"Charlotte?" Sadie ventured carefully. Something didn't feel right.

Charlotte ignored Sadie and continued to remove and

replace books. She felt Cameron at her side.

"I tried to warn you," he whispered. "She's … a *ghost*."

"No, no that's not right. She's right here," Sadie murmured, shaking her head. She reached out and touched Charlotte's arm. "She's solid."

"I don't understand it either. But we tried to get through to her and … nothing. No response. She just keeps doing that," he gestured at Charlotte, who was removing yet another book from the shelf.

"She's like the rest of them now," Travis said, coming up behind Cameron. There was no smile in his eyes, no quick joke. He looked pallid and lost.

Jenny.

"Does Jenny know about this?" Sadie asked, looking around the room for Jenny's head of brown curls.

"No. We haven't seen her since we split up," Travis replied distractedly, his eyes glued to Charlotte. "It's so strange seeing her this way. I keep expecting her to turn and make fun of me or something."

Aiden and May stood silently, watching Charlotte's mechanical motions. Sadie made eye contact with May, hoping for some genius solution, but May just shook her head. *So that's it, then.*

"We can't let Jenny see this," Sadie told the others firmly. "It'll kill her. She's already been through so much."

"We just have to keep her from coming into the library. Shouldn't be too difficult," Aiden agreed.

The group nodded slowly in unison.

"Well," Sadie started again, turning her back on the ghost of Charlotte. She tried to ignore the presence behind her and focus on anything else. "I'm guessing you haven't found the book yet?"

"Nope," Travis said, shaking his large head.

"Do you have any of the keys?" May asked.

"The room keys?" Cameron replied, "No, Ryan took them all. They're searching the rooms while we search here."

"Great," Sadie groaned. "Where did they start?"

"Top floor, but that was a while ago," replied Cameron. "I have no idea where they are now."

"*Super* great."

"Well, good luck in here," Aiden said, moving toward the door. "We have to go find those keys."

Sadie followed, and May hesitated a moment before catching up with them. They headed slowly to the stairs. It seemed like May and Aiden didn't want to go up there either.

A ragged cough drew her attention away from the stairs and to the front desk. Rumpelstiltskin sat motionless on the tall stool behind the desk, as if he had never left. Sadie had forgotten just how disturbing the man was. He had a liver-spotted bald head and saggy skin. His white orb eyes were staring ahead of him at nothing-or worse, *something*. He opened his mouth and another riddle came out.

"*What you wish is to be free,*
For that you'll need a special key.
Lucky for you, I know where,
Look around the final stair."

"Is he actually trying to ... help us?" Sadie muttered to Aiden and May.

"He's been trying to help us the whole time, actually," May said, sounding surprised herself. "All the riddles were warnings. We just didn't listen to them."

"Right." Sadie thought about the riddle he had given her about Hannah—it *had* actually helped to save her, hadn't it? Without it, she never would have brought Jenny with her, and she herself would be trapped below with Hannah, dancing with monsters until death.

Sadie wearily made her way over to Rumpelstiltskin, and the others followed close behind.

"Isn't there more you can tell us?" Sadie asked as nicely as she could under the circumstances. "Like where the book is?"

"The path you're on is true not tried,
You're the first who hasn't died!"

"Well that's comforting," Aiden mumbled behind her.

Sadie remembered that the last time they had spoken to Rumpelstiltskin, they were only allowed to ask yes or no questions. She thought for a moment then asked, "Is the book in the tower?"

Rumpelstiltskin grinned his grotesque broken-toothed smile.

"What you wish is to be free,
For that you'll need a special key—"

"Yeah, yeah," Sadie interrupted. "We heard you the first time."

"Wait," May said, throwing Sadie an annoyed look. "Please, sir, tell us the riddle again."

The old man made a rattling sigh sound, then repeated the poem again:

"What you wish is to be free,
For that you'll need a special key.
Lucky for you, I know where,
Look around the final stair."

"Final stair? You mean the top stair?" Sadie asked, hoping he was being literal and not using some stupid symbolism she didn't understand.

He grinned once more, reached to his head with both hands, and tore himself in half.

40

"I really didn't like that one," Rain said once they were outside of the room. "That little boy ..." Rain shook her head sadly.

Jenny knew what she meant. She tried to tell herself he wasn't real, that it was just a story, but she didn't know what was real or not anymore.

"Do we need a break before the next room?" Ryan said, eyeing the two girls.

"No, no, let's keep going," Rain said. "I want to get this over with."

They continued to the next room, then the next, until they were finished with the fourth floor, then they headed down to the third.

"We can skip a couple of these rooms," said Ryan, "Mine and the one Travis and Cameron were in. Right?"

Jenny nodded. Two rooms they wouldn't have to search made the long hallway feel slightly less overwhelming. They started with the first door they came to, and when they entered, they were transfixed by a large painting hanging over the single bed. It was a gorgeously painted picture of a wild boar, its tusks large and gleaming. Each coarse hair had been carefully painted onto its dark skin. Jenny felt a strong urge to run her fingers along the brush strokes but shook it off and reminded Ryan and Rain not to touch it. They nodded, still a little mesmerized by the beautiful boar. They managed to pull themselves away and began searching the room for the book. As they searched, Jenny thought she heard a voice singing very far away. She stopped pawing through a dresser drawer to listen. It was a little voice singing faintly, but she could just make out the words:

"I sing my song of woe,
For my brothers murdered me long ago!
They buried my body and carried off the wild boar
And stole the king's sole daughter."

"Oh, great," Jenny groaned. "Just what we need."

"What?" Ryan asked from a few feet away.

"Do you hear it? The singing?"

Ryan and Rain stood still, listening. The song repeated and their eyes widened.

"The king's sole daughter, huh?" Rain said, rolling her eyes.

"It doesn't even rhyme," Ryan said. "Where is it coming from?" Ryan walked slowly around the room, tilting his head slightly to listen better.

"I don't know. It doesn't matter," Jenny replied, frowning. "Just try to ignore it and finish the search."

They went back to looking through the room for the book when Rain let out a high shriek and scooted away from the bed she had just been looking under.

"Ew, ew, ew!" she cried from the floor.

"What?" Ryan asked, walking the few feet over to his sister and resting his hand on her shoulder.

"I found where the singing is coming from! There's a little bone underneath the bed. A finger bone, maybe? It's ... *singing*." Rain looked even paler than usual.

Ryan dropped down to the floor and peered underneath the bed.

"Don't touch it!" Jenny called.

"I know, I know, this ain't my first creepy fairy-tale thing," Ryan grumbled back at her from the floor. With a little difficulty, he pushed himself back up with one hand. "Yup, there's a singing bone down there."

"I'm out," Rain said, making her way toward the door.

"The book isn't here, anyway," Jenny said, following Rain out the door.

The next few rooms were simple. Some of the items were even a little comical, though Jenny knew not to underestimate them. The pot of porridge taught them that much.

When they entered the next room, Jenny noticed immediately that it was different from the others. This one had *things* in it. *Normal* things. A suitcase, some shoes on the floor, and a basic little makeup kit on the vanity desk. "Someone is staying in this room," Rain said softly, looking around as if she felt awkward for imposing.

"Or they *were* staying here," Ryan said darkly.

Jenny picked up a thick notebook she found lying on the bed and opened it. The first page had all their names written on it, with their room numbers next to each name. Jenny recognized the handwriting.

"This is Mrs. Braun's room," Jenny whispered. She set the notebook down on the bed and opened the closet. There she saw Mrs. Braun's clothes all hung up, with a few garments on the floor in a small pile. Jenny noticed a familiar dark blue jumpsuit with bright yellow canaries printed on it, the one Charlotte had liked so much. "These are her clothes."

"So she didn't really leave, like Eckert said," Rain frowned at the clothes hanging in the closet.

"We never really believed her." Jenny sighed. This was true, and when they had questioned Rumpelstiltskin on whether Mrs. Braun had really left, he had replied *no*. Still, seeing her teacher's abandoned things like this made it real. Tears began to form in the corners of her eyes. She remembered Mrs. Braun's warm, sweaty hug when Jenny was too afraid to cross the hanging bridge. They hadn't even tried to look for her. Guilt seeped into Jenny, and she began to feel hot and sick.

"Can ... can you guys search this one without me? I need some air."

"Sure, of course," Rain replied as Jenny left the room.

Jenny had intended to just wait outside the room for them but felt herself moving farther away, down the hallway and toward the stairs. The air inside the castle felt hot and thick, and she was filled with a need to get outside. As she reached the landing, she felt a cool breeze on the back of her neck, and a soft voice whispered in her ear, "Finally, we're alone."

Jenny whirled around to see Bannan standing behind her.

"What is it with you and sneaking up behind me all the time?" she yelled, annoyed.

"Sorry, I didn't mean to startle you."

"You didn't startle me. It's just annoying!"

Bannan dipped his head and looked down at the ratty carpet. "I'm sorry. I've just been waiting a long time to catch you alone. We need to talk."

Jenny shook her head. "No, we don't. Unless you're going to tell me where the book is, there's nothing you have to say that I want to hear."

"Jenny, please," Bannan said, grabbing her arm. She wrenched it out of his grasp.

"You're never going to find the book," he said gently. "You can look all you want—no one has ever found it. I've searched for it for *centuries*. Wherever it is, it's out of reach."

Jenny shook her head. She couldn't let herself think that way. Finding the book was the only way they would get out of this nightmare. She would search for the rest of her life if she had to.

"Jenny, please. Consider for a moment an alternative. You can keep searching for the book, of course, but why not search with *me*? I'm sure I could be of more help than those two ... people."

"You said yourself you've been looking for centuries and never found it. I think I have a better shot finding it with them."

Bannan nodded. "Would it be so bad," he started again,

gazing into her eyes with his own turbulent gray ones, "living here, with me?"

Jenny froze. *What is he saying?*

"I could make you happy," he continued, pleading. "It's not so bad here, if you avoid the fairy tales. You could have a life here, with me."

Jenny thought about the *life here* Eckert had had. She managed to grow up here and learn the castle's rules. She'd still be alive if she hadn't gone after the gingerbread witch. For a moment, Jenny let herself imagine what life at the castle would be like. She'd never have to decide what to do after high school, would never have to work a boring job, could spend hours in the garden or reading in the library. She could learn to cook from Sophie, could maybe even find some way to bring Charlotte back.

Jenny remembered Eckert's room. The drawer of knives, the pages and pages of the same fairy tale. Would Jenny end up like Eckert? Obsessed with finding a way to bring someone back who was gone forever?

"No," she said aloud. "We're going to find that book, and we're going to get out of here. Don't try to stop us."

She pushed past Bannan and made her way down, not sure where she was going. She stopped at the bottom of the stairs and looked back to see if Bannan was following her, but he was gone.

She didn't understand Bannan—one minute he was trying to help them escape and the next he's asking her to give up and stay at the castle with him. If they never found the book, she'd be trapped here with him forever. Forever was a long time, and she realized it might be better to have him on her side. *I should be playing along.*

She thought of the old idiom *keep your friends close and your enemies closer.*

She just wasn't sure which one he was.

41

May screamed and fell backward, into Aiden. Sadie remained still, staring in horror at the place the little man had just torn himself apart. There was nothing there now. Just empty air. But for a second, she had seen the insides of the man. She had seen his skin split apart as the halves of his body fell away from each other. She clenched her teeth together, forcing back the urge to vomit.

"Was that really necessary!" Aiden yelled, holding May up. "He could have just left!"

Sadie didn't know what to say. She looked at the bottom of the staircase and tried to focus on that instead of the gruesome image of Rumpelstiltskin's ... what ... suicide? Was he even really dead or just hiding again? Sadie tried to shake the gruesome image of his split body out of her head.

"Come on," she said, starting toward the staircase. "Let's find that key and get out of here."

Sadie didn't see Jenny—or anyone—as they made their way up the stairs to the fourth floor. She ignored the various portraits decorating the wall as they ascended and tried not to trip in the dim light. Rumpelstiltskin had told them that they would find the key at the final stair, which they assumed must mean the very top stair. As they got closer, she saw the blank wall ahead of them and couldn't help but stare at it, knowing Charlotte's body was on the other side.

"Is that where ..." Aiden trailed off, unable to finish the question.

"Don't touch the wall," Sadie said harshly. "Don't even look at it."

She turned away from it herself and began searching the small area for a key, but saw nothing. She swore under her breath.

"Maybe he meant the first stair," Aiden offered.

Sadie glanced over at May, who was staring at a large portrait hanging on the wall next to them. She recognized the man in the portrait immediately—it was Bannan, standing in a forest, one foot up on top of a tree stump and the other on the ground.

"That guy gives me the creeps," Aiden said.

"You're not the only one," Sadie agreed.

"Look," May said, pointing at Bannan's hip. Sadie leaned closer and squinted. It was hard to make out in the dimly lit hallway, but she saw what May had noticed. A key ring.

"Okay, but ... those aren't real keys. How are we supposed to use them?" Sadie said, frowning at the painting. She felt like there was something she was missing. *Is the whole painting the key? Can we cut the keys out of the painting somehow? None of this makes sense.* It was a real, literal keyhole in the tower door. It needed a real key.

May slowly reached her hand toward the painting, and Sadie saw her palm and fingers were covered in puss-filled yellow blisters. She reached out and grabbed May by the wrist.

"What happened to your hand?"

May yanked her arm away and pulled her sleeve back over it. "Nothing, just a fairy-tale thing," she muttered.

Sadie knew this must have something to do with what had really happened after they'd been separated in the woods. She considered pressing May again, but she forced herself to keep her mouth shut. Now wasn't the time.

Sadie shook her head in frustration and stared back at the painting of Bannan. She reached out and grabbed at the key ring in the painting hard, not caring if she damaged it.

She felt heavy, cool metal fall into her hand. She stared, stunned, at the very real key ring now resting in her hand. She looked back at the painting and saw it was no longer in the portrait.

"I ... it worked," she mumbled.

"Amazing," Aiden said, wonderstruck, and poked one of the dangling keys with his finger. Then his face fell, and he groaned. "There are like twenty keys on that ring."

He was right. The key ring had at least twenty keys, all in different shapes and sizes and colors. Some were gray, others were black, and few, gold. At first glance, none of them stood out as being *the key* they needed.

"We'll just try them all," Sadie replied with a shrug. "Let's go."

They made their way back down the stairs and paused in the lobby.

"Should we tell the others?" Aiden asked, peering down the hallway toward the library.

Sadie hesitated. "No. I'm not sure this is going to work, or if the book is even really up there. They need to keep looking in case the book isn't in the tower. I don't want to get their hopes up just to disappoint them."

Aiden nodded, and May was already halfway to the door.

They left the castle and made their way back through the ruins, past the broken gate and sleeping statues. Sadie was getting really tired of walking back and forth between the castle and tower. It was hot in the ruins, too, with no cover. She could feel her scalp starting to burn.

She eyed May, who was drifting along a few steps behind her and Aiden, and thought about her burnt hand. She knew none of the fairy tales she'd been in with May had caused the burn, so it must have been a fairy tale they'd experienced after splitting up in the woods. Sadie tried to figure out why Jenny,

May, and Ryan would lie to everyone about it. She shook her head, unable to come up with any theories as to why they didn't want them to know. The mystery was killing her, and she didn't have much to go on. She glanced at Aiden beside her. She knew he wouldn't want her asking May again, but she couldn't stand it. She had to know.

She stopped in the middle of the trail and turned to face May. She'd tried to be delicate, and that hadn't worked. Time to try something else.

"What happened in the woods?" Sadie asked, staring intently at May.

Aiden glared at her and stepped between her and May. "Sadie, don't—"

"It's okay, Aiden." May sighed. "You both deserve to know what happened. It's going to come out eventually, anyway."

Aiden raised his hands up in defeat and moved out of the way. He picked a nearby peach-pink rose and started slowly plucking the petals off, letting them float slowly to the ground. Sadie turned away and focused back on May.

"Go on," she urged.

"I don't regret what I did," she continued, raising her eyes to meet Sadie's. "I would do it again."

Sadie didn't know what to make of that, or how to respond. She didn't say anything, hoping May would just keep going. She did.

"It's a long story, so I'll just sum it up: we were given a wish and I stole it."

Sadie looked at May, confused. A burnt hand, Ryan and Jenny acting strangely. Neither of these things were explained by a stolen wish.

"What do you mean, you stole a wish?" Sadie asked. "What wish?"

"Mother Holle gave us one wish—and I took it. I wished ..." May looked down and fiddled with the bracelets on her wrist. Sadie held her breath, waiting for the answer to all her May questions.

"We don't have time for this," Aiden said, dropping the now-petalless stem to the ground. "Let's just go to the tower and get this book and get out of here. We can talk about this later."

Sadie looked at Aiden, stunned. He had once again blocked May from telling her the truth. He met Sadie's eyes and slowly shook his head *no*. His eyes pleaded with her to drop it. She wondered why he was so averse to hearing what May had to say. What did *he* know?

May looked up, confused. "But, don't you want to—"

"Later, May," Aiden told her softly.

May's mouth opened slightly in surprise, her eyes wide and wet with fresh tears. Sadie glared at Aiden and May and shook her head in annoyance.

"Fine," Sadie said through clenched teeth. "Let's go then."

She hurried them through the rest of the ruins, tunnel, and courtyard in complete silence. She fought the urge to throw the key ring at them and storm out of there. Instead, she swallowed down the frustration and tried to focus on the task at hand. He was right, they could talk about it later. They approached the door to the tower, and Sadie turned to face May and Aiden.

"Well, who wants to do the honors?" Sadie asked, holding the key ring out. Neither Aiden nor May said anything. She rolled her eyes. "Okay, guess it's me."

Sadie pulled apart the ring so she could slip the keys off, then started with a large iron key. Didn't fit. She threw it on the ground and tried the next one—a silver key with wavy teeth. No go. She threw it on the ground with the first one. She went through key after key, tossing the spent ones on the ground until she reached the last key. If this key didn't work, they'd have to go back to square one.

She pulled the key off the ring and looked at it. It was a

dingy gold color with three jagged teeth. *You better work*, she thought fiercely as she jammed it into the lock.

Click.

The door eased open, and instead of being taken back to the ruins they'd come from, she saw a small room, bare except for a few lit candles in holders on the wall. A black wrought-iron staircase spiraled upward in front of them. Aiden grabbed both handrails and gave them a hard shake. The staircase didn't move.

"Seems sturdy enough," Aiden said, apparently satisfied with the results of his shake test. Sadie tried not to roll her eyes at him and started up the stairs. She heard May make some sort of objection but ignored her, and a few seconds later, she heard May and Aiden following her.

Sadie led the way up the tower, step by miserable step. It was stifling hot inside the tower, with no windows and barely any light to see by. All she heard from May and Aiden behind her was their ragged breathing.

For the hundredth time, Sadie went over what May had said as she forced herself up the staircase. *She stole a wish.* Sadie set aside the question about how they got the wish and considered what May could have used it for. They were all clearly still here, nothing had changed for them. So it was something else. Something not in the Black Forest, or the castle, or Germany. It was something back home. Something more important than getting them out of this nightmare. Sadie didn't want to try and imagine what that might be, but she was sure it was a nightmare of its own. She was starting to feel like maybe it was none of her business.

Sadie's lungs burned, and her calves felt painfully tight as she continued up the spiral staircase. She looked up and groaned when she realized they were only about halfway up. She pushed herself to keep going until she finally took the last step and found herself in front of another door.

"Not another door!" Aiden groaned from behind her. "We left the rest of the keys outside!"

Aiden looked horrified, and Sadie quickly realized what he meant. This door might also require a key—a key that was lying in the dirt a million steps down. The thought of having to go back down and back up again made her feel like crying.

"Look," May said softly, gesturing at the door. "No keyhole."

Sadie looked at the bare wooden door and felt a mix of relief and fear. *What if we can't get in? This would all be for nothing. Or worse, what if we can?* She had no idea what could be on the other side of that door.

Sadie took a deep breath, placed her hand on the door, and pushed.

42

Jenny was halfway across the lobby and almost to the castle door when she heard someone coming down the stairs behind her. She prayed it wasn't Bannan and was relieved to see Ryan and Rain standing in front of her.

"I didn't know what happened to you," Ryan said as he pulled her into his arms. Just as quickly, he pulled away and stared at her seriously. "You can't just wander off like that by yourself, not here."

"I know. I'm sorry," she said, looking into Ryan's eyes. For a moment, it felt like they were back to normal, that nothing had happened and that they were the same Jenny and Ryan they'd always been.

"Look what we found in Mrs. Braun's room!" Rain said, smiling excitedly. She held out a small stack of dark blue passports. *Their* passports.

"Well, that's something, at least!" Jenny said. She felt bolstered for a brief moment before remembering the passports were useless if they couldn't leave the forest.

"What do you think happened to Mrs. Braun?" she asked them.

Ryan and Rain shook their heads simultaneously. "We've been gone," Ryan reminded her, though that was something she'd never need reminding of. "I have no idea what could have happened to her. But at least we know she's not in any of the rooms we've searched."

Jenny considered what she knew about Mrs. Braun's

disappearance. Jenny knew that Eckert had lied to them when she told them Mrs. Braun had left. Rumpelstiltskin had said she hadn't left. Which meant she must still be in the castle—or dead. Jenny hated herself for not asking Eckert about Mrs. Braun when she had found her at the gingerbread house. There had been so much happening, she just hadn't been thinking about her teacher.

"All we know, or at least I think we know, is that Eckert did something to get rid of Mrs. Braun. Ryan, did Eckert say anything to you about her?"

Ryan thought for a moment but shook his head. "We didn't talk much," he said darkly.

"We should search Eckert's room again," Jenny said. "You guys weren't there last time, and we know a lot more now about ... everything. Maybe we missed something last time."

"We should look for the book there too," Rain offered. "Which one is her room?"

"This way," Jenny said, leading them to the end of the hall where the door to Eckert's room was resting at an angle on the doorframe. Bits of wood were scattered on the floor from when Cameron had kicked it in. Ryan took a step forward to pull the door away, but remembering the embarrassment from that morning at breakfast, Jenny quickly stepped in front of him.

"It's okay, I can get it," she said, reaching for the door.

"I can do it, Jenny!" Ryan snapped. "I'm not completely useless."

Jenny retreated a step, stunned at his sudden outburst. He grabbed the door by the handle and threw it to the side with his one hand, the muscles in his arm bulging with effort. He walked into the room without looking back at them. Rain gave her an apologetic look and followed her brother inside.

Jenny shook her head and felt stupid for thinking things would ever go back to the way they were. Too much had changed.

Inside Eckert's room, it looked like a wild animal had been let loose. The blankets on the bed had been ripped apart by Marble's claws, and clothes, papers, and books littered the floor. They hadn't bothered to put anything back together the last time they'd searched her room.

"Wow," Rain said, looking around. "You guys really did a number on this place."

They searched through Eckert's things in silence. Jenny began undoing the damage and examining items as she put them back where they belonged. She filled the dresser back up with clothes, put the papers back into a pile on the desk. She saw the little red flower with the pearl in the center. The flower that she had hoped would transform Rain back into a human—except it turned out they didn't need it. She turned to look at Rain, who was sitting on the floor and examining each book before placing it back in the bookshelf. Her long golden hair flowed down her back, and for a moment, Jenny saw the deer she had been. She blinked, and Rain returned to human form.

After his outburst, she tried to avoid Ryan while they searched the room. There was an angry electricity all around him, and she didn't want to get too close. She tried to ignore what he was doing and sat down on the floor with Rain to help her with the books.

"These are all in German," Rain said. She lifted a heavy-looking book with a black cover and gold writing on the front. "For all I know, this could be titled *The Magic Book That Will Solve All Your Problems*, and I wouldn't know it." She slid it on the bottom shelf next to the last one she'd placed there. She looked at Jenny seriously. "We're never going to find this book, are we?" she asked softly.

Jenny didn't answer. She was exhausted from fighting fairy tales all morning and was still reeling a little from Ryan's outburst. The many books scattered all around them just made her feel more tired and overwhelmed.

"We'll have May come and take a look when they get back," Jenny said. "But I'm pretty sure none of them have that title."

Jenny heard a loud crash and turned to see Ryan pulling out the drawers of the desk all the way and tossing them onto the floor. Jenny remembered that when she had searched the desk, most of the drawers had been empty. She'd been careful to put everything back, including the knives they didn't take, but now Ryan was making a complete mess of the desk. She heard a crack as the next drawer he threw broke into pieces. He pulled out the drawer with the knives and set that one down more gently, then continued to tear apart the desk. She and Rain watched quietly as he grew frustrated with the desk's lack of contents and kicked the whole thing over onto its back. Jenny flinched at the loud *bang* it made as it fell, and the floor vibrated slightly underneath her. The vase with the flower rolled over the floor, miraculously still in one piece, while the pile of papers scattered all over the room. She stole a glance at Rain, who looked terrified. Jenny bet she'd never seen her brother act this way before. Jenny certainly hadn't.

Ryan must have felt them watching because he turned his attention from the desk to them, and for the first time, she felt afraid of him. His expression softened as he looked at the girls sitting on the floor surrounded by books.

"Sorry," he said, looking down at the desk as if he had just noticed it for the first time. "I'm just ..."

"It's okay," Jenny said hurriedly, standing up. "We're all stressed out right now. Let's just take a moment."

Jenny didn't know what she meant by "take a moment." It just seemed like the thing to say. She glanced around the half-cleaned-up, half-destroyed room. They hadn't found the book or anything that told them where Mrs. Braun might be.

"The book's not here," Ryan said, stepping over one of the drawers he'd thrown on the ground. He walked past Jenny and toward the open space where the door used to be. "Since we're down here, let's go check in with the others," he said, turning away. "Maybe they've had better luck."

Jenny watched as he walked out of the room and disappeared around the corner.

She let out a breath and looked over at Rain next to her on the floor. She looked back at Jenny and attempted a wobbly smile.

"He's never going to be the way he was before, is he?" Rain asked, her hands trembling slightly in her lap.

Jenny stared at the empty doorway and didn't reply.

43

The door opened. Sadie paused in the doorway and peered into the small room at the top of the tower. The room was circular with just a single little window set into one of the walls. In the center of the room was a large, striking statue of a woman in bed crafted from smooth black obsidian. She was carved to look like she was sleeping on her back in an elaborate nightgown that almost looked real. Her eyelids were closed, and her arms were wrapped around a large book with a gold cover. The book reminded her a little of a set of ancient encyclopedias her dad kept in their living room but that no one ever used. It was covered in a worn gold fabric, and there was no writing on the cover.

"That has to be it, right?" Aiden said excitedly as he rushed over to the statue.

"Aiden, wait! Don't touch anything!" May shrieked.

Aiden froze and looked down at the book sheepishly. "Well, what do we do?"

Sadie walked the few steps to the stone bed and looked down at the sleeping woman. Sadie tried to calm the excitement rushing through her as she looked down at the large, ornate book clutched in the statue's arms. *It could still not be the book*, she told herself. *Don't count your chickens.* She smiled weakly at the familiar phrase her mother used all the time.

"Well? What do you think?" She said, turning to May. May bit her lower lip as her gaze jumped around the room.

"I ... I just don't know. It has to be the book, right?"

"Right!" Aiden answered. "Right?"

"Well, only one way to find out," Sadie said as she reached forward and wrapped her hands around the bottom of the book to pull it out from the stone woman's embrace.

"I must admit, I'm impressed!" an annoyingly familiar voice said, making Sadie jump and withdraw her hands from the book. She turned to see Bannan standing in the doorway, an odd grin on his face. "You're the only ones to ever make it this far!"

"What? What do you mean?" Sadie asked, and even as the words left her lips, a cold knowing began to fill her stomach. *Oh, no.*

"I can't let you actually *get* the book, of course," Bannan continued conversationally, ignoring Sadie completely. He walked casually over to where the three of them stood next to the sleeping statue, causing them to break away to keep space between themselves and him. May and Sadie were on one side of him, Aiden on the other.

"Who are you really?" May asked softly, her eyes darting to the door behind them, then to the sole window.

"I'm Bluebeard! The robber bridegroom! The big bad wolf!" He laughed, and Sadie started to feel ill. "I didn't lie completely. Bluebeard *is* my story. They are *all* my stories."

Sadie's mind raced as she started to put it all together. *They are all his stories.* He wasn't a fairy-tale character, he was the *creator.*

"That story you told us, about Jacob Grimm. *That* was your story. Your *real* story," Sadie said slowly, her eyes on May, who was still eyeing the door.

"Ah, mostly. I may have left some things out," Jacob replied nonchalantly as he stared at May and Sadie, an irritating smile playing on his lips. Sadie shook her head angrily. She'd always known there was something wrong with Bannan, but she had gone along with what he had told them because there was no other choice. But she had assumed he was just a fairy-tale villain. This was so much worse.

"So, *Jacob*, what happens now?" May asked. "How does this story end?"

Jacob smiled and took a step closer to them. Sadie tried not to flinch or back away. She stared back into his cold gray-blue eyes, unwilling to show weakness. He smiled, and she clenched her teeth in response.

"Why? Why did you tell us about this book if you knew where it was all along? If it was just a trick?" Sadie asked, her voice shaking with rage.

"Well, you stopped playing my other games," he said with a shrug. "I had to come up with a new one."

"*Games*?" Sadie yelled, losing control. "All of this has just been a *game* to you?"

He grinned, and something inside Sadie snapped. Every time she'd ever been scared or vulnerable flooded her mind, and she struggled to push through the bad memories. She thought about that man who had stolen her bag and put her in the hospital. He'd never been identified or found. He had just *gotten away with it*. A hot rage she had worked so hard to control filled her body and blinded her to rationality.

Sadie's whole body trembled, and her hands balled into tight fists at her sides. Adrenaline rushed through her, giving her a new strength she'd never felt before. Jacob was taller and stronger than she was and had unknown magical abilities. Part of her knew she was no match for him, that she was no threat.

Sadie told that part of her to shut up, and she lunged forward without thinking. She rammed into Jacob, whose look of shock gave Sadie a moment of joy. They fell to the ground together, Sadie on top of Jacob. Then she started swinging.

She'd never punched anyone in the face before, and she wasn't positive she was doing it right, but it sure *felt* right. She ignored the pain in her knuckles as she made contact with his cheekbone, his chin. She got two good hits in before he disappeared from underneath her.

Sadie fell the rest of the way to the ground with a soft thud, and she was breathing in long, harsh, ragged breaths. She looked up at Aiden and May, who were standing, dumbfounded, above her, their mouths agape and eyes wide.

"What are you doing? Grab the book!" Sadie screamed. She stood and pushed her still-stunned friends back toward the sleeping stone woman and the book. She reached for it, but it was stuck firmly in the statue's rigid arms.

Sadie screamed in frustration and tried to rip the book out with her fingernails. She felt one of her nails snap, and she pulled her hand back. She'd broken one of her nails just below the flesh. She brought it to her mouth and chewed off the hanging piece of nail and spat it onto the ground. She stared down at the wretched woman statue and the trapped book and tried to collect herself. She looked around the small room at the other objects. A large wooden spinning wheel sat in the corner covered in dust, a small chair beside it. A small stone object was on the floor next to it. Sadie squinted to see what it was and moved toward it, realizing as she approached that it was a small stone cat. It was curled into a sleeping position, its eyes closed and head resting on its paws. Sadie felt a little guilty as she picked the heavy stone cat off the floor.

"What are you doing with that?" Aiden said, watching her nervously.

"I'm going to smash it against the woman's arms and see if I can't break them off the book."

"There's no way that's going to work," May said, shaking her head. "That black stone looks a lot stronger than the gray rock that cat is made of."

"Well it can't hurt to try!" Sadie said as she lifted the stone cat above her head and brought it down as hard as she could against one of the statue's arms.

The cat broke into two pieces, leaving barely a scuff mark on the obsidian woman.

"Told you," May muttered.

Sadie dropped the pieces of broken rock on the ground in frustration. She stared at the stone woman clutching the book—the one thing that could end this nightmare. Her long, flowing hair almost looked real, and the creases in her dress were so realistic that Sadie wondered if they would smooth out if she ran her hand across them. Something about the woman bothered her. She'd seen plenty of gray stone people and animals; she'd seen Jenny's wolf when he was carved from the swirly white, gray, and black stone, but she hadn't seen anything carved from this solid black stuff before. *Yes you have,* a little voice whispered from the depths of her memory.

Sadie ran her hand down the arm she'd just tried to break, feeling the smoothness of the stone, and remembered.

"My knife," Sadie groaned, letting her hand slip off the statue and fall to her side. She looked up at the ceiling and exhaled as the fight drained away from her. As the adrenaline and rage ebbed, pain began to come into her knuckles where she had hit Bannan and into her finger where the nail had been broken off. Her hand throbbed, and she avoided looking down at the mess she'd made of it.

She walked away from the statue and sat in the dusty, little wooden chair by the spinning wheel. She bent over and hugged her legs, hiding her face. She stared down at the cobblestone floor despondently. *I knew that knife was important,* she thought. *That damn gnome...*

If her knife was the only thing that could cut through this stone woman, it was over. The knife was long gone, deep in the forest somewhere. They would never find it again.

"Okay," she said finally, looking up at May and Aiden. "If we can't remove it, we just have to destroy it."

"I don't think that's a good idea," May said slowly.

"How do we destroy it?" Aiden said, his dark brown eyes glittering with excitement.

"You still have your knife, right?" Sadie asked.

"Yeah!" Aiden pulled the red-stone-handled knife from his waistband and tried to hand it to her. Sadie shook her head. "You do it. Just stab the stupid thing as many times as it takes."

"Wait," May said, grabbing Aiden's wrist. "We have no idea what will happen if we set the book on fire! We could be destroying the only way home."

Aiden looked at May, then at Sadie. "She's got a point."

Sadie didn't respond, just stared at the book clutched in the statue's arms. She ran through everything she knew about the book in her head. Bannan ... no, Jacob ... had been the one to tell them they needed to destroy the book. Jacob had been playing games with them this entire time. He had tried to stop them from getting the book, which meant he thought they were *able* get the book.

"Jacob tried to stop us," she said aloud. "Which means he thought we would destroy the book, and he didn't *want* us to destroy the book."

"Yeah, and?" May said as she let go of Aiden's wrist.

"So ..." Sadie felt like she had lost her train of thought. Where was she going with this?

"Jacob doesn't want us to destroy the book, so we *should* destroy the book?" Aiden offered.

May shook her head. "No, not necessarily. Destroying the book could be bad for him *and* for us."

"Well, what do you think we should do, then?" Sadie asked, exasperated.

A long silence stretched out between them as they all thought. May twisted her long hair around her finger and looked around the room. "I ... I don't know."

Aiden sighed, then sat down on the floor and leaned against one of the cobblestone walls. "My feet hurt."

Sadie considered their options. Jacob could return at any moment, and in fact might still be there, invisible, watching them with amusement. She glanced quickly around the room, looking for any sign that Jacob was still there. *If Jacob isn't here ... then where is he?*

Jenny. She'd been so concerned with the book she hadn't considered where Jacob might have gone, or what he might be doing. Jenny and the others were all in danger. Sadie stood up quickly, a new concern fueling her.

"The others," she said, "We have to tell the others about Bannan."

"Oh, no," Aiden said, realizing the same thing she had. Sadie moved toward him and offered him a hand. He took it, and she pulled him up from the ground.

"We can't just leave the book here!" May said, gesturing wildly at the stone woman. "It's our only chance, what if he comes back and moves it? We'd never find it again. We got *lucky*, because he underestimated us. He won't make that mistake again."

Sadie knew May was right, but what choice did they have?

"Do you want to stay behind and guard it?" Sadie snapped. "My friends are in danger. I can't just do nothing."

May's face drained of color, and she looked away.

Sadie felt Aiden's hand on her arm, and she turned to look at him. He looked down at her with warm eyes and smiled reassuringly.

"I'll stay and guard the book," Aiden said, not breaking eye contact. "Just promise you'll come back for me."

Sadie thought about that moment on the bridge, when the troll had her by the ankle and Aiden had come back to save her. She knew she would always come back for him.

"Sure," she croaked out, and her face burned with embarrassment at her sudden loss for words. She looked at May, who was still refusing to look at her.

"I can stay with Aiden," May said softly. "You don't need me."

Leaving Aiden and May together, alone in this tower, was pretty close to the last thing Sadie wanted.

"No, go with Sadie," Aiden said, surprising Sadie. "We've hit a block here, but maybe you can help Sadie and the rest of the group. I'll be fine, I have my boomstick!" Aiden lifted his knife in the air dramatically. Sadie looked at Aiden in confusion.

"Your ..."

"It's from a movie... I'll explain on the way back to the castle," May said with a slight shake of her head. Sadie rolled her eyes and headed toward the door. She paused and let May slip past her, then took one last look at Aiden, the obsidian princess, and the book. She had a terrible feeling she would never see any of them again.

44

Jenny entered the library behind Ryan and Rain and began scanning the room for her friends. Her eyes landed on a familiar girl in a bright red dress standing at a bookcase. *Charlotte?*

Jenny left Ryan and Rain and made her way toward the girl that might be Charlotte. Jenny's heart pounded, and she tried to calm down, telling herself it might not be her. *Don't get your hopes up.* But the place was full of random magic, maybe Charlotte had been brought back somehow while they were gone. The girl was wearing one of Charlotte's classic bright-red outfits. It *had* to be her!

The girl had her back to Jenny and looked like she was considering one of the books on the shelf. Jenny grabbed her by the arm, but she didn't seem to notice she was even there.

"Charlotte?"

The girl didn't turn, but Jenny moved to see her face, and it was definitely Charlotte. She had the same cherry-red lipstick she always wore, the same bright blue eyes with perfectly drawn cat-eye makeup.

"Charlotte, why aren't you answering me? Are you okay?"

"So much for Sadie's plan," she heard Travis say behind her. She turned around and gestured at Charlotte. "It's Charlotte! But ..."

Jenny's eyes fell on the group of girls she had asked to borrow a chair from the last time she was in the library. They had ignored her, just as Charlotte was ignoring her now. The pieces fell together, and she felt herself break apart. Hannah rushed to her side and wrapped her arms around her.

"I know. I'm sorry. We didn't see you come in! We were hoping you wouldn't have to see her like this," Hannah said.

Jenny felt like she'd been cracked open and everything good had leaked right out of her. For those few seconds, she'd been so happy. For those few seconds, she'd had her friend back.

"She's a ghost, like the rest," Jenny whispered, her legs starting to wobble underneath her. She felt Ryan guiding her to a seat.

Jenny looked up at her friends in a daze. They were all looking at her with the same hangdog sympathetic expression. As if this were only her pain to bear, as if she were the only one who cared that Charlotte had died. She hated them then—all of them, even Ryan. Even Hannah. She couldn't bear to look at them a second longer.

"I'm sorry, I was just surprised," she said, forcing a smile. "Seeing Charlotte like that ..."

"We know," Cameron said somberly. Jenny wanted to slap him. His I'm-so-sorry look made her sick to her stomach.

"I'm just going to go outside for a minute." She turned to Ryan, who she knew was about to object. "I'll be right back. I promise. I just need a minute alone."

Ryan looked at her with concern but didn't argue, and Jenny drifted out of the library, not looking at anyone as she left.

She walked slowly toward the castle's front doors in a fog. Outside, the sun blasted her face and hurt her eyes, but she ignored it. She sat down on the steps and tried to gather herself. She knew her anger wasn't fair, that she wasn't the only one upset that Charlotte had died. It had started to feel like it, though. No one ever talked about her. It was like they had all just moved on, forgotten, gotten over it. She thought about Charlotte and how close they had become the last few months. She realized that while people were always drawn to Charlotte, it always seemed surface level. Charlotte was entertaining, fun, and beautiful, and she made people feel important when she listened to them. But Jenny had been her only real friend. Her heart hurt thinking about the last time she'd seen Charlotte alive. Charlotte had been cruel to her, but Jenny knew now that it hadn't really been her, it had been the story. She wanted to scrub that night from her memory, wanted to forget seeing Charlotte's body in the wall.

She thought of Charlotte's ghost in the library and felt like crying. Somehow knowing she was stuck there as a ghost made everything even worse. Charlotte had been vibrant, alive, a force to be reckoned with—and now she was a shadow of herself, drifting forever through a library in the middle of nowhere.

Jenny stared down and watched as her tears fell and disappeared into the dirt. She'd met Marble here, she remembered. This is where she had named him and where he'd transformed from a statue to a living thing. She had been trying not to think about the wolf; with so many other things to focus on, it hadn't been that difficult, but here, now, she missed him so much it hurt.

She knew she could never keep a magical wolf as a pet forever. If they left, *when* they left, she wouldn't have been able to bring him with them. This was for the best, she knew, but it didn't make it hurt any less.

She thought about everything she had lost to the Black Forest and its fairy tales. Charlotte, Mrs. Braun, Marble—even Ryan felt lost to her, though he was there with them. She felt carved out and empty and was losing faith they would ever find the book that would be the key to their escape.

She just felt so tired.

A hand rested on her shoulder, and she turned around angrily.

"Leave me alone!" she screamed. The last person she wanted to deal with right now was Bannan.

Ryan removed his hand and backed away a step. Jenny looked at him, horrified. "Ryan! I'm sorry, I thought you were ... someone else."

Ryan eased himself down next to her and stared at the ground between his feet.

"Who did you think I was? Bannan?"

Jenny didn't reply. She didn't have to.

"What ... what exactly went on between you two, while I was gone?"

"Nothing!" Jenny said, a little too quickly and a little too loudly. "I was in his story, the story that took Charlotte. He ... he keeps saying he's in love with me, but that's ridiculous."

"It's not that ridiculous," Ryan replied softly, wrapping his arm around her. She felt awkward underneath his arm. He had blown up at her not long ago, and she had put her guard up. She found it difficult to relax but made herself rest her head on his shoulder as she knew he expected her to do. She stared at the creepy fountain in front of them, the crying girl with no hands with water running from her eyes. A little blue-and-yellow bird landed on top of the fountain girl's stone head and seemed to be staring at her.

Is that the same bird Hannah released? Jenny wondered, then shrugged it off. It didn't matter if it was the same bird or not, it was just a bird.

Jenny looked down at Ryan's other arm, the one not wrapped around her shoulders. She saw the empty space where his hand should be. She felt guilty for closing herself off to him. After everything he'd been through, maybe his blowups were normal. He was still grappling with his new existence.

"I'm so sorry for what happened to you," she whispered. "I'm so sorry we didn't get there sooner."

"Hey, don't do that," Ryan said into her hair. "It's not your fault."

Jenny knew it wasn't her fault, but it still felt like it was.

"I'm ... I'm sorry about May and the wish too," she said slowly.

She felt Ryan's body tense up.

"I understand why she did what she did," he started, "but I'll never forgive her for it."

Jenny let out a breath and didn't respond. It didn't matter now, anyway. The wish was gone, and they were still here—might be here forever.

Jenny moved away from Ryan and felt his arm fall from her shoulders. She looked out into the woods and wondered if there were other wishes out there—lost among the trees. If they didn't find this book that may or may not exist, there were still wishes. They would start looking for wishes.

She would never give up trying to find a way home.

45

Sadie walked out of the tower as if inside her own dark cloud. She didn't like leaving Aiden alone up there. Even if he had the fire knife, he was still vulnerable. Anything could happen to him while she and May were gone. She ran her tongue across her chapped lips, feeling the rough, dry skin caused by so much time spent outside. Her scalp felt hot from the sun beating down on her, and her eyes struggled to adjust to the brightness outside after being in the dimly lit tower.

May drifted behind her in silence, and Sadie didn't mind it. She was tired of talking, tired of being around people all the time. More than anything, though, she was tired of walking through these ruins. She made her way across the courtyard, following the path of pressed-down weeds they'd created. She ducked into the dark tunnel without hesitation and made her way quickly to the other side. She glanced down at the two sleeping stone guard dogs, comforted somehow by their existence.

Sadie stepped over familiar chunks of broken wall and past stone chickens and other animals she recognized. She knew the way by heart now and didn't have to think as she made each turn. May followed just a step behind her, lost in her own thoughts.

"You know why I like—or *used to* like—fairy tales so much?" May asked softly as she caught up to walk next to Sadie. "Because they always had happy endings. Evil was always defeated, the good guys always won, and if someone was killed, they could always be brought back."

Sadie glanced at May, who was staring ahead of them at something Sadie couldn't see. She wondered if May was waiting for her to respond, or if there was more she wanted to say. Sadie wasn't sure what she did to give May the impression she was up for a heart-to-heart.

"Last year my brother murdered forty-two people and himself."

Sadie stopped walking. May continued a few feet before stopping too.

"You wanted to know where I'm from so badly," May continued. "I'm from Sunset Springs."

Sadie's stomach tightened. *Sunset Springs. Forty-two people. The school shooting.*

It had been all anyone talked about for a few weeks, and then it, like every shooting before and after it, had faded into history. She didn't remember the name of the shooter, or anything about him. She hadn't even remembered the name of the town until May made the connection for her. Sadie thought about how often she had pushed May to tell her where she came from. How cold she'd been to her since that first day at the castle. Sadie wished she could disappear.

"You used the wish," Sadie croaked, "to undo what your brother did?"

May nodded. Sadie put it together easily now that she had all the pieces. May had stolen the wish to save the people her brother had killed. Ryan had been angry when they came out of the woods, and Jenny clearly had been covering something up. Now Sadie knew and wished she didn't. She couldn't feel angry at May for using the wish the way she had. But it still pinched to know they'd been so close to escaping this horrible place.

"It doesn't matter," Sadie said as she resumed walking. "We have the book now. We'll figure out how to use it, and everything will be fine."

Sadie wasn't sure if she was trying to convince May or herself.

They continued walking through the ruins, toward the castle. They easily avoided the thorny rose vines that grew wild all over the walls and ground. Sadie's mind ticked away at what she'd just learned.

"If your wish changed the past," Sadie thought out loud, "why are you still here?"

"What do you mean?"

"Well, if your brother never killed all those people, then your family never would have moved to Crescent Bay, right?"

May thought for a moment, then nodded. "Yeah, I guess if that never happened, we would have stayed in Sunset Springs."

"So why are you still here, with us?" Sadie asked.

"I don't know," May answered, shaking her head. "I hadn't thought about that. Maybe the magic only affected what happened *outside* of the forest?"

Sadie wasn't sure if she believed that May hadn't thought about it. May thought of everything. She wondered if May had expected to be magic-ed back to the States, never knowing about any of this. She didn't wonder why Ryan had been so angry. She knew.

"Are you going to tell the others?" May asked quietly.

Sadie thought about this. Ryan and Jenny already knew, but the rest of them didn't. Aiden didn't. Sadie couldn't see any good coming from telling the others.

"No," she answered.

Ahead of her, Sadie saw the broken gate and picked up her pace. She'd been so distracted by May's revelation she'd forgotten what they were doing. *I need to warn Jenny about Bannan.*

She moved faster, and May picked up her own pace to keep up. They ran out of the ruins and around the castle to the front.

She slowed when she saw Jenny and Ryan sitting next to each other on the front steps. Relief washed over her. Jenny was safe. For now, at least.

46

Jenny looked up and saw two girls with long dark hair making their way toward her and Ryan. Jenny squinted and realized it was Sadie and May. *Just* Sadie and May.

"Wasn't Aiden with them?" Ryan asked, voicing Jenny's own worried thoughts.

Jenny didn't answer, just stood up as Sadie and May hurried over to them.

"Jenny!" Sadie called out as she approached. She stopped and bent over, clinging to her side, out of breath. May was sweaty and disheveled and wouldn't meet her eyes.

"What's going on? Where's Aiden?" Ryan asked forcefully, taking a step toward Sadie and May. Jenny moved herself between him and Sadie and waited a moment for Sadie to catch her breath.

"Bannan is Jacob!" she blurted between ragged breaths.

"What? Who is Jacob?" Jenny said, confused.

"Grimm brother," May added as she wiped sweat off her face.

Grimm brother. The story Bannan had told them just last night about the two brothers and how they had created this castle full of horrors. How Jacob was hiding in one of the stories. How Jacob controlled the book. If Bannan was Jacob, then ...

He's the bad guy. Sophie's warning echoed in her head. *Why didn't I listen to her?*

Jenny couldn't believe she'd been so stupid. It'd all been

right there in front of her. She'd wondered why Bannan was the only fairy-tale character who could move around the entire castle and go outside. She'd thought it strange that he happened to know all this information about the Grimm brothers when all the other characters didn't know much, if anything, outside of their own stories. If she had just stopped and thought about it for five seconds ... She groaned and rubbed her forehead.

"So there's no book, then?" she asked numbly, her worst fear realized.

"Well," Sadie, who had finally caught her breath and was standing straight again, said. "There *is* a book."

"A book Jacob really didn't want us to get our hands on," May added.

"Where's Aiden!" Ryan yelled from behind her. Jenny jumped a little, forgetting for a moment he was there.

"He's with the book, in the tower. Calm down!" Sadie yelled back.

"Where's Ban—*Jacob* now?" Jenny asked, her eyes darting around the yard. She expected him to pop up at any moment.

"No idea," Sadie answered. "He disappeared from the tower. We were afraid he was going to come after you, Jenny. We came back to warn you."

Jenny's mind raced as she tried to figure out what to do. She'd never been completely sure that what Bannan—*Jacob*— had told her was true, but now nothing was certain. There was really a book, though, she consoled herself. A book that was being guarded by Aiden.

"Why didn't you bring the book with you? Why is Aiden guarding it?"

"Right, that's another annoying thing," Sadie grumbled. "The book is locked in the arms of a statue. Nothing we tried could get it to budge. But get this ... the statue is made of the *same stone* my knife was!"

Jenny thought about her own knife, how its swirly stone

matched Marble and the lion's fur. How it had been able to kill the lion by turning it to stone.

"You think your knife would have ..."

"I don't know! I just know that we'll never find out because I lost it to that gnome and that stupid forest!" Sadie gestured wildly behind her at the woods.

"There are other knives," Ryan said, seemingly regaining his composure. "In Eckert's room. Maybe they do something?"

Jenny thought about the knives they had taken—each one had served a purpose. Aiden's could start fire, hers turned animals to stone, Travis's had injured the nixie, May's had cut the bread in Mother Holle's story. The knives they'd left behind probably did things too. But what?

"He's right. We should check those out again," she said. "And, May, we could use your help translating some book titles while we're in there."

"What about Aiden?" asked Sadie. "We can't leave him up there all alone for too long. Jacob might come back."

"I'll go join him," a rough voice said from behind her. She turned to see Travis standing just outside the castle door. He stepped into the sunlight and down the steps, with Hannah, Cameron, and Rain close behind.

"Did you hear all that?"

"Yeah we got the gist. Where is the tower?" Travis continued.

"It's ..." Sadie's expression darkened. "You won't be able to find it by yourself. I'll take you."

Jenny didn't argue. They needed May's help inside; there was no other choice but to have Sadie bring Travis to Aiden. "You can't wait? This won't take long."

Sadie shook her head, turning to look behind her. "We've already been gone too long. Come on, Travis. We'll stay at the tower and guard the book." Sadie turned to Jenny. "Join us when you've found whatever it is you're looking for."

Sadie began walking away, with Travis's body eclipsing her

as he followed close behind.

"Wait!" Hannah squeaked, running after them. "I want to come with you!"

Jenny blinked, stunned that Hannah was suddenly volunteering to go into the unknown. Cameron, too, looked surprised, but he drifted after Hannah without a word.

Jenny watched as half of their group disappeared around the castle's corner, feeling a bit whiplashed from the hurried revelations.

She turned to Ryan, Rain, and May and took a deep breath. "You know the way."

47

Sadie trudged through the rose-choked ruins for the fifth time that day. Travis followed close behind her, a little too close for her comfort, but she didn't say anything. Hannah and Cameron walked together behind Travis, and Sadie just hoped they would keep up.

She passed the stone pig, the stone chickens, the sleeping stone people, then stopped at the opening to the tunnel. The two stone guard dogs still slept soundly on either side of the entrance. Sadie didn't hesitate this time, just headed into the darkness and walked quickly through to the other side. She waited a moment for the others to come through, and when they did, she turned and moved determinedly to the other side of the weedy courtyard.

Sadie's legs ached from all the walking she'd done that day but didn't let that slow her down. She didn't know what was going on in that tower, and she needed to make sure Aiden was okay.

She paused at the closed door to the tower, and her stomach turned. She had forgotten to prop the door open when she and May left. Sadie ran her hands over her pockets even though she knew she had left the key in the tower with Aiden.

"What's the hold up?" Travis asked.

Sadie looked up at the sky in frustration. *How could I have been so stupid?*

"I left the key up there," she grumbled.

"What?" Travis asked, leaning closer to her.

"I left the key up there!" she yelled, surprising Hannah and Cameron and causing Travis to back quickly away from her.

"Can't we just force it open? Like the castle doors?" Travis offered, looking toward Cameron.

"No, this door is different. You need a special key, or it won't open to the right place," Sadie explained.

"Hey, is that a window?" Hannah asked, shielding her eyes from the sun as she pointed up at the top of the tower.

Sadie backed away from the tower and looked at where Hannah was pointing. There was a small window cut into the tower at the very top. Sadie remembered seeing it from the inside.

"We just need to get Aiden's attention, and he can throw it down to us!" Hannah said, clapping her hands together like that would solve all their problems.

"How are we going to get his attention from way down here?" Cameron asked, giving voice to Sadie's thoughts.

"We can throw stuff," Travis said, picking up a small rock from the ground. He threw it at the window—at least that's where Sadie assumed he'd been aiming. It hit the tower a good ten feet below the window and fell back down to earth.

"Great." Sadie thought about Jenny's superior throwing arm and wished she were there.

She watched as another rock flew up and hit an embarrassingly low spot on the tower. *Maybe if we make enough noise...*

Sadie picked up a rock and chucked it as hard as she could at the window and didn't wait to see where it hit. She picked up another, and another, pitching them as hard as she could at the tower, and the others followed suit. Soon a hailstorm of rocks were flying up, accompanied by all four of them yelling for Aiden. Sadie thought she saw movement behind the windowpane.

"Stop!" she called out to the others. "I think that's him!"

The window opened, and there was Aiden's head looking down at them. Relief rushed through Sadie at seeing him alive.

"What are you doing?" Aiden called down from the tower.

"Rapunzel, Rapunzel, let down your hair!" Travis called back. Sadie rolled her eyes and cupped her hands around her mouth to amplify her voice.

"We need the key!" she yelled up at him.

"What?"

"WE. NEED. THE. KEY," they all yelled in unison.

Aiden's head disappeared and a moment later reappeared. He stretched his arm out the window. "You want me to just throw it down?" he yelled.

"YES," the group chorused.

Sadie really hoped Aiden's aim was better than theirs.

She tried to keep her eye on the tiny shiny object falling toward them, but it was so small and the sun was in her eyes. She heard a featherlight thump from somewhere in the courtyard but hadn't seen where the key had fallen.

Sadie looked at the knee-high weeds that covered the courtyard and groaned. Nothing was ever easy.

"Okay, I think the key probably fell ..." Cameron said, walking a short distance away from the castle and trying to gauge the angle at which it would have fallen from the window, "around here." He waved his arms over a large section of the courtyard. "If we line up together and start here and work our way toward the tower, we should find it pretty quickly."

They followed Cameron's directions, and Sadie winced as her bare knees pressed into the hard ground. She crawled forward, patting the ground with her hands, with Hannah on one side of her and Travis on the other.

"This sucks," Travis said next to her, as if she didn't know that.

She flattened the weeds as she crawled forward, wincing as tiny rocks cut into her knees and hands. Sadie played it back in her head, how easily this could have been avoided. All she'd had to do was grab the key before she left the tower. Or prop open the door. She grew more and more annoyed with herself as they continued to search for the key. They patted the ground for another fifteen minutes before Hannah popped up out of the weeds.

"I found it!"

Sadie stood up and brushed off the tiny pebbles that stuck to her bare knees and hands and held her hand out to Hannah. Hannah gave Sadie the key, and Sadie moved quickly back to the tower door.

She inserted the key into the lock and turned, her heart pounding. Part of her was afraid it wouldn't work again, that it was a one-use key and she would open the door to nothing.

But as the door opened, Sadie breathed a sigh of relief— they were inside the tower. She recognized the flickering candles and the seemingly infinite spiral staircase of torture. She paused, then reached down and picked up a chunk of rock and pushed it against the door to hold it open. She didn't want to have to throw the key out the window or run back down the stairs when Jenny and the others joined them.

Sadie gestured for them to follow her up. She had never wanted to climb these stairs again, but here she was. Her legs felt tight and ached with each step, and it became harder and harder for her to breathe as she made her way up. She glanced behind her to see Cameron, then Hannah, and a few more steps back, Travis. All three of them were huffing as they pulled themselves up the stairs. Travis's face was dripping with sweat. Sadie was hot too, and the higher they got, the hotter it became.

Sadie started to feel dizzy as she walked around and around the spiral staircase. She wished she had grabbed some water when she was back at the castle instead of hurrying back here so quickly. She was hot, thirsty, and sore, and was starting to feel weak. She wasn't sure how much more she could put her body through.

Finally, she made it to the top. She didn't wait for the others before pushing into the room where the obsidian princess slept and Aiden waited.

The room was the same; the book was safely clutched in the princess's arms. Aiden stood up from the one chair in the room and smiled at her.

"You came back!"

"Of course," she said roughly, still breathing hard. "I ... brought reinforcements."

As if on cue, Cameron and Hannah entered the room behind her. They looked around and made a beeline to the princess.

"Oh, wow," Cameron said, leaning down to examine the statue.

"So you can't get the book out?" Hannah asked, pushing lightly at the bottom of the book sticking out from the statue's arms.

"No, and I've been trying," Aiden said. "Won't budge."

"Don't wait for me or anything," huffed Travis as he half fell through the door and into the room. He was covered in sweat, and his face was bright red from the exertion of walking up the staircase.

Sadie rolled her eyes and turned back to Aiden and the statue.

"The others are searching Eckert's room for anything that might help us with this," Sadie explained. "But if they don't find anything ... I think we should destroy the book."

"Okay, hear me out," Travis said, still breathing hard, "What if I try kissing her?"

"*What?*" Sadie blurted. "Yeah, because that really worked out great for you last time." Sadie shook her head, annoyed. Snow White had turned to ash when Travis had kissed her ... *oh.*

"Travis, you're a genius! Go ahead, lay one on her!"

"Hold on, I feel like I'm missing something here," Cameron said, pushing his glasses farther up his nose. "What 'last time'?"

Sadie realized when Travis had caught Cameron and Hannah up on their time in the woods, he had left out Snow White.

"Um ..." Sadie glanced over at Travis, who was examining the floor and scratching his head.

"How about we just stick with I'm a genius and move on?" he said, giving them a wobbly smile.

"Right!" Aiden said, clapping his hands together. "Okay, Travis, pucker up."

48

Inside Eckert's room, Jenny dumped out the drawer of knives onto the bed. Ryan, Rain, and May gathered around her and stared down at the knives. None of them knew what they were looking for.

Jenny stole a glance at May, and May threw her hands up. "What am *I* supposed to do? I don't know anything about knives!"

"You knew about that bread knife, didn't you?" Ryan hissed. May's face reddened, and she looked away from him. Rain looked between Ryan and May quizzically, then at Jenny. Jenny avoided Rain's eyes and looked down at the knives on the bed. She wasn't going to be getting into any of *that* right now.

There were twelve knives of all different shapes and sizes, a few with crystal handles, some gold and silver, some wood. Jenny didn't know what she was looking for. It wasn't like they came with labels or instruction booklets. She picked one up with a short, sharp blade and a handle made of what looked like clear quartz. As she examined it, her mind started to feel clearer, and something clicked. *Instruction booklets.*

"Hey!" Jenny said, looking up from the knife excitedly. "I don't think Eckert would just have these knives in a drawer without cataloging them, do you?"

May shook her head. "No. She seemed like the type that would keep track of everything."

"So I bet there's a notebook, or something, that explains what these knives do!"

Jenny dropped the knife she'd been holding back onto the bed and started looking around the room for a notebook. The others followed suit, and soon they were tearing apart the room—*again*. May went through all the books on the shelf and the ones still lying on the floor, stacking them as she ruled each out. Rain pulled out the sheets and blankets on the bed and threw them on the ground.

Jenny drifted over to the desk, which was still lying on its back, empty of drawers. She bent down to pick up one of the still-in-tact drawers when she noticed it. A black notebook perfectly wedged into the top of the desk, where the top right drawer should be. She dropped to her knees and carefully pried the notebook out with her fingernails from its hiding spot. It popped out, and Jenny flipped the cover open to see pages and pages of writing she couldn't understand, then she stopped.

It was a drawing of a knife with some writing below it. As she flipped through, she saw more and more pages with drawings of knives, and Jenny's heart raced as she realized she had found it.

"I found it!" she yelled so loudly it was almost a scream. She stood up and made her way back to the bed and handed the notebook to May, who took it with wide eyes.

"I can't believe it," May said, flipping through the pages. "This is everything. Everything we need!"

Jenny smiled proudly until May looked at her with her eyes narrowed.

"You were the one that searched the desk the first time."

Jenny's smile faded as she realized what May was saying.

"Yeah, but—"

"You should have found this before. I can't even imagine what might be different! We might have been home by now!"

Jenny took a step back from May, stunned at how quickly she'd turned on her.

"It's not my fault," Jenny snapped. "And you're one to

talk—we *definitely* would be home by now if you hadn't—"

"Stop it!" Ryan yelled. "We have enough to deal with right now. We can't start fighting with each other!"

Jenny felt like she was on fire, and all she wanted to do was tear into May. *How dare she*, Jenny thought, *after I protected her all this time. I kept Ryan from telling everyone what she did, and for what?*

"If May hadn't what?" Rain asked, taking a step toward them.

"Not now, Rain," Ryan hissed. "Jenny, you need to calm down."

Calm down. Jenny was tired of calming down, tired of trying to be strong and keep everything—and everyone—together. She wanted to storm out of the room and slam the door as hard as she could—but she knew she couldn't even do *that*, since the door was still lying on the floor.

She'd been so happy to find the notebook, and May had immediately extinguished it.

Ryan leaned close to Jenny and whispered in her ear, "We need her. Just hold it together a little longer."

Jenny glared at Ryan and clenched her teeth. "Just translate the notebook," she spat at May.

May glared but turned back to the notebook in her hands. She consulted the drawing and picked up a knife that matched it. It looked like a steak knife with a handle made of the same cherrywood the table in the Red Room was made of.

"Turns food to wood," May read flatly, then dropped the knife back on the bed, away from the others. Jenny didn't know how *that* would ever come in handy. May picked up another, this one a small dagger with an ornate gold handle. "Turns straw into gold." May dropped it onto the bed, next to the first one. She picked up another small dagger. This one had a handle that looked like it was crafted from hammered metal. "Turns clothes into armor." May dropped the knife back on the bed.

"That could be useful, right?" Ryan said, picking it up and examining it. May shrugged and turned the page in the notebook.

She continued this way for a few minutes, reading off what each knife's power was—one grew plants, another caused eternal sleep—until she got to the last one, the knife Jenny had picked up earlier with the clear quartz handle.

"For clarity," May read. She didn't drop it on the bed with others but instead looked it over carefully. "This one could be useful."

Jenny had felt something when she'd held that knife. Her mind, usually so full of conflicting thoughts and feelings, had cleared, and she'd been able to focus. May was right, that knife could be *very* useful. Jenny eyed the knife in May's hand and considered how to get it back. May wasn't going to just give it to her, and Jenny knew she couldn't just grab it.

"Why do you think Eckert left all these behind?" Rain asked.

Jenny considered. "Well, none of them were going to be useful against the gingerbread witch," Jenny replied. "Though if she had brought the clarity knife, maybe things would have gone differently."

"She probably didn't want clarity," Ryan said bitterly. "If she could see clearly, she never would have done what she did."

Jenny nodded to herself. Deep down, Eckert must have known what she was doing was wrong and would probably fail. She hadn't cared—she hadn't wanted to see the truth. She hadn't wanted to see that she'd be far too late to save her brother.

"Some of these might come in handy," Jenny said. "But we're not any closer to figuring out how to get the book out."

Ryan grabbed a beaten-up leather satchel from the floor— one of Eckert's things that had been unceremoniously tossed during their search. He put all the knives into the bag, then glanced at May, who was still holding the clarity knife.

"I think I should hang on to this one," she said. "It might help me figure stuff out."

"Right," Ryan said, nodding. "Good idea."

Jenny glared at the back of May's head, then brushed past her to the opening where the door once was. She hadn't thought this through, didn't know where she was going. She just wanted to get away from May. "I'm ... going to get some water."

"I'll come with you," Ryan replied, moving toward her. He turned to his sister and hesitated. "Rain, stay here with May. We'll be right back."

Rain nodded and glanced over at May, who was sitting on the bed and staring a little *too* hard at the open notebook in her lap. Jenny bit back a thousand bitter comments and said nothing as she left the room.

Jenny moved quickly down the hallway toward the kitchen, but Ryan caught up with her, grabbing her by the arm and turning her around to face him.

"What is going on with you?" Ryan asked as she pulled her arm from his grasp.

"Me? May started it! And last I checked, you hated her. So what is going on with *you*?" Jenny couldn't believe Ryan was taking May's side. She'd spent most of the day trying to protect May from Ryan, and now here she was, being ganged up on by both of them.

"Nothing is going on with me, Jenny," Ryan said softly, tilting her chin up so her eyes met his. "You know we need May. We don't have time for this."

Jenny turned away from Ryan and looked up at the ceiling as she tried to calm herself. Ryan was right. They needed May to do the translating. Jenny would have to suck it up and get through this. They had found the book; they were so close to getting out of here.

"You're right," she forced herself to say. "Sorry."

"Great, now can we go back?"

Jenny nodded and followed Ryan back toward Eckert's room. Inside, May was bent over Eckert's notebook, her lips moving soundlessly as she read. She looked up as they entered and shook her head, slamming the notebook shut.

"I don't know," May whined, tossing the notebook at Jenny's feet. "I know some German, but I'm not fluent, and her handwriting is a mess. I didn't see anything about the book, though, and most of it seems to be about the gingerbread witch."

Jenny stared down at the notebook on the floor in front of her. Just a few minutes ago, that notebook had been *everything*. Now it was nothing.

"Nothing about the sleeping-princess statue?" Ryan asked, leaning down to pick the notebook up.

"Briar Rose," May corrected. "And no. From what I can tell, Eckert didn't know about the book or Briar Rose at all."

Jenny thought about the *Sleeping Beauty* fairy tale. It had been one of her favorites as a kid. Briar Rose is born, and her parents throw a big party but neglect to invite one of the fairies. She comes to the party anyway and curses Briar Rose to die on her sixteenth birthday by pricking her finger on a spindle. Another fairy softens the curse by changing it to sleep instead of death, and the whole kingdom sleeps with her until her prince arrives to kiss her awake.

It's a simple story, and the solution was, once again, a prince's kiss. That hadn't worked on Snow White in the forest, and Jenny doubted it would work on the statue in the tower.

"So that's it then?" Jenny asked, refusing to look at May and instead pretended to look around the room. "We have nothing?"

"Well, we have the knives. That's something, right?" Rain chirped. Jenny shrugged. She didn't know how any of the knives they had found would help get the book out of Sleeping Beauty's arms, but it was something.

The four of them stood around awkwardly, not speaking, for a few long moments. They'd done all they could here. It was time to join their friends in the tower. Jenny winced as she realized May was the only one who knew how to get there. Once again, they needed May. Jenny hesitated; she didn't want to be the one to suggest it.

"Well, if this is all we got, it's what we got," Ryan said with a shrug. "Let's go see a tower about a book."

One by one they left Eckert's room, for the last time, Jenny hoped. They walked down the hall to the lobby, and Jenny thought about the rolled-up painting of the brothers Sadie had stuffed underneath Rumpelstiltskin's desk. If they couldn't get the book out before dark, at least they would have a satisfying bonfire later.

49

Travis hesitated a moment before leaning over the princess statue and carefully kissing her on her cold, stone lips. Sadie held her breath, hoping the same thing that had happened to Snow White would happen to the princess. If the statue turned to ash, they could just pluck the book out. She stared intently at the statue, willing it to disintegrate. A minute passed, then another.

Sadie's heart sank. *Why did I think it'd be that simple?* she chastised herself.

"Well, worth a shot!" Aiden said, shrugging. He pulled out his knife with the red-stone handle. "So back to the stabbing plan?"

"Let's wait for Jenny and the others to get here," Sadie said. She hated waiting, but they might have found something important. It was worth holding off until they arrived. Sadie lowered herself to the ground and leaned back against the stone wall. It was far from comfortable, but she was tired of standing and her feet were killing her. Hannah continued to examine the stone princess, running her hand along the waves of the statue's hair, the smooth folds of its dress.

"She's so beautiful," Hannah whispered.

"Yeah, you don't get called Sleeping Beauty for nothing." Sadie sighed.

"She doesn't turn to stone in the story," Hannah said. "Are we sure this is Sleeping Beauty?"

Sadie considered this. May had said the story was *Sleeping*

Beauty, and they had just gone along with it because May was always right. But what if she wasn't always right? What if they were in an entirely different fairy tale?

"I don't know. I mean, there's a spindle." Sadie gestured at the spinning wheel in the corner of the room. "That's specific to *Sleeping Beauty.*"

"Yeah, that's true," Hannah agreed, nodding, "But not just *Sleeping Beauty.*"

"What do you mean?" Aiden asked.

"Well, I had a lot of time to read while you guys were gone. I got through most of the fairy-tale book. There are a few stories that have spinning wheels in them. *Rumpelstiltskin* is one, actually. You know, spinning hay into gold? Then there's another about a king who forces his daughters to constantly be spinning."

Rumpelstiltskin. Sadie felt a chill run through her body. Rumpelstiltskin was the one who told them where the key to the tower was. Sadie looked around the room in a new way.

"Remind me—what's the *Rumpelstiltskin* story again?" Sadie asked weakly.

"Oh, sure," Hannah said, brightening. "So there's a father who likes to brag about his daughter and one day claims she can spin hay into gold. Someone tells the king about it, and the king commands the daughter to be brought to the castle. When she arrives, the king locks her in a room full of hay and tells her she must spin it all into gold by morning. She panics, because she can't spin hay into gold. So Rumpelstiltskin appears and tells her he'll do it if she gives him something. So she gives him some jewelry, and he spins the hay into gold. Same thing happens a few more nights, and each time, she gives him some jewelry. The last night, though, she runs out of jewelry, so Rumpelstiltskin makes her promise to give him her firstborn child. She agrees. The king eventually marries her and for some reason never makes her do the hay-into-gold thing ever again. She has a baby, and Rumpelstiltskin comes to collect. She refuses, so he tells her if she can guess his name, she can keep her baby."

"Right, I know this part," Sadie said. "She hears him say his name, or something, and guesses it, and he goes away and she keeps the baby. Right?"

"Yeah, basically," Hannah said.

"So ... what does any of that have to do with this?" asked Travis, gesturing around the crowded room. Sadie wondered the same thing. The only connection the tower had to the *Rumpelstiltskin* story was the spinning wheel, and that wasn't even a particularly strong connection.

"Nothing, probably," Sadie said bitterly. She looked around the room, hoping she'd see something new she hadn't noticed the first thirty times she'd looked. Her eyes fell on Cameron and Hannah, standing *very* close together by the statue. She raised an eyebrow as she studied them, and Hannah caught her staring. Sadie watched as Hannah made her way around the large sculpture in the center of the room and sat down next to her.

"What's up?" Hannah said, her green eyes wide and innocent. Sadie couldn't think about the book anymore; her imagination was burned out, and she needed a break. She needed to think about something—*anything*—else. Sadie noticed Cameron pretending to look around the room, but his gaze kept returning to the poppy-haired girl next to her.

Sadie leaned close to Hannah and in a soft voice asked her what was going on with her and Cameron. She smirked as Hannah's face lit up bright red.

"Nothing!" she insisted, not meeting Sadie's eyes.

"Uh-huh, sure doesn't look like nothing to me," she said, giving Hannah a playful nudge.

"Let's talk about it later," Hannah whispered, "when he's not *right there.*"

"Fine." Sadie sighed.

"How are you doing?" Hannah asked in a slightly louder tone. "What you went through in the woods—it all sounded terrifying."

Sadie remembered the troll's meaty hand wrapped tightly around her ankle, the nixie almost killing her, Eckert's head. She had asked Hannah about Cameron because she wanted to talk about something not related to their current situation, to feel normal for even a minute. Sadie wondered if she would ever feel normal again. She wasn't sure she even knew what the word meant anymore.

"I'm fine," she replied as she rested her head on Hannah's shoulder. "We made it out of the forest. We found the book that will somehow get us out of here. Everything is going to work out."

Sadie felt like she was telling a bedtime story to a small child. She didn't believe the words she was saying, at least not enough. They'd found the book, but even if they did manage to remove it from the sculpture, they had no idea what to *do* with it. They'd been relying on Bannan to help them use the book once they found it, but Bannan didn't exist.

They were on their own.

50

Outside, Jenny, Ryan, Rain, and May made their way around the castle and paused in front of the banged-up metal gate that led into the rose-choked ruins. Jenny had only been here once before, that first day. It was where she'd met Bannan—*Jacob*, she corrected herself—the first time. She shook her head at how stupid she had been. She couldn't believe she'd actually trusted him.

She followed Ryan through the broken gate and down the mazelike path. May led them expertly through the ruins, never even pausing to consider which direction to go when they reached a fork in the path. All around her, thorny rose vines reached out to snag on her clothes or scratch her bare skin. The blooms gave off a strong, cloying scent that was quickly starting to give her a headache.

"What is this place?" Ryan asked, reaching out to touch one of the pale-pink, double-petaled roses.

"Briar Rose's castle, I guess," May answered from ahead of them. "What's left of it."

Jenny stepped over rubble and sleeping stone animals as they made their way through the ruins and toward the tower she could see looming in the distance. They approached the bench she had sat on that first day, and her face grew warm as she remembered how she had felt when Bannan sat down next to her, how close she had let him get. She pushed the thought away angrily. *It was the bracelet that made me feel that way*, she thought. *It wasn't real.*

As they passed by, she looked longingly at the empty place where she'd seen Marble the first time. He'd been made of smooth stone then. *He was posed in a funny, playful bow.* She smiled softly, remembering how his butt had been up in the air, his head looking up at her with a wide grin.

She fell back a little, distracted by her memories of Marble, and she hurried to catch up to the rest of the group. But the faster she tried to go, the slower she went. She watched, bewildered, as Ryan, Rain, and May retreated farther and farther away.

Jenny blinked, and everything was different. The ruins, the rose vines, her friends—they were all gone. She looked around, groggy, as if she'd just woken up from a deep sleep. She wasn't in the ruins anymore; she was in a lush garden full of every kind of flower she could imagine. Stargazer lilies the size of her head bobbed in the slight breeze, and soft clouds of white baby's breath floated among thousands of indigo cornflowers, bright yellow marigolds, and white and red windflowers. Butterflies in all colors and sizes floated in the air around her, and she was mesmerized by the slow flap of their delicate wings.

She looked down to see herself in a shimmering gold dress so long it touched the ground. She felt something heavy on her head and took it off to look at it. A tiara covered in diamonds and emeralds sparkled in her hand. She stared at it in awe, tilting the tiara left and right to admire how it shimmered in the sunlight. She sensed someone coming up behind her, but she felt sluggish and slow, and she couldn't turn around to look. Hands appeared and took the tiara from her, then placed it back on her head.

"My queen," someone whispered in her ear. "I can give you anything you wish for."

She tried to turn toward the voice, but movement ahead of her grabbed her attention. A curtain of pink jasmine vines parted, and out stepped a unicorn—pure white with shining silver hooves and a silver horn. Jenny couldn't believe what she was seeing; it was so beautiful she felt like she might cry. The unicorn approached Jenny and stopped right in front of her. She stared into the creature's big, impossibly blue eyes, and her breath caught. When she was little, she'd been obsessed with unicorns. She remembered how badly she had wished they were real. She reached out and stroked the unicorn's silky neck and breathed in its freshly cut grass scent. She eyed the silver horn gleaming on the animal's forehead but didn't dare touch it.

"All you need to do is tell me what you desire," the voice continued from behind her.

The voice was soft and soothing, and Jenny found herself wanting to lean into it. She looked around, at the beauty of the garden, the unicorn, the butterflies, and wondered what else she could possibly want. This fantasy world was more beautiful, more perfect, than anything she could dream up.

She felt a strong arm wrap around her waist and pull her close. She turned and stared into familiar gray-blue eyes. Dark, wavy hair fell across his forehead, giving him a rakish quality. *Bannan. Jacob.* The names swirled in her head confusingly, and she couldn't quite remember who either of them were, but she did recognize the warning bells that started ringing throughout her body.

Jenny pulled away and took a few slow steps backward, putting space between her and Jacob. She removed the crown and threw it to the side. Her memories came flooding back, and the dreamy calm state she'd been in was replaced with hot rage.

"You lied to me! I know who you *really* are, *Jacob*!"

"Yes, I figured as much. That's why I brought you here, to show you what I have to offer." Jacob ran a hand through his hair and took a step toward her. She took two steps backward, and he stopped.

"Are you not even a little tempted?" he said with a smirk. "Anything you want, I can create. Anything at all."

"I want Charlotte back," she spat.

"Of course."

The pink jasmine vines swayed apart again, and Charlotte appeared in a bright cherry-red dress. Her short white-blonde hair was perfectly styled. Jenny felt as though she'd been stabbed in the chest.

"Charlotte? Is that really you?" Jenny took a step toward her, wondering if this Charlotte would ignore her the way ghost Charlotte in the library had.

"Of course it's really me," Charlotte said with a smile. Jenny paused, examining the girl in front of her. Something in her eyes wasn't quite right, and the tone of her voice was just a little bit off. Or was she just imagining things? Jacob had been tricking her this entire time. She wouldn't let him trick her again.

"What did you say to me when we first met?" Jenny asked. She wanted nothing more than to hear the answer—the right answer. The real Charlotte would know. Jenny swallowed and watched Charlotte's reaction.

Charlotte blinked her bright blue eyes at Jenny and looked over at Jacob. Jenny knew, then, that this wasn't Charlotte, no matter how badly Jenny wanted her to be.

"Nice try," Jenny said, waving the mirage away. The thing that looked like Charlotte disappeared into pink smoke. "Charlotte was one of a kind. You can't trick me with a shoddy approximation."

Jacob lowered his head, feigning contrition.

"Why are you doing this? I know you're Jacob Grimm. I know this has just been a big game to you—and I'm not playing anymore."

Jacob laughed, and Jenny cringed. The sound of his amusement made her physically ill.

"Of course you're still playing," Jacob said. "You'll always be playing—as long as you're here. And you'll *always be here*."

Jenny's heart pounded inside her chest. She looked around

the garden, frantic to find a way out, a way back to the ruins and her friends.

"The only thing you can control, *the only thing*, is which side you're playing on," Jacob continued. "Believe me, the game is much more fun when you play *with* me instead of *against* me."

"I choose against," she said, lifting her golden gown so she could walk without tripping over it. She started determinedly in the opposite direction of where Jacob stood, even though she had no idea where she was going. She just knew she couldn't stand there listening to him anymore.

"As you wish."

The gold dress disappeared, and she was back in her own clothes. May, Ryan, and Rain were standing in front of her, their eyes wide.

"What just happened?" Ryan asked, moving closer to her.

"I ... Jacob ... did something. Took me ... somewhere. It doesn't matter. Let's keep going." She brushed past Ryan but then stopped, realizing she didn't know which direction to go.

"What did he say to you?" May asked seriously, her eyes dark. Jenny didn't want to tell her, didn't want to give her anything.

"Jenny? What did he say?" Ryan echoed. Jenny rolled her eyes and tossed her head back in frustration.

"Nothing useful. Just the usual *blah blah stay here and be my queen* nonsense."

"Be his *what?*" Ryan moved toward her, his expression pinched.

"It's just part of his game. It doesn't mean anything," she explained. "Now come on. I don't want to be here one second longer."

May looked at her suspiciously but turned and started back down the path. She followed with Ryan and Rain behind her.

"You're sure he didn't say anything else? Anything about

the book?" Ryan insisted.

"You mean did he tell me how to get the book? What to do with it? No. No, I think I'd remember that," Jenny snapped and immediately regretted it. It wasn't Ryan she was mad at. She stopped and turned around to face him. "I'm sorry. I just can't take it anymore," she said. "I hate it here. I hate what he's doing to us. I just want it to end."

He nodded and wrapped his arms around her. She allowed herself to enjoy the comfort of his embrace for a brief moment, then extracted herself from his arms. Jenny turned and saw May was already a few yards away. She went after her and wondered how May could remember where to go. The ruins were a mess of broken rock and vines, and it all looked more or less the same. But May took each turn without hesitation, and they moved quickly through the broken walls and stone creatures until they stopped at the opening of a dark tunnel. Jenny couldn't help but smile faintly at the two sleeping guard dogs curled up on either side of the opening.

"It's through here," May said, then ducked inside. The darkness swallowed her, and for a moment, Jenny didn't want to follow. But then Rain slipped into the darkness, and Ryan pushed Jenny gently forward.

"You're never going to be behind me again," he said softly. "Every time I take my eyes off you, you disappear."

Jenny smiled faintly and walked slowly into the dark tunnel, bending down slightly so as not to hit her head. It was a short tunnel; Jenny could see Rain's and May's silhouettes bobbing along against the bright light coming from the other side. In a few moments, she was through and standing in an open courtyard overrun with weeds and vines.

May hadn't waited for them; she was continuing forward to the other side of the courtyard toward a tower that loomed above them menacingly. Jenny looked up at it, wondering if the way out of here was really up there.

She walked on a small goat path through the tall weeds the others must have made, with Ryan close behind her. Ahead, May had finally stopped and was waiting impatiently for them at the base of the tower.

"This way," she said, and entered the tower through a door propped open by a rock. Statues of slumped, sleeping soldiers were on the ground on either side of the doorway. Jenny hesitated. She could see inside the dark tower, could see the flickering candles and the start of a spiraling staircase she assumed would take them to the top. Sadie and the others were waiting for them up there, waiting for them to arrive with a solution to their problems. She felt tired looking up the seemingly endless staircase, and she wished she had more than a few useless knives to offer. She felt Ryan's warm hand on her lower back and let him guide her over the threshold and into the tower.

51

Sadie tried to make herself as small as possible as the circular room at the top of the tower became more and more cramped. It'd been tight before, but with the addition of Jenny, Ryan, and Rain, there was now nine of them. Nine people in a room that only comfortably fit six or seven. There being so many bodies was also making the room feel hot, stuffy, and disgustingly humid. She could smell everyone's sweat mixing together in the stagnant air and felt herself gag.

"Can someone open that window?" Sadie yelled.

Aiden squeezed past Travis and Cameron to the only window and pushed it open.

"Better?" Aiden called back to her.

It was not better.

"So, did you guys find anything in Eckert's room?" Sadie asked.

The chagrined looks Ryan and Jenny exchanged told her no.

"Sort of?" Jenny said, taking a satchel from Ryan and holding it up for the rest of them to see. "We brought the rest of the knives. They all do something special."

"Special—but nothing related to this," May added sourly.

Sadie had known better than to let herself get her hopes up too high, but she had still hoped just enough for this news to make her feel deflated. She'd told Hannah everything was going to be okay, but they were no closer to solving their book problem than they were before. Sadie knew there was only one thing left for them to try.

"If we can't remove the book," Sadie said seriously. "We can always just destroy it."

A hush fell over the room as they considered this. Sadie knew May would be against it, that they might all be, but at this point, they had run out of options.

"How would we destroy it?" Rain asked.

Aiden held up his fire knife. "We light it on fire."

"I still think destroying it is a mistake," May said predictably. Sadie looked over at Jenny and was surprised to see the dark look she was giving May.

"Do it. Torch it," Jenny said, her jaw tight and eyes hard.

Suddenly Sadie wasn't so sure destroying the book was a good idea after all.

"Should we take a vote?" Cameron asked, shifting awkwardly away from Travis, who had sweat stains blooming from his armpits and staining his shirt.

"Sure, why not," Jenny replied. "All in favor of torching the book?"

Hannah and Cameron raised their hands first, surprising Sadie. Ryan hesitated, glancing at May and then Jenny, then slowly raised his hand. Aiden raised his hand and so did Travis. Sadie lifted her own hand in the air.

The only two people with their hands down were May and Rain. May, she had expected, but Rain? What was going on inside *her* head?

"Well, majority rules," Jenny said, lowering her arm. "Aiden, go ahead. Stab away."

"Don't you think it's strange Jacob isn't here, trying to stop us?" May insisted. "If he was so concerned about us getting this book, where is he?"

"Maybe he's afraid of Sadie's right hook," Aiden joked.

Sadie smirked a little, remembering the one good punch she'd gotten in before Jacob pulled his disappearing trick. She remembered how good it felt making contact, even though it had probably hurt her more than it had him.

"The book is too important to destroy," Rain argued. "Who knows what it could do? We have time. We can figure it out without setting it on fire."

The heat inside the tower was really getting to Sadie. She was feeling a little dizzy. She pulled her sweaty, sticky T-shirt away from her body and shook it, trying to release heat and cool down. She was starting to care less and less about what they did with the book. She just wanted to get out of the stifling tower.

Jenny pushed past Cameron and Travis, determination carved into her face. Sadie watched, stunned, as Jenny took the knife from Aiden, and in one quick movement, stabbed it into the book.

"What is wrong with you!" May yelled at Jenny. Jenny glared back and let go of the knife, leaving it standing straight up in the book. Black flames whipped up the blade from where it met the book, and they all backed away as much as they could in the small room.

"Is that what's supposed to happen?" Hannah asked softly next to her, her eyes fixed on the black flames whipping high into the air.

Part of Sadie had expected nothing to happen, for the book to be under some magical protection, but the pages burned quickly, crisping black, then white. Bits of burnt paper floated through the air around them, and the book began giving off a smoke so dark purple it was almost black. The smoke billowed off the book and filled the room quickly. *Too quickly*, Sadie thought. In mere moments, it was pitch black inside the room, and her lungs were burning from the smoke.

"We need to get out of here!" Sadie yelled as she blindly grabbed for Hannah and pushed her toward the only exit. Chaos filled the tower as they all tried to get out of the door at the same time. Sadie pushed Hannah through the door and followed her out. She felt Travis's heavy steps behind her as they made their way to the spiral staircase. Sadie watched Hannah start to descend the stairs, then stepped aside to let Travis pass. He gave Sadie a confused look but continued down the stairs as the dark purple smoke poured out of the room toward them. Ryan broke through, coming out of the room coughing, an unconscious Rain draped in his arms, her long golden hair swaying back and forth as he walked.

"What happened?" Sadie asked, placing a hand against Rain's pale cheek.

"Her heart," Ryan gasped, tears flowing down his face. "She just collapsed. It's too much for her, she can't—" Ryan broke off as a coughing fit seized him. Sadie guided him to the stairs and pointed down. "Go! You need to get her out of here!"

Ryan stopped at the first step and turned back to Sadie, "But Jenny—"

"I've got her. Go on, move!"

Ryan coughed again and made his way slowly down the stairs, his sister's limp limbs swaying in his arms. After they'd taken a few steps, Sadie couldn't see them at all—the black smoke was all around her, filling every corner of the tower. She heard a clatter and squinted at the doorway to see Cameron as he half fell out of the room, coughing, his eyes streaming tears from the smoke.

"I can't find Hannah!" he yelled, his voice high and tight. "I have to go back—"

"Hannah's fine! She already went down the stairs. Now, go!"

Cameron paused the same way Ryan had, and for a brief moment, Sadie felt a little jealous of her friends. He looked at Sadie like she might be lying to him. She couldn't blame him—even if Hannah hadn't made it out, she would have still told him she had. Sadie had one goal, and that was to get *everyone* out. Everyone.

"She was the first one down!" Sadie yelled through the smoke. To her relief, Cameron turned away without any more arguing and headed down the stairs. Sadie pulled her shirt over her nose and mouth, but it didn't really help. She coughed so hard her throat and lungs felt like *they* were on fire, and her eyes burned. May, Aiden, and Jenny were all still inside the room.

They should be out by now, Sadie thought, trying not to panic. She took a step toward the room but stopped when a figure emerged from the thick smoke. Sadie could just make out May's colorful bracelets through the black fumes. She grabbed May by the arm and pulled her toward the stairs. May looked like she was about to vomit.

Jenny fell out of the room after her, tripping on something and collapsing onto the floor. Sadie helped Jenny up, then guided her toward the stairs. Her lungs burned, and she felt dizzy. She didn't know how much longer she could last. Jenny took a few steps down the stairs, then turned, looking back at May, who was still at the top of the stairs.

"Aiden is still in there!" May yelled, twisting to look behind her, as if she could see him through the thick smoke still pouring from the room.

"I'll get him. You two, go!" Sadie answered, waving them ahead. May started down the stairs but stopped. Jenny was blocking her way down, looking up at Sadie. Sadie's throat and lungs burned so badly she didn't think she could talk anymore. She waved at Jenny to keep going and turned back toward the room full of smoke. She waited a beat, hoping Aiden was right behind them, but when he didn't appear, she dropped down to her knees to try and get underneath the smoke. She forced herself to crawl forward, into the room, and toward the book that was still pouring smoke, though it should've been nothing but ash by now. Sadie couldn't understand how one book could cause this much chaos. Sadie blinked smoke-wrought tears away and tried yelling Aiden's name, but each time it devolved into a coughing fit that shook her whole body. The stone floor hurt her knees as she crawled toward the statue, where she'd seen him standing last and stopped when she bumped into a large, soft mass on the floor.

She could barely see Aiden through the smoke, but he wasn't moving. Sadie grabbed him underneath the arms and as quickly as she could, scooted back toward the door, dragging his heavy, limp body out of the room.

Sadie dropped him on the floor at the top of the stairs and slapped him across the face. "Wake up, Aiden, or you're going to die!" she yelled, then burst into a painful coughing fit. She was struggling to think clearly. The smoke was filling her lungs and head. She was growing weaker by the second; she could feel her body slowing, and her limbs felt heavy as she struggled to keep herself upright. She knew if she didn't get out of the tower soon, she was going to pass out too. She slapped him again, and miraculously his eyes burst open and he let out ragged, painful-sounding coughs.

Sadie grabbed Aiden by the hand and tried to help him up, but it felt like he was anchored to the floor. As her own strength quickly waned, she began to panic. She wasn't strong enough to carry him down the stairs; she couldn't even get him up off the ground. She wasn't even sure she could get *herself* down anymore. She felt so sluggish and heavy. Something next to her moved, and she flinched. She couldn't see through the smoke but recognized Jenny's voice.

"On three," Jenny said as she leaned down and grabbed Aiden by one arm. Sadie felt tears rolling down her face and wasn't entirely sure they were just from the smoke. She pushed through her own exhaustion and leaned down to grab Aiden by his other arm.

"Three!"

They both pulled and were able to get Aiden on his feet. They half dragged him down the first few stairs, then stopped.

Sadie looked at Jenny, whose face was covered in ash and sweat, and shook her head. This wasn't working. They would never make it down at this rate. If they didn't drop Aiden and run, all three of them were going to die. *I am not going to die in this tower,* she told herself firmly. *And neither are they.*

Sadie kicked Aiden in the leg, hard. He swiveled his head to look at her, drunk from lack of oxygen. "Whayoudofor?" he mumbled. She kicked him again. His eyes widened as he tried to focus on her. She felt some of the weight lessen as he regained control of his legs. Sadie let go of his arm and took him by the hand. Jenny let go, too, and fell behind him. Sadie turned and moved down the stairs as fast as she could, dragging Aiden behind her like a heavy, wobbly kite.

The farther down the stairs she went, the less smoke there was, but she'd been breathing it too long, and she felt light headed and nauseous. She tried to keep it together and felt a rush of relief when she finally stepped off the last stair. She and Jenny pulled Aiden out of the tower and moved as far away as they could before collapsing onto the ground. She took in deep breaths of clean air and tried not to throw up. Beside her, Aiden was holding his head and staring at the ground, his chest heaving. Jenny was a few feet away, still standing but leaning forward and gasping for breath.

Sadie looked for the others and saw Hannah, May, and Ryan standing over something in the center of the courtyard. Jenny rushed over to Ryan, and Sadie slowly got up and made her way to the group. She pushed between Hannah and May and saw Rain lying on her back on the ground, her peaches-and-cream complexion smeared with gray ash and her long hair loose in a golden puddle around her face. Cameron was at her side, pressing on her chest rhythmically and then breathing into her mouth.

"Is she okay?" Sadie whispered.

"He's doing CPR," Hannah whispered back, her eyes full

of tears. "Sadie, she's not *breathing*."

Sadie watched Cameron work on Rain, the blood pumping in her ears and her eyes stinging. She glanced at Ryan. His face was twisted in fear. Jenny held on to his arm and seemed to be saying something quietly to him. Sadie felt powerless as she stood there, just watching as Cameron tried to save Rain's life. She thought of the last time she'd seen Rain like that—a couple years ago at their town's annual Radish Festival. Rain had been taken to a hospital after riding a small roller coaster. After everything Rain had gone through the last few days, Sadie felt it was a miracle this hadn't happened sooner.

She felt a movement behind her and turned to see Aiden peering over her at Rain and Cameron. He was covered in ash, and his eyes were bloodshot from the smoke. He looked like he was barely able to stand.

"Her heart couldn't take it," she heard Ryan gasp. She looked over at him to see tears streaming down his face, leaving clean streaks on his own ash-covered cheeks. "This never should have happened! I should have—"

A rattling gasp burst out of Rain as she tipped her head backward. Cameron leaned back to give her room as she tore at her throat, gasping for air. Rain rolled onto her side, and hard, painful-sounding sobs poured out of her.

"Please, I don't want to die here, please," she cried.

Ryan dropped to his knees at his sister's side and wrapped her in his arms. He rocked her gently back and forth as she cried and coughed into his shoulder. "Shhh, you're not going to die," he whispered to her. "You're going to be fine. We're all going to be fine."

Sadie felt awkward, watching this intimate moment. As she turned, she noticed the same black-purple smoke that had caused this start to pour out the door they'd escaped out of. Sadie squinted as the smoke started to take shape; seven separate streams grew out of one. As she watched, more intrigued than afraid, the seven smoke streams started to take shape. They grew serpentine heads, and each one opened its mouth to reveal long smoke tongues. Arms that ended in sharp claws grew on either side of the original stream of smoke. *It's a dragon*, she thought, stunned. *A seven-headed smoke dragon*. It was heading straight for them.

"Guys, we need to get out of here," Sadie croaked, her throat burning and swollen from the smoke. Ryan stopped rocking, and Rain looked up from his shoulder, her eyes red and her face smeared with tears and ash. Sadie pointed at the smoke dragon that had formed just outside the tower, and they all turned to gawk at the immense creature weaving its way toward them. Each of the seven heads opened its jaws and spit black flames out at them. She could feel the heat. She gestured toward the tunnel, and they moved as quickly as they could toward it, with Ryan struggling to carry Rain, who was too weak to walk. Sadie paused when she got to the tunnel and watched them go in one by one, making certain everyone had made it through before ducking in herself.

Outside of the courtyard, they stopped and stared at the dark opening of the tunnel, wondering if the smoke dragon would slither its way through. Sadie didn't want to stay to find out. She waved for the others to keep going, and she brought up the rear. As they made their way through the ruins, she paused and looked back at the tower against the skyline. She didn't see any sign that the smoke dragon was following them.

They continued to move quickly through the ruins, past crumbling walls and shrinking vines, stone chickens, and statues of sleeping people. The roses around them, which had been a rainbow of pinks, reds, yellows, and whites, had all changed to the same dark purple of the smoke. Sadie eyed the roses nervously, uncertain what the color change meant. They moved faster through the maze of ruins until they reached the banged-up old metal gate. As she crossed the threshold and left the ruins behind her, she relaxed at little. They had made it out, and she hadn't seen even a wisp of the purple smoke behind them.

They made their way around to the front of the castle. Sadie eyed it with uncertainty; she didn't know what to expect now that they had destroyed the book. As they came closer, she saw that it was unchanged, and there, standing on the front steps with an obnoxious grin that made her fists clench, was Jacob.

52

Jenny's whole body ached, and her throat hurt from breathing the dark purple smoke in the tower. As they approached the front of the castle, she allowed herself to feel hopeful—now that they had destroyed the Grimm brothers' book, they should be able to leave. She took a deep breath of clean air and tried to tame the excitement bubbling up inside of her. When her eyes locked onto Jacob, casually standing on the castle steps grinning at them, her heart sank, and she felt a chill roll through her. *No.*

"Why is he still here?" Ryan whispered to her. "I thought destroying the book would destroy him."

"Destroy me?" Jacob echoed Ryan and laughed. It was a cringe-inducing sound and added fuel to the fire of hatred burning inside of her. "You can't *destroy* me! Everything here is *because of me.* I am all-powerful!" He laughed again, and Jenny's jaw started to ache from clenching her teeth.

She had been *so sure* that destroying the book would end Jacob's reign of terror. But here he was, completely unaffected. The blood drained from her face as she realized she might have destroyed the only thing that could have told them how to beat Jacob. *And* she had released some sort of smoke monster. *Maybe he wanted us to destroy the book*, she thought miserably. She could feel May's eyes on her, but she refused to turn.

"Did you enjoy my tower?" Jacob said slyly as his gaze moved across them. "Tsk, looks like you all survived. I was sure at least one of you wouldn't make it out." He eyed Rain, then Aiden.

"*Your* tower?" Cameron asked as he moved in front of Hannah.

"Of course. Everything here is mine. You aren't the brightest, are you?"

Before she could stop it, Jenny felt a sharp laugh burst out of her. Everyone turned and stared at her, but she didn't care. She felt out of control—the laughter was strained and crazed and sounded like it was coming from someone else. She wondered if she had finally snapped.

Ryan grabbed her by the arm and leaned in close. "What are you doing?" he whispered.

"Nothing," she said breathlessly, the laughter hurting her charred lungs and throat. "Just, *Cameron,* not bright!" she couldn't help it, she laughed again and winced at the pain it caused. "He just saved Rain's life! He's probably going to be valedictorian!"

Thinking about Cameron being valedictorian quickly sobered her. Cameron wasn't going to be *anything* if they never left this place. The book she had been relying on had been a lie, and they had no other options. Jenny looked around at her friends and felt a deep sadness for all of them. For what they had wanted to be, for what they had wanted to do with their lives, and how none of that was going to happen. They were stuck here forever, or until Jacob succeeded in killing them all off, one by one.

She thought about Charlotte. Beautiful, charismatic Charlotte. She would have been something important, Jenny was sure of it. Charlotte could have done anything she wanted to. Now she was just a mindless ghost. She couldn't stomach the thought of the castle filling up with all of her dead friends. She had only one card left to play.

"What if I agree to stay here with you," Jenny offered, her eyes glued to Jacob. "Would you let the others go?"

Jacob tilted his head slightly as if considering, his dark

wavy hair falling across his eyes. "Why would I do that? You're already here with me."

Jenny's heart beat painfully inside her chest as she walked over to Jacob.

"Jenny, what are you doing?" Sadie hissed at her as she walked past. She ignored the question and continued until she was directly in front of Jacob. She looked up at him. On flat ground, he was taller than her, but standing a step up caused him to tower over her menacingly. His dark, windswept hair fell across his forehead, and his stormy, gray eyes bore into her. She swallowed and tried not to waver.

"Sure, I may *be* here, but if you don't let my friends go, I'll *never* be yours."

She looked up at him as seductively as she could but wasn't sure what the result was. She was filthy, covered in ash and dirt, and her bare arms and legs were still peppered with unsightly welts from the shrunken apple heads. She was a mess, but that didn't seem to matter to Jacob. The cruel smile he'd had melted away, and he looked down at her the way he had when she met him, when he introduced himself as Bannan. He was looking at her like she was *interesting*. Like she was something he'd never seen before. She didn't know if he really had feelings for her or if he was even capable of having feelings. All of it could easily have just been part of his game, but it was her last chance. Her only chance.

"And if I let them go," Jacob said as he reached out to wind one of her loose ringlets around his finger, "You'll be mine?"

He let her hair slip away from his finger and brought his hand down to rest against her face, then her neck. She could feel the blood pounding throughout her body and was starting to feel light headed. She forced herself to remain still, forced herself not to jerk away from his touch.

"Get your hands off her!" Ryan yelled as he stormed toward them. Jenny quickly turned around and gave him the hardest look she could muster. *Don't.* Ryan stopped a few feet away, looking like a slapped puppy—confused and hurt.

"What if I let them go and you don't hold up your end of the bargain?" Jacob said, unmoved by Ryan's outburst. She turned back to face him. His arms were now folded across his chest. Jenny's pulse was beating in her ears.

"I'm sure there are lots of things you could do to me if that happens."

Jacob smiled, a disconcerting twist of the lips that was neither warm nor happy.

"That is very true," he replied. She hated the way he was staring at her; there was an intense hunger in his eyes she knew could never be satiated. She fought the urge to back away from him. She had to remain strong. For them.

"It'll be dark soon," he said without taking his eyes off her. "Why don't you prove to me that you're mine tonight, and if I'm satisfied, I'll let them go in the morning."

Jenny hated this idea.

"Jenny," Sadie snapped from behind her. "You can't do this."

Hannah walked over to them, her pale skin flushed and her eyes shining. She grabbed Jenny by the arm and glared up at Jacob.

"Wait, just wait a minute," Hannah said as she pulled Jenny away from Jacob. The group moved toward Jenny and surrounded her, blocking her from Jacob's view.

"This is disgusting," Hannah said in a harsh whisper. "You aren't seriously considering doing ... *that* ... are you?"

Jenny looked down at the ground, her face flushed with shame and fear.

"We won't let you sacrifice yourself," Rain said softly.

"Yeah, I mean, it's not so bad here," Aiden said, a forced brevity in his voice. "We can make it work. Might be, you know, fun. Living here together. Forever."

"I won't let you do this," Sadie snapped, her dark brown eyes blazing. "So just forget it. It's not an option."

"It *is* an option," Jenny argued, her voice low so Jacob wouldn't hear. "You think I want to do this? Be with ... *him*? Of course not. But I'd rather do that than have to watch all of you waste your lives and die here. If I have a chance to save you all, I'm going to take it."

She watched as her friends shook their heads sadly. Ryan grabbed her by the hand, and she met his gaze. He looked shattered, like he knew he had no choice. There was no other way. He pulled her into a tight embrace, and she felt his lips lightly touch her ear.

"If it was just me, I'd never let you do this," he whispered, his voice strained. "But Rain ... "

Until then, Jenny had been holding it together pretty well. She felt her eyes start to water, and a powerful feeling of injustice swelled inside of her. *This isn't* fair.

She pulled away from Ryan and tried to look unmoved. She swallowed the lump in her throat and turned away from him. She was determined not to cry. Not in front of Jacob.

Jenny pushed through the wall of friends and made her way back to Jacob, who was still waiting for her on the castle steps. She had to get this over with before she lost her nerve. He had an amused smile on his face.

"Okay," she said. "Deal."

"You know, I've thought about it, and I've changed my mind," Jacob said with a slight tilt of his head.

"What? You can't do that!" Jenny's heart beat faster. *No, no, no. He can't take it back!*

"Don't worry, my darling, I'll still let *most* of them go," Jacob said, his eyes passing over her friends behind her. "All except one. I'd like to have some insurance that you'll behave. I'll even let you pick which one stays." Jacob grinned.

Jenny turned and looked at her friends who were all looking

at her with similar stunned expressions. Her stomach twisted and it felt like the blood had drained from her body.

"No," she argued, trying to keep her voice strong and even. "You have to let them *all* go."

"Tsk, you're not in control here," he said. "Pick one to stay, or they *all* stay."

She thought that offering herself to Jacob would be the worst thing she ever had to do—but she had been wrong. This was so much worse. How could she possibly choose? She would be dooming whomever she chose to stay. She would be taking their life away. Jenny didn't want to entertain this, but her mind was already rolling through the options.

She couldn't make Ryan stay, force him to be trapped in this castle watching her get used by Jacob. No. And she couldn't take Rain away from Ryan either. Cameron's parents had already lost one son, she couldn't take their remaining child from them. Hannah couldn't handle it here—she was barely holding it together as it was.

That left May, Travis, Aiden, and Sadie. A small part of her wanted to choose May, knowing she would be the most helpful. But then she'd have to be trapped with May in the castle for the rest of her life, and Jacob was bad enough.

She locked eyes with Sadie. If she had to spend forever trapped in a castle with just one person, it would be Sadie. The time Jenny had spent alienated from her had been the worst part of her life, until this. But the love she had for Sadie, the love that made her want to choose her, was the same love that wouldn't let her take Sadie's life away. She glanced at Aiden and noticed how close he was standing to Sadie. Jenny wouldn't take him away from her either.

"I'm sorry," Jenny said, her heart pounding painfully in her chest. "Travis."

53

Sadie watched, stunned, as Jenny chose Travis to stay behind with her. She had been certain Jenny would have picked her, and was slightly hurt she hadn't. Sadie struggled to get her thoughts straight—she was hurt Jenny hadn't chosen her, but she was relieved too. She wanted to leave this horrible place just as much as everyone else. But *Travis*? She never would have thought he'd be Jenny's choice to stay.

"It's alright, I understand," Travis said glumly. "I'm the only one no one would miss."

Sadie jerked her head to stare at Travis, who she saw, *really saw*, for the first time. He was no longer the bully in the donut shop, no longer the class clown vying for attention. He was just a boy. A boy who thought no one would miss him. Sadie's vision blurred as her eyes watered, and she wiped angrily at the wetness that fell down her cheeks. *Stop it.*

No, Sadie thought fiercely, *this can't be how this ends. The bad guy cannot win.* Sadie chewed on her bottom lip until she felt it crack open. She licked the sliver of blood away, hot copper on her tongue. *There has to be a plan B.*

Then it occurred to her: maybe this had always been *Jenny's* plan B. The book was a complete waste of time, but there had to be another way. Any other way than leaving her best friend behind to the whims of an ancient psychopath. Sadie glared at Jacob with a hatred so strong it made her veins tremble. Sadie wanted to scratch his eyes out. In that moment, it was all she could think about—how his eyeballs would feel underneath her fingernails.

Sadie looked at the others, who had been given the golden ticket out of the Black Forest. The others who had so easily allowed Jenny, and Travis, to pay for their freedom with their lives. She hated herself for being one of them. Hannah's face was buried in Cameron's shoulder, and Cameron was looking at the ground. Ryan was staring out into nothing; any anger he'd had fizzled out and was replaced with defeat. He was supposed to love Jenny, and he was just going to let this happen? He wasn't going to fight for her? His weakness sickened Sadie.

"No," Sadie spat. She pushed herself in front of Travis, who had already started walking toward Jenny and Jacob. "I'll stay."

"Sadie, no!" Jenny hissed.

Travis paused and looked from Sadie to Jenny to Jacob. His broad, sunburned face was blank with confusion. She tried to maintain her confidence, but it was already faltering. *What have I done?*

"No," Jenny repeated, turning to Jacob. "I chose Travis. You said I had to choose."

Jacob rubbed at his chin and looked back and forth between Travis and Sadie, as if considering.

"To be honest," he finally said, "I wasn't thrilled with your choice, Jenny. I find this one"—he waved a hand at Travis—"the most boring of your little group."

"Rude," Travis mumbled.

"This one, though," Jacob stepped down off the steps and closed the gap between himself and Sadie. She shifted backward, trying to keep some space between them. In a movement too quick for her to stop, he reached out and removed her hair tie, causing her long dark hair to fall loose down her back. "Is much nicer to look at, at least."

"No," Jenny whispered. Sadie tried not to look at her.

"I accept your offer!" Jacob said gleefully, shooing Travis away. Travis lumbered backward, as if in a fog. "Come now, ladies, it's starting to get dark."

Jacob turned his back on her and Jenny, walked back up the steps, and opened the heavy castle door. He waited, holding the door open for them. Jenny turned and followed, passing Jacob as she entered the castle. Sadie hesitated, still not believing what she had just done. Aiden grabbed her by the arm. Surprised, she turned to face him.

"Why?" he asked, a hurt in his voice Sadie had not expected. "Why did you do it?"

Sadie wasn't sure how to answer that question. Going home with Aiden was all she wanted—and she had been *so close* to having that wish come true. She looked up at him; his deep brown eyes had shadows underneath them, his mouth was just inches from her own. After she entered the castle, she might never see him again, she realized. He and the others could be gone come morning. This might be her last chance.

She pulled him close and kissed him—her first, and last, kiss. She wasn't sure she was doing it right, but it was warm and soft, and she didn't want it to end. Her bottom lip stung a little where it had split open, but the pain just made it feel more real. She felt his hands in her hair and let her body relax against his. Finally she pulled away, her face flushed, and avoided meeting his eyes. She felt a buzzing inside of her, all over her—it was a feeling she'd never had before. *A feeling*, she thought sadly, *I will never have again.* She looked up, and Aiden was staring at her, his mouth slightly open and his eyes wide. He awkwardly ran a hand through his hair and looked like he was about to say something. Sadie didn't want to hear whatever it was. It would either be dumb or mean, and it'd ruin this moment, or he'd say something sweet and perfect and it would make walking away from him even harder. She turned away quickly, before he could get a word out, and hurried up the steps after Jenny. As she reached Jacob, who was still holding the door open, she paused and glared at him before stepping over the threshold and into the castle.

The door shut behind her with a very final-sounding *thud*. She had a feeling that even if the others tried to get in, they wouldn't be able to. The entrance was warm with candlelight, and Rumpelstiltskin's front desk was still unmanned. Jenny stood awkwardly in the center of the lobby, just underneath the dusty chandelier. Her arms were crossed, and she slowly shook her head at Sadie. Sadie ignored her and turned around to face Jacob. She thought of how much this man—who should be long dead—had taken from her. Her life. Her chance with Aiden. Her best friend. For what?

"I just want to know—why did you make that whole thing up about the book?" Sadie asked. "Just to torture us?"

Jacob's eyes flicked to the empty space on the wall where the portrait of he and his brother used to be. Sadie smiled, remembering how much fun she had tearing it down earlier that morning. She relished the thought that she had taken something, however small, away from *him*.

"I told you in the tower—you stopped playing my other games, so I had to start a new one. You are so gullible. Feisty, but gullible." His eyes flicked to the empty space on the wall again. Something stirred inside Sadie's mind. Something about the painting. Sadie forced herself not to look at the desk where they had shoved the portrait after trying to destroy it. Jacob shouldn't care about a stupid painting, unless it wasn't *just* a stupid painting. Then it struck her: maybe he hadn't been *completely* lying before.

She remembered how she had reached into a painting of him to take his key ring, how the painted object had become solid in her hand. *He likes hiding things in paintings!*

Excitement surged through her as she realized she knew where the book was. The *real* book. It hadn't been a lie, and it was right *there*, shoved underneath Rumpelstiltskin's desk, just a few feet away from her. She just didn't know how she was going to get to it without Jacob noticing and stopping her. She needed him out of the room.

"Excuse me," Jacob said as he brushed past her and rested an arm around Jenny's shoulders. Jenny seemed to shrink underneath his arm, her eyes full of seething anger. "I think I'd like to play with my new pet," he said, pulling Jenny closer to him. Sadie felt sick watching him, felt sick thinking about what that meant. She could try to delay him, try to keep him down here as long as possible. But she needed to get that book, so she said nothing. *Sorry, Jenny.*

Jacob smiled and looked down at Jenny. "Come, pet. Let's get you cleaned up."

Jacob took Jenny by the hand and pulled her toward the stairs. Jacob paused at the bottom and, instead of continuing up, turned around to face Sadie again.

"I'd offer you a room, but"—he gestured at the rack behind the desk, empty of keys from when the others were searching the rooms—"I'm sure you'll figure something out."

Jacob grinned, and it took everything Sadie had not to lunge at him. Instead, she didn't move a muscle as she watched him lead Jenny up the stairs.

Once Jacob and Jenny were out of sight, she ran behind the desk to grab the painting. She dropped to her knees and pulled it out. *This whole time*, she thought, exhilarated but terrified that she might be wrong. She unrolled the canvas and stared at the open book in the portrait—Jacob's lap. How could they have been so stupid? *It was right there.*

She swallowed and reached for the book in the painting. Her hand slipped into it just like last time, and when she pulled it back, she was holding a book, and Jacob's lap was empty. It was the largest—and heaviest—book she'd ever held. It had a simple black leather cover and was at least three inches thick with gold-trimmed pages. The book was open about halfway when she pulled it out of the portrait, and Sadie stared down at the pages covered in scrawled German. She flipped through a few pages to find more writing, in what looked like two different sets of handwriting—Jacob's and his brother's, she guessed. She couldn't read any of it, but she knew they must be the stories, the stories that had been trying to kill them.

"I was wondering where that went."

Sadie whipped her head up to see Jacob standing just a few feet away from her. She slammed the book shut and held it tightly to her chest. She noticed his eyes flick down to the painting on the ground.

"You ruined it," he said, his previously teasing tone now infused with icy anger. "That's the only portrait of my brother I have."

Sadie briefly glanced down at the painting. Her and Jenny's footprints were all over the two men's faces. The paint was scratched off in some places. She looked past Jacob, toward the stairs, and didn't see Jenny.

"Where's Jenny?" she asked, her stomach twisting.

"I left her upstairs when I felt you take the book. The book and I are connected, you see. It's *part of me.*"

Sadie cursed herself for not getting as far from the castle as possible when she got her hands on the book. She should have taken it and ran, not sat there on the floor of the lobby just waiting to get caught. Jacob towered over her and made her feel small, insignificant, and most of all, vulnerable. She scrambled to her feet, the book still clutched tightly to her chest.

"It's foolish, what you're doing," Jacob said, clucking his tongue. "Perhaps I won't let *anyone* leave now."

Sadie's heart rattled harshly in her chest, and her head spun as she tried to come up with an exit strategy. He was stronger than she was, in all ways—he could just pluck the book out of her hands right now. The same fury that had fueled her in the tower when she attacked him burned through her now. She had hurt him then, she remembered. Not much, but enough for him to magically remove himself from the situation. She thought about everything she'd seen Jacob do—and realized it actually wasn't much. The only magical thing she'd witnessed him do was disappear and reappear. She thought about the story he had told them about him and his brother, how their power came from the book. The book *she* was holding.

She backed up toward the door, and he took a few steps forward. If he reached his arm out, he could almost touch her. Sadie was starting to panic; she had one chance to do the exact right thing, and she had no idea what the exact right thing was. She looked around her for a weapon, for anything that might help her, but found nothing. She looked down at the book in her hands and wondered—if Jacob could use the book against them, couldn't she do the same thing? She didn't have anything to write with, nothing she could use to write a new story into the book. *Doesn't matter*, she thought bitterly, *he'd stop me before I got a single word down.*

She looked down at the book, the top of the gold-edged pages shining up at her. It was just paper. Old, brittle paper. She opened the book, and Jacob took a step toward her. She quickly grabbed a few pages and tore. Jacob let out a glass-shattering scream, and she looked up to see not the handsome young man Jacob had been pretending to be but an ancient man with paper-thin skin and white hair. The skin on his face sagged, and his hands turned into bony claws. The only recognizable thing was his searing gray-blue eyes.

Sadie was horrified, and elated, by Jacob's transformation. *She* had the power now. She grabbed another few pages and tore them out, letting them drift to the floor as Jacob screamed again. His arms and chest looked like they'd been shredded by an invisible wolf. Blood dripped down from the long claw marks, and Sadie hesitated. Jacob howled in pain and lunged at her, grabbing her by the arm and yanking her toward him. His other hand reached for the book and tried to tear it out of her grip. She struggled against Jacob, who was still surprisingly strong in his elderly body. His long nails dug into her bare arm, and she let out a scream of her own. The book started to slip out of her arms as he pulled at it. She saw a small flash of blue and yellow as something fell—no, *flew*—down at Jacob's head. A small bird was dive-bombing Jacob and scratching at his eyes with its tiny talons. He let go of the book to slap at the bird, but his other hand remained firmly attached to her arm. The bird was able to blind one eye before he smacked it away. Sadie winced as she saw it hit a wall and tumble to the floor. The little bird was oddly familiar to her, then she realized it looked like the bird Hannah had freed from Eckert's room. She watched as it twitched but did not get up.

She tried to pull away from Jacob's grasp, but his grip was vicelike, and he was reaching to grab the book again. She noticed movement behind Jacob and looked around him to see Jenny standing at the foot of the stairs a few feet away. Jacob was so close she could smell the repulsive perfume of rotting roses wafting off him, and his attention was fixed on her and the book. He hadn't noticed that Jenny had come down. Sadie knew she didn't have any time to think it through, so she went with the first thing that came to mind. She threw the book.

It landed with a loud thud at Jenny's feet, and Jacob released Sadie's arm to chase after it.

"It's the book!" Sadie screamed to Jenny, who grabbed it off the floor moments before Jacob reached it. "Destroy it!"

Sadie rubbed at her arm, which was raw and red from where Jacob had been grabbing her. She ran after Jacob, then threw herself at his back, knocking him to the ground. She just needed to keep him occupied long enough for Jenny to destroy the book. Jenny opened it and must have seen where Sadie had ripped pages out, because she began doing the same thing. Sadie struggled to hold Jacob back as Jenny tore out a few pages and crumpled them in her fist. Jacob screamed, and the arm Sadie had been holding on to crumbled into dust in her hands. Jenny was frantically tearing pages out now, and every time she did, Jacob let out a hellish shriek and part of his body crumbled to dust. The castle around them began to shiver, the massive chandelier tinkling as it trembled above her. Sadie pushed herself off the floor and scooted around the mess that used to be Jacob. He was still alive somehow, screaming and writhing on the ground in a furious anguish. When she reached Jenny, the book was still about half-full of pages. Sadie stopped Jenny's ripping and took the book from her.

"They are connected," Sadie explained. "If we completely destroy the book, he will also be destroyed." The castle's shaking grew more intense, and paintings began falling from the walls. "I'm guessing it'll destroy the castle too."

Jenny nodded, then looked down at the ground. Sadie followed her gaze to see the little blue-and-yellow bird had managed to make it over to them and was emitting the softest chirps she'd ever heard.

"Is that the bird from Eckert's room?" Jenny asked, bending down to get a closer look.

"I think so. It came out of nowhere and attacked Jacob before you got here." Sadie watched the broken little bird; its wing was bent out of shape, and its feathers stuck out at strange angles. *Why would Eckert's bird try to help us?*

Jenny picked the little bird up and held it in her hands. She stared at it for a second before looking back up at Sadie.

"Rumpelstiltskin told us that Mrs. Braun never left the castle," Jenny said.

Sadie looked at the bird in Jenny's hands, and something snapped into place. "The flower I saw Eckert pick that first day! It transforms people who have been changed into animals back into people. She must have intended to change her back at some point!"

"The flower is still in her room," Jenny said excitedly. "I saw it earlier."

The castle continued to shake around them, as if the structure was slowly weakening. "We need to be quick. I don't know how much longer the walls are going to hold," Sadie said as she turned toward Eckert's room.

They ran the length of the hallway, leaving Jacob behind writhing in agony on the ground, powerless. When they got to the room, Sadie paused, stunned at the disarray the room was in. They'd left it a mess before, sure, but it hadn't been *this* bad. The desk was tipped over on its back, and all the drawers were pulled out and scattered on the floor.

"What happened in here?" Sadie asked as she scanned the room for the flower.

"Ah, doesn't matter. The flower is over there." Jenny gestured to a small glass vase on the floor that had been tipped on its side. The red flower was sticking out of it. Sadie hoped it hadn't been ruined or the magic hadn't dried up along with the flower.

Sadie leaned down and picked up the vase. As she did, she heard a faint rattling sound. She started to remove the flower from the vase, but Jenny stopped her.

"Let's do this outside," she said. "The bird is injured. If this really is Mrs. Braun, she will probably be injured too. We won't be able to carry her out."

Sadie nodded at the logic and moved toward the door, the book in one hand and the vase in the other. The castle was shaking harder now, and she heard the creaking of strained wood beams. If they didn't get out soon, they may never get out. They ran back to the lobby where Jacob was still writhing in agony on the floor. He stared up at them with his remaining eye and focused on Jenny.

"Jenny, don't do this. You can still fix this. I'll give you anything, please."

Jenny stopped and stared down at him, then turned to

Sadie.

"Give me the book," she said, holding the bird out to Sadie.

"Jenny, what are you—"

Jenny shifted the bird into one hand and took the book from Sadie, then handed her the bird. She couldn't do anything but take it. It was warm and soft in her hand, and she held it close to her body to make sure she didn't drop it. She looked at Jenny, who was standing over Jacob, the book open in her hands.

"That's a good girl," Jacob murmured from the floor. "Now, all you have to do is—"

Jenny ripped a large section of pages out, and Jacob's tongue crumbled to dust in his mouth.

The castle shook harder, and rocks began slipping out of the walls and falling with a crash around them. The lit candles in the chandelier and the wall sconces fell from their places and dropped to the floor. The small flickering flames spread quickly across the ancient carpet, blocking them from the only exit. Sadie couldn't believe how fast the flames moved; they jumped easily from the carpet to the hanging tapestries and paintings. The front desk caught and became one big flaming torch.

The heat blasted them as Sadie searched for a path out of the castle. The fire had consumed a section of the carpet and moved on, leaving behind black ashes and a few glowing embers.

"Come on," Sadie yelled over the roar of the fire. She hugged the vase with the flower and the small bird to her chest and ran as quickly as she could across the smoldering carpet. She made it to the doors and turned to make sure Jenny was with her. Jenny had made it around the fire but was turned away, watching the thing that used to be Jacob being eaten by the flames.

"We need to get out of here!" Sadie yelled at Jenny over the roar of the fire and creaking of the failing wood beams. Jenny nodded, and together they pushed through the heavy double doors and fell into the cool, clear night air. Sadie breathed deeply and started down the steps when Jenny called out to stop her.

"Wait! What do we do with this?" she asked, holding up what remained of the ripped up book. Sadie looked at the book, then at the castle being consumed by fire.

"Toss it in."

Jenny hesitated, then opened one of the doors and threw the book inside to be consumed by the fire. They hurried down the steps and moved a safe distance away from the castle, but not so far that she couldn't still feel the warmth emanating out at them. They stood together, watching as it caved in on itself and the fire licked the sky.

"Hey," Jenny said, turning to Sadie.

"Yeah?"

"We got to have that bonfire after all."

Sadie smiled and then everything went black.

54

Jenny opened her eyes and saw a pale blue sky. Her entire body hurt, and she winced as she forced herself to sit up. She was surrounded by rubble and debris, all that was left of the castle. Her mind was foggy, but it was starting to clear, and everything came rushing back to her. She and Sadie had been watching the castle burn when it suddenly exploded. She must have been knocked unconscious by the blast.

Sadie was just a few yards away from her, sitting next to a completely naked woman with short gray hair. Jenny pushed herself up and made her way carefully over to Sadie and the woman, stepping around sharp rocks and broken wood beams.

Mrs. Braun was scratched up, and one of her arms was bent at an unnatural angle. "I was holding the bird and flower when the explosion happened. They must have touched when I was knocked down."

"Is she ..." Jenny peered down at their unmoving teacher.

"She's alive, just unconscious," Sadie replied. "We should get something to cover her up."

Jenny nodded and looked around the clearing for anything they could use. Everything was covered with rubble and dust. A sharp intake of breath behind her made her turn.

Cameron was lying a short distance away, his eyes focused on the large piece of rubble on top of one of his legs. Jenny hurried over to him, careful not to trip on any of the rocks or other debris littering the ground. The rock on Cameron's leg was large, but not too large for her to move. She just had to do it *carefully*. She grabbed on to the rock with both hands and slowly lifted it off his leg. He cried out as the weight was removed, and she saw tears squeeze out of the sides of his eyes. She dropped the rock to the side and knelt down to examine Cameron's leg.

"How is it?" Sadie called.

Jenny wasn't sure how to answer. She certainly wasn't a medical professional, but even she knew bone belonged *underneath* the skin, not jutting out. Blood poured from where the bone had ripped through the skin.

"Oh god," Cameron said as he saw his leg.

"Don't look!" Jenny begged, too late. "Just ... It'll be okay. We just need to get you to a hospital. It'll be fine."

But Jenny didn't know if it would be fine. All around her was rubble and wreckage and despair. The castle was gone, but the woods were still there. She and Sadie had destroyed the book, the castle, and Jacob, but they were still in the middle of the woods with no way out. There was no way Cameron would be able to walk out on that leg. She scanned the clearing for the others, her heart rattling inside of her as she imagined all kinds of horrible things. She was afraid to find out what had happened to the rest of them.

She saw Sadie get up and leave Mrs. Braun's side, walking slowly away from them through the rubble toward something Jenny couldn't see.

"Jenny," Cameron forced out, pain tightening his voice. "I need you to help me out here. You need to stop the bleeding." He tore off his shirt, the buttons popping off, and threw it to her. "Wrap my leg as tightly as you can with that, where the blood is coming out. We need to apply pressure."

Jenny stared down at the shirt in her lap, then back at Cameron's leg. She knew she should be moving quickly, but she felt paralyzed. Everything had been fine, they'd *won*, but then she had woken up to this new nightmare.

"Jenny!" Cameron yelled, breaking her reverie.

"Yes, sorry," she gasped as she wrapped the shirt around his leg with shaky hands and tied it off. He let out a scream as she tightened it, and she quickly let go of the shirt. "Sorry! I'm so sorry. Are you okay? Should I take it off?"

"No, no, leave it. Just ..." Cameron looked around, and panic filled his eyes. "What happened? We were all standing outside, we saw you and Sadie come out, but then—"

A look of recognition passed across Cameron's face. "There was an explosion. Hannah. Where's Hannah?" Cameron gasped, his neck craning every which way as he searched for her.

"Don't move," Jenny said as she pushed herself up to stand. "I'll find her."

Jenny made her way through the rubble, looking for Hannah and the others. Sadie was sitting a short distance away on the ground, rocking something in her arms. Something with a shock of bright poppy-red hair. Jenny ran clumsily toward the two, her legs barely working. Her heart was in her throat, and tears stung her eyes.

"Hannah, no, Hannah, come on, please, please wake up," Sadie begged the limp girl in her arms. Tears streamed down her cheeks, and she didn't seem to notice when Jenny crouched down beside her. Hannah's eyes were closed, and bright red blood poured from her head and smeared across her pale face. Sadie continued to rock Hannah's body, her head bent down, ugly broken sobs overcoming her.

Again, Jenny didn't know what to do. *This isn't right. No, not at all. No, Hannah must be okay. It doesn't make any sense.* An odd quiet filled Jenny and cleared away her thoughts. The tears that had threatened to fall moments earlier dried up. Her throat hurt a little, but nothing else did. She saw what was happening in front of her, but it couldn't touch her. The quiet wrapped itself around her like a protective coating, and she felt her heart harden.

She stood up and walked away from her best friends, one broken and the other breaking. She had to find the rest of their group. She focused on that task, pushing Hannah to the back of her mind. She couldn't let herself feel *that* right now. She had to help the others.

She picked her way across the rubble and found May first. She was dirty and bruised but otherwise uninjured. She remembered how carefully May had tended to Travis's wounds after the nixie attack.

"May, we found Mrs. Braun. She's over there." Jenny gestured in the direction Mrs. Braun was lying. "She needs clothes and first aid. Can you handle that?"

May looked up at her from the ground, dismayed, but she nodded. Jenny continued her search and saw Travis getting up from the ground. He had a gash across his forehead and was covered in soot and dirt. He wrapped his arms around her when he reached her and squeezed so hard she felt the air press out of her body.

"I thought everyone was dead!" he cried, gripping her harder. She extracted herself from his arms and gave him a soft pat.

"Come on, help me find the others. Ryan, Rain, and Aiden are still missing." Jenny considered sending Travis to help Cameron, but he was okay for the moment, and Travis was the only one strong enough to carry anyone else they might find that needed help.

He gave her a slightly hurt look, and she realized she should have acted happier to find him alive. She pushed the concern away. She didn't have the energy or time to be dealing with *feelings* right now.

They called out for Ryan, Rain, and Aiden but didn't get a response. Jenny became increasingly worried as they searched the rubble. Finally, Aiden called back. He'd somehow been blasted so far back he was at the tree line. He waved and walked over to them, and as he approached Jenny, she noticed he wasn't harmed at all. He was filthy, like the rest of them, but she didn't see any gashes or broken bones.

"Hey, what happened? One minute I was walking away and the next I woke up on the ground. Where's Jacob?" Aiden scanned the wreckage, an anxious look pinching his face.

"We killed him. I'll explain it all later. Cameron has a broken leg. Can you go over and help him?"

Aiden's eyes widened, and he nodded. She pointed to where Cameron was still lying, and Aiden hurried toward him.

"You didn't tell me Cameron had a broken leg!" Travis shouted, looking after Aiden as he retreated.

"I know, sorry. He's going to be okay, I think. I might need your help with Ryan and Rain, we don't know …" Jenny broke off and tried to maintain her composure. She wasn't going to let herself imagine what might have happened to Ryan and his sister, but the fact that she hadn't found them yet was making her increasingly concerned.

They continued to pick their way through the wreckage, tossing broken paintings aside, pushing pieces of bed frames out of the way. The fire had incinerated most of the first floor, it seemed, but hadn't touched any of the other floors before the explosion happened.

They had searched the front of the castle and started making their way around the side, toward the bridge that led over the river. There she found Ryan, his body covering Rain's far smaller frame. Neither of them were moving. Jenny rushed to them and gently removed some light debris that had fallen on top of them. Travis helped her gently pull Ryan off his sister and roll him onto his back. Rain looked awful. Despite Ryan's attempt to shield his sister from the falling debris, her face was covered in quickly forming purple bruises and her breathing was labored.

Next to Rain, Ryan looked much worse. His blonde hair

was darkened with dirt and blood, and his arm—the one he'd already lost a hand from, was smashed. His stump was reinjured and bleeding, and his forearm had sharp bone fragments breaking through the skin. Jenny forced herself not to look away, but smoothed the hair from his face and with a shaky hand checked his pulse. She could feel it beating weakly against her fingertips. She let out a breath she hadn't even realized she'd been holding. Ryan was alive.

She turned to Travis, who appeared to be talking softly to Rain next to her. To her surprise, Rain's eyes were open, and her lips moved to respond to Travis, even if the rest of her body was still. Jenny turned her attention back to Ryan. His eyes were still closed and his eyelashes trembled against his cheeks. She cupped his face in her hands and leaned down and kissed him as softly as she could. She knew the fairy tales were over, that the magic was gone. She didn't expect her kiss to magically revive him, but she hoped it would call him back from wherever he had been pulled to. His eyes fluttered slowly open, and she smiled down at him. "Hey, there."

Ryan groaned and carefully sat up. He looked over at his sister and made a quick movement to turn toward her but cried out in pain. Jenny couldn't tell which of his injuries was causing the pain. He needed help, and quickly.

Jenny's mind raced through what she needed to do next. Four of them couldn't walk, so hiking out of there as a group wasn't an option. She could go for help, bring help back here, but she had no idea how long that would take and by then ... Jenny didn't want to imagine what she'd be coming back to.

Jenny looked up at the cloudless blue sky. The sun was creeping its way higher, and she felt the air around her start to grow warmer. She could feel the shell that had grown around her begin to crack. She hadn't beaten the bad guy to save her friends only to watch them die out here anyway. She looked around, frantically, for anything that might help them.

Then she saw it.

A short distance away, next to one of the higher remaining chunks of wall, was the missing van.

55

Sadie looked down at Hannah's sweet face now covered in blood and ash. She closed her eyes tightly and willed Hannah alive. *Open your eyes, please. Please, just open your eyes. Be okay. You have to be okay.*

But Hannah didn't open her eyes.

Sadie had told Jenny to throw the book into the fire. She was certain that had been what caused the explosion, what caused the wreckage they were now in. *She* had done this. This was *her fault.*

She sensed someone behind her and saw Aiden, a little scratched up but mostly unharmed, holding Cameron up. Sadie eyed Cameron's hurt leg. The shirt wrapped around his shin was soaked in blood. Cameron's face fell as he looked down at Hannah in Sadie's arms.

"No." It was a small sound. Cameron's non-broken leg gave out, and Aiden struggled to hold him up. "Let me go," Cameron said, pushing Aiden away.

Cameron pulled himself closer to Sadie and touched Hannah lightly on the face. Tears fell down his cheeks and onto Hannah's dirty T-shirt. Travis lumbered up behind them, drawing their attention away from Hannah.

"We found the van," he said slowly, his eyes dropping to rest on Hannah. "Is she ..."

Sadie sniffled and shook her head.

"Where's Jenny?" she asked, her voice strained and breaking from crying.

"She's with Ryan and Rain by the van. She asked me to come get you guys."

His eyes lingered on Hannah's body, then looked away.

"How did you find the van?" Aiden asked. "I thought Eckert got rid of it."

"I don't know. It was just sitting there on the other side of the castle, near the bridge," Travis replied with a shrug. "We think she hid it with magic, or something."

By the bridge? Sadie shook her head. They must have walked past it countless times without even realizing it.

"That's something, at least," Aiden said solemnly, his gaze slipping to Sadie and Hannah.

"Yeah, we just need to find the keys."

Aiden sighed and rubbed his forehead. "We don't have the keys?"

Aiden looked at the wreckage spread out all around them. "We'll never find them in this mess. If they're even here at all."

Sadie felt the bump in her pocket. When she woke up, she had found Mrs. Braun transformed back into a human and the glass vase shattered, revealing a set of keys. She'd pocketed them, knowing they must be important if Eckert had hid them in the vase. If they were the keys to the van, which she was now sure they were, they had a way out. She looked out at the ruins and knew there was nothing left to stop them.

She looked down at Hannah in her arms. She wished as hard as she could for Hannah to be alive, repeated it over and over inside her head, but she knew the magical world they had been in was gone. Wishes didn't come true in the real world.

"I have the keys," Sadie said softly, her throat hurting. "Travis, help me with Hannah."

Sadie transferred Hannah's limp body into Travis's arms, and he carried her princess-style toward the van. Sadie tried not to cry as she saw her friend's head loll lifelessly back and forth over his arm, like a broken doll's.

They made their way slowly across the broken furniture and stonework, Cameron leaning on Aiden and Sadie. They came to May sitting next to Mrs. Braun, who was now covered with what looked like a slightly singed maroon drape. May looked up as they approached, her mouth turned down with worry.

"She's breathing, but she's not responding to me," she explained. "I ... I don't know what else to do."

"Mrs. Braun!" Aiden shouted in surprise. After finding Hannah, Sadie had forgotten all about their teacher.

"We found the van and the keys. We're leaving right now," Travis told May. "I'll be back to get Mrs. Braun."

"I'll wait here with her," May said.

When they reached the van, Sadie saw Ryan sitting up against a partially intact wall. Rain was next to him, resting her head on his shoulder. They both looked rough. Every inch of Rain's bare skin was covered in bruises and small cuts. Jenny was on her knees in front of Ryan, examining his bloodied arm.

"Sadie has the keys!" Travis announced as they approached. Jenny turned and stared at Travis with Hannah in his arms, her expression blank. Sadie couldn't understand how Jenny could be so detached, so cold. Jenny stood up and faced them as Travis gently set Hannah down on the ground. Sadie tried not to look at her.

"That's amazing," Jenny said. "Did you see Mrs. Braun? Is she still alive?"

"Yeah, but not awake," Travis replied. "I'll go back for her."

Sadie felt like she was in a bad dream. Everything that was happening made perfect sense—and yet it didn't make any sense at all. Dazed, she helped Aiden lower Cameron to the ground next to Ryan and Rain. She pulled the keys out of her pocket and handed them to Jenny without a word.

Travis disappeared and then returned with Mrs. Braun, struggling underneath her dead weight, with May beside him.

He awkwardly set their teacher down, trying to keep the drape wrapped around her. Sweaty and red-faced, he lowered himself down onto a rock and rubbed at his arms.

Sadie stood like a sleepwalker, staring at the broken and bleeding people on the ground.

"Sadie and I destroyed the book. The castle is gone, Jacob is gone," Jenny said, drawing their attention to her. "I think we'll be able to leave now. But first we need to come up with a story."

Sadie stared at Jenny, bewildered. *A story?*

"No one is going to believe us if we tell them what really happened," Jenny continued. "They'll think we did something terrible, or that we're all crazy. We have to be smart about this."

Jenny's hard eyes scanned the group, but no one made a sound. Sadie tried to swallow, but her throat was swollen and raw from crying. She didn't have anything to offer anyway.

"We came out here on a school trip," Jenny started, "and then something happened that resulted in all our injuries. What is that something?"

"Landslide?" Aiden offered weakly.

"Maybe, but they might want us to take them to it," Jenny replied.

"Why don't we just use a version of the truth?" said Cameron. "We were staying at this castle and it collapsed."

"We'd get way too many questions we wouldn't be able to answer," Travis replied. "A good lie is simple. Don't include too many details that you can get caught up in later."

"We need to fake a car accident," May said from the edge of the group, her arms crossed. "It's the only thing that would explain everything."

Silence fell over the group as they considered this. Sadie searched her mind for an alternative but came up with nothing. May was right. It was the best option they had.

"What about my hand?" Ryan asked from the ground. "They won't be able to find it. And what about Charlotte?"

Sadie had no idea how they would explain Charlotte. They didn't have her body. She was just *gone*. Jenny's face darkened, and Sadie watched as she drifted away from the group toward the river. Jenny stood at the edge of the cliff, and for a second, Sadie was afraid of what Jenny might do.

Jenny turned back, her expression serious. "We need to push the van into the river."

"We can't do that! We need the van. How else are we going to get out of here? Half of us can't even walk," Travis argued.

"Some of us will go for help," Jenny said. "The rest will stay here."

Sadie started to tune out as the others argued about who should go, who should stay, and if they should even do this at all. Sadie felt wiped out and, in that moment, didn't even care what they did.

In the end, it was decided that Jenny, Sadie, Aiden, and May would go for help while the others stayed behind. Sadie wished they could leave May behind, and Jenny seemed to feel that way too, but they knew they'd need someone who could speak German when they found help.

They put the van in neutral and Travis, Aiden, and Jenny pushed it toward the edge of the cliff. "Are you sure this is the best idea?" Ryan called from the ground, voicing what Sadie was thinking.

"No, I'm not sure," Jenny replied. "If anyone has a better idea, speak now or we're pushing this thing over the cliff."

Jenny waited a few moments in the silence that followed, then nodded her head to Travis and Aiden. With one last push, the front of the van tipped over the edge, then gravity did the rest. Sadie watched their only mode of transportation disappear over the edge and flinched when she heard it hit the rocks below. Those who could stand gathered at the edge of the cliff and looked down. The entire front was smashed in, and the river was fighting it, trying to force it down stream.

"There's no way we would have survived that," Aiden said. "They aren't going to believe us."

"They'll have to believe us," Jenny replied firmly. "The only alternative is the truth, and they definitely won't believe *that*."

Knowing they couldn't waste any more time, they said their goodbyes and started off toward the road. Already, the grass was growing over the rubble, the wood beams and broken furniture were decomposing, and the stones were darkening with age and moss. It was like time was catching up with the castle. Soon, she realized, there would be nothing left that proved the castle had ever existed at all. The Black Forest was covering its own tracks, hiding its own sins. *Maybe there is some magic left in these woods after all,* she mused wistfully.

As they reached the road, Aiden turned back, a question in his eyes. He turned to Sadie and asked softly, "Where did all the fairy tales go?"

Where did all the fairy tales go? Sadie didn't want to think about it. She didn't want to know. She turned and fell in step with Jenny, their arms lightly touching as they walked down the road that had brought them there.

Ever After

Jenny adjusted the rearview mirror in her new van. She'd bought it from a local guy who had grown tired of the nomadic vanlife and decided to settle down in Crescent Bay. It had everything she needed—a bed, a kitchenette, ample storage, and solar panels. The only thing she added was a secure booster seat for her slightly overweight corgi, Hamilton. She looked over at her canine copilot and smiled. With his ginger-colored fur and stubby legs, he was nothing like the massive wolf she'd bonded with in the Black Forest, but he still stirred up memories of Marble. She felt a soft ache in her chest and shook the memory away.

She carefully backed the van out of the driveway and took one last look at her childhood home. Her dad was at work, so there was no one to watch her leave, no one to say goodbye to. She had planned it that way.

She pulled out of her neighborhood and drove down the long stretch of Highway 1 going south. She drove through town, past the fast-food restaurants and her high school, past the beach she had met Ryan at, and then she turned down Sadie's street. She stopped the van in front of Sadie's house and looked at it for a long moment. The navy-blue craftsman was nicer than her own ugly tract house, with its white trim and tidy flower boxes in the windows. She remembered all the sleepovers she and Hannah had had there, all the movies they used to watch, the late-night sharing of secrets. Thinking of those times made Jenny's chest hurt. She got out of the van and walked over to Sadie's mailbox, hesitated, then slipped her letter inside. She lingered for a moment at the mailbox and considered changing her mind, considered throwing the letter away and walking up to the door to say goodbye to Sadie in person. To tell her the truth. But she didn't. She turned and got back into her van and drove away.

She pulled back onto Highway 1 and continued driving south. She watched the Now Leaving Crescent Bay sign as it quickly approached and then disappeared behind her.

After she had burned the book, the magic that had trapped them there let go and they were able to leave. They hadn't been walking long before they ran into the German police. Their group had been reported missing when they never checked in to Schloss Lieser, the castle they were supposed to have gone to, and none of their parents could get ahold of them. They told the police that Charlotte had died in the car accident and the river had taken her body away. Jenny knew they were suspicious, that there were holes in their story. Mrs. Braun had gone along with their story, blaming memory loss whenever the police asked her something specific. They had no choice but to believe them. The police said they would send out a search party for Charlotte's body, but she knew they would never find it.

When they returned home from Germany, everything was different. Their parents had believed their story, too, or at least acted like they did, but their classmates looked at them differently. At school Jenny could feel their eyes on her, hear their whispers as she passed by. It had been hard for her to get back to normal life. She'd had trouble seeing the point of any of it. Classes, softball, prom—after what had happened in the Black Forest, it all felt so trite and insignificant. The constant nightmares didn't help either.

Her senior year flew by in a blur, and she barely remembered any of it. She was either half-asleep or drifting off into her own dark thoughts. She had managed to squeak by and graduate, but she suspected her teachers might have felt sorry for her and passed her out of pity. Mrs. Braun retired early, though they all knew the school district forced her out. They couldn't keep a teacher on, no matter how beloved, after what had happened. She had visited her afterward. Mrs. Braun seemed relieved to no longer be teaching and had gotten really into bird-watching.

Jenny had told Sadie that she hadn't gotten into any of the colleges she applied to, but that was a lie. Jenny hadn't applied to any schools. She didn't think there was a point after her grades had tanked, and she had no idea what she wanted to study anyway.

She visited her mother at Redwood Grove Hospital just once, right after they had returned from Germany. She had wondered if she'd understand her mother more after what she had just gone through. When she got there, her mother was the same as she had ever been, her eyes wide and darting around like she could see things Jenny couldn't. She left after only a few minutes when her mother started screaming at her. It was the usual things, blaming Jenny for her being locked up there, paranoid ramblings about how Jenny wasn't really her daughter but a spy sent to destroy her. Jenny couldn't take it anymore. When she left the room, she knew it would be the last time she'd visit. There was nothing for her there.

As she was leaving the hospital, she saw May with her parents in the parking lot. They locked eyes, and May gave a soft nod but did not approach her. May had gotten her wish—the shooting had never happened. Instead, her parents had found a gun and a notebook with pages and pages of murderous ramblings in her brother's room. They still moved to Crescent Bay, not to get away from their town, but because Redwood Grove was the best mental institution on the West Coast. Either way, May had ended up in Crescent Bay, had ended up on that trip to Germany—that was something her wish *hadn't* changed.

Jenny had tried to make it work with Ryan, but they had broken up by Christmas. They were both different people from who they'd been before entering the Black Forest. He just didn't understand her anymore, and she didn't need him the way she used to. He had left Crescent Bay with his band the day after graduation, for a summer tour, and Jenny was happy for him. He couldn't play the instruments he used to anymore, but he could still sing and wasn't going to let a missing hand destroy his dreams. Ryan would always be part of her, but that part was now firmly in the past.

Rain got into art school and was moving to San Francisco at the end of the summer. Her girlfriend, Farrah, had been surprisingly understanding of what Rain had gone through. Jenny didn't think Rain had told her what really happened in the forest; they had all sworn to never tell anyone, but there seemed to be an odd *knowing* in Farrah's eyes. Farrah had gotten into University of California, Berkeley to become an architect. Last Jenny heard, they were talking about getting an apartment together. The artist and the architect.

The sky was clear and bright blue as she took the winding road south. Dense forests of cedar trees and eucalyptus grew on either side of the highway, but every now and then, they would clear to show her a peek of the sparkling blue-gray ocean on her right. Jenny felt a rush as she drove farther and farther away from Crescent Bay. She gripped the steering wheel and carefully maneuvered the van around the tight turns. She snuck a quick glance at Hamilton next to her, his paws on the car door, his tiny stump of a tail wagging vigorously as he looked out the window.

As she drove, she thought about what she was leaving behind. She hadn't been close with her dad before Germany, and afterward, it was even worse. He'd been supportive, at first, when they'd returned without Charlotte. But he didn't understand why her grades had fallen, why she'd quit the softball team, why she'd broke up with Ryan. She couldn't explain any of it to him, so they'd spent the last few months just trying to avoid each other. When she told him she wasn't going to college, he lost it. All the tension, sadness, and disappointment burst out of him, and he said things Jenny knew she would never forget, no matter how hard she tried. She hadn't told him she was planning on leaving. She'd just left.

Jenny rolled down her window and let the cold, salty air flow into the van. The ocean was so close she could hear the soft crash of waves as they rhythmically hit the beach. She thought about Travis and the story about a shark he always started but never seemed to finish. Travis wasn't going to college either. Instead, he was joining the FEMA Corps. Jenny would have thought he'd had enough disasters to last him a lifetime, but he'd told her he wanted to help people instead of wasting his time in boring classes. *That* she could understand.

The road curved left, then right, and Jenny smiled as she saw her favorite road sign: Shifting Sands. There was only one sign like this that she'd ever seen, and she'd always loved how poetic it sounded. It meant to warn of sand slipping from the dunes into the road, but to her it always seemed to hint at something more.

She couldn't see very far down the road. Its turns and dips kept her focused on what was right in front of her, and she liked it that way. Her first stop was Joshua Tree. She'd felt the desert calling to her, but she wasn't sure where she was going after that.

She'd know it when she got there.

Sadie sat down and pulled out the letter Jenny had left in her mailbox that morning. She'd seen a van pull up in front of her house and had been surprised to see Jenny get out of it. She watched from the window as Jenny left the letter and got back into the van. She'd known Jenny was going to leave Crescent Bay, she just hadn't known when. If Jenny didn't want a messy goodbye, Sadie could respect that.

She pulled the letter from the envelope and remembered how they used to slip notes into each other's lockers all the time, before. They used to fold the paper in various designs, though Sadie had always been better at it. The letter felt oddly flimsy in her hands. Fragile.

She unfolded it and started reading it out loud.

"'Dear Sadie,

I'm sorry I didn't come to say goodbye in person. I just thought this would be easier for both of us. I wanted to thank you for always being such a good friend. I wish I had done better at being yours. I've been selfish, and I took you for granted, and I'll always regret that. You're such an amazing—'"

Sadie stopped reading it out loud, embarrassed by Jenny's over-the-top outpouring. She read through the cheesy parts in her head and started again.

"'I don't know where I am going, but I'll give you a call when I get there. Good luck at college. I know you're going to be a kickass attorney someday. Tell Hannah I love her, and say goodbye for me. Love, Jenny.'"

Sadie set the letter down in her lap and gave Hannah's hand a soft squeeze. Sadie had spent countless hours inside this cramped hospital room, listening to the hums and beeps of the machines keeping Hannah alive. She'd been unconscious since Germany, lost in some coma dream world that Sadie hoped was pleasant. The doctors said there wasn't a good chance that she would ever wake up, but Sadie clung to that small chance. Hannah's parents and little sister were clinging to that chance too.

"I'm moving onto campus this weekend," Sadie told Hannah. "I won't be able to come visit you as often, but I promise I'll come as much as I can. I won't be that far away."

Hannah's eyes shifted slightly underneath her eyelids, and Sadie hoped that meant she understood. She felt a sharp stab of guilt as she let go of Hannah's limp hand and set it down gently on the hospital bed. She watched her friend sleep and wondered if this was really better.

Sadie was excited about starting college in the fall. She hadn't decided on a major yet but knew she wanted to go to law school after she finished her bachelor's. She was sick of constantly seeing bad people get away with their crimes. When she thought about all her possible futures, the only one that really excited her was one where she put criminals behind bars.

As she left Hannah's room, she nearly ran into Cameron. He had a bouquet of sunflowers in his hand, large bright-yellow heads nodding in every direction. She smiled. She didn't know how often he visited Hannah, but she knew there were always fresh flowers in her room. She patted Cameron's arm, and he nodded politely, his face grim.

They'd all been devastated over what happened to Hannah, but Cameron had taken it the worst. He'd spent so much time in this hospital when his brother was dying of cancer. Sadie was sure he'd never wanted to come back here, and yet here he was. She'd heard from Jenny that he'd gotten into most of his top schools but had deferred to take a gap year. Sadie hoped he wasn't planning on spending it in that hospital room waiting for Hannah to wake up.

Outside the hospital, Aiden was waiting for her. They'd been dating in secret ever since coming back from Germany. Not even Jenny knew. She didn't know why they had decided to hide it, maybe it was because of how guilty they felt. For a long time, she felt a stab of guilt whenever she let herself be happy. Falling in love with Aiden as one friend lay in a coma and the other struggled with depression and a breakup had felt wrong. Now, though, she was learning to let those feelings go.

He was going to be at the same college as her, studying film. He wanted to make his own movies, but until then, he gained endless enjoyment making Sadie watch all his old favorites. Now she understood almost all of his little references. Sometimes she'd even quote some of the movies back to him, and whenever she did, his face would light up. She loved nothing more than seeing him happy.

Sadie walked up to Aiden and gave him the best smile she could muster. He wrapped her into a hug and rested his head on the top of hers. She sighed into his chest, her heart hurting and her eyes becoming misty.

"Are you okay?" he mumbled into her hair. She took a deep breath and pulled away to look up at him.

"No. But I will be."

Black Forest Burning